shattered CROWN

KOZLOV EMPIRE BOOK FOUR

MONICA KAYNE

ISBN 978-1-7782704-4-4

Book Cover by Opulent Swag and Design

Editing & Proofreading by Romance Editor, Nina Fiegl s.p.

First edition 2024

This book is dedicated to my grandmother, who passed away at the age of 99 just as I was finishing this book. She wanted me to marry a doctor, but I'd like to think that a part of her would be proud that I am supporting my family by writing smut.

Author Note

Shattered Crown is a dark mafia romance with mature themes and profanity. Please check my website for trigger and content warnings.

https://monicakayne.com/trigger-warnings

Prologue

Present Day

KIRA

One month ago, I made a bargain with the devil and today the bill is due.

That devil is none other than Maxim Belov. Billionaire. Business magnate. Crime lord.

And the man who killed Aunt Masha—the only mother I've ever known.

"Do you, Kira Antonov, take Maxim Belov to be your lawfully wedded husband..." the priest begins, his voice echoing in the vast cathedral. His words become a distant murmur as I fix my gaze on the man I'm about to wed.

Maxim's cold eyes meet mine, filled with a calculating appraisal. A faint smirk tugs at the corners of his mouth. He's undeniably gorgeous, his jet-black hair peppered with salt and pepper at the temples, highlighting piercing blue-gray eyes, a chiseled jawline, and defined cheekbones that lend him an air of ruthless nobility.

The cathedral falls into a hushed silence, the weight of

countless expectant eyes bearing down on me. Sweat beads along my back, and I struggle to keep my breathing steady, knowing there's no turning back once this commitment is made.

But the only thing more terrifying than calling him my husband is not avenging Masha's murder. And without his ring on my finger, that will be impossible. So I allow my need for vengeance to outweigh my fear. I've walked through fire to get here; now, I need to take the final leap.

The priest looks from Maxim to me, his brow creased with concern, and repeats, "Do you, Kira, take Maxim as your husband?"

Maxim drags his thumb across his bottom lip, tilting his head in a silent query. I can almost hear his mocking tone in my mind. *"What's it going to be, lastochka? Will you run away, or will you see this marriage through?"*

I draw upon every shred of anger and grief, letting it steel my resolve. *This is for Aunt Masha and the justice she deserves.*

When I finally find my voice, it's strong and clear. "Yes." So help me God.

And just like that, I've bound myself to a monster for as long as it takes to exact my revenge.

Chapter One

One Month Earlier

KIRA

I fan myself with one hand while grabbing a chilled glass of champagne with the other. *Haute couture* in summer is never a good idea. But then again, nothing about tonight is.

The luxurious ballroom is filled with Russia's *crème de la crème*, celebrating Maxim Belov discovering his long-lost daughter, Alyona Nikitin. But like everything associated with Maxim, the happy union is just an illusion.

Glancing around the lavishly decorated room, I spot Alyona—my best friend and ride-or-die—in one corner, caught up in a discussion with Maxim and the interior minister. A familiar sense of anger prickles my spine. Despite the story that Maxim spun for his esteemed guests, this is no happy reunion.

One week ago, he abducted Aly and me from a safehouse in Croatia and whisked us away to his grand Black Sea estate. At the time, we had no idea who had captured us or why, until Maxim sat Aly down and basically said, "Nice to meet you. By the way, I'm your biological father—here's the proof. From here on out, you're going to rule my empire by my side. And if you don't, I'll kill everyone you love."

The last thing Aly wants is joining forces with Maxim, a man entrenched in organized crime as he is in legitimate business. What she yearns for—what she's *always* yearned for—is a regular life, far from the bratva upbringing she's known. Well ... that, and my brother Leo, but that's a whole other story.

So yeah, not the warmest of reunions with dear old dad. But here we are a week later, at Maxim's version of a "debutante ball", where he's parading Aly around like his newest acquisition, which is exactly what she is to him. Property to be owned and controlled.

But no one in their right mind would challenge Maxim. His influence extends far beyond business and politics, deep into the underworld. He's not bratva; he's the king to whom the bratva *pakhan*s report. If he's the king, then Alyona is his reluctant princess.

And I'm the joker that got caught up in this mess. Truth of the matter is, Maxim has no business with me. I suspect I'll be free to go after tonight, but there's a fat chance that's going to happen. When the opportunity presents itself, I'm getting my friend out of here—one way or another. Aly is strong in her own right, but I'm a born fighter. Along with my half-brothers—Andrei, Daniil, and Leo—I run Brooklyn's Kozlov Bratva, the most powerful crime syndicate on the US East Coast.

I take another sip of champagne and watch the couples on the dance floor before scanning the room again. But this time, Aly is nowhere to be seen. I'm about to go look for her, when I'm met with a pair of familiar green eyes.

"Liza?" I exclaim.

Elizaveta Ivanova, an old friend and roommate from boarding school, stands in front of me. Her teenage braids have been replaced by cascading chestnut waves, and her striking eyes are winged-tipped and sophisticated, but they still light up with the same genuine warmth as always.

My lips curve into a surprised smile.

She chuckles, wrapping me in a tight hug. "I can't believe it! The last I heard, you'd moved to New York and found your brothers. The Kozlovs, is that right?"

"It's true," I confirm. "I'm back in Russia for a ... visit." If you consider abduction and forcible confinement a visit. "And what about you? What have you been up to?" I ask, eager to change the subject.

"Not much has changed since we were schoolmates. I've been living the life in Moscow—the parties, the society events, the usual. Papa allowed me to go to university, but now that I've graduated..." She takes a solemn breath and lifts her left hand with a less than thrilled expression.

My gaze is drawn to a flashy diamond ring on her third finger. "You're engaged?"

I'm not surprised. She's always been the dreamy, romantic type. Unlike me—I'm happy to never get married. I prefer the freedom to work and run the family business. Plus, in most bratva families, marriage means losing all freedom.

"You remember Anatoly Petrovich, from the grade above us?" she asks without a trace of enthusiasm.

I wince. "He's not exactly who I pictured you with."

Liza is beautiful, chic, and sweet down to her marrow, and Anatoly is the exact opposite. My memory of him is of a self-important, pompous ass, who used his family name and connections to get good grades and only targeted the drunkest girl at any given party.

She grimaces. "Trust me, he's not who I pictured myself with. He's still the same *mudak* he was at school." My parents are pushing this 'advantageous alliance' with the Petroviches,"

Liza mimics, using air quotes. "I think you can imagine our situation. Nothing has changed."

Liza's father, Boris Ivanov, has a hearty appetite for drinking and gambling. Her mother used to regularly be at the headmaster's office, pleading for more time to settle Liza's tuition fees. It was well-known among the students that, despite the Ivanovs' supposed wealth, they frequently fell behind on payments due to Boris's vices.

Anatoly might be a creep, but he's a rich creep from a shipping magnate family. With the Ivanovs' underworld connections, it's a match made in mafia heaven.

I sigh and take her hand in mine. "I'm sorry. When is the wedding?"

"Sometime next year. But to be honest, never is my preference."

We look over to see Anatoly, slightly paunchy with thinning blond hair, attempting to engage a waitress in a conversation that seems too friendly. Watching him, I feel a fresh wave of sympathy for my old friend.

"Want me to help you do a runner?" I offer. "I can commandeer one of the helicopters on the back property and get us the hell out of here."

Liza pauses in thought, sipping her champagne. "If anyone is capable of stealing a helicopter from Maxim Belov, it's you."

An involuntary shudder passes through me. His name alone is distasteful.

She smiles nostalgically. "Do you remember when we... Well, actually, *you* stole the headmistress's car to get to that party in St. Petersburg. The look on Sister Olga's face the next morning. Shit. I think she whipped us for that one."

"I think she did. If it hadn't been for my aunt pleading our case to the headmistress, we definitely would've been expelled." The memory brings a bittersweet smile to my face.

While other parents would have been outraged, Aunt Masha had a rebellious streak—much like me—and understood the thrill of bending the rules. "She always said life was too short to live by the rules set by nuns."

Liza studies me, her expression growing serious. "I know how much you loved her and struggled after she ... died. I wish I could have been there for you more than I was."

I shake my head, swallowing the pain that threatens to drown me every time I think of her. Aunt Masha raised me. Until I found my brothers, she'd been the only person who ever loved me. The only person I ever loved. The person whose absence in my life still leaves a hole as big as a continent in my heart.

Liza is one of the few people that know my aunt was murdered ... and how it was all my fault.

"I'm the one who should be apologizing to you for not reaching out. When I settled in New York, I needed to move forward with my life. Thinking about Russia and the people I left behind" — I squeeze her hand — "was too hard."

"Of course, I understand." She smiles sadly. "What brings you here now?"

I clear my throat. "I'm close friends with Alyona Nikitin, Maxim Belov's daughter. I'm here to support her during this time of ... transition." *Forcible* transition. But I leave that out as it doesn't fit the narrative Maxim is spinning.

She shakes her head. "It must have been a real shock to find out her biological father is one of Russia's most powerful men!"

"You have no idea," I say, swallowing the knot in my throat when I think of how trapped Aly is in a world she never chose.

"I don't, but I'm dying to know." Liza raises her eyebrow, clearly intrigued.

I can't help but smile—she's always been one for gossip, but this story is not mine to share. I'm about to change the subject when she curses softly, her attention shifting to something behind me.

"Jesus, that man. I need to get him out of here." There's panic in her eyes.

I understand why. Liza's father is swaying and pontificating loudly into the ear of the Polish Ambassador, who looks less than impressed.

"I'll help you," I offer.

Boris is built like a bull—there's no way petite Liza could take him on her own. With the promise of a cigar and a fresh glass of liqueur, we're able to cajole him outside to one of the empty terraces off the main ballroom.

"Sit, Papa," Liza demands, settling him into a chair and handing him a glass of water.

"Vodka?" he asks hopefully.

"No. You don't need any more to drink," she hisses. "You need to sober up."

"My Elizaveta." He chuckles. "Always taking care of your papa. A good girl, right?" He looks at me to make his point, and that's when he tilts his head to the side, squinting. "Who are you? I recognize you from somewhere."

Liza crosses her arms over her chest. "It's my old friend, Kira Antonov. You remember her—we were roommates in school."

His eyebrows knit together. "Oleg Antonov's daughter?"

"Papa! She doesn't want to be reminded of that."

He points in my direction. "Hard to believe, looking at her, that this little thing was behind the coup to kill Oleg and take over the Antonov Bratva."

My stomach twists. My family's legacy is ugly and brutal, and it's all because of my father. The man who stole me from my mother's arms as a newborn and shipped me off to Russia to be raised by his sister, Masha, while he stayed in the US.

By the time I turned twenty-one, Oleg had completely unraveled. His drug and alcohol abuse escalated, he ventured into human trafficking and started cutting the street drugs he sold with fentanyl. His senior lieutenants were fed up. They came to Russia and secretly met with me and Aunt Masha, urging me to dethrone my father and claim my place as the rightful heir.

Leading the Antonov Bratva was not the future I'd pictured, but I hated my father and what he was doing. Only, the attack that we planned went south when someone tipped him off. In the end, my father survived, but most of his senior lieutenants were killed. After that, Oleg became hell-bent on revenge. He had my aunt murdered, and would have done the same to me if he could.

But he wasn't about to. I got to him first.

Liza's eyes widen and her mouth falls open as she prepares to scold her father, but I stop her with a hand on her shoulder.

"It's okay," I assure her. "It's been said before."

Boris starts to laugh like I told him the funniest joke in the world, and Liza and I exchange looks.

"Why are you here?!" he asks, wiping a tear from his eye. "Out to get revenge on the host?"

"Why would you say something so ridiculous? She's a guest here, like us." Liza flashes me an apologetic look, but there's something about Boris's tone that sets my teeth on edge.

"What do you mean, get my revenge?" I ask cautiously.

Leaning in closer, his voice drops to a conspiratorial whisper. "You know, considering the rumors about how Maxim helped kill Masha Antonov."

"Ex-excuse me?" My breath catches in my throat, and everything around me spins as his words hit me like a freight train.

"You don't know what you're saying!" Liza's voice quivers with rage. "You're drunk!"

"I am, but I still know what I'm talking about."

My blood freezes in my veins. I'd love to dismiss Boris's revelations as drunken ramblings, but I've long known that while my father ordered the hit on my aunt, someone else lured her out of hiding. "Why would Maxim Belov help my father kill Masha?"

"Why? Who knows." He shrugs, his words slurred and his eyes glassy. "Maxim Belov does whatever he wants. No one would dare challenge him."

Liza shakes her head in disgust before her worried eyes meet mine. "Please tell me you don't believe a word. He can barely stand."

"Why would he make up something like that?" I stumble back, trying to get control over my racing thoughts. "Last summer, when I was back in Russia cleaning out my aunt's secret cabin—the place she'd been hiding out in—I found the diary she'd kept in the days before she was murdered. In the entries leading up to her death, she mentioned someone she knew and trusted who had vowed to protect her. Although she didn't disclose their identity, she planned to meet them in Moscow. But whoever this person was did the exact opposite. They led her like a lamb to the slaughter."

Liza frowns. "It's still a jump to think Maxim had anything to do with it."

I swallow the lump of emotion clogging my throat. "He knew my aunt—he told me so. And he's one of the few people powerful enough who could have protected her from my father."

Liza blows out a breath. "What would his motivation be?"

I pause, my hands curling at my sides. "Well, I don't know, but I certainly plan on finding out."

"No! You need to drop this." She grabs my shoulders, and she fixes me with a stern look. "Maxim is dangerous. You know that as well as I do. He'll kill you—his daughter's friend or not—if you start sniffing around his business."

My lips form a firm line. "If it's true, there's no way in hell I'm leaving it alone, even knowing what Maxim Belov is capable of."

"You don't even know if it's true—you just admitted that yourself. My father's drunken ramblings and a vague diary entry aren't proof."

We both look down at Boris, now passed out in his seat.

"Then I'll find the proof."

"Like that's easy. Maxim is better guarded than the gold reserves at Fort Knox."

I sigh. She's not wrong, but a challenge won't dissuade me. I vowed to myself I'd never forget—I'd avenge Masha's death when the opportunity arose. This is the first solid lead I've had, and I'm sticking to my promise. Her murder will not go unanswered, no matter what it costs me.

"I don't know how, but I'm going to figure this out," I announce before breaking from Liza's hold and striding towards the main ballroom.

She calls to me, but I don't turn around.

I need to see Maxim for myself. Scanning the room, I spot him surrounded by a group of men, all hanging onto his every word. His gaze lifts to mine, and in an instant, I'm caught, unable to look away from his commanding stare.

A chill runs down my spine. His lips twist into a smirk, clearly amused by my unease, but I stand my ground.

Whatever secrets he's hiding, I will unearth them before I burn him alive. I don't know how, only that I'll find a way. And somewhere in all of this, I'll free Aly from his grasp too.

* * *

Fifteen minutes later, I've done two laps of the ballroom, staked out the washroom, and checked the hallways, but I can't find Aly anywhere. I feel bad that I left her to fend for herself for so long. I'm sure tonight feels never-ending for her.

As I push through the crowd, a waiter grabs my elbow, guiding me to the side. Irritated, I'm about to pull my arm away, but as he steps forward into the light, my breath catches in my throat.

"Andrei?" I whisper.

My eldest brother, the Kozlov Bratva pakhan, stands before me disguised as a waiter, complete with a wig and an absurdly fake mustache. Under any other circumstances the situation would be laughable, but right now it feels surreal.

I've never been so relieved and horrified to see anyone in my life. Relieved because Andrei always makes everything better, but horrified by what Maxim will do to him if he's discovered.

"Are you hurt?" he whispers darkly. "Has he mistreated you? I swear to God, if he put his hands on you—"

"He hasn't hurt us..." I hesitate. Aly will be furious if I tell my brother the truth because she's convinced Maxim will make good on his promise to kill her loved ones, especially Leo. But I can't pretend everything is fine. "The situation isn't great."

Andrei glances around, ensuring we're not overheard. "No kidding. That's why we're here. To get you guys out."

"Who else is here?"

"Only Daniil, Leo, and Yulian," he replies, referring to our other two brothers and Aly's brother, Yulian. "We snuck in as..." Andrei pulls a face and gestures to his ridiculous waiter costume. "We've looped the security cameras, but we don't have long. We need to put some distance between us and Belov's men before they realize you're gone."

I clasp my hands together tightly, our grim reality crashing down. "He has a damn army. Leaving here unnoticed won't be easy."

Andrei grimaces. "There are helicopters waiting for us a few miles out. We won't have a chance like this again—we need to take it."

My heartbeat quickens. Escaping from Maxim is reckless, dangerous, but Andrei is right. This is likely our only opportunity to break free. Even if it makes uncovering the truth about Masha's death all the more difficult, I have to do what's best for my friend. And what's best for her is escaping Maxim, even if I can't shake the feeling that he'll pursue her to the ends of the earth.

Anxiously, I scan the room. "I don't know where Aly is," I admit.

"She's in the wine cellar with Leo, which is where we're all to meet. Walk out of here like you're heading towards the washroom and then make your first sharp right. Go down the stairs heading into the basement. I'll meet you there."

Taking a deep breath, I force myself to appear calm and composed, even though my nerves are stretched tight like piano wires. Walking across the expanse of the room, I keep my gaze fixed straight ahead, silently praying I don't encounter Maxim on my way out.

My shoulders drop an inch as I reach the basement and Daniil and Yulian step out of the shadows. The sight of them floods me with relief. Daniil's eyes light up, and without a word, he strides forward, lifting me off the ground in a quick, tight hug.

"I can't believe you guys pulled this off," I marvel. "You're all crazy, you know that?"

My brother gives me one of his signature roguish grins. "Like we were going to leave you here in Belov's evil clutches."

Evil is exactly right. But there's no time to focus on tonight's revelations. That's for later.

Yulian steps forward, his hand clapping onto my shoulder in a reassuring gesture. I give him a small nod and smile as Andrei appears beside me.

His first line of business is to rip off his fake mustache with a wince. "How did I get stuck with the shitty fake mustache? This is humiliating," he grumbles. Daniil opens his mouth, but Andrei cuts him off with a sharp look. "You are to never mention this. Ever."

Daniil shrugs. "I make no guarantees."

"Save the bickering until we're out of here," Yulian grumbles, expression tense. "Follow me." He leads the way towards what I assume is the wine cellar. Swinging open the door, he's the first one in the cellar-like room, sweeping Aly up in his arms. "Thank fuck you're okay."

"I am," she reassures him.

"We need to get moving." Yulian points towards the exit. "Van's out back."

Aly's expression drops, hands clasped together. "I can't," she says. "You go. I need to stay for now. It won't be forever, but—"

Yulian's head snaps back. "What are you talking about?"

"If you stay, I'm staying. I'm not leaving here without you," Leo declares, his eyes locked on Aly—the love of his life he's only just gotten back.

Before the argument can continue, the lights stutter, blanketing the wine cellar in sudden darkness.

This isn't good.

Dread pools in my stomach, and all I can do is brace myself for whatever nightmare is about to unfold.

Chapter Two

KIRA

The creak of the door breaks the silence, followed by the heavy tread of boots. My heart pounds like a drum as the lights flicker on, bringing Maxim and his cold fury into sharp focus.

His guards stand behind him, weapons drawn, and his own gun is aimed directly at Leo. "A family reunion. And I wasn't invited?"

Leo glares back at him with hate. "You're not her family, even if you do share blood with her."

My muscles tense, fear pooling low in my belly. We're cornered, outnumbered, and facing the wrath of a man who knows no bounds.

"Let them go," Aly pleads with her father. "We had a deal. I'll stay, but you have to let them all go."

The words are barely out of her mouth before Leo steps in front of her. His eyes are fierce with challenge as he raises his arm, a pistol pointed at his opponent's chest. It's a useless standoff, each man with a gun drawn at the other. The only difference is that Maxim has an army to back him up.

Maxim chuckles and casually lowers his weapon, a demonstration that he has all the power. "What's your endgame here, Kozlov?" he asks Leo, reclining against a wine cask. "Do you think you can rescue Alyona and gallop off into the sunset as a happy couple? You—the man who abandoned her for the brotherhood—are suddenly the knight in shining armor?"

A tingle of unease prickles my neck. How Maxim knows about Aly and Leo's past is beyond me, but one thing is certain: he's a man accustomed to getting his way. What he wants is a partner to rule alongside him. Whether it's Aly or another, bound by blood or oath, does it really matter to him?

While Maxim and Leo continue to face off, an idea begins to take shape in my mind, one that could alter everyone's lives here.

"This doesn't change anything," Maxim snarls, snapping my attention back to the present. "Alyona is still needed by my side."

"It is a choice. Her choice," Leo roars. "I'll do whatever it takes to secure Aly's freedom. Kill me if you must to make your point, but it will only drive your daughter away and deepen her hatred for you."

Goosebumps dance across my skin. Provoking Maxim is like taunting a lion in his den—it's only a matter of time before he strikes.

Andrei must have the same thought because he steps forward and tries a diplomatic approach to negotiating Aly's freedom, offering Maxim a lucrative alliance with the Kozlov Bratva.

"More money, more power... That means nothing to me," Maxim says with a dismissive wave. He comes to stop in front of Leo, his face as hard as granite. "While I applaud your loyalty to my daughter, I require an heir, a blood relation to lead by my side. And make no mistake" – his mouth settles into a hard line as he tilts his head towards Aly – "you may not want this, but you will learn to be a leader. As my daughter, it's in your blood. Are you willing to walk away from our agreement, Alyona?"

Aly's fear is palpable as Leo steps forward, looking ready to rip Maxim limb from limb.

"Stop!" All eyes are on me as I stride through the room and position myself directly in front of Maxim. Curiosity dances in his gaze as it settles on me. "You want an heir, someone to rule by your side..." The room takes a collective breath. "Then take me."

I'm gambling on Maxim's willingness to consider a different arrangement—one that offers Aly the freedom she craves while allowing me to infiltrate his inner circle. Because what better way to unearth Maxim's dark secrets than by his side ... as his *wife*?

"I'll marry you," I say, my nails pressing into my palms. "I will become your wife and lead by your side, but let Alyona go."

Maxim's expression morphs into one of intrigue, his eyebrows arching. One side of his full mouth quirks upwards.

"Kira, no!" Aly's voice is thick with panic, but I give her a pleading look. This plan serves us both.

"Now, why would you want to do that?" Maxim questions, eyes narrowed.

My skin feels electric with tension, but I keep my head high. "Because I want to be in power. I was born to rule. Even if I despised my father, royalty is in my blood. It's my fate. This will be nothing more than a business arrangement. No romantic entanglements, nothing that could get messy." I'm not sure if what I say next will sweeten the deal, but I'm desperate enough to try. "But I will give you heirs if that's what you want."

Maxim's face gives nothing away, his fists tight at his sides. It's surprising he's even considering my proposal, but it means I was on the mark—he wants someone bound to him to rule by his side, and he's smart enough to realize that he can't force his daughter into that role.

Maxim's demeanor remains composed as he turns to Aly. "What do you have to say on the matter?"

Her expression darkens. "I'd like to speak to my friend alone. Without you and your guards breathing down our necks."

"You have five minutes." With a sweep of his arms, Maxim and his men clear out of the room.

Aly is the first one to speak. Or rather, yell. "Are you crazy?! I won't let you do this," she hollers, stomping her foot. "You can't bear him a child! I won't allow you to sacrifice your happiness for mine."

"You're not allowing me to do anything," I point out. "It's my choice."

Leo turns to me. "*Sestra*, it means the world that you offer yourself like this, but there is another way."

"Leo is right." Andrei crosses his arms in front of his chest. "I can't stand the thought of you tying yourself to that monster for the rest of your life. We'll figure something out."

"I don't get it." Alyona's face falls. "You hate him. You hate him more than I do!"

"Oh, I hate him, alright." I sigh deeply. "But he's a means to an end." That's all I'll say on the matter. If I tell them my true motivations behind this marriage, they'll fight me bitterly. Because marrying Maxim Belov for the sole purpose of investigating him and possibly killing him is dangerous. I know it is, but it's a risk I'm willing to take.

Leo throws his hands in the air. "Money and power we have... What could he possibly give you?"

"Trust that I have my reasons. I can't tell you what those are right now, but I'm going into this with my eyes wide open."

"There is no 'wide open' with a snake like Belov," Daniil snarls. "At least take some time to consider. You can't decide your entire future under pressure like this."

"Aly and I can stay here while we try to work things out with Belov," Leo offers. "I can't allow you to throw away your future on a whim."

I hold up my hand. "This isn't a whim. And this is not a case of altruism. Although, you know I would do anything for you, Aly." I give her a weak smile. "This is for me."

"I don't know what to say." Aly gives a small shake of her head, her lower lip caught under her teeth. "'Thank you' doesn't seem sufficient."

"Not 'thank you'." I hug her. "How about 'good luck'?"

The hair on the back of my neck rises, and the air shifts in the room as Maxim comes back in. "So?" He raises his eyebrows at Alyona.

"What do you want me to say?" Aly's gaze hardens. "You've left us with no choice."

Maxim approaches me, standing so close I can smell his musky aftershave. One of his fingers tips my chin upwards, our eyes meeting. Something about how he looks at me, how close he's standing—all of it—causes a strange heat to stir within me. A flutter of nervous energy dances in my stomach, an uneasy mix of anticipation and dread. It must be the thrill of knowing I'll soon avenge my aunt's death.

"Is this what you want, lastochka?" It means swallow bird, a term of endearment, but he's using it to mock me.

"'Want' is a strong word, but I accept this arrangement."

His shrewd eyes sweep across my face as if unraveling my

true intentions. "I look forward to learning exactly what it is you're really after, Kira. And make no mistake, I *will* find out."

I have to bite the inside of my cheek to keep from reacting.

His gaze sweeps the crowd, his smile wolfish. "It's settled, then. Kira and I will marry. And that makes us all family."

The room is so silent you could hear a pin drop.

I refuse to look at Maxim or anyone else. From here on out, I'll act the part of his wife while digging up every dirty secret my soon-to-be husband is hiding.

Chapter Three

Present Day

KIRA

I burst onto the balcony, struggling to catch my breath as the French doors slam behind me. The cool night air floods my senses and clears my head—a welcome break from the cloying perfumes and vodka shots filling the wedding reception.

I press a hand to my racing heart, the lace fabric of my gown harsh against my skin. One breath, then another.

It's done. I'm officially a Belov.

We went right from the cathedral to the glitzy reception held in Moscow's finest hotel, a who's who of the country's elite milling about, satisfied they got an invite to the event of the year.

I didn't invite anyone, no friends or family. What's the point of anyone I'm close to witnessing this charade of a marriage?

Away from curious eyes, I find a stone bench against the

wall and sit down, drawing deep breaths and giving in to the vulnerability I've avoided since saying "I do".

I may be impulsive and hot-headed—Alyona and my brothers would certainly agree, especially if they knew why I really married Maxim—but in this, I'm resolute. I've spent the last few years quietly chasing leads on Masha's killer, and none of them were solid. This is the first time all the cards line up.

A tremor of cold runs up my spine, not because of the night's chill but because of a movement in the far corner of the balcony.

"Is someone here?" I shoot up to a standing position. A near panic attack is a bad look for a bride.

I don't see anything, just sense it, until a single flame pierces the darkness. It ignites the end of a cigar, followed by an inhale and the wisp of smoke that fades into the night.

And then an achingly familiar voice—deep and powerful, and one I've come to hate—says, "Was it really that bad?"

My husband.

I'm quiet for a moment before I answer. "Being trotted around like a show pony? What every girl dreams of on her wedding day, no?"

He's still bathed in shadows, a halo of smoke surrounding him, but I hear his soft chuckle. The only soft thing about him. "It comes with the territory of being my wife. Isn't that what you wanted? If I recall correctly, *you* suggested marriage, not the other way around."

"Yes, but..." The words die on my lips.

Maxim rises like a phoenix out of the flames, and same as every time I see him, my heart stutters in my chest. Only his profile comes into the light, the sharp contours of his jawline and the slight curve of his lips casting a striking silhouette. This alone is enough to make grown women weep. My new husband might be a psychopath, but he's the very definition of rugged male beauty.

I clear my throat and try again. "I saw a business opportunity, and I took it. Alyona didn't want to be part of your world, and I didn't want to see her dragged in kicking and screaming, and miserable, when I knew I would be much better suited to rule by your side."

He advances on me, all traces of his charming public persona wiped away.

I step back because having Maxim this close short-circuits my brain. I swallow hard and look up at the man I'm bound to for life. Or at least until I murder him.

But I won't kill Maxim until I know exactly what he did and why.

"Ah, yes. A business opportunity." He takes a puff of his cigar and blows a ring over my head. "In that case, shouldn't we work out the terms of our agreement?"

There's something in his tone that catches me off guard. A shiver runs down my spine.

You'd think I would have spent time negotiating the terms of our agreement, but right after agreeing to the marriage, Maxim allowed me a month before settling in Moscow by his side. I spent most of the time in Brooklyn, packing up my apartment and sorting out my affairs, not reaching out to anyone I know because they'd have questions I didn't want to answer.

I swallow hard. "I agree. We need to talk." I look behind me through the glass doors at the party still in full swing. "But, right now?"

He flicks a wrist dismissively. "Our guests will wait."

Ideally, access to his business would be the best way for me to investigate his connections, alliances, enemies—anything that can shed light on his past involvement with the Antonov Bratva, particularly if he owed my father any favors. What motivates him—is it money, power, retribution? Beyond business magnate, beyond being the man that Russia's crime syndicates report to, who is he really?

A little late for that.

Apart from the few public details, all I know is that he's nearly twice my age, my best friend's biological father, and he was married at one time. That juicy tidbit, he confided in Alyona.

I swallow hard, my throat feeling dry and tight. "I'd like to help run your syndicate business. As you know, I've been involved in the Kozlov Bratva for several years and—"

"I wanted Alyona—my daughter, my heir—to help lead my empire. That's not what I require from you." He tilts his head, assessing me quietly. "What I need from you is a society wife. Host parties, involve yourself in charities, attend events with me, look good on my arm—"

"What!" Anger presses down on my shoulders. "You're looking for a trophy wife? To throw dinner parties and look hot? You could have mentioned that earlier."

"I never said anything about dinner parties." His voice is as dry as paper.

I don't know whether to laugh or punch him. He leans in, the close proximity forcing me to tilt my head up to meet his dark blue orbs. A flicker of unease drips down my spine because Maxim, up close and personal, is intimidating as fuck.

"This is a business arrangement, Kira, and in business, I always do what's best for me."

I stomp a foot. "I am capable of much more than shopping and hosting parties. Surely, you see my value as something more than a Stepford wife."

He stills, nostrils flaring as he runs a thumb down the center of his lips. "A few hours ago, you pledged to obey me. Are you breaking your vows already? Because I don't think you'll like the consequences of disobeying me." His lips curl up at the corner but not in a friendly way.

His threat burrows under my skin, making my collar feel like a noose. I take a step back and suck in a full breath. "You wanted Alyona in your business, so why not me?"

"Because my circumstances have changed." With deliberate precision, Maxim grinds his cigar into a nearby ashtray, ensuring every ember is extinguished before his eyes cut back to mine. "As you know, my business interests are ... varied." I take that to mean legal and not-at-all legal. "We're having some trouble with a powerful triad based in Hong Kong, and things are about to get messy. I don't need bad press complicating matters, so I'm feeding them a juicy story to ensure they're distracted."

Realization dawns slowly. "I'm the story. We're the story." Moscow's most eligible bachelor off the market is what headline dreams are made of. It certainly explains the media covering our wedding—something I wasn't entirely prepared for.

"I think you understand now."

My mouth opens and closes, then opens again. "You ... you misled me. I thought I was going to be your partner, not just a pretty distraction." Heat blooms under my collar, and yet I don't know why I'm the least bit surprised. Maxim is as slippery as they come.

A muscle ticks in his jaw. "Perhaps you should have clarified the terms before you suggested marriage."

I take a deep, calming breath and assess the situation. Fighting him will get me nowhere—he's as impenetrable as steel. If Maxim wants a society wife, fine, but it won't stop me from learning what I need to.

"You're right. I should have." The soft light from the ballroom dances across the sharp angles of his face. It seems like a cruel joke that a man this hot could also be so damn cold. "But here we are. Let's set the terms now. I'll be what you need me to be—I'll throw the parties and the dinners, and play the part of a perfect wife, but in return, I want you to take me seriously. In time, I want an expanded role in your world, one with real power."

That smirk, which I've already come to loathe, curls his lips. "Your role will be expanded," he says, catching me off-guard. I'm pleasantly surprised until he finishes the thought. "You'll bear me children. Did you forget so soon, Kira? When you offered yourself up as my bride, you promised me heirs."

My promise in the wine cellar comes back to haunt me. It was never a promise I intended to keep. I'd consider having kids someday, but certainly not with this monster. Still, I'll let him believe I'm willing, long enough to learn what I need to.

"I didn't forget, but I need time." My mind spins out, trying to grasp onto a length of time that seems reasonable. "One month. Give me one month to settle into your world, and then we can ... we can..." The words stick in my throat, and for some reason, it seems to amuse Maxim. "Start a family. But before then, there will be no physical relationship between us. Sleep with whomever you want. I don't care. Between us, it's strictly business."

I'm no prude. I like sex. No, scratch that—I love it. I usually have plenty of it in the form of one-night stands and temporary flings, but I'll never sleep with my aunt's killer.

"Good to know that I have your blessing, but just so we're clear, I don't need it. I take what I want, when I want it." He grasps my chin, our gazes clashing. His thumb skates deliberately over my jaw. "I'm not extending the same permission to you." His grip on my chin tightens ever so slightly, his eyes burning with a possessive intensity. "I never want to hear of another man touching, no less looking your way. Business arrangement or not, I don't share what's mine."

My head snaps back, disgusted by his alpha-hole chauvinism. He may be the consummate politician in public, but he doesn't maintain the gentleman's façade with me. "One month," he rasps. "That's all the time I'll give you."

"Great, then we understand each other." I rip my chin from his hold, desperate to regain my composure. Balling my hands into fists, my eyes flick towards the French doors.

Inside, the party continues to celebrate in our honor. The guests are happy to toast our supposed wedded bliss, lost in the illusion of a love story that couldn't be farther from the truth.

"We should get back to our wedding," I tell him. Not because I want to, but because plastering on a fake smile and shaking hands is easier than staring at him any longer.

His strong hand circles my wrist, and the heat from his grip sends an unexpected jolt through me.

"One month." His words ghost over the shell of my ear, and then he's gone.

A month. That's all the time I have to figure out what involvement he had in my aunt's murder. After that, my hands will either be soaked in his blood after I take my revenge, or... Well, the alternative is bleak. I'll be six feet underground.

Because one thing is for certain: crossing Maxim Belov is a death sentence.

Chapter Four

MAXIM

"Has the motherfucker opened his mouth yet?"

Yuri, standing sentry by the door to our interrogation room, stares at me dumbly, about to take a bite of a sandwich. When he registers my presence, he lowers the sandwich and stands. "Not yet, boss. Roman is still working on him."

I toss my bow tie and cufflinks at the kid and roll up my sleeves.

Yuri's eyebrows press together. "Isn't it your wedding ... like, now?"

"Just came from the reception."

"Uhh ... congratulations?"

I nod, although I'm not sure what there is to congratulate me on. I broke a promise I made to myself long ago to never marry again. Not when the first time brought a betrayal so deep it tore my world apart.

I push past the soldier into the barren room.

Roman, one of my two right-hand men, turns as I enter and fixes me with a questioning stare—the question being, *What the fuck are you doing here on your wedding night?*

My unspoken response is simple. *Don't fucking worry about it.*

Most men would be taking advantage of their bride, especially one as gorgeous as Kira. Almond-shaped hazel eyes flecked with green and gold, shoulder-length wavy blonde hair, and curves that could drive a man to madness. But as hard as she makes my dick, she's a means to an end and nothing more.

I approach the man tied to a chair in the center of the room and punch him square in the jaw. The violence soothes the restless energy that's flowed under my skin since Kira walked down the aisle towards me, looking forlorn and fierce like a wild storm dressed in white.

When I abducted Alyona, Kira was collateral damage because she was hiding out with my daughter. I'd heard of Kira by reputation only, but I had no business with her. My focus was entirely on bringing Alyona into my world, but I misjudged her. Because Alyona doesn't care about privilege and power. What she wants is a normal life with the man she loves—Leonid Kozlov. Even though I was prepared to force her hand, it was clear she would never accept her place in my world. That she would come to hate me more than she already did, and that hate would poison her soul. I'd already lost one child, my little boy, Ilya—the one bright star in my world. I refused to lose another.

This union has its purpose, and it's to keep the world focused on the trivial and away from the war brewing with the Black Company.

As much as I'm a legitimate businessman with investments in tech and real estate, I'm also involved in fraud: art, finance, and now luxury wine—a market dominated by the Black

Company Triad ... until now. The man tied to the chair in front of me is proof that they don't welcome the competition. Too bad for them because I have no intention of backing down.

My prisoner's cries bring me back to the present. His blood and spittle cover my white dress shirt, and the smell of copper and dirt filters through the air.

Henri Blanchet looks like he's been to hell and back. He's a European wine expert that we paid a stupid amount of money to, to help us craft high-end counterfeit wines. But recently, my hackers figured out that he was double-crossing us. Taking our paycheck and then spilling our secrets to the Black Company. Which is why he's tied to the chair in front of me. Roman worked him over but kept him alive until I could join.

"Let's get this fucker talking," I spit.

Roman walks behind Blanchet and uses a blade to nip the skin of his neck, watching blood drip over his hands. The man groans, fear and hate warring in his expression.

I grab Blanchet by the hair, jerking his head back, forcing him to meet my gaze. "Talk now, and I might make your death quick." I hoist a drill into view, flicking it on long enough for him to catch my drift. Blanchet's eyes widen in a silent, horrified plea.

His lips tremble and he starts spilling everything, the words tumbling out in a frantic rush, proving a universal truth—fear is a powerful motivator.

* * *

An hour later, one less soul graces God's green earth and I'm back in my office, pouring a generous two— no, make that four —fingers of whiskey. The fiery liquid disappears quickly, and I'm pouring a second glass as Pavel and Roman enter the room.

These two men have proven their worth, especially after

Ilya's death. They're my right hands that help me run my empire.

Pavel's cold gray eyes are sharp against his slicked-back blond hair. His suit, black and impeccably tailored, wasn't just picked for my wedding earlier—it's his uniform. I'd wager he even sleeps in Armani. Pavel views the world in absolutes; there's no gray area for him. You're either loyal or a traitor. Friend or foe. From the day we met in a boxing studio on the wrong side of town, he's shown an unwavering loyalty.

Roman, on the other hand, is a study in contrast to Pavel. Not only physically with his deep brown eyes and dark, wavy hair, but his personality too. It's lighter, friendlier, less intense. Roman wouldn't be caught dead in a suit; his preference is for leather jackets and washed-out jeans.

Like most opposites, they complement each other well.

Pavel sinks into a high wingback chair across from my desk as Roman pours himself a whiskey.

"So what did you learn in school today, children?" Pavel inquires.

"Nothing we didn't suspect already." I drag my hand down the side of my face. "Blanchet was compromised a few weeks ago, which lines up with when our hackers noticed large sums of money funneled into his account. Money in exchange for information. They wanted to know everything about our operations: the wines we're crafting, the volume of our output, when we plan on hitting the international auction market." I thread my fingers in front of me.

Stirring his drink, Roman adds, "Blanchet's job was also to sabotage our production. Fuck up the labels somehow so the auction houses would find a tiny discrepancy. The Black Company doesn't want to outdo us. They want to end us."

"Almost can't blame them." Pavel shrugs. "We're fucking good."

We can flawlessly reproduce bottles of the finest vintage wines in taste, appearance, and packaging. Wine fraud isn't my most profitable venture—not by a long shot—but I love nothing more than parting rich people with their money and putting it to better uses.

I rest my elbows on the desk and steeple my fingers under my chin. "His Black Company contact was a guy named Chun Leung. He only ever dealt with Leung in person, which means he's in Moscow, but Blanchet doesn't have a number for him. Leung would always call him on a burner phone to set up their in-person meetings."

Pavel's leg bounces in a steady beat. "I'll speak to our guys about hacking into Blanchet's phone, digging out the dates and locations of their meetings."

I nod. "Then we can comb through CCTV footage from around the city to help us identify Leung."

Our goal is to find the elusive leader of the Black Company. If we can figure out who he is and take him out, the war is ours. His soldiers will be lost without his direction.

"Looks like you've married in time for us to go to war." Roman sits back and leans his hands on his head.

I down the rest of my drink, feeling the usual churning in my gut when it comes to a ring around my finger. But marriage to Kira was too good of an opportunity to pass up—I could use the media attention to distract from the shit storm that is brewing with the Triad. And marrying Kira, Alyona's best friend, also keeps my daughter in my orbit. Despite impressions to the contrary, I want my daughter to be happy.

Roman chuckles as he flips through images on his phone. His eyes flick up to mine. "I don't suppose you've seen the social media coverage of your wedding." He angles his phone towards me and imitates a chirpy entertainment reporter. "It seems Russia's most eligible bachelor has been swept off his feet by a half-American beauty, leaving the nation breathless. Everyone wants to know more about the most surprising love story of the year."

I give Roman a dry look. "Remember, there's a loaded gun under this desk and I'm not shy about using it."

Pavel scoffs. "Kira barely said yes to you at the altar today."

Her flushed cheeks and clenched fists revealed her hesitation, even as she tried to appear brave. Twenty-five years old is a child, even if she doesn't look like one with curves for days. Curves that I need to put out of my head if I know what's good for me.

I raise an eyebrow at Pavel. "Is there something you want to say?"

"Nothing I haven't said before."

Pavel doesn't trust Kira's motivations. Despite her insistence that she wants the power that comes with my last name, it's hardly the full story. As part of the Kozlov Bratva, she had money, power, and privilege. Not at my level, but she wasn't exactly struggling. Either she's a martyr who wants to save Alyona from her big bad father, or she has ulterior motives. Whatever her reason, it doesn't matter—she's in my world now, and I hold the reins.

"Like I've said, I don't trust the little minx either. It's why I'll need one of you to serve as her personal bodyguard."

"No, fucking thank you," Pavel says at the same time as Roman says, "That'll be a hard pass."

I blow out a breath. "It wasn't a question. We need eyes on her, and you two are the only ones I trust. I'm not arguing the issue, so work it out."

"Fuck me!" Roman exclaims after a particularly aggressive rock, paper, scissor game. Despite both of them being only five years younger than my forty-three, I swear sometimes they act like boys.

Roman slumps down on the couch. "I've been demoted."

Pavel smirks. "Good. Maybe it will teach you some humility." Turning to me, Pavel says, "You'll need to put a lock on her room at night or I guarantee she'll slit your throat in your sleep."

I grin at that. "No need. She'll sleep in my bed. It's the best way to keep a close eye on her." It's also going to be distracting as fuck, but I refuse to dwell on that.

"In your bed?" Roman's eyebrows shoot up to his hairline. "Might as well leave a dagger under her pillow."

My jaw tightens. "I'm quite sure I can defend myself against a woman."

She's built for fucking, not fighting. But I won't be doing either. What Kira doesn't know yet is that I have no intention of bringing another child into this world. I've only let her believe I want an heir to keep her in line.

"Don't underestimate her, that's all I'm saying." Pavel runs a hand through his short hair. "Her father did, and it didn't end well for him."

"Please say you're not comparing me to Oleg Antonov. I'll take that as a grave insult."

Pavel raises his hands. "I wouldn't dream of it. Just a friendly reminder to sleep with one eye open."

Standing up, I signal the end of the discussion. I point at Pavel. "You handle the Black Company. I'll handle my wife."

Chapter Five

KIRA

"And this is the marital bedroom." Nadya, Maxim's personal assistant, flings the door open and charges in ahead of me while I'm still contemplating the term "marital bedroom".

I better have misheard her because my feelings towards Maxim are anything but domestic. He disappeared after the reception last night, leaving me alone at the hotel where we were married. Frankly, it was a relief that he had no wedding night expectations. I tore off my dress like it contained the plague, ordered fries and a milkshake from room service, sank into the luxurious cloud of a bed, and binged *The Golden Girls*.

This morning, reality came calling. A car came for me, whisking me to the high-end Rublyovka area Maxim calls home. It's my first time seeing the house or meeting any of his staff. And this *delight*, Nadya Petrovna, appears to run the joint with an iron fist.

Stern, with silver-streaked hair pulled back into a tight bun and hawkish brown eyes, I can sense her territorial instincts flaring. According to her, she's been running Maxim's home and life for the last fifteen years as his personal assistant. I've stepped into her territory, and she's clearly not happy about having to deal with a new lady of the house. Especially one young enough to be her daughter.

I turn to her and force a friendly smile. "I think there has been a miscommunication. Maxim and I won't be sharing a bedroom."

Her lips tighten. "According to Maxim, you will."

There's no way I'm getting cozy with that mudak at night, especially since I bought myself a whole sex-free month. But the other factor is the nightmares I have about my aunt's death. I don't have them every night, but when I do, they leave me shaken and sweaty, the images haunting me long after I wake up. It's not something I want Maxim to witness. Who knows what I'll reveal in my sleep.

"If you call him," I say between clenched teeth, "you will find that the arrangement between us has changed."

Nadya sniffs and raises her chin, fingering the cross around her neck. "Maxim would have informed me. He's not a man who acts on a whim." She changes the subject, like my objection means nothing. "Your clothes are in the closet, and your personal belongings have been unpacked. I suggest you make yourself at home."

Home? Please. There's nothing cozy about this place. When Nadya rushed me through the mansion, from the fancy entrance to Maxim's room, I noticed the dark-paneled walls covered with modern art, sleek leather furniture, and a whole lot of glass.

Sure, it looks nice, but the space doesn't exactly feel inviting.

Nadya's lips press into a thin line, like she's daring me to argue with her. I'd love to tell her off, but she could be a valuable source of information. It might take her time to accept my new role in the house, but hopefully she and I can come to an understanding.

I break our silent face-off with a peace-making smile. "Alright then. I'm sure you know what's best."

"I do. And it will benefit you to realize that sooner than later." *Touché*! But her shoulders lower an inch at my placating words.

I certainly have no plans of sharing a bed with Maxim, but Nadya doesn't need to know what happens behind closed doors.

With a victorious sniff, she informs me, "Breakfast will be served in half an hour. Maxim will be expecting you in the dining room."

"Got it," I say, attempting to sound enthusiastic but falling short.

I breathe a sigh of relief as the witch takes her leave.

Alone in Maxim's bedroom, I feel a million miles from home. His room is as generic as a hotel. Like the rest of the house, it lacks the personal touches that make a space feel lived-in and warm. Everything is beautiful and expensive, of course, but the only sense of Maxim is his aftershave lingering in the air.

Sitting down on the bed, I fish my cell phone from my purse and prepare to make the call I've avoided for ... oh, an entire month. But now that we're married and the wedding was certainly covered by the press near and far, there is no putting off the inevitable.

Aly answers on the first ring. "Kira! Oh my God, I'm looking at your pictures online right now. Holy shit, you actually went through with it."

I stare at the four-carat ring weighing down my finger. "I did," I confirm.

She sighs. "Why didn't you tell us it was happening so soon? I feel bad that we weren't there for you."

"Don't feel bad, please," I say, shaking my head even though she can't see me. "There's so much bad blood between everyone and Maxim, and I didn't want it to be uncomfortable."

"We would have sucked it up in order to be there for you," Aly counters.

"I know it's hard for you and my brothers to understand, but this is something I have to do on my own. I'm fine, really. I promise you."

She releases a wary breath, and I can tell she's holding back a barrage of questions. "How are you and Leo?" I ask, changing the subject. "I bet he's the happiest man in the world right now."

Aly and my brother, Leo, have been circling each other since they were teens. The one good thing that came out of Maxim attempting to abduct Aly is that it brought her and Leo back together. When my brother found out someone was pursuing Aly, he dropped everything and whisked her away on a yacht to keep her safe.

A puff of laughter slips from her. "He's good. We're both good. We're planning our wedding in a few months. I hope you can come."

My heart sinks in my chest because I have no idea what the future holds for me. "Maybe," I offer. "Keep me updated, okay? I have to go, but it was so nice to hear your voice. I miss you. Send my love to everyone."

"I miss you too. And, Kira?"

"Yes."

"You know we're always here for you, whether you change

your mind or need help. Whatever the situation, I'm a phone call away."

I fight the ball of emotion that threatens to choke me. "Thank you. You're the best."

"Right back at you, babe."

I hang up, struggling to contain my tears. The weight of everything bears down on me. My family wants to help, but getting them involved means putting them right in Maxim's crossfire.

I check my watch and realize I only have five minutes before I'm expected downstairs. With that, I make my next call.

Liza answers on the first ring. "Allo?"

"Hi. It's me, Kira."

"Oh, I know who it is," she quips. "You married Maxim fucking Belov, and you didn't think to ... oh, I don't know ... give me advance warning! Seriously, what the fuck?"

Welp, I had to see that coming.

"I know it seems nuts, but the opportunity presented itself, and... What can I say?" I haven't spoken to Liza since the night of the ball. I knew she'd try to reason with me, and frankly, that's exactly what I wanted to avoid.

"I'll explain everything in person," I promise. "Can we meet today? Somewhere private, where we can be alone."

"Alone?" She sighs as if this is all too much. "You'll never be alone again. Maxim is going to assign a legion of guards to you."

I puff out my cheeks. "Let that be my concern. Pick a place and text it to this number."

She snorts. "I hope you know what you are doing, Kira. *Da ty yobanulass.*"

Am I out of my mind? Maybe. I've certainly been accused of worse.

Chapter Six

KIRA

"*Syrniki*," Nadya announces, unceremoniously dropping a plate of Russian cheese pancakes in front of me.

Why Maxim's assistant is serving me breakfast when there's a cook and an army of waiters nearby is a mystery. I assume it's to spread her loving joy first thing in the morning. Or possibly to poison me.

Across the table, Maxim is hidden behind a raised newspaper, effectively blocking me from his view. The only part of him visible is his hand, occasionally darting out to grab his tea cup. I think I see a bruise on his knuckles, but it could be the lighting playing tricks on me.

Flanking Maxim are the two men I met briefly at our wedding. Pavel Ivanovich is the one with blond hair. Strikingly handsome but cold, he looks like he stepped out of a Viking legend. The other is Roman Vasiliev, with deep brown eyes and dark wavy hair that many women would pay good money to run their fingers through. He seems the friendlier of the two. Exactly what these men are to Maxim isn't clear, but I get the feeling they're his right hands.

Pavel is vibrating with intense energy, one foot tapping under the table while he stares at a spot directly above my head. Roman is sitting back, lounging like a king, and sexting God knows who. The look in his eyes as he concentrates on his phone can only be described as devilish.

Nadya slides into the seat next to me, a plate of toast as dry as the conversation at this table in front of her. She raises an eyebrow at my plate, judging the stack of jam-drenched pancakes in front of me.

I take an extra-large bite, letting out an exaggerated moan of delight for Nadya's benefit. She eyes me with disapproval.

"Mmm, you guys are missing out," I say with a little grin. The pancake is ridiculously good, and I'm not going to pretend otherwise. As I catch Nadya's eye, I add an extra flourish, swirling the pancake in the jam. I know I need to get on her good side, but I'm starting to wonder if she even has one.

Maxim snaps his newspaper shut and folds it into a crisp rectangle, clearly preparing to get down to business. Everyone else follows his lead, sitting up straighter. Roman even stows his phone.

"Give me a rundown of my schedule?" he says to Nadya.

Like an efficient little robot, she pushes her plate away, and without missing a beat, picks up her tablet and starts scrolling. "At nine, you have a meeting with the board of directors at XD Industries," she begins, her voice crisp and business-like. "Then at ten thirty, there's a conference call with your European contacts regarding the new shipping routes. Lunch at noon with the finance minister at The Grand. It's about—" She glances up briefly, looking at me like my presence is a nuisance. "Well, you know." Returning her gaze to the tablet, she continues, "At three, you're inspecting the new construction site, and there's a video conference with the legal team about the recent acquisitions at four." She swipes her fingers across the screen. "Your night is reserved for a private event with the—"

"Clear my schedule for tonight."

Nadya looks up from her tablet, bewildered. "But the ambassador—"

"Can be rescheduled."

Maxim's gaze settles on me, and for some reason, a blush climbs up my neck and warms my face. When Maxim gives me the full weight of his attention, it steals the breath from my lungs.

"What are your plans today?" he asks me, like I have a life here. Like we didn't only get married yesterday. Although, in this instance, I actually do have plans.

"I am going shopping with an old friend of mine, Elizaveta Ivanova. I'm sure you know her father," I say, sipping my black coffee.

If Maxim is surprised at my acquaintance with Liza, he doesn't show it. "Good," he remarks, his eyes scanning my outfit—a sleek, leather jacket paired with distressed jeans and a form-fitting top that says *What Would Joan Jett do?* "You'll be expected to join me at various public events in the next few weeks. You'll need to elevate your wardrobe accordingly. I'm sure Nadya can advise on what's suitable."

Uh, yeah right I'm taking fashion advice from someone who looks like she's perpetually attending a funeral.

I lift my chin. "I'm sure I can choose my clothes without her *expert* guidance."

He runs a palm over his jaw and assesses me carefully.

"I guess we'll see, won't we? Roman will be your guard from now on. He will accompany you everywhere. And unlike fashion, that's not up for debate."

"Great." I force a smile. "What I always wanted. A babysitter." Roman might seem laid-back, but I have no doubt he's tasked with spying on me, which means I have to tread carefully around him.

Roman snorts and shrugs his shoulders. "Babysitter? Please. I'm like the cool uncle but with a gun."

Maxim leans back, stretching in a way that showcases his powerful frame. I look away as butterflies flutter in my stomach. Even in a suit, he can barely conceal his ripped physique. Shit, this is not where I want my focus.

"I need a word alone with my wife," Maxim announces.

Everyone seems to do a double take, and I wonder if it's because he referred to me as his wife for the first time ever. Roman and Pavel rise and leave the room without another word, but I can sense Nadya hovering. One sharp look from Maxim sends her packing.

I'm curious what he has to say to me privately since everything else about our arrangement seems to be known within this small circle.

Dropping his napkin in front of him, Maxim drums his fingers on the table. "Have you spoken with Alyona recently?"

I'm surprised by his question. Now that he has someone else under this thumb, I don't see why he cares. "What? You're not monitoring my communication?"

His jaw ticks. "No, but if you keep on being a brat, I'll start."

"Whatever," I mumble. "It's none of your business. It's not like you care about her. You demonstrated that very clearly."

A shadow crosses Maxim's face. "I'd still like to know how she's doing."

I gesture to my phone. "You're welcome to call her."

"I doubt she'd like to hear from me." He sneers.

"True." I look at my nails. "Is that all you wanted to talk to me about?"

A muscle in Maxim's cheek twitches, and I have to suppress a grin. He reaches into his front pocket, retrieving a sleek brown wallet. From it, he pulls out a black Amex card and slides it across the table towards me.

I don't reach for it.

"I have my own money," I say, not liking the idea of being in his debt.

"That's not how this works, Kira. You're no longer the New York mafia princess, free to do whatever you like. You're a Belov now. My wife. What is expected of you is a level of decorum and respect fitting the Belov name."

I'm tempted to ask what exactly defines the Belov name—abduction, perhaps dark rituals?—but he leans forward and runs a thumb over my knuckle, and I swear my brain checks out.

"When you're out with me, I need you to look every inch my equal."

We lock eyes for a moment, the room crackling with unspoken tension.

"What does it mean to be your equal?"

His eyes briefly dip to my lips, before meeting my stare. "You're smart. You'll figure it out."

Before I can ask what the hell that means, he's already exiting the room, not sparing me another look. On his way out, I catch a glimpse of a pistol concealed beneath the hem of his Armani jacket.

Respectable businessman, my ass.

Chapter Seven

KIRA

An hour later, accompanied by Roman and a small contingent of Maxim's men, I arrive at the high-end boutique in central Moscow Liza recommended.

Despite the size of my entourage, I bet Liza has come up with a way for us to talk privately. She's the think-ahead type, balancing my spontaneity. My aunt used to tell me, "You leap without looking, and Liza's there to build the bridge under your feet." While I could be impulsive, Liza's always been my level-headed anchor—the one who organized our group study sessions at school and wouldn't let me drink too much at parties.

We enter the store to find Liza waiting. Attentive assistants flit about her, and with a sigh of relief, I realize she had the foresight to close the store to the public.

"Kira." She rises and wraps her arms around me, before pulling back and taking in the handsome man by my side. Her eyebrows raise in a silent question.

"Liza, this is Roman Vasiliev, one of Maxim's—" I'm about to say guard dogs when he steps forward, his eyes running curiously over my friend.

"An associate of Maxim's," is all he says. "And now personal guard to Mrs. Belov."

"Nope. Please never call me that again," I hiss.

He ignores me completely. "And this is the lovely Elizaveta Ivanova, I take it."

He sticks his hand out in greeting, and Liza eyes it like it's a dead fish before giving it a cursory shake.

"I'm acquainted with your father and fiancé," he adds. "But I only know you by reputation."

Liza's eyes narrow. "Yes, well, don't believe everything you hear."

When I tilt my head at Liza, she gives me a subtle shake of her head. *Oh-kay.* Clearly, I've been out of the gossip loop in this city for far too long.

"So, shall we get to shopping?" Roman rubs his hands together like he's been waiting all day for the pleasure of retail therapy.

I pull myself to my full height of five feet, two inches. "We will. As in, Liza and myself. I suggest you and your men go grab some coffee or the blood of angels, whatever it is that you drink, and leave us in peace."

"No can do." He shrugs apologetically. "My job is to keep you safe from harm, and I can't do that on a coffee break."

When I bristle at his words, Liza mumbles under her breath, "Who's going to keep you safe when you piss off Kira?"

Roman can't be swayed. I'm sure Maxim gave him explicit instructions to watch my every move—whether to keep me safe or because he doesn't trust me. Likely both. But it's clear Roman isn't going anywhere.

I gesture around us. "Do what you need to. We have some shopping to do."

Roman settles on one of the nearby settees, being fawned over by the female staff desperate to offer him a cappuccino, while his men fan out throughout the store.

Liza pulls me deeper into the boutique, where the evening wear is hung in elegant rows. When we're out of earshot, she points at my wedding ring and whisper-hisses, "Explain!"

"Keep it down," I say, busying my hands with rummaging through the racks.

When one of the many store assistants comes over, I scare them away with a sharp shake of my head. I dare a glimpse upwards and see Roman is already on his phone while the other guards are out of earshot. So I tell Liza exactly how and why I got myself into this mess.

She scrunches her forehead. "I still don't understand why you had to marry him."

"It was the only way to get close enough to figure out what role he actually played in Masha's murder," I whisper. "And to get my revenge if it comes to that."

Liza's eyes go wide, and she practically drops the skirt she's been admiring, staring at me like I'm mentally unbalanced. Which, frankly, maybe I am.

"I love purple on you," I say loudly. "It really brings out your—"

"You're going to get yourself killed. I know how much your aunt meant to you and how devastating it's been, but you have to let it go and get on with your life. Go back to New York. Go back to... Well, I don't know what, but leave here and forget about what my drunkass father told you."

"It's too late." I hold up the rock weighing down my fingers. "I have to see this plan through. I understand if you can't help me, but I'm not changing my mind."

"Jesus," she curses, shaking her head.

I get a sense of déjà vu, but this time, we're not talking about sneaking out of the window to get drunk with the boys at the adjacent boarding school. This is life or death. Maybe it's unfair of me to involve Liza, but I only need information from her—I'd never put her life at risk.

Glancing at Roman, I notice his attention has shifted from his phone to us, which is a bad sign. I quickly grab a few pieces off the hanger and pull Liza into a changing room with me.

I hear Roman's chuckle on the other side of the door. "Two of you in one changeroom. Is that a girl thing?"

"Yes," I bark. "In case I need help with a zipper. And so she can give her opinion without me leaving here."

"I actually might have a valuable opinion. You know, I'm often told that I dress very dapper—"

Liza, looking as intense as I've ever seen her, wrenches open the door, stopping him mid-sentence. "I'm sure you know exactly what's appropriate for Kira, but unless you can tell me the designer on the latest cover of *Vogue* or the shade of green that's selling out the runways right now, we don't need you to weigh in."

I'm stunned for a moment, impressed by my usually restrained friend's forceful response. I brace for a sharp retort.

"Sheesh, touchy," Roman mutters before wandering away.

"Girl, that was amazing," I say after she shuts the door, but she's still focused on our earlier conversation.

She drags her eyes up to meet mine and rubs her temples. "I don't understand," she says. "If Maxim is Alyona's father, why did he wait until she was in her twenties to contact her?"

I release a weighty sigh because it's complicated, but if I'm going to be asking for her help, she deserves to know the truth—all of it.

"Maxim and Alyona's mom had a fling. She was older, married to Aly's dad, but it happened and nobody knew. Aly's family moved to the States when she was a baby, and Maxim never learned he had a kid." I pause, letting the gravity of the story sink in. "He discovered Aly was his daughter when she was a teen. He wrote to Aly's mom, and they made a deal. Maxim would stay away until she turned twenty-five so she could have a normal life. After that, all bets were off."

Liza looks at me wide-eyed. "That's a crazy story. But it also means Maxim's your best friend's father. Are you really willing to kill him?"

I take a deep breath, searching for the right words. "Aly hates him, but regardless, if Maxim was involved in Masha's death, he should be held accountable. I don't care who he is or how powerful and connected he may be."

That's the problem—men like him never answer for their sins. But he will answer to me, if it's the last thing I do.

"Nothing is worth dying for. Nothing. Masha wouldn't have wanted this for you."

"Maybe not," I acknowledge. "But I can't let it go." I'm willing to accept however this is going to end. Even if the end is me staring down the barrel of a gun. I've crossed a line, and there's no turning back now.

Liza studies me closely, like she's trying to get a read on my mental state. I stare back at her, unflinching, because I'm as clear-headed as I've felt in years.

"Fine." She throws her hands in the air. "Tell me what I can do to help you."

I smile gratefully. "I need to talk to your father. Can you arrange a meeting or something? I won't drag you into this more than necessary, but I need to know what he knows."

She shakes her head. "He's in Poland now and hard to

reach. But when he's back, I'll try. He might not even remember what he said."

"He'll remember," I assure her. *He better.* "By the way, do you know what the story is with Maxim's first wife?"

She blows out a breath that flutters her bangs. "Honestly, she disappeared one day. Whether he had her killed or sent her packing, no one really knows." Liza chews on her bottom lip as if considering what she's going to say next. "It's rumored they had a child together, but I can't say if it's true."

"A child? Aly's the only child he's ever spoken of. But he wants me to bear his heirs." Liza crosses herself, and I can't help but grin. "It's okay. I negotiated a one-month delay on any *relations*."

One month should be long enough for me to figure out Maxim's involvement in my aunt's death, but if it's not... Well, I'll cross that bridge when I come to it.

"Girl, you need to get yourself on birth control," she nearly shouts. "Birth control he doesn't know about!"

"Shhh, would you keep it down?"

She's not wrong. If for some reason I'm still around after a month, I need to ensure I don't get knocked up by him. I can blame his geriatric sperm for me not getting pregnant. Except, instinctively, I know Maxim's sperm is far from inferior. I bet he has super sperm; one look from him would impregnate any sad, unsuspecting female in his midst. But I won't be one of them.

"Do you know a doctor who could get me the pill?"

"I know one. Give me some time, and I can get it for you." Her eyes scan the small changing room stuffed with designer outfits. "We need to pick out a new wardrobe for you." Liza tosses a sparkly black off-the-shoulder dress at me. "Start with this one."

As I zip up the dress, I gesture around the room. "Buy

whatever you like. In fact, buy whatever you don't like. I have Maxim's Amex, and I intend to do some real damage."

Liza quirks her lips. "You think he'll notice?"

"He will if we head to the Bugatti dealership after this and get matching convertibles."

Liza snorts. "Sounds like a plan."

When the dress is all zipped up, I raise my arms and spin in a what-do-you-think gesture.

She raises her eyebrows. "Smoking hot. We better get you on birth control sooner than later."

"Please." I throw my shirt at her head. "Maxim can eat his heart out because I won't be spreading my legs for that man. Ever."

* * *

After a full day of shopping, I'm exhausted on the drive home. Beside me, Roman navigates Moscow's traffic with ease, expertly weaving through the maze of cars. I'm surprised he opted to drive me personally, and even more so that he allowed me to sit in the front with him. Of course, we're flanked by two other vehicles, and there's no doubt this car is bulletproof.

I'm still trying to figure Roman out. It's unclear whether he's actually younger than Pavel, who seems to be in his late thirties, or if he just dresses better. Instead of a suit, Roman's wearing dark jeans, a charcoal V-neck T-shirt showing off his chest tats, and a worn-in leather jacket. As a part of Maxim's inner circle, he's by default an enemy, but there's something about his dimpled smile that makes him hard to dislike.

"Do I have something on my face?" Roman breaks the silence and swipes at his chin.

"No." I sit up straighter. "You're fine."

"Then why are you staring a hole into the side of my head?"

Was I? Jeez, I'm too tired to be sneaky. "I was zoned out. A lot on my mind."

He sighs. "It's a pretty big life change, huh? Leaving New York, moving here, getting married."

I sink lower in my seat. "It's what I signed up for. Of course, I didn't think I was going to be relegated to a society wife."

He chuckles. "What's so bad about being a society wife? You seemed to enjoy yourself today, trying on dresses and giggling over the latest styles with Liza."

"Sure, that's fun for, like, a day. But I'm capable of so much more, and Maxim knows it."

Roman looks over at me thoughtfully. "Is it true you killed your father?"

My head snaps towards him. Talk about getting right to the point. I debate how much to reveal. The truth of the matter is, my history is well-known in bratva circles, and this might be the perfect opportunity to ask about Masha's death.

I twirl the ring about my finger. "Unfortunately, I'm not the one that pulled the trigger, but I would have if given the chance. After my failed attempt to take over the Antonov Bratva, my father hunted me for months. He'd already tortured and killed my aunt, Masha, to learn my whereabouts, and I was next." I hold my breath for a minute and then casually add, "You must have heard about that?" I watch him closely, trying to discern if there's any sign of recognition or guilt in his expression about my aunt's fate, but I can't find anything. Only ... sympathy.

He scratches the back of his neck. "Yeah, of course. We were in Japan on business at the time, but I remember hearing about it. That really sucks. I'm sorry."

"Japan? With Maxim?" The surprise in my voice is evident.

"Yeah, we were working on some deal with the Yakuza. Maxim was there for part of it. It was four years ago, hard to remember the exact dates. Why does it matter?"

"It doesn't. Just curious." My heart races.

What does this mean? Even if Maxim wasn't in the country, he could've still orchestrated her murder from afar. But the way Boris spoke, it sounded like Maxim was directly involved in the killing.

"So how did you end up hooking up with the Kozlovs?" Roman asks, interrupting my thoughts.

I smile. At least this part of the story is happy. "I didn't know at the time that they were my half-brothers. I knew the Kozlov Bratva was a powerful New York player and my father's biggest rival, so I approached them to help me take him down." I huff out an amused breath. "By approach, I mean blackmail... Maybe not my smartest move."

Roman looks over at me, eyebrows raised.

I shake my head. "Long story short, during a very tense standoff with the Kozlovs, I discovered they're actually my half-brothers—my father seduced their mother and then stole me from her when I was a newborn. Anyway..." I tuck my hair behind my ears. "My brothers helped me take down my father, and as you know, we've all grown quite close. A happy ending to a really messed-up situation."

Roman whistles through his teeth. "Shit. Your story's even crazier than I could've imagined. But also more badass." He takes one hand off the wheel and high-fives me.

"See? I'm capable of a lot more." My eyes dart out the window. "Maxim underestimates me."

Roman's knuckles tighten on the steering wheel. "Yes, well, Maxim's cautious about who he lets into his world. It'll take him some time to fully trust anyone, even his own wife."

He pauses. "*Especially* his own wife," he adds under his breath.

Okay, mysterious much?

"In the spirit of sharing..." I lean in slightly, lowering my voice. "I know Maxim was married before. Alyona told me. I don't understand why it feels like it's some big secret." I pause, sitting on my hands to stop myself from fidgeting. "I also don't understand how it ended. I thought there was no divorce in this world." Unless he had his wife killed. Which, honestly, I'm not ruling out.

Roman shakes his head. "That's a story that's best left in the past. You won't win any favors with Maxim if you ask about Irina."

Irina? Is that her name? I'm tempted to ask if they had a child together, but considering Roman shut me down, maybe I won't push it. "Do you realize how fucked up that sounds? I'm married to the guy, and I can't ask about his past?"

"What did you expect? That you'd be braiding each other's hair and swapping secrets all night?"

His words strike a chord and I turn away sharply, feeling more upset by what he said than I have any right to be.

"Sorry, that came out harsher than I meant it to."

I press my heated cheek to the window pane, acutely aware of Roman's intense stare. "Maxim doesn't need time. He needs an attitude adjustment," I grumble.

We've pulled up in front of the mansion, but Roman doesn't make a move to get out of the car. "He's not all bad. After my father left my family, I was lost. Angry. Confused. I lashed out. No one wanted anything to do with me. I would have been on the street if it wasn't for Maxim. He gave me purpose and direction when I had none."

It's great that Roman can see some redeeming qualities in

him, but I'm not there yet. All I've seen is the cold, hard side of Maxim. "A real modern-day hero."

Roman rolls his eyes. "I'm not saying he's a saint, but he's lived through shit. And seeing as you're wearing his ring, even if it's an arrangement, you might want to consider there's more to him than meets the eye."

I shift my gaze straight ahead. My fingers idly touch the ring on my hand, its weight a constant reminder of the game I'm playing. "I'll take that into consideration."

Chapter Eight

MAXIM

A few hours from sunrise, I drive the silent streets of Moscow, heading to my home.

My knuckles around the steering wheel are raw and bruised—fresh from a win at the city's most notorious underground fight club. There, I'm no magnate, no business tycoon. I'm just another fighter, finding solace in the brutal ballet of fists and blood. I doubt anyone there knows who I am. And if they did, they'd know better than to blab it to anyone.

The fighting ring is a place as familiar as home to me. My father was an underground fighter. Unlike my mother, he managed to stay alive until my fifteenth birthday. Not that he was much of a father—my grandmother did the bulk of raising me. He didn't care if I went to school, brushed my teeth, ate vegetables, or any of the things a typical parent might worry about. But he did care if I could fight. That, he taught me well.

In the ring, I was invincible. At a young age, I mastered the art of ducking and weaving, ensuring my face stayed untouched. Quick jabs, strategic right hooks, whatever it took to send my opponent sprawling. It didn't matter if my opponent was twice my size. Fighting was what I was good at. When my father died, it was how I made money to survive.

It's also what got me noticed by Oleg Antonov, Kira's father. The Antonov patriarch had not passed on the reins yet, and Oleg was eager to impress his father. When he saw the damage I could inflict with my fists, he brought me into his bratva—not as a made man but as his secret weapon—taking me along on collections. He used to get a thrill commanding me to break bones and crush skulls. Treating me as though I were his damn pet he could order around. I'd still be under his thumb if it wasn't for my skill in investing and aligning myself with the right people. From early on I knew that a man like Oleg—with his vices and ferocious temper—was not someone I wanted to hitch my wagon to.

The irony that I ended up marrying his daughter isn't lost on me. At least we have one thing in common. She hated him as much as I did. The daughter whose cat-like hazel eyes, tousled blonde hair, and creamy thighs I tried to drive from my mind tonight with every punishing blow I landed.

I'm not sure how successful I was. Because it's not only about how she looks. Few people are willing to stand up to me like she does, and apparently, that gets my dick hard. Not that I'll be doing anything about it. I don't like her, I don't trust her, and most of all, I don't want a wife. Our relationship will remain strictly business.

Parking in my underground garage, I nod as I pass the guards patrolling my main floor, before taking the stairs two at a time to my bedroom.

Pavel was right. I didn't do myself any favors by demanding Kira and I share a bed.

Do I believe that keeping Kira close is the best way to keep an eye on her? Absolutely. Is it the only reason I want her near in the dark of night? No comment.

I open the door to my bedroom, bracing for the view of Kira nestled under the gray silk sheets, but the expanse of my bed is untouched, empty. My eyes dart around the room, searching for any sign of her, but she's not here.

Did something happen to her? My mind races through scenarios, but the obvious answer is usually the right one.

Exasperation consumes me. Pulling my cell from my pocket, I dial the guard on duty in the control room.

"Boss," Anton answers promptly.

"Check the cameras on this floor. It seems my wife was confused about where she was expected to sleep." I don't believe for a moment Kira was confused about anything, but let Anton believe what he will.

There's a brief pause, the clacking of keys on a keyboard providing background noise. "Looks like she entered the south-facing guest bedroom in the east wing earlier in the evening. She hasn't come out yet."

A smirk tugs at the corner of my mouth. So, she's playing a little game of hide-and-seek. Doesn't she know I'll always win?

It's exhilarating, though. A challenge like this is rare; it's not often someone dares to test me.

I hang up the phone and prepare to teach Kira what it means to disobey me.

Chapter Nine

KIRA

A shock jolts through me, ice seeping into my bones, wrenching me from blissful oblivion. Gasping for breath, my eyes shoot open to find I'm still in bed, except I'm drenched in freezing water. Bolting upright, I blink away the droplets clinging to my eyelashes, trying to make sense of what happened, when my gaze finds Maxim standing over me, an empty bucket dangling casually from his hand.

"Fuck you," I splutter, pushing the wet strands of hair out of my face, my temper flaring as I scramble out of the soaked bed. My T-shirt clings to me like a second skin, heavy and cold against my shivering frame. "What the hell do you think you're doing?"

"I suppose I can ask you the same thing." Maxim's eyes narrow, a flash of irritation crossing his features. He steps closer, his voice edged with authority. "You are to sleep in my bed, or did my order somehow slip your mind? I know for a fact that Nadya was clear that was a requirement."

"I'm a wife in name only. You said so yourself. Just because you decided sleeping together is part of the arrangement doesn't mean I agreed," I shout, drenched and shivering.

"You belong wherever I say you belong. This ring" — he grabs my left hand in his much bigger one — "binds you to me. It gives me the power to determine your future."

All my pent-up anger boils over, and I reach for a bedside lamp, hurling it in his direction. He bats it away before it hits him, breaking with a loud crash onto the floor. Regret immediately consumes me because I know there will be consequences.

He forces his next words out between gritted teeth. "You shouldn't have done that."

Panic constricts my lungs, yanking away my breath. At one time, I believed he wouldn't hurt a woman, but now... The way his eyes flash with violence, I'm not sure of anything. I inadvertently step back, toppling a chair with a loud thud, but I can't tear my eyes away from Maxim to check the damage.

I'm shivering—whether from fear or cold, I don't know. Maxim frowns as I wrap my arms around my shaking form. My nipples harden sharply, almost like diamond points, and Maxim doesn't fail to notice. His eyes linger, bold and unapologetic, and it sends a jolt through me—part embarrassment, part something else I can't quite name.

I wrap my arms tighter around myself, acutely aware of a weird kind of electricity in the air. A pull that's hard to ignore, even though every rational part of me is shouting to do just that.

"Let's call tonight a misunderstanding." His voice is low and menacing, and I know better than to argue. "But from now on, know that I expect you in my bed every night."

"Why?" I demand, even as anxiety pulses in my chest. "We won't be intimate. You said—"

"We are married. Even if this is an arrangement, I won't have my staff gossiping about us keeping separate rooms."

I scoff. "I don't care about appearances. This marriage isn't what I signed up for, anyhow."

His expression turns thunderous, and every instinct tells me to drop it, leave the issue be. But as is often the case, my defiance wins out.

I rear back to slap him but his hand darts out, gripping my wrist. In the pale light coming from the window, I catch sight of his battered knuckles, the heat from his touch like fire.

"You keep on testing me, Kira. I'm starting to believe you want a reaction. Are you so eager to see what happens when you provoke your husband?" His dark voice presses against my ear.

I refuse to question why his words cause moisture to flood between my thighs and an ache deep in my core. Nope. No way. Not going there.

Instead, I run.

Rebellion drives me as I bolt from the room. My heart hammers against my ribs, adrenaline fueling my sprint. I can hear Maxim hot on my heels. What did I expect? And what the fuck is my plan? He knows this place like the back of his hand, and I'm soaking wet, running into the abyss.

His voice is mocking. "You want to run and me to chase you, don't you, lastochka?"

My breath comes in sharp pants, equal part fear and excitement.

"How about this?" he continues. "I'll close my eyes and give you a ten-second head start. But guess what happens when I find you?"

His footsteps cease behind me, and I continue down the stairs—more places to hide on the first floor. Or maybe I need to go straight out the front door into the streets of Moscow. But when I picture his legions of guards that stand at the entrance to the home, I think against it.

My mind races, trying to map out the floor plan in this labyrinthine house. My muscles scream in protest, but stubbornness keeps me moving. And the knowledge that, by running, I've already made the outcome worse.

Slipping into the kitchen, I quickly scan the room for a hiding place. The space under the island seems too obvious, and the cabinets are too small to conceal my frame. My gaze flits to the large walk-in pantry. Maybe it can lock from the inside.

I dart inside, pressing my back against the shelves laden with spices and canned goods. I fight to control my breathing, attempting to be as silent as possible. Even though I'm delaying the inevitable.

He'll catch me, and I know my little outburst is going to come at a cost, but what that cost is remains to be seen. Will he take me over his knee or something worse? Tie me up and have his way— Shit, my mind is wandering into dangerous territory. Dangerous because I get a little thrill from defying him, the push and pull of power that underlies our every interaction.

I strain my ears, trying to discern his movements over the pounding of my heart. The kitchen is eerily silent, save for the distant hum of the refrigerator. Then the faint sound of footsteps on the tiled floor reaches me, slow and deliberate.

I hold my breath. The tension rises as he comes closer.

He doesn't sound the slightest bit out of breath when he speaks. "You should have stopped to grab a towel. The water droplets from your clothes led me straight to you."

I can feel Maxim's presence on the other side of the door, mocking me. I clench my fists, cursing him, because he's the reason I'm all wet.

As if he could see me, he chuckles softly, and it's a sound that sends shivers down my spine. "Are you going to come out or do I have to come in and get you? Because if that happens, I won't be responsible for my actions afterwards."

I grit my teeth. As if I have a choice. My best bet is to walk out of here with my head held high and scream bloody murder if he attempts to put his hands on me. Which, in this house, wouldn't matter since it's Maxim's, but if he's worried about what the staff think, maybe that'll dissuade him from the worst of his plans.

Chin lifted, I push the pantry door open and step out, meeting Maxim's broody gaze head-on.

"Ah, so you want me to go easy on you?"

"I want you to leave me alone," I reply, my voice as steady as I can manage.

With measured steps, he closes the gap between us and presses me against the wall, his hands landing on either side of me, caging me in. He's barely touching me, but my skin tingles all the same.

"No such luck," he whispers.

I should be a shivering mess right now, but I'm not—the warmth radiating off him is a stark contrast to the cold dampness of my clothes.

He leans forward and inhales deeply against my neck, sending goosebumps through my traitorous body. "That was fun," he says darkly. The air is thick and charged. "Now, what do you have to say for yourself?"

Closing my eyes, I attempt to shut out his closeness and the inexplicable draw I have towards him. "You're a psychopath."

Maybe I'm crazy too.

"You were the only one who ran in the first place. You *wanted* me to chase you." He lifts his dark eyebrows as if daring me to argue with him. "You knew this is how it would end, didn't you? With you begging for my forgiveness."

"The only thing I'd ever beg of you is to leave me the fuck alone."

His eyes flash with heat that has me on edge. "In that case, beg me to leave you alone."

This moment is not only a physical standoff; it's a clash of everything we are—his control against my dissent, his power against my stubbornness, his secrets against my determination to unearth them.

I refuse to back down, to show any sign of weakness, even as my pulse races and my breath comes in short gasps.

"No." I stand my ground.

"So defiant, lastochka." His hot breath grazes my ear. "Beg me to let you go," he purrs.

My jaw hardens and I turn my head, looking purposefully away from Maxim. "I will do no such thing."

"Hmm, have it your way." His hands lower and grip my hips, holding me in place.

What the fuck?

He raises his knee, his thigh planted firmly between my legs.

Oh. Shit.

The gusset of my panties is the only barrier between my pussy and the fabric of his expensive Italian suit.

"This feels good, doesn't it?"

I don't bother voicing my objection as I struggle in his grasp. It turns out to be the wrong move. He's holding me firmly in place, and all my thrashing about is bringing my core in contact with his very hard thigh, again and again.

A whimper escapes my lips, heat blasting through my veins.

Holy shit.

As if he knows the effect he's having on me, he only holds

me tighter, pressing his leg firmly against where I need him most.

My brain cells are scrambling, too busy fighting against the pleasure I shouldn't be feeling. Each movement, each brush against him sends waves of unwanted sensation through me. It's like my brain has short-circuited, unable to process anything beyond this raw, physical response.

"That's right. Get yourself off on my thigh, *wife*." He spits out the last word like an insult.

He runs a single finger along my collarbone, a deceptively innocent touch. I shudder, releasing a low moan, surrendering to the sensation. How can I be responding like this, under his control and in a situation so twisted? I'm infuriated with myself, with my body's betrayal, but I'm helpless to stop it.

"That's it. Keep going. Rub yourself on me," he growls, licking his lips and watching me with dark intensity, like he's enjoying my conflicted pleasure. "Beg me to come."

It's as if every logical part of me has taken a back seat, leaving me at the mercy of these overwhelming, primal sensations. Maxim's gaze grows more hazy, his breathing uneven as I hover on the edge of need and bad decisions. His hold on me tightens, his fingers pressing into my skin, the moment taking its toll on both of us. If I'm going to fall, he's going down with me.

Just as I'm cresting the peak, unable to fight the wave building inside of me any longer, the kitchen light flicks on.

Nadya stands in the doorway, her eyes wide with shock. Her usual composed demeanor crumbles for a moment as she takes in the scene before her—me, drenched and disheveled, pressed up against the wall by Maxim.

I stand there, trying to catch my breath, feeling a thousand different shades of awkward and exposed.

Maxim doesn't even flinch. He releases me casually, stepping back with a grin that doesn't reach his eyes. The sudden absence of his body against mine leaves me feeling cold, despite the warm flush still covering my skin. My T-shirt clings to me, my hair a wet mess around my face. I desperately want to shrink into myself, away from Nadya's penetrating gaze and Maxim's unsettling calm.

"I heard a noise," is all she says, her expression shifting from surprise to disapproval. She's seen much in this house, but I bet this is new. I'm sure it'll only give her further reason to scorn me.

"We're perfectly fine," Maxim assures her, picking a piece of lint off his suit jacket as if nothing out of the ordinary has happened. As if I wasn't dry-humping her boss's leg, about to reach orgasm.

Nadya's eyes flick to me, heavy with judgment. Maxim being a lunatic, soaking me in ice water and chasing me around the house is certainly not my fault, but I bet she won't see it that way.

Well, fuck her. And for that matter, fuck him. Maxim seems to be deriving way too much amusement from this moment.

"Excuse me," I say, attempting to brush past Maxim to go... Where, I'm not sure, but I do know I need to get the hell out of this kitchen and as far away from Nadya's intrusive glare as possible.

Of course, Maxim doesn't allow that to happen. "So what will it be, lastochka? Will you be joining me in my bed, or would you prefer to sleep outside with the dogs?"

The dogs? This man is as savage as they come.

"Fine," I hiss back. "I'll sleep in your bed, but don't expect anything else from me. My legs are sealed shut."

"We'll see about that," he murmurs, his voice a low rumble.

Before I can react, his hand clasps my upper arm in a firm

grip, guiding me past a frowning Nadya, towards the grand staircase.

Choosing the most remote bedroom in the house for my temporary sanctuary was my bright idea to hide from Maxim. I thought distance might grant me freedom. But now, as Maxim's unwavering hold steers me, I see there's no escaping his grasp. Maxim Belov is capable of finding me anywhere on his property. Anywhere in the city. Hell, I get the feeling he could find anyone anywhere in this world if he really wanted to.

As we enter his bedroom, a shiver racks my body. Maxim frowns like he disapproves of me being cold. Which is insane since he's the reason I'm feeling this way.

Without further discussion, he grabs a dress shirt off the back of his chair and holds it out for me. "You need to get out of your wet clothes. Put this on."

Perhaps if I was thinking straight, I'd argue that I have a closet full of clothes ten feet away, but I'm so desperate to be out of this wet T-shirt and for this night to be over with that I reach for his clothing.

"Turn around," I demand, trying to reclaim some control.

Maxim responds with a cocky half-grin. "No, I don't think so," he drawls. "I think I'll sit right here and watch you." His eyes glint with intrigue.

I'm about to tell him to go to hell and stomp off to the bathroom to change, but something stops me: the realization that I don't entirely hate the idea of him watching me. In fact, the thought of making him squirm by looking at something he could never have, adds a wicked thrill. It's payback time.

"Suit yourself." With deliberate slowness, I peel off the drenched fabric clinging to my skin and toss it directly at him, maintaining unflinching eye contact.

Refusing to be intimidated, I stand my ground. He may think he holds the upper hand, having brought me to the brink of orgasm and now witnessing me strip, but I'm determined to show him differently.

I don't cover my body, my full curves on display. He goes still, his gaze slowly lifting to examine my every inch. His eyes darken, and his body holds tension like a coiled spring ready to snap.

There's twisted pleasure in knowing I have the power to affect him just as he affected me. Slipping on his shirt, I'm immediately wrapped in his rich scent. It smells like leather and something smoky—aged whiskey, maybe? Rich and undeniably masculine. Like him.

When I finally look up, there's a slight quiver in his clenched jaw. Without another word, he turns and storms away towards the bathroom. Moments later, I hear the shower running.

I sure hope it's a cold one.

Chapter Ten

KIRA

Sunlight seeps into the room, its rays piercing through the open curtains in sharp, golden streaks. I reluctantly open one eyelid, confirming Maxim is no longer in the bed, before opening my eyes fully.

Before going to sleep, I built a pillow barrier between us to maintain some semblance of personal space, a feeble line of defense in a situation where I felt utterly defenseless. The barrier did its job because I had no sense of Maxim beside me. I thankfully fell asleep well before he turned in.

Slipping out of the stupidly comfortable bed, the first thing I notice is a note on the nightstand beside where I sleep.

Nadya has reviewed your wardrobe and removed any unfitting items.

- M

Charming. As if I needed another reminder of the gem I married. My restful night's sleep is now a distant memory, replaced by a wave of irritation.

I make my way to the bathroom and take in my reflection in the mirror. I look disheveled. My hair is a rat's nest after that asshole drenched me in ice-cold water and then chased me through the corridors of his mansion. With the first few buttons of Maxim's oversized dress shirt undone, it looks like I had a lot more fun last night than I actually did.

I may not have had fun, but I nearly had an orgasm. I blame it on the heightened tension and nerves. Not on the thread of desire that unspooled when Maxim chased me through his house, forced his leg between my thighs, and—

Nope. Stopping that thought right there. Instead, I focus on my sour mood as I enter the glamorous walk-in closet and confirm that Nadya did, in fact, get rid of most of my wardrobe. Some of the clothes I purchased with Liza remain, but that's pretty much it.

Maxim's side of the closet is exactly what one would expect from a control freak. Designer suits hang in neat rows by shade. Next to them are racks of crisply pressed dress shirts in whites, blacks, and muted colors, organized with an attention to detail that borders on obsessive. The far end is dedicated to a collection of leather shoes, from Oxfords to loafers, each pair polished to a sheen and all looking more expensive than my entire wardrobe. Definitely signs of an obsessive-compulsive personality.

Not that it comes as a surprise. But it does give me an idea. I'm alone, surrounded by Maxim's personal belongings. Maybe he has a diary or a calendar covering the dates of Masha's death? I still can't decide if his being in Japan is relevant or not. Either way, I'd like to know what I'm dealing with.

Yanking open the top drawer of his mahogany dresser, I

find neatly folded rows of monogrammed handkerchiefs organized by color. The next drawer down is the same story. His ties are displayed in an array that rivals a color wheel, with everything from deep burgundies to cool silvers.

Without further thought, I dip my hand into the drawer and mess up the ties, mixing up the meticulously arranged colors. This way, he'll think I'm fucking with him rather than purposefully snooping.

I go for the bottom of the drawer next, groping along and looking for anything that's not a handkerchief. I come up empty. My search continues—opening drawers, flipping through rows of stacked shirts, and scanning shelves—seeking anything that could be revealing. It's strange that I haven't come across any personal items somewhere here. A journal, a stray condom packet, a picture of his mistress... Anything.

I'm giving up hope when I open the bottom dresser drawer. There, I find perfectly organized socks in various shades of black and gray. Reaching out, I give the contents a little stir, and that's when my fingers brush against something that is definitely not a sock. It feels like a flimsy piece of plastic.

I pull it out, revealing a faded polaroid. In it is a little boy, no more than four or five, with tousled dark hair and eyes that are unmistakably familiar. They're Maxim's eyes.

This must be Maxim as a child. He's grinning, looking like any ordinary, carefree kid, a front tooth missing, dirt smeared across his sweet round cheeks. It's a stark contrast to the cold, impenetrable man he is today.

Who was he before the world turned him into the man I married? What happened?

I doubt I'll ever find out.

Chapter Eleven

KIRA

For what feels like the millionth time today, I find myself drifting into the forgotten sitting room at the mansion's rear, seeking a peace that's out of my grasp. Settling by the window, I press my palm to the cool glass, staring outside at the golden carpet of fallen leaves covering the expansive grounds.

I like this room. It's in the farthest reach of the mansion. Judging by the layer of dust and cobwebs, this room is barely used, so it's become my secret sanctuary.

It's just me and a pint of ice cream, a box of tissue, and a smutty novel Alyona gifted me.

Today would have been Masha's fifty-sixth birthday and, like every birthday since she passed, I'm haunted by the weight of her absence. She had a tradition of showing up at my boarding school and hauling me away for the day to do something fun. We'd go exploring art galleries, eat amazing food, and end the night with an avant-garde theater performance or something equally outrageous.

That was Masha. Bold and unconventional. She would hate that I'm moping today. She'd actually hate that I've spent the last few years weighed down with grief. If she were here, she'd make me change into something fabulous and call up Liza insisting we hit the town. She'd want to be celebrated, not mourned.

But how can I celebrate her when I haven't learned a single thing about her death? I've been living under this roof for a week, and my opportunities to investigate Maxim have been nonexistent. When I suggested marriage, I thought I'd be involved in running his business, which I hoped would give me an opportunity to learn his whereabouts around the time of Masha's capture and murder. I stupidly thought I'd be Maxim's equal—that is so far from reality it's almost funny. Almost.

Masha may not have condoned moping, but she definitely did condone drinking champagne in a bubble bath. So fuck it. That's what I'm going to do.

I drag my body off the couch, when the door barrels open and the wicked witch of Moscow walks in.

Nadya. She's my least favorite person in this household. The woman looks at me with contempt for merely breathing, but Nadya is as tightly knitted into Maxim's world as Pavel and Roman, meaning I can't dismiss her entirely. She'll never be a friend, but it's worth trying to sweeten her up. Though I can't shake the feeling that, in her eyes, no woman could ever be worthy of her precious Maxim.

"This room is off limits," she announces in her usual brusque tone.

"Sorry. I didn't realize," I say, collecting my things. It makes me wonder if there's something in here that she doesn't want me to see, which only furthers my curiosity. Pressing a finger to my lips, I tilt my head. "Can I ask why it's off limits?"

Nadya crosses her arms in front of her chest and taps her foot. When I'm convinced there will be no details forthcoming, she finally says, "This was the sitting room Irina liked to entertain in. Maxim wanted it sealed off after..."

After he killed Irina? Thinking about it sends a shiver down my spine.

I survey the room more closely, now aware of the feminine touches scattered throughout—sheer white curtains framing the windows, porcelain figurines placed on the mahogany shelves, a fine persian rug underfoot.

Nadya's vague mention of Irina is an opportunity I can't ignore.

"I didn't know." I tuck a strand of my hair behind my ears. "I feel like we got off on the wrong foot, and I never meant for that to happen. I know how important you are to Maxim, and I want us to be able to ... get along."

"Get along? Like you're worth a second of my time." Her words are cold and brutal. "You're temporary. You'll be gone as soon as you've served your purpose. Don't mistake yourself for someone of importance in Maxim's world because you never will be."

Okay, still a bitch.

I grit my teeth and try again. "Maxim agreed to this marriage for a reason. Because it serves us both. I'm sure he'd appreciate it if you took me under your wing. Help me adapt to this household, provide guidance—"

"The only guidance you need is to understand your place. You're here for Maxim's benefit, nothing more. And you'll be put out like yesterday's trash sooner than later. Now, leave."

My fingernails press sharply into my palms. I know they say you can attract more flies with honey, but I tried being nice and it got me nowhere. If I can't win Nadya over, then she needs to understand I'm no doormat. In fact, I'm a bad bitch.

"Fine, you want me to leave?" We lock eyes, neither willing to look away. "Then tell me what happened to Irina."

Her mouth tightens with disapproval. I expect her to shut me down, but she doesn't. "She betrayed Maxim in the worst possible way." I don't miss the tremor in her hands as her eyes turn arctic. "Do you know what happens to traitors in this world?"

Her words set me on edge. My aunt and I were called traitors by those still loyal to my father. "I know very well what happens to traitors. Is this your issue with me?" I advance on her and she notches her chin, holding her ground. "You think I am going to do the same to your precious Maxim? Betray him?"

"You should be ashamed of yourself," she whispers darkly. "To work against your own blood."

Her words are like a punch to my gut. "What did you say?"

I've never brought up my father in this household, but anyone connected with the Russian underworld knows who he was and what he did. How I retaliated.

"How can you say that?" I retort sharply. "Do you know what he was doing? Involved in human trafficking, including children, cutting his drugs with fentanyl without a care for the lives lost. Addicted to painkillers and booze. He was an animal needing to be stopped. And yet you stand here, judging me for doing my duty."

Her nostrils flare. "You're so naïve. You know nothing about the world. Even if your father was flawed, he deserved your loyalty. That's the bratva code." Her face is a mask of fury, her hands clenched by her sides. "Maxim should never have married you. You're a delusional child."

Nadya's not the first person with the bratva's old-guard mindset to sneer at my actions. I can't convince her that I was in the right, but at least I know what her issues are with me. I wonder if Maxim feels the same way—not that he's ever expressed that.

I meet her disdain with a steely gaze, my voice unwavering. "I'd rather be naïve than blindly loyal to a corrupt ruler."

"I'm sure you would."

"What's going on here?" Maxim's deep voice cuts through the tension like a cold blade.

My gaze snaps up to find him leaning against the door frame, the dim light from the hallway casting shadows across his imposing figure. His eyes, dark and inscrutable, focus on Nadya.

A flicker of alarm crosses her features before she regains her composure. "I was letting Kira know that we don't use this room any longer."

Interesting. Nadya's certainly giving him a watered-down version of our conversation. If she doesn't want Maxim to know how she really feels about me, I'll play her game. And I'll win.

He runs his tongue over his upper teeth. "I see." His gaze settles on me. "Is there a reason you're here?"

"It's a little more private, and I like the view." I shrug. "I didn't know that it was off limits."

Maxim looks from Nadya to me and back again. "If you like it, it's yours. Redecorate as you see fit."

"Really?" I don't know why, but somehow, this feels like a small win. I can't resist giving Nadya a smug, triumphant glance.

"Did Nadya mention that you're expected to accompany me to a public dinner in a few hours?"

"No, not yet, Maxim. I was about to," Nadya says hastily. "Hair and makeup are scheduled for this afternoon, and a stylist from my selected list will soon bring some fitting outfit choices."

No, fucking thank you. Using one of Nadya's stylists is

where I put my foot down. If I'm going out tonight—on Masha's birthday of all nights—I am going to make sure I look damn good. My aunt wouldn't have it any other way.

"As much as I value your fashion advice" — I nod at Nadya's plain gray dress while Maxim barely conceals a smirk — "I think I'll contact Liza for some stylist recommendations of my own."

"But—"

Maxim cuts her off. "Kira says she can handle it."

Is Maxim defending me? My heart gives a little thump in my chest.

"Very well, then."

I can feel the steam rolling off Nadya in waves, and I take that as a small win. For now. But I know whatever issues she has with me are far from resolved. This is only the opening act in what promises to be a long, drawn-out battle of wills.

Maxim adjusts his cufflinks. With a final look, he says to me, "Tell the stylist we're going to Probka tonight. Everyone in Moscow knows the restaurant. Be ready to go by eight. And for the love of all things holy, don't wear any piece of clothing that's ripped, frayed, or references Joan Jett."

Chapter Twelve

MAXIM

I'm juggling a lowball of whiskey in one hand while pressing the phone to my ear with the other, when the limo pulls up to the curb beside Probka, the city's hottest new restaurant that I have a majority stake in. It's a favorite among the city's eager-to-see-and-be-seen socialites, partly due to its celebrity chef owner, Daria Amelin. It's not my usual choice, but it's exactly what I need tonight.

"All is set," Nadya confirms on the other end of the line. "The restaurant is full, and the press has been notified. No one will miss your appearance."

I take a sip of my whiskey. Its warmth contrasts with the cool looks Kira is throwing at me from the opposite seat. When she catches my eye, she crosses her arms in front of her generous chest and averts her gaze out the window.

"Did you let Daria know?" I ask Nadya.

"I did, and she's thrilled." Nadya pauses, and I know what that pause is about. My wife. "I still don't think this is a good idea. She's still so ... *much,*" she says with distaste. "Given some time and training from me, I could mold her into a more suitable wife. Although, I'm afraid she'll never be good enough for you."

And there we have it—no woman will ever be good enough for me in Nadya's eyes. She either has me on way too high of a pedestal or she doesn't want to have to share the 'lady of the house' title with anyone else. Both, likely. I've spoiled her. Ever since Irina, I've kept my home a fortress—no women, no distractions. My affairs are short, to the point, and never where I lay my head.

But the idea of molding Kira, now that's laughable.

I eye my wife carefully. There's no question she's a firecracker. Despite my earlier warning, she's chosen thigh-high boots with bold stiletto heels. Yes, her black dress is simple and classic, but on her body it looks ... it looks smoking hot. It's not so much the dress I'm thinking about but what's underneath it.

Now that I know what she looks like naked—her generous ass, creamy thighs, her pink tinged nipples—I can't get the vision out of my mind. It's been a full week, and the memory of her bare skin lingers like a constant torment.

"It's fine, Nadya," I say, an edge to my voice. "I'll take it from here."

What Nadya fails to grasp is that Kira's youth and beauty are part of her public appeal. Our mismatch, our age difference—everything—works in my favor because the press is fascinated by the opposites-attract love story.

Outside the window, the paparazzi are already swarming like vultures waiting for their moment. Or rather, our moment. It's our first public outing together, a carefully planned display of post-wedding bliss. Although, from the expression on Kira's face, no one is going to believe the bliss part.

“Is that all for us?” she asks, gesturing out the window with a frown.

“It is,” I acknowledge. “Do you think you could try and look happy when we step outside? Not like I kicked your dog?”

She frowns. “Seriously, why would you even say that? What kind of person would even think of kicking a dog?”

I huff out a laugh. “A proverbial dog. I wouldn’t kick an actual dog,” I clarify. I’ve kicked men—done a lot worse to them, in fact—but I have nothing against animals.

“You’re a modern-day saint.” She scoffs. “Anyhow, don’t worry. I’ll flash my pearly whites for the cameras.” With a sneer, Kira pastes a smile so forced it borders on comedic.

One side of my mouth tips up at the corner. “You might want to try again. Didn’t quite buy it.”

“Chill, okay? I faked it at our wedding. I’ll be fine. Let’s get this over with.”

I take a deep breath and hold out my open palm to Kira. She hesitates momentarily, before taking my hand as the limo door opens and the charade begins.

* * *

"For your next course, we have beautiful pan-seared scallops on a bed of truffle-infused cauliflower purée, garnished with microgreens, and a delicate saffron and citrus emulsion."

Kira hangs on every word as Daria places the dishes before us. “Are these local truffles?" she asks.

“They are, indeed,” Daria replies. “Few people know these mushrooms grow in Russia. I’m impressed that you do.”

Kira's face lights up with a wide, genuine smile, the kind that reaches her eyes and transforms her entire expression. It hits me how beautiful she is when she’s not flinging insults my way.

An hour earlier, we had posed for photos in front of the restaurant, the paparazzi's cameras flashing away. As promised, she smiled broadly for the pictures and posed beside me. But her expression was brittle, her pose stiff. I doubt anyone else noticed, so captivated by our appearance, but I did. That's why seeing her now, at ease, with real joy on her face, stirs something inside me.

"My aunt was a real foodie," Kira responds, a hint of emotion in her voice. Not surprising, considering the way she lost Masha. "She took me to nearly every Michelin-star restaurant across Europe. I learned to appreciate fine dining from a young age." Kira flicks a quick, assessing glance my way as she takes a sip of the Chenin Blanc that was paired with this course.

"Thank you, Daria," I say. "Everything has been outstanding so far."

"I'm glad to hear it." With a nod, Daria heads back to the kitchen and Kira sits back, smoothing the napkin in her lap.

"So, you're on a first-name basis with the chef?" She raises her eyebrows. "That's cute."

I'm not sure what Kira is getting at. Yes, Daria is young and attractive, but our relationship is strictly professional. "It's not cute, it's business. Daria needed help to open this place, and I was in a position to help her."

She looks at me doubtfully. "You don't seem like the type to invest in small businesses. What's in it for you?"

I lean back, scanning the restaurant's sleek black-and-gold modern decor while a sultry beat injects life into the room. "Money. But investing in Probka isn't only about financial returns. It's about supporting someone with real skill and vision. There's not enough of that in today's world."

Kira carefully swipes her fork through the cauliflower purée and releases a little moan that travels straight to my dick.

"I agree." She arches an eyebrow. "And yet, you don't seem that interested in the food. You haven't even mentioned how well the yuzu and saffron taste together."

I huff out a dark laugh. "My background was far from this world of fine dining. I came from a place where any meal on the table was a blessing. So, while I enjoy these elaborate dishes, I'm not particularly picky about the specifics like yuzu and saffron."

Talking about my past isn't something I usually do—it opens doors to memories I'd rather keep at bay. But there's something about her genuine curiosity that makes me lower my guard.

She leans back, studying me. "So, from simple beginnings to the kingpin of Moscow's bratvas," she muses. "That's a story I'd like to hear."

I ball my fists under the table. "It's not a happy one."

She raises her glass to me. "Who among us has a happy history? You know mine. It's only fair that you tell me yours."

Usually, I'd shut down any talk of my past, but fuck... Maybe it's the wine or the way she's looking up at me with those big, curious hazel eyes, but I don't have it in me to deny her. "I was born in the Chertanovo district. They call it Moscow's forgotten periphery for a reason," I say wryly. "My mother died when I was young—two or three years old. I don't remember her. I was mostly raised by my paternal grandmother. My father too, but he'd come and go, never really a constant presence. But he taught me one valuable thing—how to fight."

Kira leans forward, her expression intense. "Is that how you survived on the streets?"

"It was helpful for self-defense, but it was more valuable as a way to make money. There weren't many choices for moving up in life, not beyond stealing or drug dealing. So, I used my fight winnings to invest. I started small, with investments in real estate, gradually expanding to bigger, more lucrative deals as I built my empire."

What I don't tell her is that her father, Oleg, was my introduction to the world of the bratva. But he was only that, an introduction. It was my work ethic, my drive, and my smarts that opened doors in the underworld. But does Kira really want to hear about my short-lived connection to her asshole father? I doubt it.

For some reason, I don't want to ruin this surprisingly normal moment between us.

"That's quite a story," she admits, holding eye contact. "Why do you keep your past so tightly guarded? You should be proud of the fact that you overcame a difficult childhood and made something of yourself."

"Pride is a useless emotion. What good has it done anyone?"

I was proud of the life I had built, right up until I lost my son. After that, everything changed. Pride didn't bring him back nor heal the pain. The harsh reality is that life can be cruel and unforgiving, no matter who you are.

"I prefer to look forward, focus on what's next. Not look back," I say, clearing the ball of emotion from my throat.

Kira tilts her head in thought. "Is that why you gave Daria a chance? To invest in her future?"

"That, and she was good in bed."

Kira looks horrified.

I bark out a laugh. "I'm kidding. God, you're easy to rile up."

Her eyes flash with irritation. "Trust me, I don't care."

An amused smile plays across my lips. "Sure you don't. Jealousy is perfectly normal. I'm not judging."

She exhales sharply in annoyance. "You can sleep with whomever you want until ... *you know*."

Oh, do I know. Until the month is up.

"But there's only one person I want to sleep with," I say, drinking her in.

As soon as the words leave my mouth, I realize two things. One—it's true. And two—that's a problem. Because I don't do marriage and relationships. Once burnt, twice shy.

Kira grips the edge of the table and gives me an unreadable look.

Blyat. I curse internally, pushing my wine glass away. Clearly I've drunk too much. "Tell me stories about Masha jet-setting you off to fabulous restaurants."

She freezes, her glass of wine halfway to her mouth. She lowers it and stares at me through narrowed eyes. It's like I've asked her to reveal state secrets rather than happy memories of her childhood.

"Why do you want to know about that?"

I shrug. "Why not? I'm sure you have some good stories."

She leans her jaw into her hand, and looks away from me briefly as if cataloging her memories. Finally, her lips quirk upwards. "She once took me to Australia for three days so we could try pavlova in the country it was invented."

"Pavlova? Like, the meringue dessert?"

"It was her favorite." She tilts her head, focused on her next bite. "Little known fact: pavlova is named after Anna Pavlova, the Russian ballerina, but it was invented in Australia or New Zealand. There's some debate over where."

"I didn't know that."

"Do you like ballet?"

"I like it as much as the next man. I can appreciate it as an art form, but it's not exactly my idea of a good time."

"So what's your idea of a good time then? I haven't seen you do anything for fun."

My idea of fun is pummeling an opponent in the ring, torturing a confession out of traitors, and orchestrating hostile business takeovers. "I like golf," I tell her.

"Bullshit." She snorts. "Haven't seen you play a game once."

"I'm a busy man. Recently married, actually." I wink at her.

She rolls her eyes. "Newlywed life running you off your feet?"

"Something like that." I bring the glass of wine to my lips, not taking my eyes off of her. "And what about you? What do you do for fun?"

Her fingers toy with the edge of her napkin, a wistful look crossing her face. "I used to dance ballet, you know. Not professionally, but it was something I did for *fun*."

"Dancing, huh?" The disciplined precision of ballet contrasts with her stubborn, brash personality, but I like that she's a contradiction. "Why did you stop?"

Kira shrugs, her gaze drifting off. "Life, I guess. Responsibilities. Family stuff."

I can read between the lines. Her asshole of a father was becoming more unstable, and she had to step up to take the reins.

"Do you miss it?"

"Not as much as you'd think. The instructors were always telling me to lose ten pounds, and it pissed me off." She exhales softly. "To be honest, what I liked most about it was that my aunt loved to watch me dance." She looks over at me as if gauging my reaction. "Masha loved the arts—any form, really. Dancing, singing, theater, visual arts. She always came to my final recitals with two dozen red roses and a bottle of champagne. Not sure the nuns at my school appreciated the champagne as much as I did."

"Masha was one of a kind," I say, stretching my legs under the table. "You're a lot like your aunt."

Kira's brows pull together, and she looks at me like she's weighing everything I've said.

"How well did you know her?" Kira's voice sounds accusatory.

Does she think I had a thing with her aunt? She was a beautiful woman, but it was never like that. "I didn't know her that well, only in passing."

"Did you know my father—"

Before she can finish the thought, the grating voice of Mayor Rashnikov assaults my ears, ruining the moment.

"Maxim, never thought I'd see you here, but it's a pleasure nonetheless."

By here, he means a hot new restaurant that attracts the glitterati. He's right—despite it being a good investment, it's definitely not my scene, mostly because douchebags like him are regular guests.

I turn, barely concealing my irritation with a nod. "Funny. I'm not surprised to find you here." I take a sip of my wine. "Where's Zoya?"

He pulls a face. "At home, where wives should be," he says dismissively.

Kira's expression sours.

Pyotr's attention shifts to her, his eyes bright with unwelcome eagerness. "And who might this be?"

"My wife," I say, letting the word hang for a moment for my own satisfaction, then add, "Kira, may I introduce you to Mayor Pyotr Rashnikov?"

Kira, keeping her poise, offers a restrained smile that

doesn't reach her eyes as she extends her hand and murmurs, "Nice to meet you."

Pyotr, seizing the opportunity, grasps her hand and leans down to kiss the back of it.

She stiffens noticeably, and it takes all my control to not to stab him with the steak knife beside my plate.

"Ah, yes, the young beauty everyone in the city is talking about. I regret missing your wedding; I was away on business," Rashnikov claims, though his kind of business likely involves gambling and whoring. "I'm hosting a dinner at my house soon. You and Kira must come." A smarmy grin spreads across his face as his eyes drag over Kira.

As much as I loathe the mayor, interacting with him is an unavoidable part of doing business in this city, be it above or below the law.

"We'll see if our schedule allows it." I give him a terse get-out-of-here nod.

"Excellent! I'll have my secretary send over the details to Nadya."

"Perfect," I deadpan.

Pyotr shifts his attention back to Kira. "I must have been living under a rock to miss that Maxim snagged a young gem like you. I look forward to getting better acquainted with you, Kira."

My hand wraps around the knife and before I'm conscious of it, I'm standing, about to plunge the blade into his carotid artery because how dare he fucking look and talk about *my wife* that way.

"Maxim," Kira hisses, her sharp tone snapping me back to reality.

Seizing the moment, the mayor quickly excuses himself, disappearing into the crowd.

Once he's out of sight, Kira hits me with a questioning look. "What was that?"

I sink back into my chair and signal the waiter for a whiskey. "That's the mayor of fucking Moscow." I spit.

"God help us all." She pulls a face.

"I can't stand him," I confess, swirling my wine. "Pyotr plays dirty. He's got incriminating info on almost everyone in this city. Uses blackmail, threats, whatever it takes to get what he wants. He's not a man of honor."

"Isn't that a common tactic in business, politics, whatever?" Her eyes bounce over to where he's holding court with a group of men.

I sigh, grateful that my whiskey has shown up. "True, it's common, but Pyotr takes it to another level. He doesn't just play dirty—he revels in it, using people's vulnerabilities to his advantage without any moral code. Even bad men like me have lines we don't cross, but he has no such boundaries."

She smiles tightly, her eyes hardening. "Really? You want to talk about boundaries? Should we call up Aly and ask her about your moral code?"

I gnash my teeth. Would Kira believe me if I said I acted in what I believed were my daughter's best interests? Yes, my methods were shitty, but it was all in the name of protecting Alyona and giving her a better life.

"I did what I thought was best for her at the time," I grit out. "But I don't want you anywhere near Rashnikov. He's especially slimy when it comes to beautiful young women."

She swallows and eases back in her chair, her eyes drifting to the mayor. "But you do business with him, right?"

"I can't avoid it."

"Then I suppose we can't avoid his dinner."

Her words give me pause. There's a note in her voice I can't quite place.

"We'll see," I say. "Now, put on your brightest smile. The paparazzi are waiting outside and require one more show."

Chapter Thirteen

MAXIM

My eyes pop open at five, as they've done nearly every morning of my life. But this morning, something is different.

The wall of pillows Kira constructed between us to avoid any contact has been kicked away, and her lush, perfect body is flung over mine. The silk tank top she wore to sleep has crept up her stomach and is showing off her every smooth curve, while her amazing tits are pressed against my arm, her leg hooked over one of mine. Dangerously close to my rapidly hardening cock.

Jesus fucking Christ, what did I do in a past life to deserve this sweet torture?

Or maybe the question should be: what did I do in this life? *Plenty*.

I'm sure she's seeking out my warmth, and if she were to wake up like this she'd be horrified. She'd probably accuse me of knocking away the pillows between us—which is definitely not the case, but I'm not exactly scrambling away.

Truth is, this feels ... nice. Having Kira soft and warm against me. Compliant. It's been a week since we had dinner at Probka, and we've barely seen each other since then. Blame my busy schedule, or the fact that I fall into bed after she's gone to sleep and wake up well before her, but our distance only heightens my awareness of her now. Which is why I need to get the hell out of my bed and on with the day.

Carefully, I slide out from under her, ensuring she remains undisturbed. I take one last look at her, feeling a pang in my chest. Asleep, Kira loses the fierce edge she carries during the day, her features softening and her expression calm. Quietly, I make my way to the bathroom for a shower, the image of her sleeping form lingering in my mind.

As soon as I step under the showerhead, all the lust brewing under my skin hits me like a ton of bricks. Damn, I can't seem to make the shower cold enough, and I know the only thing that will take the edge off.

My hand reaches down and curls around my cock—swollen and thick for her. With one hand braced on the wall and cool water falling overhead, I stroke myself up and down a few times, thinking about Kira's naked body the night after I doused her, chased, and demanded she change into my shirt. My command was meant to put her in her place, to show her that I would always have the power in this dynamic, and maybe that would have been the case if Kira had a demure bone in her body. But instead, she notched up her chin and held my gaze, fierce as a lioness as she stripped naked before my eyes.

Stroking myself, I imagine what would happen if that night had gone differently. If instead of allowing her to put on my shirt, I ripped the fabric from her hands and pushed her down onto her knees. Would she obey my command like she did when I made her take pleasure on my leg in the kitchen, or would she fight me? I'm not sure I'd care either way.

I picture gripping a handful of her hair, pulling her head back until I have her positioned perfectly, before I surge forward, burying my cock in her hot warm mouth.

"Look at me, Kira," I'd demand. "Look at me while I fuck your mouth."

The moment I picture her eyes locking with mine, a fiery blend of desire and anger dancing in her gaze, I can't hold back. I crave her defiance as much as I crave her submission. With a silent roar, cum erupts, blasting all over my stomach.

I stand under the stream, catching my breath, wondering if I've officially lost my mind. Our arrangement is supposed to be nothing more than business. Chasing her around the house and making her strip in front of me was definitely not part of the deal. Neither is allowing her to curl up to me in her sleep, and I *definitely* shouldn't be jerking off to the thought of her choking on my cock. Yet here I am, breaking all my own rules.

After turning off the shower, I shave and get dressed in my usual black Armani suit, ready for what promises to be another busy day. I have to approve the final Romanée-Conti forgery, meet with international investors, and then do a photoshoot for *Society Magazine*. With Kira.

Exiting the bathroom, I spare Kira one final glance—her lips parted, her blonde hair spread messily across the pillow. My hand lands on the doorknob but before I can turn it, Kira cries out.

The sound stops me cold. It's not a normal whimper or mumble of sleep; it's a sharp, panicked cry, full of fear.

I turn around. Her body is tense, her hands clenched in the sheets, face contorted. She's trapped in a nightmare, one that seems to grip her with an intensity that's almost tangible. I approach the bed slowly, watching her struggle against the invisible demons of her dream. Her breaths are quick and shallow, her brows knitted together.

I have no idea what to do or if I should do anything, but witnessing her torment makes my throat constrict. Gently, I reach out and run my hands over her hair, pushing the strands back from her forehead.

"Kira," I whisper.

She doesn't wake up. Still, as I stroke her head, she gradually begins to relax. Calm returns to her features, her breathing evens out, and her grip on the sheets loosens.

Good. I have a million fucking things to do today, and this isn't my concern.

I pull my hand away and turn to leave when her body jerks violently, a muffled cry escaping her lips. It's more intense, more frantic this time. Her hands claw at the air as if fighting off an unseen assailant.

I should turn and walk away—I don't have time for this shit. That's what I should do, but the urge to help her, to do something—anything to ease her distress—seizes me. *Fuck.*

I whip out my phone and blast an email off to Nadya to delay my morning meetings. Irritated, I turn back to the bed, ignoring the inner voice warning me that I'm crossing the line I've set for myself. *Don't get close, don't get attached, don't care.* Not to mention if Kira wakes up in my arms, she will most definitely get the wrong idea.

But here's the thing about the voice of reason: it's easy to block out.

Without shedding my suit jacket, I slip back under the covers and pull her into my arms. I stroke her head and let her nuzzle into my chest. She doesn't wake, but again, the nightmare seems to recede under my touch.

Maybe I've lost the plot because I've never cared whether the woman in my bed sleeps soundly or not. All that mattered was that my dick was wet and she wasn't disturbing me. But Kira's vulnerabilities speak to my own. I understand how past pain haunts you in your sleep. Even if you evade those thoughts during the day, they come for you at night. Perhaps that's why I only sleep a few hours each night—to avoid the painful dreams of the car Ilya was in exploding before my eyes.

Twenty minutes later, Kira is sleeping peacefully on my chest, her beautiful face relaxed, her breathing soft and rhythmic against my skin.

I should have been at my desk long ago, with a million tasks waiting, but they can wait a little longer. For the first time in a long while, I'm content to just be still.

* * *

Gabriel, my master vintner, holds a wine glass up with an air of self-congratulation. When he takes a sip, he closes his eyes momentarily, letting the flavors flood his palate, and exhales a contented sigh.

I slam the glass down on the tasting table in front of me and turn to Gabriel. "It's good."

The wine *is* good. It's even exceptional. But it's a hair shy of perfect, my usual standard. Still, this is a moment worth celebrating. Except today, my mind is elsewhere.

"I'm glad this meets with your approval," he says cautiously, like he thinks I'm fucking with him.

He looks at me as if I've grown two heads because I never give my okay so readily. I always have notes, always push for better. But right now, there's a storm brewing in my head, and it's got Kira's name all over it. I'm glad she didn't wake up when I finally slipped out of bed an hour after soothing her in my arms.

I run my tongue over my teeth, giving a small shake of my

head. Word will get around that I've gone soft if I act out of character, and that's a dangerous proposition. "The finish isn't long enough, the tannins are too pronounced, and the label texture doesn't match the original. Try again."

My unflinching feedback is more in line with what he's used to. He gives me an efficient nod and turns back towards his laboratory.

Back at my office, I slam the door and sink into the chair behind the desk. My gaze immediately lands on the clock hanging on the wall, its hands inching closer to the hour I've been dreading all day.

As if I needed the reminder, Pavel strides into my office, the smug look on his face inspiring violence.

"Don't say it," I tell him before I'm forced to throw him through the nearest window.

He lifts both palms innocently. "Then you don't want me to remind you that you need to leave soon?"

In an hour, I'm expected home to play the doting husband for a *Society Magazine* feature and photo shoot with Kira. The charade of playing the perfect newlyweds, forcing smiles and answering invasive questions, is bullshit I could do without today. The looming pretense already feels like a weight on my chest, especially after this morning when I broke all my damn rules to comfort her. Because seeing her tormented like that, even in her dreams, caused a tight knot to form in my heart.

Blyad. I'm getting weak.

I don't know the source of Kira's nightmares, but I'm guessing it has something to do with her ruthless father.

Pavel sighs and takes the seat across from me. "Your marriage is a necessary evil—you said so yourself."

My earlier words come back to haunt me. That was before I knew what she smells like, how she likes her pancakes smothered in jam, how she cries out in her sleep and can only be soothed by pressing her body to mine.

When I don't respond, Pavel takes the seat across from me. "No woman will ever have power over you again."

"I know that." His words make me itchy under my collar. I'll never let a woman mean anything to me—that's a straight-up fact. "What exactly is your point?"

Pavel's expression is unreadable as he crosses one leg over the other. Few can address me as he does, but Pavel isn't just anyone—he's my oldest friend. We both cut our teeth in the same gritty boxing gym, a place of refuge from the brutal streets. Pavel cleaned the place in exchange for training and a handful of rubles. While I had some family, Pavel was orphaned at twelve. He was thrust into adulthood prematurely, hustling on the streets to provide for his younger sister. Her disappearance—a void that swallowed his hopes—brought us together. I helped him search through the darkest corners of the city. We never did find her alive.

And when Ilya was taken from me, Pavel was one of the few who understood my anguish. He kept me going during my darkest days.

Our grief is a bond that goes deeper than blood.

"My point is that a woman will never have power over you like that again. Once Kira serves her purpose, you can send her back to her brothers or whatever it is you plan to do once the war with the Black Company is behind us."

"You're forgetting that Kira is my only connection to Alyona."

"Lots of good that's doing you. Have you spoken with Alyona once since getting married?"

"And say what? 'So sorry I threatened to kill everyone you love. I was prepared to coerce you into doing what I want but ...

what, had a crisis of conscience?' I'm not sure she's ready to hear from me."

"I'm no expert," Pavel says, lifting his arms in the air. "But 'sorry' is always a good start."

Sorry is not part of my vocabulary but if given the chance, I would apologize to Alyona because she deserves it.

Discovering Alyona was my daughter years after losing Ilya was like a little piece of me coming back to life. Alyona shares the same eyes as Ilya—a striking shade of blue—and the same dark thick hair. Looking at her reminds me of what I'd lost and found again.

Alyona was in her teens when I discovered she's my daughter. I had to wait eight years before I could reach out and tell her I was her biological father because of a deal I'd made with her mother. She made me promise I wouldn't disrupt Alyona's life until she turned twenty-five. Maybe it was because I had to wait so long, but when I could finally contact her, I was impatient. I wanted her safe and in my world, ASAP.

But my impatience blew up in my face. And now, I'm paying the price.

"She's not ready to hear from me yet," I grumble, rubbing the back of my neck, exhaustion pulling at me after a lifetime of not enough sleep. I stand, indicating that this conversation is done. "Let's get this over with."

"There is no 'us' in this. It's all you," Pavel adds with glee.

"Don't you have something better to do?" I straighten my tie.

"Actually, I thought I'd tag along for the lovey-dovey newlyweds' shoot—"

My glare cuts him short.

"So that's a no then?"

"That's a fuck no."

Chapter Fourteen

MAXIM

I'm immediately assaulted by the chaos. Bright lights, a busy photography team, and elaborate floral displays fill the grand hall. It feels more like a film set than my own home.

Society Magazine spared no expense for this feature, and it's not a mystery why. Everyone wants to know more about the woman who sank her talons into Russia's most eligible billionaire, the man no one believed would settle down again. Not that the details of how my marriage to Irina ended were ever made public, but rumors have a way of spreading like a virus. Being featured in a *Society* spread is my idea of hell. I'm a private man, and even though this is all bullshit, I despise having to play a part.

Nadya has briefed Kira on what's expected of her, but I can't help but wonder how today will play out. When I catch sight of her across the room, my focus narrows; the noise, the lights, the people—they all blur into the background. All I can see is her.

Kira's hair, usually a wild cascade, is tamed into gentle waves that rest on her shoulders. She's dressed in a classic pink Chanel suit, the color complementing her peach and cream complexion. Like her subtle makeup, it downplays how damn young she is, which I suppose was Nadya's instruction to the stylist and hair-and-makeup team who put her together today. She looks perfect, comfortable and composed as if this bustling scene around her is an everyday occurrence.

Kira laughs at a comment from Maria Tokarev, a well-known entertainment journalist. She's an elegant woman in her forties and one of the few in the industry I trust to not fuck this up.

Taking a deep breath, I cut through the room, a smile held tightly on my face. I may not like to play the game, but I'm certainly good at it. "Good afternoon, ladies."

Kira turns to me, a glint in her eyes that I can't quite decipher. "There he is," she purrs. Without waiting, her lips meet mine, delivering a not-so-chaste kiss.

Holy hell, that's unexpected. Her lips are soft, tasting of berries with a hint of mint, and it's all I can do not to push my tongue into her mouth for more.

But she pulls back first, her eyes flashing with what looks like a challenge. She's playing the part of a doting wife, though I hadn't anticipated this level of ... *enthusiasm.*

I place a hand on the curve of Kira's lower back.

She tenses for a moment, then eases into my touch. "Maxim, I'd like to introduce you to Maria Tokarev. She'll be writing about us for *Society*."

"Maria," I greet, leaning in to give her a polite peck on the cheek. "As always, it's a pleasure."

A frown momentarily creases Kira's forehead. "You two know each other?"

Maria tilts her head. "I've been covering Moscow's elite for a long time. Though Mr. Belov here isn't one for media spot-light, he is a man about town, so we've crossed paths. However, he's never agreed to an interview until now. You must have worked your magic on him," she says, winking at Kira.

"Maybe I have."

Kira's words catch me off guard. Does she have any memory of what happened this morning, or is she playing the part for Maria?

Turning to me, Kira says, "Honey, how about we do the photo shoot first, and then we can settle in for the interview."

"Whatever works best," I murmur, pleased that Kira is at least acting the part.

"We're all set up over here." Maria gestures towards my sitting room, where a photographer is adjusting his camera on its tripod, with a few strategically placed lights illuminating the space.

The photographer—a nerdy-looking guy in his thirties, wearing black-rimmed glasses and a casual shirt—looks up from behind his lens and gives us a welcoming smile. "Good to see you again, Mr. Belov," he says, nodding my way.

I recognize him from past events but never had a formal introduction.

"Maxim, meet Ivan. He's the best in the business," Maria chimes in.

I acknowledge him with a nod. "Let's get this started."

"Of course," Ivan replies, directing his attention to both of us. "If the two of you could get comfortable... Don't worry about posing—I prefer more natural shots. Why don't you sit down on the couch and relax," Ivan encourages. "Pretend we're not even here."

I raise my eyebrows. Relax? Act natural?

I'm about to tell him I don't have all day for this crap, but Kira doesn't give me time to argue. She pulls me towards the couch and settles down, ensuring there's just enough space for me beside her.

Ivan starts fiddling with the lights as I sink into the cushions beside Kira.

I lean in close to her. "You did good," I praise. "Who said you wouldn't make a good society wife, after all."

She raises a brow, her lips tilting upwards. "Hold your praise. We're only getting started."

As if that's not ominous. Does the little vixen have something up her sleeve?

When I meet her stare, she just blinks up at me innocently. I lean back, wrapping my arm around the couch and search her face for any sign she remembers this morning—me holding her through the nightmare—but there's nothing. Not a flicker of recognition.

"How did you sleep last night?" I ask, voice rough.

Her eyebrows pull together. "Fine. Why? Did I ... say something in my sleep?"

I consider mentioning the nightmare, but there's something about her, a flash of vulnerability that makes me decide to drop it. "You seemed restless, that's all," I say, keeping my tone light.

"We're good to go anytime you are," Ivan calls across the room. "Show me what you've got."

Kira's lips form a mischievous smirk. "Just follow my lead," she whispers into my ear, her warm breath tickling my skin.

Before I can process her words, she's crawling into my lap, her lush ass flush against my crotch. My hands instinctively grasp her hips.

"What are you doing?" I murmur.

With a sly grin, she turns her head and winks at me. "Is there a problem?"

If there is, the photographer doesn't see it. "Perfect. Hold that." He captures a few shots, then suggests, "Maybe a bit closer, Kira? Imagine you're sharing a secret."

Following his guidance, she moves in even closer, her lips brushing against my earlobe. The warmth of her breath sends a shiver up my spine. Then she squirms in my lap, and my brain short-circuits. I release a hiss as she very deliberately readjusts her position, her soft ass nestling tight against my cock.

"You okay, honey?" she coos in my ear as Ivan clicks away. "You seem a little out of breath."

Between clenched teeth, I bite out, "Maybe if you stop fidgeting like you have ants in your pants, I could have a moment to ... pull myself together."

With that, she provocatively rolls her hips against my groin in a slow, sensual motion, deliberately teasing. A deep, involuntary grunt escapes me as she shifts back in my lap, my cock swollen and weeping in my pants. Pretty sure my eyes roll up to the back of my head. The little vixen is playing a game—one that is rapidly spiraling out of my control.

"What is it you think you're doing?"

"I'm sorry, are you uncomfortable?" She twists around, her gaze lazy and knowing, taking in my desperate state. She comes in close, her light floral scent filling my nostrils. It only adds to the maddening sensation. "Would you compare it to having a bucket of freezing cold water dumped on you in your sleep?"

"Kira, behave," I spit out.

The only thing I can do to stop her unofficial lap dance is grab her hips and pin her tight against me. It might limit her wriggling, but it doesn't help my ragged breaths, pumping heart, or the fact that I couldn't stand up and walk away if I needed to.

My problem would be way too obvious.

"Man, this is smoking," Ivan praises, scrolling through the pictures on his camera. "There's real chemistry here."

Maria leans in, and he shows her the snaps. She nods approvingly.

"Are we nearly done?" I grit. My knuckles whiten as I struggle to keep Kira still.

"Almost. Can you look up at Kira like she's the most precious thing in the world to you?"

I'm sorely tempted to tell Ivan to fuck off, but taking the path of least resistance seems wiser. The quicker I get this over with, the sooner I can distance myself from Kira.

I inhale a deep, cleansing breath. It's like prepping for a fight—I need to center myself. Pushing all other thoughts aside, I focus on getting through the next few minutes without losing control. Because that's the effect Kira has on me. Maybe if her body wasn't so warm and soft, if she didn't feel so damn perfect pressed against me, I could focus on something other than the urge to bury myself in her tight cunt.

"One more," Ivan instructs. "Almost like you're going to kiss. I want to capture this tension."

Kira leans in towards me, her plump lips close but not touching mine. Her hot breath flutters against my mouth, and it takes everything in me not to capture her lower lip between my teeth.

"You will pay." I keep my voice light and pleasant, but the threat is anything but.

Her expression remains unchanged, but the thumping pulse at her throat betrays the impact of my words. Maybe she's imagining how I made her pay after she ran from me.

She lays her soft hand on my face, pressing into my jaw while her lips brush against mine like a ghost caress. The shudder of arousal that moves through my body is fierce. It's the sweetest form of torture, and she knows exactly what she's doing.

Her mouth hovers over my ear as she whispers, "This is *my* payback, Maxim. I won't be pushed around by you. I won't bend to your every whim or be bullied by you. I don't know how it was with your first wife, but I'm not like that."

I freeze, unease creeping over my body. Ripping myself from her hold, I search her eyes.

Why is she mentioning Irina? What does she know?

Somewhere beyond us, Ivan declares, "That's perfect."

The space around us comes alive, buzzing with the crew doing whatever it is that they need to do, but Kira and I don't move as I watch her for a reaction. The weight of the past clings to me, making it hard to breathe.

"What do you know about my first wife?" My tone is arctic.

She seems to realize she wandered into very ugly territory, whether on purpose or not. "Forget I said that." She swallows, quickly sliding off my lap. "I was making a point."

My jaw tightens. "Never bring her up again."

Kira shoots me a defiant look and then strides away to join Maria. I take a moment to rise, straightening my cufflinks, smoothing down my tie.

When I look up, Nadya watches from the sidelines. Maria might have missed this interaction, but Nadya hasn't missed a thing. She never does. She cocks her head as if to ask, *Do we have a problem?*

Of all the people that know my personal history, Nadya is the most protective of me. Maybe because she saw the true devastation and raw grief from that time, how the only way to survive was to close my heart, harden the shell around my soul, and attempt to carry on.

I clear my throat and give a slight shake of my head. I don't need Nadya running interference. I can handle Kira all on my own.

Except when I can't. Like when she's grinding on my dick in a room full of people.

Well, two can play that game, and I'm more than capable of matching her step for step.

* * *

KIRA

Maybe I should have considered my devious little plan more carefully because it wasn't just Maxim who got all worked up—I was feeling rather needy myself. In fact, everyone in the room seemed a bit hot and bothered.

Of course, Maxim doused the heat of the moment when I mentioned his first wife. I guess it makes sense to not want to discuss the woman you *killed*. Whatever, if you can't stand the heat, get out of the kitchen.

I don't have time to stew over his words because Maria is already settling into the sitting room, where tea and refreshments are set up. Poised, she takes a seat first, smoothing out her skirt before reaching into her bag and pulling out a digital recorder, which she places in the middle of the coffee table.

"Mind if I record this?" she asks. "So I don't miss anything."

"That's fine." I lower myself onto the plush loveseat beside Maxim, leaving a small gap between us—a careful space that speaks volumes.

Maxim is not having it. This time, he's the one to close the distance between us, sliding towards me so that our legs are touching. Still irked by his reaction to my mentioning his first wife, I shoot him a look that says, *Back off*. Maxim is unfazed by my annoyance. He flashes one of his panty-melting smiles and drapes an arm casually around my shoulders. I stiffen at the unexpected intimacy, but with Maria sitting across from us grinning from ear to ear, I can't knee him in the balls, so I do my best to relax.

"Alright," Maria begins, looking between us with keen interest. "Let's get started." She presses the record button. "I think the first question on everyone's mind is: how did you two meet? As I understand it, Kira was living in America at the time."

"I have connections to Kira's family in the US," Maxim says, keeping it vague. "We met when I was in New York last winter, and when Kira visited Russia a few months later, I invited her to stay at my Black Sea home." I scoff quietly. This version of events is so far from the truth it's almost comical. Maxim's hand drops to my knee, giving it a subtle squeeze in warning. "It was there that we really got to know each other," Maxim continues. "We spent hours strolling through my vineyard, enjoying picnics on the beach, spending time together."

Maria writes something in her notebook, shaking her head. "What a romantic you're turning out to be. Kira, were you surprised by the softer side of the famous Maxim Belov?"

"Was I ever," I say emphatically. "The Maxim I know is quite different from the one everyone else sees."

Maria smiles knowingly. "Tell me something surprisingly romantic Maxim did during your courtship."

"Oh, we can't give away all our secrets," he jumps in before I can say anything. "Some things are just for us." His words are sweet, but his eyes flash with warning as he lifts my hand and drops a kiss on the inside of my wrist, sending an involuntary shiver up my arm.

I push aside the fluttering sensation in my belly. "Oh, come on, don't be coy. We can share a few things." I give him a sugary sweet grin before I address Maria again. "Maxim refuses to spend a night apart. He'd rather douse me in freezing cold water than not sleep by my side."

"Douse you in water?" Maria's eyebrows pull together.

"Is that what I said? I meant himself." Beside me, Maxim stifles a laugh, disguising it with a timely cough. "And his proposal was something else. We were surrounded by our family and friends, in the wine cellar of his Black Sea home. It was all so romantic."

Maria nods eagerly, scribbling down every word. "That sounds like a fairy tale."

"I'm glad you have such fond memories of that evening," Maxim murmurs so only I can hear as he brushes the pad of one finger over the pulse point at my wrist. I shoot him a hands-off look.

"Not sure 'fond' is quite the word," I whisper back.

Maria shifts in her seat, tilting her head in thought. "Maxim, what made you choose to settle down again at this point in your life?"

Maxim stiffens beside me but quickly masks his discomfort with a practiced smile. "Maybe I've been waiting for the right woman to come along and sweep me off my feet." His eyes lock on mine.

A charged undercurrent shifts the air between us and I have to look away, breaking the connection that suddenly feels too real.

"Last question," Maria's voice rings out. "Do you have any plans for a honeymoon?"

Maxim's hand, warm and steady, covers mine and a heady rush coasts over my skin. For some reason, I don't want to play our game anymore.

"I have something very special planned for Kira. A surprise."

"Ooh, that sounds lovely," Maria coos as I steal back my hand.

He's saying it for her benefit. Like his put-on charm and those politician-perfect smiles, his smooth words are another layer masking who he really is. But I will uncover that truth.

Maria informs us she has everything she needs and then thanks us warmly for the interview. She shakes Maxim's hand.

When she turns to me, I gesture towards the door. "Let me escort you out," I offer.

Maxim's eyes narrow as if questioning my motives, but he doesn't say anything, and I don't offer an explanation.

As we walk through the hall towards the entranceway, Maria turns to me. "You know, I've covered Maxim for years, and I've never seen him like this. So alive."

I don't know what to make of her revelation. Obviously Maxim is a great actor when he wants to be.

"Like what? How was he before?" I realize this is the perfect opportunity to get some answers, not only about Maxim's past. As a journalist, she might know something about my aunt.

"There's a spark that's been missing for a long time. But I see it again, and it's all because of you."

I'm about to ask her why he lost his spark in the first place when a dark shadow appears out of nowhere.

"Mrs. Tokarev, I trust you got everything you required," Nadya says, inserting herself between us.

Maria smiles, but I sense an underlying annoyance. "I did. Thank you for arranging everything. It's been such a delight to meet the wonderful Kira that everyone is so curious about."

I don't want to miss the chance to pick Maria's brain. "Maybe we can meet for coffee one—"

"Thank you again for your time," Nadya interrupts me. "I have arranged a limo for you. It's waiting outside." The older woman gestures towards the door, leaving no room for argument.

Maria takes my hand in hers. "It was truly a pleasure, Kira. Thank you." With a final nod, she turns and leaves, her steps echoing through the foyer.

As soon as Maria is out of earshot, I whirl around to face Nadya. "Stay out of my business," I snap, my frustration boiling over. "I don't need you to monitor my every move."

Nadya steps closer, her gaze sharp, fingers absently playing with the cross around her neck. "You have no right to befriend a journalist. It's not only *your* reputation at stake," she fires back with a stern tone. "You'd do well to remember that."

"And you'd do well to remember that I'm the lady of this house, and I certainly don't answer to you."

Nadya's eyes narrow, and she lets out a slow, measured breath. "We'll see about that," she says, her voice laced with thinly veiled contempt. "I was here before you, and I'll still be here long after you're gone." With that, she turns and walks away, leaving a tense silence in her wake.

A realization dawns on me, sharp and unbidden. Nadya must be in love with Maxim. It's the only thing that makes sense, the only reason she'd act so possessive over him.

I'm quite sure Maxim doesn't reciprocate her feelings, but the whole thing is so weird. I really need to hurry up and dig harder into Maxim's connection with my aunt's murder.

And the mayor's dinner party in a few days is the perfect place to do some digging.

Chapter Fifteen

KIRA

"Does that man ever give you a moment to yourself?" Liza shoots Roman a disdainful look from across the living room. Not that Roman's noticed. He's busy pacing, alternating between talking and typing on his phone. It's been like this all morning.

"Ignore him. He's too busy with whatever is going on to care about what we're doing." I shift, reaching for the pot of tea and pouring us each a cup.

It's not like he doesn't give us space, but I understand her annoyance—having him shadow me everywhere is irritating. On the bright side, at least it's not Pavel. That would be a nightmare I wouldn't wish on anyone.

We've decided meeting at her family's estate is the safest bet. No Nadya hovering nearby and less chance of listening devices planted on the property, or at least here in the living room only the women use to entertain. We're seated around a small table, fashion magazines spread out in front of us.

When Roman thinks we're thumbing through the latest styles, he's happy to ignore us. Which is the point. But when I turn back to get a better look at him, his eyes are glued to us as if we're actually doing something of interest.

No, correction. Not glued to me. Glued to Liza. He's returning her dark scowl. I suppose the feeling is mutual.

"How do we get rid of him?" She glowers his way, the midday light casting soft shadows across her face.

I laugh. "We don't. Ignore him. He's staring to be a dick." I stick my tongue out at Roman, and he returns a one-finger salute, then goes back to typing furiously on his phone.

Since Roman was assigned as my guard, we've settled into a kind of sibling-like relationship. I tease him, he rolls his eyes and acts like I'm not hilarious, but overall it's an easy vibe between us, which is more than I can say about the others in the household.

Since the *Society* photo shoot, I have seen little of Maxim. He falls into bed in the early hours of the morning and is always gone by the time I wake. The only sign he's slept in the same room as me is his scent still clinging to his pillow. A scent somewhere between musk, leather, and man. Not that I've spent too long analyzing it. Not that I bury my face in his pillow and inhale deeply. Who would do that?

Back when I lived in New York, I used to jolt awake, heart pounding, drenched in guilt over Masha's death. But lately, that hasn't happened. The nightmares come, but they also fade away before they wake me up. Which makes no sense because I literally sleep in her killer's bed.

Maybe peace comes knowing I'll get my revenge soon. Not that I've made much headway. Snooping around the house is near impossible with guards and cameras everywhere, and Maxim's inner circle is tight-lipped. Tonight will be my first real opportunity to dig.

We have dinner at Mayor Rashnikov's home, along with other prominent guests. Earlier today, Liza gave me a lay of the land—a who's who of Russian politics, business, and culture. Much has changed since I left nearly five years ago. But it's the mayor that I will be focused on. Liza agreed he knows everyone's secrets—blackmail is his stock in trade—and he has a weakness for women. Which is super icky, but it also makes him a perfect source. I just need to get him alone.

When I glance up from the magazine I was casually flipping through, Roman is in front of me, a phone pressed to his ear.

"Hold on," he says into the receiver. To me, he says, "I have to go out and deal with something. Will you be okay here for a bit?" His eyes ping between Liza and me.

She picks up another magazine and thumbs through it, purposefully ignoring Roman's presence.

"It's fine. Go deal with what you need to. I'll be right here."

Roman nods. "I won't be long."

I shoo him away with my hands.

Liza's family has plenty of guards around. It's probably the only reason he feels comfortable stepping away. While it hasn't been explicitly said, I can tell things are heating up with the Black Company. Maxim, Pavel, and Roman have been locked up in meetings most days, and everyone seems ... I don't know. Tense. Although, maybe they are always like this. It's not like they tell me shit. I'm only the arm candy.

Liza watches him walk away, a curious expression on her face. "Shocker. He's leaving you unattended for more than five minutes."

I bite out a laugh. "Guess I've been on good behavior. But now that we're alone..." I scoot forward in my seat. "Have you spoken to your father yet?"

She looks down at her hands and fidgets. There's something she doesn't want to tell me.

"Out with it," I demand.

"He's still in Poland, but we spoke on the phone. He told me not to stick my nose into other people's business. Said I was going to get myself into trouble asking questions about Belov."

My heart sinks. I was really counting on Boris and his loose lips. "But ... didn't you remind him he's the one who spilled the beans in the first place?"

"Of course. It doesn't mean anything, only that my father is now sober enough to be scared of Belov." Her eyes soften with a hint of sympathy.

I slump back into my seat. "It makes getting the mayor alone tonight that much more important."

"He's a major creep, Kira. I'm really not sure it's worth it."

"Come on," I plead. "It's my only chance."

She sighs. "Promise me you'll be careful."

When I agree, she gives me a mischievous smile.

"By the way, look what just went live online." She holds her phone between us, and I realize we're looking at *Society Magazine*'s website, featuring pictures of Maxim and me.

"Holy shit, that was fast. It's only been a few days since we did the shoot."

"Uh, how about: holy shit, you guys look like you're about to rip each other's clothes off and go at it in front of the crew."

"What?" I grab the phone from her to take a closer look.

I'm seated on Maxim's lap, my back pressed against his chest. One of his strong arms snakes around my waist, pulling me closer, while the other hand rests possessively on my thigh. My head is tilted to the side, our lips inches apart. Maxim stares at me like he wants to throw me down and fuck me into the floor, and I look like I wouldn't mind it one bit.

A nervous laugh bubbles up my throat. "It's not how it looks."

"I'm sure. I know how it is with the photographer posing you and all. Obviously, you don't want Maxim. He's the enemy."

"Exactly!" I bite my lip.

These pictures certainly bring the heat. Truth be told, my big plan to tease Maxim also affected me. My panties were soaked by the end of the photo shoot. If some higher power exists, my first question when I get to the pearly gates will be why they had to give the devil incarnate a panty-melting smile and a voice that drips like honey.

Ugh. He really is the worst.

Liza takes her phone from my hands and scrolls through the image gallery. "This photographer sure is talented. I can see why they rushed to publish these. Well ... that, and everyone wants to know more about the elusive Maxim Belov and the young beauty who captured his heart." She winks at me.

"Puke," I say, with an eye roll. "The real version would be much more shocking. 'Young bratva princess marries her aunt's suspected killer'. Or 'Evil oligarch marries his daughter's best friend to improve his public image'."

Liza dissolves into a fit of laughter. "Truth is *always* stranger than fiction. Anyhow..." She wipes her tears. "Do you know what you're going to wear tonight?"

I shrug. "One of the dresses we bought together at the boutique."

Usually I'd feel more excited about the possibility of dressing up, but today my heart is feeling a little heavy. Back at home, Aly would be my unofficial stylist, choosing my outfit and suggesting accessories. It's not like I had time for that shit. I was running a bratva with my brothers. Here, I do nothing but swan around the mansion all day and meet with Liza.

I try to remind myself that this is the only way, a means to an end. Once I've avenged my aunt's murder, I can go back home. I can be close to Aly and join my brothers again. I miss strategizing with them in our office above a garment factory in Brooklyn. I miss being asked my opinion on important matters. I miss our big family dinners, buzzing with conversation and banter, the table crowded with everyone and their spouses.

Homesickness washes over me, tugging at the corners of my heart.

I lean my elbows onto the table, resting my hand on my jaw. "I'm sure Nadya will have something to say about whatever I wear."

Before the interview and photoshoot with *Society Magazine*, she gave me a full morning of instruction on how to be a proper lady as if I didn't go to the finest boarding schools in Europe.

"*Khuy*." Beside me, Liza hisses, calling someone a dick between clenched teeth.

I raise my head, expecting to find Roman back too soon. Instead I find her fiancé, Anatoly, strolling into the living area, head held high as if he owns the property, which given the debts Liza's family owes him, he might. Spotting us, he arrogantly nods his chin and makes his way towards us.

"Fuck me," Liza grates. "Definitely not an invited guest."

Yeah, I wouldn't think so. She is not fond of the man she's being forced to marry.

As distasteful as I find him, something occurs to me. He could be a source of information. He's well-connected and, much like the mayor, seems like the type who'd try to have dirt on everyone.

"Kira Antonov. Or should I say, Mrs. Belov?" He smirks at me, but it's slippery. Like everything else about him. "Congratulations are in order. Although, I admit I'm a bit sore that we didn't get an invite to the wedding, seeing how we're old school chums."

Sure, if that's how he wants to remember it.

I give him a patient smile. "I had nothing to do with the invite list. I let Maxim's people take care of all the logistics."

"It's about time we had a chance to catch up. Liza's been hiding you away." He takes a seat at the table, his shirt straining against his generous midsection as he sits.

He hasn't bothered to greet Liza, who seems to have shrunk into herself at his arrival. Her arms are crossed over her chest while her gaze is fixed on the table, avoiding direct eye contact. I hate seeing my vibrant friend so diminished in his presence.

"Hardly. She hasn't been hiding me away. I've been busy settling in."

"Oh, I'm sure Belov's kept you very busy." He smirks, the insinuation clear. "I saw the *Society Magazine* spread, after all. It's all the city is talking about."

Great.

"Anatoly," Liza finally acknowledges her fiancé, her voice flat. "Why are you here so early? Dinner's not until eight."

He gives Liza a patronizing grin as he sits back in his seat, his fingers intertwined and resting on his gut. "I had business with one of your father's men," he says with a wave of his hand. "Since our old friend was visiting, I thought it was only polite to say hello."

I manage a tight smile as Anatoly pours himself a cup of tea, making it clear he's not going anywhere. He was considered handsome back in school, but with his receding hairline and paunch, he's now not the shining star he once was. Though, his swinging dick attitude suggests he hasn't yet received the memo.

"So," I ask through gritted teeth. "How have you been?"

"Fine, fine." He dismisses my questions with a little wave.

"I'm sure Liza told you everything there is to know about us. I'm more curious about you."

My heart lurches. Somehow, I don't like the sound of that.

"The *Society* article said Belov is connected with your family in New York. Is that how you met? Through your brothers—the Kozlovs, right?"

"That's right," I confirm. "Maxim and I met in New York, and eventually" — I force the next words out — "we fell in love."

"Ah, yes, you fell in love strolling through his vineyard and curling up to watch movies together. How quaint."

Liza scoffs. "Wake up, Anatoly. It's how most couples get together these days, not because they're the solution to their family's financial sins."

Anatoly's dead shark eyes cut to Liza. His mouth settles into a grim line. "Aren't you lucky that in Russia we still observe the old way of doing things, or else your family would be on the street."

Liza looks away, her knuckles turning white as she grips the armrest of her chair.

"We're all friends here, Kira. You don't need to feed me the same drivel you feed the press. I know how you really met."

My stomach drops. What is he suggesting?

I lock eyes with Liza, who subtly shakes her head.

"I have no idea what you mean." I fight to keep my expression neutral.

"Your father, of course." Anatoly's smile is razor-sharp as he cocks his head my way. "Are you saying you're not aware of Belov's connection to Oleg Antonov?"

I swallow, deliberately keeping my tone light. "Maxim and I don't talk about my father. It's unpleasant."

Anatoly's eyes narrow, a hard glint appearing in their depths. "Your father was a real piece of work, wasn't he?" He pauses, rubbing his chin thoughtfully. I know I won't like what he says next. "Oleg discovered your husband in an underground fighting league in Moscow's slums. He's the one who brought Belov into the world of the bratva."

Nausea swirls in the pit of my stomach. If this is true, and Maxim and my father did have a connection, it explains why Maxim would help my father kill Masha.

Fuck.

Liza frowns. "What? I've never heard that before."

"It's a well-known fact in certain circles. I'm surprised your husband never mentioned it to you." The way he says that, it's clear he's enjoying having information I don't. "Then again, Belov rose far above the ranks of your father. I'm sure he wanted to distance himself from that disgrace as much as possible."

Anatoly's words buzz through my brain, but I can't focus on what he's actually saying. Questions run through my head, pieces of a puzzle scattering and rearranging themselves.

How close were Maxim and my father? Why did he keep this connection from me?

I should be elated by this revelation—it's the first lead I've had that connects Belov with my aunt's death—but for some reason, it feels like a betrayal. Which makes no sense. I've been digging for the truth, but now it feels like I'm buried under its weight, unable to breathe.

Anatoly worms forward in his seat, seeming to take delight in my shocked silence. "Don't be too hard on the man. I'm sure he planned on telling you at some point."

"Leave her alone," Liza snaps at her fiancé. You know how she feels about her father."

I should be asking a million questions, but they all feel too heavy, stuck in my throat. I stand abruptly, cutting off further conversation. "Thank you for the visit, but I should get going. Maxim and I have an event tonight."

"Certainly," Anatoly chortles. "Wouldn't want to keep the mighty Maxim Belov waiting, would we?"

Liza looks between Anatoly and me, her face a mix of confusion and concern.

I lean down, placing a soft kiss on Liza's cheek. "I'll call you later."

Chapter Sixteen

MAXIM

I swirl the whiskey in my glass and stare out my office window into the darkness beyond, my phone pressed against my ear.

"We have a lead on Chun Leung, the Black Company operative in Moscow," Viktor tells me. He's my head of security and intelligence. As a former special forces operative, his security and surveillance training is an invaluable asset to my operations. "Check your phone. I just sent a picture over."

I put my phone on speaker and swipe until I'm looking at a grainy black and white image. It shows two men on the steps of a building. One is Henri Blanchet, and the other must be Leung.

"They were last seen together here, in front of the Tretyakov Gallery. The security cameras didn't give us a super clean image of him, but it's enough for our team to work with."

I allow a rare smile. "Finally some fucking good news. Make finding Leung a priority."

Things have been quiet with the Black Company, but it's the calm before the storm. I'm planning on taking our first wine forgery to auction in New York soon, and that will surely light the fuse, setting off a war with them.

"We will," Viktor assures me. "Now that we know what Leung looks like, we'll use facial recognition software to sift through the city's CCTV footage and track him down."

"Keep me updated," I say and hang up the phone.

I check my watch. Kira is keeping me waiting. Not that I'm in a rush to go to the mayor's dinner tonight. Everything about that man sets my nerves on edge, but I do business with him, and I'll have to introduce Kira to my world eventually.

The quiet is abruptly broken as the door flies open. I turn to see Nadya, her face flushed with agitation.

"Your new wife is impossible to deal with. I give up," she declares, her voice crackling with frustration.

I set my glass down, arching an eyebrow, as a pang of irritation moves through me. Nadya is not known for hysterics, but Kira seems to push all her buttons. "Are you trying to tell me she's running late?"

Nadya bristles. "No. I'm here to tell you she's dressed like a common whore, even though I specifically chose an outfit and left it out for her."

I sigh. This shit again. Kira is a force of nature, strong-willed and independent, while Nadya thrives on control and tradition. The two were bound to clash. She wants Kira to heel to her dominance, but that's never going to happen.

"You don't have to deal with her," I remind Nadya sharply. "She's my issue, not yours."

"But your problems are mine to bear." Her voice is soft and pleading. She comes closer, laying a hand on my arm. "You know everything I do is for you. I want to make this arrangement more bearable."

"If you want to make it more bearable, find a way to get along with Kira."

Nadya was never going to be happy with any woman by my side. After Ilya's death sent my world into a tailspin, she quietly stepped up, taking on more responsibilities. With no lady of the house, she filled that void, which worked fine until now. But she's acting like a rabid guard dog these days, and it's wearing on my nerves.

Nadya sniffs disdainfully and folds her arms. "It's impossible to get along with a traitor like her."

Traitor? A prickle rises on my neck. Something about that word doesn't sit right.

Before I can respond, the door swings open and Kira enters, looking like sex on a stick. She's wearing four-inch heels, delicate fishnet stockings, and a form-fitting dress that hugs her curves like it's been painted on. Like the vixen she is, she looks right at me, gauging my reaction as she slowly rests a hand on her hip.

When she sees Nadya sneering, she flashes her a shit-eating grin before addressing me. "Ready to go?"

White heat licks the lining of my stomach. I run my tongue over my teeth and try to hold back the impulse I have to throw her over my lap and show her exactly what I think of her outfit. And the smirk on her face. And the way her tits look like the perfect handful. I manage to hold back—barely.

"Leave us," I say to Nadya, who obliges. "What kind of statement were you looking to make tonight?" I ask Kira as I lean against the wall, arms crossed in front of me. "We're going to a dinner party at the mayor's residence, for fuck's sake, not a club in the Arbat district."

Kira's eyes, heavy under thick lashes, lock onto mine. She snares her plush bottom lip with her front teeth. "No statement. It's just a dress, Maxim."

Just a dress ... that makes me want to push her against the wall and fuck her with no mercy. I guarantee I won't be the only one having this reaction to Kira tonight.

I force my face to remain neutral, but inside my blood is boiling. "You've met the mayor, Kira. You saw what kind of twisted fuck he is. So on top of the many business matters I have to deal with tonight, I also have to worry about him lusting after you?"

She shrugs. "So? Why did you marry me if not to have a hot young thing hanging off your arm? You've made it clear you have no interest in my business sense or intellectual contributions. Why not enjoy the view?"

I don't miss the note of vulnerability in her voice. Maybe because she's so young and way too fucking brash for her own good, but something inside my chests twists knowing that this ruthless world will eventually dim her light. Starting with me.

"We don't have time for you to change," I say, glancing at my watch. "Don't go anywhere with the mayor alone. And for fuck's sake, be on good behavior."

"Don't you worry, I'll be the perfect society wife exchanging recipes for borscht and talking about the latest styles to hit the runways." She blinks up at me, innocence personified.

Why do I have this nagging feeling that I've dug my own grave?

* * *

My young wife has charmed the hell out of everyone here. The mayor and his wife, Zoya, are as intrigued by Kira as the other guests: Ludmila Vetrova, the famed ballet director from the Bolshoi Theatre; Grigor Grigoriev, a distinguished conductor for the Moscow Philharmonic Orchestra; and Tim Burke, an American tech mogul.

Any subject that comes up—from the latest production of *Giselle* at the Bolshoi to the current world financial market trends—Kira holds her own. She is polite, witty, and charming, and so goddamn beautiful I can hardly look at her because it scrambles my brain.

That, unfortunately, doesn't seem to be Pyotr's problem. The mayor's eyes have been glued to her all night—her legs, her tits, even watching her lips as she speaks. I'd shank him right here if we weren't surrounded by his guards. Either Kira is oblivious or a great actor because she makes it seem like he's the most charming man on the planet, and trust me, that couldn't be further from the truth. He's as charming as a sprouted old potato, which incidentally he resembles.

As soon as the last dinner plate is cleared, I turn to Pyotr, an insincere smile pulling my lips. "I think it's time for a nightcap." Code: we need to talk business. Alone.

But his eyes are still glued to my wife's chest as she continues an animated conversation with Ludmila. "Maybe in a while. I want to show Kira my sword collection."

Not fucking happening.

"I would think you want to hear about your cut in the Albanian deal."

That sure gets his attention. He leans towards me, swirling the wine in his glass. "Is that already paying dividends?"

Kira's gentle laughter floats across the table, and his eyes are drawn back to her. I've had enough. He may be the mayor, but *I* run this fucking city.

I stand up, my chair scraping along the oak floor. "Excuse us," I say to the table, buttoning up my suit jacket. "Pyotr and I have some business to discuss."

Curious eyes land on me, but I don't acknowledge anyone

else at the table. Entering the mayor's office, I fix myself a cognac and make myself at home, taking a seat in Pyotr's office chair.

The mayor enters the room shortly after and freezes, watching me closely. I pick up the 1928 Babe Ruth signed baseball I gifted him last year after he granted my construction company exclusive rights to build a complex of skyscrapers downtown. His eyes ping pong, following the ball as I toss it from one hand to the other.

"You really need to put this behind some sort of glass," I suggest coolly. "You know, precious items can get damaged or lost so easily if not properly cared for."

"Too true. Too true," Pyotr agrees, taking the seat across from me. "I like to admire it sometimes without the layer of protection."

"We all like pretty things, but we can't play with them if they're not ours."

He misses the meaning of my words as he leans forward, rummaging in a teak box on his desk. If he wasn't so stupid, I'd swear he's purposefully baiting me.

Thwack.

The sudden noise reverberates through the room as the baseball smashes against the window. The impact is loud and startling, but the window, being bulletproof, doesn't even crack.

Pyotr's head snaps up, his gaze darting to the undamaged window and then to me, shock in his eyes. "Why would you do that?!"

"Because I require your attention and you're too busy rummaging around for a fucking cigar."

Pyotr's face tightens and he sits back down, clutching a cigar between his fingers. "I'm sorry," he huffs. "I'm too drunk to talk business right now. How about we meet at Cabaret Le Rouge Monday night? There are some new faces you don't want to miss." By "faces", he means tits and ass because Cabaret Le Rouge is Moscow's elite strip club.

"I don't have time for that."

He nods, taking a puff off his cigar, exhaling a plume of smoke that lazily drifts towards the ceiling. "Passing up an opportunity to get your dick sucked at Cabaret? Is this about your new wife? I didn't think a man like you would ever get remarried, but she is a hot piece of ass."

Fire shoots through my veins, and I consider using the baseball as a weapon to pummel his face.

"Because if I was married to a woman like that, I'd keep her bent over—"

Without clearance from my brain, I reach into the back of my waistband, my hand curling around the cold metal of the Sig. As I disengage the safety, the door opens.

Zoya pops her head through. "Please tell me you are done talking business. We're about to serve tea and *medovik*." Layer cake.

My hand slowly uncurls from the metal tucked into my waistband, and I straighten the lapel of my suit, looking down at the worm in front of me. If it wasn't for his wife, a saint of a woman for putting up with him, I'd be calling in a clean-up crew to the *mayor's fucking house*. He doesn't get to talk like that about the woman wearing my ring. No one does.

Dragging a slow, steady breath into my lungs, I stride out of the mayor's office. The urge to see Kira is overwhelming, a stark contrast to the fury that had me unraveling moments ago.

I storm through the room, my gaze scanning for her.

There she is, laughing with that American dickhead, Tim. A deep, possessive instinct floods my veins. First the mayor, then this asshole making her smile.

Kira's eyes widen as I approach. Lacking the patience for politeness, I send Tim a get-lost look. He gets the message and slinks away. I take his seat, but rather than maintaining a respectable distance, I lift Kira and set her down on my lap—right where she belongs.

She can't mask her surprise, her eyes meeting mine. "Everything okay?" she asks cautiously.

A muscle in my jaw twitches. "Everything's fine," I say tersely. "But I think it's time we started acting like newlyweds."

She nearly chokes on a laugh. "I see."

Ducking my head, I kiss her neck, eliciting a shiver from her. She smells like cinnamon and cloves, her skin unbelievably soft beneath my lips as if I'm pressing my face into satin. I go further, my hand trailing down her side to her legs. Her eyelids flutter shut for a moment, lashes casting delicate shadows on her cheeks. The contrast between the softness of her skin and the rough texture of the fishnets ignites a surge of desire.

She looks at me as though I've sprouted a second head, but she doesn't pull away, and I notice her pulse quicken at the base of her flushed neck.

"What are you doing? This is not part of the plan for tonight," she hisses through gritted teeth.

"Actually, it is," I murmur, my breath brushing her neck. The room buzzes with conversation, but it's clear we've captured everyone's attention. "We're here to put on a show, right? Let them see how your husband affects you. How much you crave his cock." She goes still, caught off guard by my blunt words, or the way I lean in and sink my teeth into the delicate curve of her earlobe. "Don't you, lastochka?

Her body tenses and she lets out a little whimper, which might have something to do with my thumb absently brushing circles on her inner thigh.

"Fuck." The word comes out of her mouth as a half-whisper and half-moan.

I like the effect I'm having on her. I especially like that

Pyotr's watching us from across the room as he reaches for another shot of vodka.

Good.

Something territorial flares inside me, a raw emotion that sparks like an uncontrollable blaze. Let the mudak understand that she's mine. Let the whole room take note and spread the word throughout Moscow. As I'm considering dragging Kira into the closest bathroom, Zoya materializes in front of us.

"Maxim, you must come and hear what Tim has in store for the Global Tech Conference. It's groundbreaking, but some advice from you would be invaluable."

I clear my throat, grounding myself into the polished businessman everyone expects, though I can't muster any enthusiasm.

"You should go," Kira says as she stands, her eyes revealing a flicker of disappointment, quickly concealed as she smooths her dress. "Grigor offered us season tickets to the Philharmonic. I should take him up on that."

I don't need season tickets anywhere; all I have to do is show up at an event, and doors open. But Grigor is a true gentleman, and I'd prefer she spend time in his company rather than Pyotr's.

"Get us the best seats in the house," I say, and because possession still pumps through my veins, I pat her ass, not caring that her response is a not-so-subtle death glare.

Chapter Seventeen

KIRA

What alien has taken over Maxim's body and replaced him with this … caveman? Sure, the touchy-feely act is just for show, but earlier tonight at dinner, he didn't seem interested in any display. He barely looked my way. Maybe the alcohol helped him loosen up enough to realize we weren't acting like a newly married couple. Then again, Maxim doesn't care about others' opinions. He doesn't need to.

I glance across the room where he's engaged in conversation with Tim, the younger man hanging onto his every word. Shivers run down my spine as I recall the rough warmth of his hand sliding down my leg and his whisper in my ear.

"Let them see how your husband affects you. How much you crave his cock. Don't you, lastochka?"

My pussy clenches thinking about his dirty words whispered against my skin in a roomful of people. He's finally abandoned his suit jacket and his tailored white shirt is casually unbuttoned at the top, with sleeves pushed up to his elbows revealing powerful forearms. The way he sits back, knees apart, causing the fabric of his pants to pull taut… My goodness, is it hot in here?

As if he senses me staring, his intense eyes connect with mine. An amused expression hints he's aware I was enjoying the view. I glare back at him.

I'd like to say I didn't appreciate his wandering lips and hands, but it wouldn't be true. I may hate him, but my body did not get the memo.

I've missed everything Grigor has said to me in the last two minutes, but I do catch him saying, "You must see this Valentin Serov piece."

He gently takes my elbow, guiding me towards the foyer, where several art pieces adorn the walls. Among them are some rare Russian masterpieces.

God, I had no idea the mayor was so stinking rich, but then again, if Pyotr is doing business with Maxim, it means he has his hands in all kinds of pots. As we're admiring the Serov painting, a slithery presence enters into the room.

I know immediately who I will find when I turn around. The creepy-ass mayor who has been throwing me lusty looks all night. Even if he's a sleazeball, he's also the man I need to talk with if I'm going to learn about Maxim's involvement in my aunt's death. Maxim warned me against being alone with him, but I can handle myself. I've certainly dealt with my fair share of assholes.

Anatoly's revelation still burns beneath my skin. Why would Maxim neglect to tell me about his connection to my father? I know we haven't had deep talks, but it's highly suspect that this never came up between us.

Turning on a megawatt smile, I turn to the mayor approaching us and carrying two full glasses of champagne.

"I noticed your hands were empty, my dear." He passes me one of the glasses and keeps the other for himself. "We can't have that."

"Thank you. So thoughtful," I say, trying not to puke in my mouth. "About that antique sword collection—I'd love to see it if you have the time."

The man's eyes widen like he won the lottery. "I'd like nothing more."

Grigor clears his throat. "I'd be interested in taking a look myself if you don't mind—"

"Sorry, not much room down there." Pyotr shrugs. "I try to control the humidity. Too many bodies... You know how it is."

Grigor shoots me a concerned look, but I don't want him to worry so I wink and murmur so only he can hear, "If I'm not back in twenty minutes, send help." It's a joke meant to disarm him, but Grigor laughs nervously.

Great.

Pyotr leads me down a long flight of stairs, the sound of our footsteps echoing in the narrow hallway. We arrive at a heavy wooden door that Pyotr pushes open to reveal a cozy room with an arched ceiling. Swords of every size, shape, and vintage are hung meticulously.

Maybe it would be kind of cool if the mayor wasn't standing so close to me I can feel his breath on my neck. I move further into the room, wanting to put as much space as possible between us.

"Impressive, isn't it?" Pyotr walks slowly along the display, a reverent touch on each piece, as I feign interest. "Each sword has a story, a part of our rich history."

"It's magnificent," I say with forced enthusiasm, which naturally Pyotr takes to mean I want to hear the history of each piece.

Twenty minutes later, I know more about Damascus steel sabers and the curved Cossack shashkas, than I'll ever need to.

"Come sit. Let's have a drink." Pyotr gestures to the far side of the room, where a little sitting area is set up—a plush burgundy sofa in front of a grand fireplace.

The mayor moves to a small bar cart and pours two glasses of amber-hued cognac. Not that I have any intention of drinking around him—I've long abandoned the champagne from earlier. But this is my chance to pump the man for information, so I lower myself onto the cushion.

No sooner have I made myself comfortable than Pyotr is right beside me, handing me a glass. His proximity is unsettling; he sits too close, his thigh almost touching mine.

There's an intensity in his eyes as he raises his glass for a toast. "To new friendships," he says, his voice low and too intimate. "Now, I want to hear all about you. Maxim has said very little about his new bride."

I smile demurely. "Oh, I'm not very interesting. But since you're such good friends with my husband, I was hoping you can tell me more about him. He's so tightly guarded, even with me."

The mayor chortles. "That's Maxim for you, a mystery. But I'd be more than happy to help in any way I can..." His fingers brush lightly along my leg.

I have to suppress a shudder of revulsion. His touch elicits the exact opposite effect of Maxim's.

I clear my throat and shift out of his reach. "I hear nothing happens in this city without Maxims' approval, is that true?"

"Maxim is not the only powerful man in this city." He puffs out his chest as if he can compete with Maxim's raw masculinity and commanding presence. "There's plenty that happens without his knowledge. In fact, as the mayor, I wield considerable power."

"Maybe you can help me then..." I pause and give him my best sweet-and-innocent look. "I've always wanted to know what happened with Masha Antonov. She's a relation, and I never really got a straight answer about how she died."

"Ah, yes. Masha." Pyotr's hand comes to rest on my thigh again.

I swallow down my disgust for a hot minute because I need to hear his answer.

"It was a shame the way she was killed, wasn't it."

Impatience blasts through my veins. "How did she end up at that warehouse in the first place? Who lured her there? It had to be someone with considerable power to hide their involvement—" The words die in my throat as the mayor's fingertips brush the inner seam of my panties.

I freeze, bile filling my throat.

"I'll share what I know ... but what will you do for me?"

"Nothing!" I try to push his hands away, but he holds firm. "I'm serious," I gasp, struggling against his grip. "I'll scream."

"Just you try," he snarls.

I sink my nails into his forearm and he bites out a curse, when the door suddenly swings open.

Maxim stands there, radiating an aura of barely-contained rage that drops the room's temperature by several degrees.

"Get your fucking hands off my wife." Maxim's voice is a deadly whisper, each word dripping with menace.

Pyotr visibly pales. He withdraws his hand and scrambles to sit up straighter. "Belov, we were just discussing—"

"How I'm going to kill you?" Maxim cuts him off, stepping further into the room, his tall frame casting an imposing shadow. "How, if I ever find you with your hands on my wife again, I will string you up by your dick and make sure you dangle there until it rips straight off of your body? Then I will personally remove each and every one of your appendages with a hacksaw until you bleed out. Is that what you were discussing?"

I'm shaken, my stomach churning with nausea from everything that's happened, yet there's a sliver of relief in knowing how fiercely Maxim is willing to protect me. But is it really about me, or a possessive claim over what he considers his?

Pyotr's face reddens with a mix of fear and humiliation. For all his bluster and bravado, the mayor looks ready to piss himself.

"Maxim—" I begin, but he stops me with a raised hand.

"Did he hurt you?" His eyes close, and he swallows hard. "Did he do more than what I saw?"

I shake my head, and a muscle in his jaw twitches. The stoic mask he always wears slips, exposing a rare glimpse of something deeper. There's a fierceness in his eyes, but it's not about possession. Could it be that he's actually concerned?

"It was nothing," Pyotr says hastily, getting to his feet. He takes a handkerchief from the inner pocket of his jacket and dabs at the sweat now running down his face. "You can't be serious. Since when have you ever cared for a woman?"

Maxim smiles, and it's frightening. "Since now." His eyes flicker towards me, a softening in his gaze that contrasts the harshness of his words. "We'll call this a misunderstanding. Now you know better."

The mayor nods frantically, like one of those bobbleheads people put on their car dashboard. At least he's smart enough to take the out Maxim is providing.

"In that case," Maxim continues, "we will bid you a goodnight." He extends his hand to the mayor to end the night with a handshake. It's a Trojan horse if I've ever seen one.

Unfortunately for Pyotr, he doesn't see the warning signs. As their hands meet, Maxim's clasp quickly turns from cordial to crushing. His tightening grip is swift, ruthless, and calculated. Pyotr's face contorts in pain, his eyes widening in a mix of shock and agony as the unmistakable sound of bones crunching under the pressure echoes through the room. Pyotr's knees buckle, his other hand instinctively reaching out to cradle the one being crushed, trying to pry Maxim's fingers away. But it's of no use.

My heart slams against my chest watching Maxim exact his revenge with a slow, icy smile. This is the cold-hearted predator that I've seen glimpses of. I wonder what would happen if we weren't in Pyotr's home with his wife upstairs, what Maxim would actually do. The thought causes a chill to travel down my spine, and it's not in revulsion. There's an undeniable thrill in knowing that this ruthless, hard man would go to any length, even risking valuable alliances, to protect me.

And there's a twisted sense of satisfaction in seeing Pyotr face the consequences of his vile actions.

Maxim finally releases his hold and Pyotr crumples, his now mangled hand trembling as he holds it close to his chest, his face ashen. But Maxim is no longer looking at his victim; his eyes have moved on to me.

"Let's go," he says, grabbing my arm. His voice, dripping with dominance, makes my skin tingle.

One part of me—the smarter part, I suppose—is telling me to shake his hand off me and give him shit. I was capable of putting the mayor in his place. But the other part of me? Feminism has completely left my body because that part is soaking her panties and allowing the beast I call a husband to escort me out of the room.

The moment we're alone in the backseat of the car, Maxim spins on me. "What the fuck were you thinking being alone with the mayor? I warned you, Kira. I warned you. That man is a predator! You could have been... Fuck!"

Hot, indignant tears threaten at the corners of my eyes, but

I hold them back, refusing to give Maxim the satisfaction of seeing how deeply he affects me. Part of my fury is directed at my own recklessness for putting myself at risk, and the rest is aimed squarely at Maxim for ... everything. Every damn thing. He's the source of my misery and the one who sends my stomach into knots—it's completely unfair.

"I know you think I'm useless, but I can and will defend myself. And don't bother pretending you give a shit about me because you obviously don't." Beneath my defiant words, an unvoiced thought creeps in—he does care, he must, even a little. Not that I want him to. He killed my aunt, for fuck's sake.

Fury radiates from Maxim like a blazing inferno. He clutches his phone so tightly that his knuckles turn white, threatening to crack the screen. "You don't get it..." he hisses. It's like watching a man at war with himself, torn between anger and frustration. "When did I ever say you're useless? When did I ever... Jesus."

With a sudden movement, Maxim pivots, facing the window. His shoulders are taut, tension radiating from his body. When he spins back towards me, his face is a mask of raw need. Before I can react, he pushes me down on my back, his bigger body crowding above me. Surprise jolts through me in a rush that leaves me breathless.

"You are mine. My wife." His nose skims down my neck slowly, and he inhales deeply, his voice a low, commanding murmur. "It doesn't matter if you want my protection or not. I will protect you at all costs."

Goosebumps prickle along my skin as his warm breath brushes my neck. I can't deny the thrill of being his, even when I want to resist.

His mouth crashes down on mine. It's hot and passionate, and sends my brain cells into a tailspin. His tongue breaches the seam of my lips, plundering and claiming me for his own.

The wild dance of my heart betrays my excitement, especially with Maxim so close because his very proximity is like a magnetic force, drawing me in despite my better judgment. I know I should throw him off me, tell him to go to hell, but the traitor inside me, the one that hasn't listened to reason all night, grasps Maxim by his lapels and pulls him even closer, matching each swipe of his tongue with my own.

His lips are softer than I imagined they would be, although there's nothing gentle about how he kisses. It's raw, untethered, as if trying to lay claim to every inch of my body, asserting his dominance.

I melt. Literally melt, because I've never been kissed like this. It feels like he would die if he didn't taste me.

He groans and presses his very pronounced hard-on against me. My God, he's big and he's rock-hard. This realization charges through me, sending a tingling thrill to my core and a warm dampness between my legs. Arousal washes over me, quickening my pulse as I rock my hips against his erection. He emits a deep, guttural grunt, and the sound of his labored breath is intoxicating.

Everything about this is wrong, but there's no chance in hell I'm willing to come back to earth. I'm beyond thought right now. Floating on a cloud of pure need, a need that is Maxim deep between my thighs.

Maybe he shares the same sentiment because he grabs both of my ass cheeks and thrusts up into my core once, twice, and then ... he tears himself away from me, scooting to the other side of the car like he's touched a live wire. My heart sinks with disappointment. Why did he stop? Was this all a game to him?

Breathing heavily, he runs a shaky hand through his hair, his eyes avoiding mine.

My cheeks flush with heat as I slowly sit up and straighten

my dress, trying to gather my self-respect off the floor. What the hell is wrong with me?

I drag the back of my hand over my lips, wiping any trace of Maxim on my skin as embarrassment steals up my throat.

Tonight was a disaster.

I learned nothing about my aunt's death.

I was nearly assaulted. No, forget that—I *was* assaulted.

And that kiss...

Christ.

Anger boils over into defiance, and before I can stop myself, my fist meets his chest. "I'm not yours, Maxim. I don't care what you say. There's nothing between us but a marriage contract."

His jaw ticks, but he continues to stare out the window, ignoring me, which only makes my blood hotter.

Words I hadn't planned on saying tumble from my lips. "Why didn't you tell me you knew my father? That you had history together. Was that not information you thought I had a right to know?"

This gets his attention. His surprised gaze meets my own. "Of course I knew your father! Half of Moscow knew the mudak in some way or another. He was heir to one of the most powerful bratvas in the city."

"You didn't just know him—he discovered you," I shoot back, my voice heavy with accusation. "He took you from underground fighting rings and introduced you to the underworld. How could you not think to tell me?!"

Dark fury crosses his face. "Oleg Antonov didn't fucking discover me. He used me, like he used everyone. Including you, his own flesh and blood. The only difference is that I had the power to walk away from him. I saw what kind of a *ublyudok* he was, and I left him in my dust."

His outburst catches me off guard, bitterness coating his every word.

So maybe he didn't like my father if he's calling him a bastard, but that doesn't prove anything. My father may have had something over him; Maxim could have been in his debt. Anything's possible. But deep down, I can't shake the weight of truth—Maxim doesn't bow to anyone.

Another thought quickly follows, hitting me hard. *He's not a liar.*

His penetrating gaze remains locked on me for what feels like an eternity, then he exhales deeply. "I never mentioned my acquaintance with your father because I assumed you don't like to speak of him. Given your family history." The weight of everything he's not saying presses between us. "I don't understand why this is important to you. Your father is long gone—you made sure of that." His lips twitch. If he didn't hate me, I would almost mistake that look for pride.

"I just..." I swallow hard, trying to steady myself. "I deserve the truth. All of it."

"You first, lastochka. You tell me your truth, and I'll tell you mine." He releases a gruff laugh. "How about you answer this question..." His mocking tone is replaced with a much darker one. "Why were you alone with the mayor tonight, after I warned you?"

A single finger lifts my chin, compelling me to meet his gaze. He remains silent, and with each weighty moment that passes, my hypocrisy burns—while I demand the truth from him, I'm certainly not willing to share my own.

"Forget it," I say and avert my gaze out the window.

He tuts, shaking his head. "You're so curious. Tell me what you're really after. What do you want to know so badly?" His hand glides down my neck, the soft pad of his thumb gently brushing against the pulse point.

A shiver moves through me. It's infuriating. I clench my jaw, refusing to be affected by this man. "Nothing. I don't like being blindsided. I felt like a total fool in front of Anatoly Petrovich today, having no clue that you knew my father."

Maxim snorts derisively. "You shouldn't care what Anatoly Petrovich, of all people, thinks of you. His dirty secrets stretch from here to the Wall of China."

"That doesn't make it any better," I whisper.

When we enter the security gates to Maxim's estate, all I can think about is jumping out of the car and darting into the house. I need to get away. I need distance from this man that sucks all the air out of a space. That makes my body feel things I desperately don't want him to make me feel.

Fuck him and his demands I sleep in his bedroom. I'll curl up in the shed with the dogs tonight for all I care.

"Seriously, Maxim, forget I said anything. Forget everything about tonight." He fixes his gaze on me, his eyes narrowing as his eyes drop to my lips. "It's late, and I need to sleep."

As soon as it's safe, I throw open the door and dart out, my heels clicking against the cobblestone drive. I'm relieved he doesn't follow me. He doesn't even get out of the car. My hands form tight fists, nails digging into flesh, as the limo speeds off and disappears into the dark night. Off to see one of his mistresses, I presume.

Good. I won't have to share a bed with him tonight.

Thank the Lord for small mercies.

Chapter Eighteen

KIRA

The warehouse looms large and ominous, but I push forward. I slip between crates and machines, my footsteps echoing off the concrete. This place, reeking of rust and neglect, is the last place I'd ever choose to be. But Masha is somewhere here—I've got to find her, somehow.

My heart pounds in my chest as I tread carefully among the crates and machinery, each step echoing off the unforgiving concrete walls, the sound almost deafening in the eerie silence.

And then, in a dimly lit corner of the warehouse, I see her. Masha, bound and helpless, her eyes wide with terror. A man is standing over her, his face a mask of cold detachment.

It's *Maxim*. He's holding something in his hand—an instrument of pain, its purpose clear even in the dim light.

I'm frozen, my heart pounding.

I call out to him, "Maxim, don't hurt her! Don't do this. Please."

He looks like a wild animal in the overhead light, sick and blood-thirsty. This is not the Maxim I know.

He smiles at me, and it's terrifying. "What do you mean don't do this? It's already done."

A mix of fear and disbelief paralyzes me. This can't be real. It must be some twisted trick of my mind, conjuring my deepest fears.

"Save yourself, Kira. Run!" My aunt's words echo through my bones, but I can't leave her here.

What should I do? How can I help her?

I fall to my knees, my voice trembling as I plead with Maxim. "Please, you're not a monster. There's still something decent left in you, I know it!" I search his eyes for a glimmer of the man I know, but Maxim stares through me, his gaze empty and void of any warmth.

He turns back to Masha, his hand gripping the knife tightly. Before I can react, he starts plunging the blade into her stomach, over and over.

I scream, a tortured sound that gets swallowed up by the warehouse walls. Blood pools beneath me, spreading rapidly, its warmth seeping through my clothes. The pool grows, and I'm certain it's going to drown me, swallow me whole in this nightmare. I open my mouth to scream, but it fills with blood, thick and choking.

That's when I feel it—arms wrapping around me, pulling me back from the brink of this horror. A familiar smell, comforting and safe, envelops me.

My surroundings begin to fade—the warehouse, the blood, and Maxim all slipping away into darkness. The arms around me are my anchor, freeing from the terrifying dream.

My eyes open, and my reality changes in a flash. I'm not in the warehouse anymore, there's no blood, no Masha, and no torture, but there is Maxim. Because the arms that are holding me, that pulled me from the nightmare, belong to him.

He's looking at me with concern.

I jerk away from him instinctively, my heart still racing. "What are you doing?" I blurt out and roll over to the other side of the bed, needing space from the man who is both my tormentor and savior.

"You were screaming in your sleep. I was trying to calm you," he explains, his eyebrows pressed together. He reaches out, smoothing a lock of hair behind my ears. "What did you dream of?"

"I don't want to talk about it." I'm shaking, the remnants of fear still clinging to me. Moments ago, in the realm of sleep, he was the cause of my terror.

It wasn't only a nightmare. I don't yet have the proof, but he killed Masha.

I mean, probably.

I'm losing focus. Maxim has somehow lulled me into complacency. I let him kiss me last night, but never again. I won't be distracted any longer. I need to dive deeper, to sift through the layers of Maxim's life more thoroughly.

He rises from the bed, his expression shifting from soft to something hard, impenetrable. It catches my attention that he's fully dressed in his usual sharp, all-black suit. Did he wear that to bed?

"You mistook my intention," he says, his voice chilling. "I wasn't trying anything other than to calm you down. You were hysterical."

His attempts to comfort me feel somehow more intimate than any physical touch. It's not just his presence but the concern in his eyes, the soothing tone of his voice—it all too much.

I flip over on my side so I don't have to face him. "Why are you here? Did your mistress kick you out of bed early?"

I hear his sharp inhale and then a bitter chuckle. "Yeah, something like that. But I won't need my mistress soon." He pauses, and I scramble to follow his meaning. "Don't forget, wife. Your one-month grace period is almost up." With those words, he walks out of the room.

Fuck! I forgot my stupid promise to give him heirs. I'd lost track of time, but in another week or so I'll need to spread my legs for Maxim. Nope, not happening. Last night alone should be enough of a reminder that Maxim is the last man I want to be tied to.

I sneak a look at the bedside clock. It's just past five in the morning, which means few people are milling about and I'd wager Maxim was heading out of the house. Which means my chance to search his office is now.

Pulling on a robe, I slip through the hallways of the mansion unnoticed. I rarely venture to this part of the house, but if anyone asks, I'll say I'm looking for Maxim. After all, I'm his wife. Who would question that?

Slipping into his office, I gently close the door behind me with a soft click, a wave of nervous energy coursing through me but I ignore it. Even if I'm discovered, his guards can't kill me—one of the few perks of being married to the boss.

His office is a striking reflection of him—masculine, neat, rich. Dark wood panels line the walls, and a large, imposing desk sits in the center, its surface clean except for a few neatly stacked documents and an expensive-looking pen set. A desktop computer sits atop his desk, something I find surprising. Most bratva don't want an electronic trail, but then again, Maxim has legitimate businesses to run as well.

I assume his computer is heavily protected, so I decide to search the room first, beginning with his heavy oak desk. The top drawer holds an array of pens and notepads, all perfectly aligned. The next one down is filled with neatly arranged files, each labeled with precision but none related to my aunt or father. In the third drawer, I find something different—a day planner.

Bingo!

Learning his whereabouts, who he was meeting with, any business deals or negotiations he was involved in around the time of my aunt's death could be useful. Flipping through his planner, front to back, my heart sinks when I realize this notebook doesn't cover the years in question. Furthermore, there's no details listed. It's almost like he writes in code.

Screw. This. I can't fuck around any longer.

Taking a deep breath to steady my nerves, I sit down at Maxim's desk, press a button, and watch as the screen flickers to life. To my surprise, it doesn't prompt for a password. *That's weird.* I had prepared myself to hack into the system, relying on the skills I'd honed over the years, but this ... this is too easy.

My fingers dance over the keyboard, navigating his system with a growing sense of unease. None of the documents are password-protected, but then again, there's nothing but mundane business worksheets and routine correspondence.

Then I find what I'm looking for. A calendar.

I open it, half expecting it to be locked out, but it too opens freely. My heart races as I scroll back to the dates around my aunt's murder. The entries for those days are detailed, and to my surprise, they show Maxim was in Japan—like Roman had said—but had returned to Moscow a few days before Masha was lured out of hiding.

Holy shit. My stomach drops, a heavy stone of dread settling deep within.

Now that I have access to his life, I'm determined to do a deep dive and see what I can uncover. With time ticking away,

I search for my aunt's name directly in the calendar app, typing in "Masha Antonov" and pressing Return. The search yields a single result, and my heart leaps into my throat.

There it is, a calendar note titled *Meeting with Masha Antonov*, dated a few days before my aunt was abducted. My finger hovers over the entry, eager to click and reveal the details, when the doorknob turns.

The sudden sound jolts me. I try to minimize the screen, but it's too late. The door swings open, and Maxim steps into the room, Nadya following close behind him.

Our gazes collide in a silent storm, Maxim's eyes flashing a message loud and clear: *Caught in the act, little spy.*

Chapter Nineteen

MAXIM

“Everything is set up for the wine auction in New York,” Nadya reports, her voice business-like as she trails me through the halls of the mansion.

I nod, only half listening, my mind preoccupied with one thing. My wife.

Last night’s dinner, seeing the mayor’s hands on her, that kiss. That fucking kiss. And then this morning, the burning hate in her eyes when she woke in my arms as she came down from a nightmare.

It’s been one hell of a twenty-four hours, and all I need is a stiff drink and a hard fuck, but it looks like neither is coming my way.

After I spent the night pummeling any opponent that dared step into the ring with me, I made the snap decision to put our forged Romanée-Conti up for auction in New York. It’s an excuse to get out of Moscow, but more than that, it’s an excuse to get away from Kira because now that I know how she feels under me, I'm practically tortured with temptation.

It has to stop. Now.

"So, as I was saying, the—"

I open the door to my office, and the sight that greets me is unexpected, to say the least. Kira, clad in her night robe, is sitting at my desk and typing on my computer. That is, until she notices me standing there. Wide and worried eyes lift to meet mine.

I should be angry—she's clearly doing something she shouldn't be—but for some reason, I'm more intrigued than infuriated.

"Maxim!" she exclaims, jumping up and attempting to pat down her robe. "I didn't expect you."

"No, I bet you didn't."

Nadya pushes past me, her voice sharp and accusatory. "What do you think you're doing in here? This is completely unacceptable!" Anger rolls off of her in waves. She turns to me, expecting me to echo her outrage, but I remain silent.

Not because I don't think Kira is out of line, but because I don't want Nadya around when I question my wife. That pleasure is mine and mine alone.

Kira's eyes dart nervously from me to Nadya and back again. She bites her lip but smartly decides to remain silent.

"It's fine, Nadya." I hold up my hand to calm her. "I asked Kira to look into something for me this morning."

"What?" My assistant whirls around, a puzzled frown creasing her forehead. "But, Maxim, you never—"

"It's under control. Thank you, you may leave us." I cross my arms in front of my chest, my tone leaving no room for further discussion.

Reluctantly, she casts one last angry glance at Kira before leaving.

Kira stands there like a trapped deer in headlights, her nerves palpable. "I can explain—" she starts, but I shake my head to stop her.

"Really? Can you do it without lying to me?" My gaze holds hers.

She swallows hard, the tension in the room thick enough to slice.

"Sit," I order, pushing out a chair into the middle of the room with my foot.

"I'd rather not."

In two strides, I close the distance between us and push her down into the seat. She looks up at me, her eyes a turbulent mix of emotions. Bracing two hands on the chair's arms, I bracket her in, letting her feel the full weight of the moment, the uncertainty of what I might do next. Then, slowly, I position two of my fingers on the pulse point at her neck, sensing the rapid beat beneath my touch.

"Explain yourself," I command softly. "If you lie, I'll know it by the speed of your pulse."

She bites her lip, her chest rising and falling noticeably. My gaze drops, snagging on her delicate throat. Slowly, my eyes continue their descent, until... Jesus. Those tits were nearly my undoing last night. How I would love to suck her nipples until she cried out my name and begged me to slide my dick inside—

"You didn't come home with me last night," she begins, her voice barely above a whisper. "After everything with the mayor and how you touched me." She swallows, pulling my attention to her mouth and her delicate throat. And the steady thump of her pulse under my fingertips. "I ... I was feeling jealous, and I wanted to find out who she is—your mistress."

I bark out a laugh. "Do you really expect me to believe that?"

She licks her lips. "Yes."

"One, you've made it clear you'd rather I fuck anyone but you. Two, the thump of your pulse" — I drag the pad of my finger over her lower neck, smiling to myself when she shivers — "suggests you're lying."

"I'm lying? You're the one who's full of shit!" Like the defiant little brat she is, she wears her venom on her sleeve. She tries to push me away, but I grab her hands, restraining her delicate wrists with one of my much larger hands. "There is no way in hell that feeling my pulse is an effective lie detector."

Restless lust simmers under my skin like an itch just out of reach. "It's not," I admit, "but it was fun to pretend."

She softens her features and attempts a conciliatory tone. "Let's forget about this. Your office wasn't locked, and your computer literally has no passwords. Obviously, you're not concerned about privacy, so I assumed there was nothing here you were trying to hide."

I smirk at her naïveté. This computer is a showpiece. It's where I play solitaire, schedule squash games. This sanitized, harmless machine is what they'll seize if there's ever an investigation into the country's billionaires. I'm confident Kira didn't learn anything of importance, but she was certainly after something.

"I have my reasons, and none of them concern you. What should concern you is how I'm going to extract the truth from you."

"And what will you do?" Her voice is throaty. If I didn't know better, I'd think there was excitement in her eyes rather than fear.

"You'll just have to wait and see." I release her hands and place my two fingers back on her pulse point.

Fuck. My wife likes this game we're playing.

She lifts her head, and I don't miss her half-lidded gaze, nor the way her nipples have hardened to peaks beneath her thin robe.

My cock throbs in response. "One more chance to tell the truth, lastochka."

She glares back. "I'll take the punishment."

"That's not an option."

She blinks up at me as the tip of her pink tongue dances out of her mouth to wet her parted lips.

Fuck me, there's only so much a man can take, especially when that sexy mouth is level with my crotch.

"Get up." I wrench her up by her hair, and God help me, instead of a cry it elicits a little moan. How did she go from shooting me death looks this morning to practically wrapping her lips around my dick?

A sudden thought surfaces—she's using sex to distract me. She knows I'm weak for her. After last night, the whole city knows I'm weak for her. I can't believe I fell into her trap, but now I'm in dangerous territory. She's a liar, and instead of throwing her in the dungeon, I'd rather teach her a lesson on her knees.

Hand still wrapped around her silky strands, I force in a deep lungful of air. "Last chance to come clean," I rasp, not bothering to hide my arousal pressing tightly against her.

Perhaps we have a different definition of coming clean. Because Kira rises to her tiptoes, parts her lush mouth, and drags her tongue over my lips.

"Kira," I growl in warning, our breaths mingling.

She's manipulating me, but that realization isn't enough for me to stop this. Not when my need for her is seeping out of my pores.

She's about to speak, but I know the only words to come from her will be lies so I don't let her talk.

My thumb hooks into her mouth, and I pull her lower lip

down with a sensual tug. "You don't get it, do you? This mouth is the fucking bane of my existence. Not only because it's always sassing me but because it's so fucking sexy. I've had detailed fantasies about plundering it with my tongue, my cock, even my fingers..."

I slide my thumb between her lips—she twirls her tongue around it, drawing it in deeply. A low groan escapes me, followed by a sharp "Fuck!" as I press my arousal against her. Delicious tension builds, and although one of us should be the responsible adult, it won't be me. I'm beyond saving. The brief taste of her in the limo only fueled my desire.

My cell buzzing in my pocket snaps me back to reality—the reality that she's a cunning little liar, searching for dirt on me, playing detective in a world she barely understands.

I pull away from her inviting mouth and eager tongue, my breaths coming in heated pants. She blinks up at me as if emerging from a trance.

"Don't think this means you're off the hook," I manage to say.

Her lips press together, still maintaining her silence. The most likely explanation is that she's gathering information about my business to pass on to her brothers. Whatever her motive, I'm determined to uncover it. She won't be out of my sight until I figure out her true intentions.

"By the way, you better get packing. We leave for our honeymoon tomorrow."

She freezes, her narrowed eyes meeting mine. "Honey-moon? That was just a story for the press."

I step back from her and straighten my tie, then adjust my cufflinks. It feels like I'm coming down from a drug high.

"I have business in New York, and there's not a chance in hell I'm leaving you here alone." So much for getting a break from her—I'm going to be glued to her fucking side. "We leave for New York first thing in the morning."

Chapter Twenty

KIRA

"Good morning, Mr. and Mrs. Belov, it's a pleasure to have you on board. Our expected flight time direct to New York is approximately nine hours at a cruising altitude of forty thousand feet. Svetlana is your cabin attendant and will take care of all your needs during the journey. If there's anything you require from the cockpit, please don't hesitate to let us know."

The pilot signs off as Maxim's private jet taxis towards the runway. I don't have to look back at Svetlana to know how willing she is to take care of any and all of Maxim's needs. She's been sending him hot and heavy glances from the galley ever since we boarded.

Whatever. Let her entertain him.

I have bigger concerns right now, starting with Maxim knowing I'm after something. I get the feeling he suspects I'm gathering intel for my brothers. I'm fine with him thinking that since it's far from the truth. But it means he'll be watching me closely. This doesn't bode well for my chances of discovering why Maxim was supposed to meet Masha before her death.

I pop my earbuds in and stare out the small window, trying to focus on the view outside as the plane takes off. The roar of the engines fills the cabin, and as the plane accelerates, my eyes meet Maxim's in the window's reflection.

I quickly look away. The unexpected consequence of using my body as a tool to distract him when he found me snooping is that I feel a jolt of lust when he looks at me. And he's been looking at me a lot today.

"Here's your sparkling water and black coffee, Mr. Belov." Svetlana bends over, offering Maxim a seductive smile and glimpse of her ample cleavage as she places the drinks in front of him. A delicate curl of her auburn hair slides forward, contrasting with her fair skin. "I remember your exact preferences," she purrs, her voice heavy with suggestions.

I roll my eyes. This woman has zero subtlety.

He clears his throat and flicks her an admonishing look. "You seemed to have forgotten my wife's drink."

"I'm so sorry," she chirps. "I didn't realize you were traveling with company." *Liar.* "I'll be sure to get another water right away. Or a Coke. You're American, right?" Svetlana finally acknowledges me with a condescending smile.

My back stiffens, and I meet Svetlana's judgemental gaze with a harsh look of my own. If Maxim is going to bring his whores on our flight, he better not expect me to be friendly.

Against my better judgment, jealousy sparks in my gut. "Actually, I'll have a bourbon. Neat. That's what us Yanks like to drink."

"Very well," Svetlana says with a feigned cheerfulness in her tone, then swiftly turns away.

"Oh, and one of those fancy little bags of peanuts," I call to her rigid back. "Dry-roasted, please, and hold the salt."

She doesn't bother turning around this time. She huffs out a breath and straightens her shoulders.

"You know what," I continue, tapping a finger on my lips. "I'd also love a coffee. I'll take half-caff, triple-shot, no foam, soy milk, one pump vanilla, two pumps hazelnut, extra hot macchiato with a dash of cinnamon."

Svetlana's shoulders hunch around her ears, and the only acknowledgement she gives is a stiff nod. A moment later, she's gone.

Beside me, Maxim lets out a low, amused snicker, the fine lines at the corners of his eyes deepening. "Don't you take your coffee black?" he asks, arching a brow.

I stare straight ahead, refusing to make eye contact. "Was it really necessary to bring your mistress to New York?"

His hand lifts, gently cradling my jaw, guiding my gaze up to meet his intense stare. "Are you jealous, lastochka?"

She's everything I'm not. Tall, sophisticated, skinny. So, yeah, I'm jealous. But I'll never give him the pleasure of admitting it.

"I don't care what you do," I hiss, shaking free from his grasp. "But it's basic common courtesy not to bring your whore on our so-called honeymoon."

His jaw ticks, and he keeps quiet for a minute. Then, like he's come to a decision, he gets out of his seat. "Excuse me," he says, buttoning up his suit jacket before walking off.

That motherfucker. He can't wait until we land—he's already sneaking off to get under Svetlana's skirt at thirty thousand feet.

I press my molars together and grab a magazine from the console in front of me, but I can't focus. The words blur together in a jumbled mess, my insides entirely consumed by my boiling emotions. I'm rubbing at the headache pounding in my temples when Svetlana materializes beside me. With

Maxim not here, she doesn't bother with her fake-as-shit smile.

"Your bourbon." Svetlana places the lowball before me with slightly more force than necessary. Following that, she holds up a bag of gourmet mixed nuts. Before she hands it to me, she warns, "Careful, these are a real calorie bomb."

A flush of embarrassment colors my cheeks. I try to think of a swift comeback, but fuck, talk about hitting a girl when she's down. I'm not particularly sensitive about my body, but like everyone on this planet, I've dealt with my fair share of body issues and I don't need to be shamed by my husband's mistress, of all people. The emotions of the day get to me. Her insult, going back to New York—which is bitter-sweet—and Maxim's suspicion of me... All of it feels overwhelming.

I stand and push past Svetlana, needing a moment alone to collect myself. As I do, her hand wavers, and the cup of coffee she's holding wobbles and splashes over the rim.

"Shit!" The hot liquid soaks through the fabric of my jeans. I grab a napkin off her tray and dab at the stain, an attempt to stop the seeping coffee from searing my skin.

Svetlana rolls her eyes, her ruby lips curling into a disdainful smirk. Cheeks burning, I make a swift exit towards the back of the plane, hoping to salvage whatever I can of my jeans and dignity.

I feel so silly. Why am I letting this get to me? I downright encouraged Maxim to sleep with other people, and that's exactly what he did. So why does it burn so fucking bad?

Blotting at my jeans with a paper towel, I'm horrified to realize that my face is damp. I'm crying, and I don't know why. Or maybe I do. I'm tired, overwhelmed, and all I can think of is how I've failed Masha ... again. I still don't have any information that ties Maxim to her murder, and when I'm around him I lose focus.

I give up patting my jeans dry and accept that I'll smell like coffee for the rest of the flight. Taking a deep breath, I sit down on the closed toilet seat and take stock of my current situation. We have another nine hours in the air, and I'm already exhausted having not slept all that much over the last few days.

Part of me wants to lock myself in this bathroom for the rest of this flight and let Maxim do whatever the hell he wants, but the part of me that's fought for respect my whole life resists. I'm not going to hide in a bathroom to accommodate Maxim or that rude bitch. I am going to walk out of here with my head held high and show both of them that I won't be pushed aside.

With one final deep breath, I march out of here and head towards an empty bank of seats. I'm sure as shit not going to sit beside him any longer. My footsteps slow as I near the galley, catching a whispered exchange between Svetlana and Maxim behind the drawn curtain. A bigger person might keep on walking, but that's not me. So I press myself against the wall, listening.

"I don't understand what I did wrong," Svetlana whines, her words dripping with feigned innocence.

"You disrespected my wife." Maxim's voice is hard and unrelenting. "If you were a man, you'd be dead by now."

"You've been married for all of five minutes, and she's young enough to be your daughter. I don't believe it's real for one second." Her voice turns breathy and intimate. "We have history, Maxim. I thought I meant more to you."

"Perhaps your definition of history includes a mile-high blow-job, but mine doesn't."

He's so ice-cold I almost feel bad for her. *Almost.* But mostly, I feel a pulse of satisfaction as he comes to my defense.

"What my marriage is or isn't is none of your business, but know this... She wears my ring and bears my name, and I won't have Kira made to feel less than the queen she is. My queen."

His queen? Am I hearing this right?

A silent beat, and then a muffled sob before Svetlana's voice—now laced with a quiet fury—hisses through the door. "How can you be so cruel?"

"You think this is me being cruel? Insult Kira again, and you'll see what cruelty really looks like. Pack up your shit. We're making a pitstop."

Huh? I'm confused about what's going on, but I don't stick around to hear more because Maxim is on his way out of the galley. Hastily, I slide back into my seat, pretending to browse for a movie on my tablet.

A minute later, Maxim settles beside me. We both remain silent. When I steal a quick glance at him, he appears relaxed, one ankle resting on his knee, his gaze fixed ahead as if the earlier exchange never occurred.

I'm prodding at the screen with my finger when the PA system activates. "Good afternoon, Mr. and Mrs. Belov. A brief note from your flight deck: We'll be making an unplanned landing in Saint Petersburg shortly. Rest assured, all is well on board. As we commence our descent, kindly fasten your seatbelts and secure any loose items. We aim to minimize our stopover duration and will promptly continue our flight to New York."

Maxim looks unsurprised.

"What is going on?" I hiss.

"A quick touchdown, nothing to worry about."

I stare at Maxim, waiting for him to say more, but he reaches across me to fasten my seatbelt as if I'm not capable of doing it on my own.

"You smell like coffee," he murmurs, inhaling my neck. "I like it."

His close proximity, the way he buries his nose in my neck,

sets off a flurry of goosebumps up and down my arm. It deeply irritates me. I scowl at him, and he grins at me.

I'm vaguely aware of the subtle jolt of landing, the wheels kissing the tarmac. When the cabin door opens, it breaks our trance—Maxim and I both pull away, looking everywhere but at each other.

Svetlana strides purposefully down the aisle, her face a cold mask of fury. Her carry-on rattles along behind her, its wheels clicking against the floor. She pauses beside us, her eyes narrowing on me with disgust. "Slumming it with fat girls."

Maxim growls as his hand darts out to collar her wrist in an unyielding grip. "You've already lost your job with me. Do you want to lose your life?"

She rakes her eyes accusingly over Maxim before ripping her arm from his grasp. Stupid woman.

"I give your marriage another month before you're crawling back to me," she bites, an ugly twist to her full lips, and then she's gone.

I keep my eyes on the now vacant doorway. "What is going on?"

"We're dropping off the trash."

"Because of me?"

"She should have never been here in the first place. I'm serious, lastochka, no one will ever disrespect you like that."

Before I can push for him to explain, someone else boards the plane, entering through the door that Svetlana just exited. Warmth rushes through me as I note that this flight attendant is male.

He stows his small carry-on bag in a cabinet near the front of the plane and makes his way towards us. "Good afternoon, Mr. and Mrs. Belov. My apologies for any disruption. I'm Gleb, and I'll be attending to you for the remainder of our journey."

"Thank you. I'll let you know if we require anything." Maxim nods, and taking the hint, Gleb continues on towards the back galley.

Minutes later, the plane begins to accelerate for takeoff. The pilot wasn't kidding when he announced a brief stop.

I glance over at Maxim—he's pulled out his phone, and it's pressed to his ear.

"Why was she working this flight?" he barks out in place of a greeting. Someone responds on the other end of the line, but he's impatient. "You know better, Nadya," he admonishes. "I'll take your word for it that having Svetlana on this flight was an oversight. In the future, no more mistakes like this. Offer Svetlana up to the mayor—she's no longer an employee of mine." When he hangs up, he doesn't look at me. He keeps his eyes straight ahead, focused on the seat in front of him.

A million questions run through my head, like what the hell the call was about. It certainly wouldn't surprise me if Nadya purposefully scheduled Svetlana on this flight. *Jesus*.

Maxim may not trust me, but he's damn possessive of me. If he has developed feelings for me, can I use it to my advantage?

"To be clear," Maxim's voice breaks the silence between us. "There is no mistress. When I go off at night, I'm fighting, not fucking. Have you noticed the state of my hands since we started sharing a bed?" He holds up his knuckles for me to see. They are as raw and bruised as any professional fighter's.

There are few moments in my life when I genuinely don't know what to say, but this is one of them. I could ask who he's fighting and why, but honestly, right now I'm not even sure I want to know.

"Okay," I tell him.

"Okay," he echoes. A small smile grows on his face, and he goes back to typing on his phone.

I close my eyes, and within moments, I'm teetering on the brink of sleep. Just before I drift off, I'm enveloped in warmth, Maxim's rich scent. He's draped his jacket over me, and it's the closest thing to comfort I've felt in a long time.

Chapter Twenty-One

KIRA

New York. New York fucking city.

The city stretches beneath me, all manic, frenetic energy, discernible even from the fortieth floor of the hotel terrace. It's a bird's-eye view of untamed Manhattan, a city I once called home. A place I still miss so much my chest hurts.

It's the last place I expected Maxim to take me on a honeymoon. I was expecting Tahiti or the Maldives—somewhere hot, exotic, and lavish. This is not a honeymoon, despite what he called it. This is business.

We arrived in New York yesterday, and later this afternoon, we're to attend a private wine auction for the first of Maxim's counterfeit wines. Of course, I'll be there on his arm, drawing in all the media buzz our honeymoon is guaranteed to attract. A juicy tidbit to distract from the real story. They call it "wagging the dog" in politics, and Maxim is nothing if not a master politician.

The door to the balcony opens, and I know it's him standing there, watching me. I'm never not aware of Maxim's eyes on me. It's like his stare is weighted with an intensity I can't ignore.

He's going to tell me that we have to leave for the auction soon, but I don't turn around, pulling the shawl tighter around my shoulders. He doesn't say anything either. Only watches.

Is he worried I'm going to jump? He should be more worried about me pushing him.

"You miss this city?" He settles beside me, resting his forearms beside mine on the railing. Like me, he's looking straight out over the urban sprawl that leads to the greenery of Central Park.

I nod. "Every damn day."

"I keep a residence here. We can visit ... or you can visit when life is more settled."

Yeah, right. There will be no settling into this life with him.

He pushes a hand through his tousled hair, and my stomach clenches. He's all bespoke suits, with ten thousand-dollar cufflinks and a perfect shave on his perfect face. But his eyes. He's got the devil in his eyes.

After my nightmare, everything came into sharp focus. I can't sit around and wait to discover the part he played in my aunt's death, and even though he's threatened not to let me out of his sight, I'll find a way to break from him. Because New York is the perfect opportunity for me to dig harder.

Pavel and Roman stayed in Moscow to run things in Maxim's absence, and we don't have our usual cadre of guards around us. Not to say we're unprotected, but things are different in the US. War doesn't spill onto the streets the same way it does in Moscow—no car bombs or daylight kidnappings off the street.

I know New York like the back of my hand. Over the next

week, wherever Maxim goes, I'll follow. If I meet someone who may have information that I need, I'm going to get it from them one way or another. No more flirty bullshit, like with the mayor. I'll use any means necessary to get the details I want. Even if it means torture.

Because in New York City, I'm Kira Kozlov. I have connections, and I'm taken seriously. People know what I'm capable of. Even without the support of my brothers, I'm someone here.

I turn to him now, notching my chin up to meet his gaze. "Why aren't we staying at your place then?"

He gives me a wicked grin. "That's not very romantic, is it? The penthouse suite of The Ritz-Carlton is what the society papers want to hear about."

I scoff. "You really know how to sweep a girl off her feet. What's next, a carriage ride through Times Square?"

His mouth twitches. "I'll consider it. That would definitely make headlines, considering carriages aren't allowed in Times Square. But I could make it happen ... if you really wanted to."

I roll my eyes. "Trust me, I don't." I'm quiet for a moment as I look out at the horizon. "But the one thing I would like to do while we're here is see Alyona. Without you."

I thought about it for a long time on the flight over here. Even though she'll ask questions—questions I can't answer yet—I miss my best friend. I want her to see that I'm fine. I know she blames herself for the predicament I'm in, and I don't want her to shoulder that guilt. It'll be good for her to see me in person, to see that I'm not beaten down and sad.

In fact, knowing that my revenge will come soon is solace. The nightmares that have gripped me these last few years have finally started to lose their hold. Mostly.

Maxim leans his forearms along the railing, continuing to stare out over the city, his eyes not meeting mine. Finally, he clears his throat. "Alyona and Leo are in Italy, scouting places for their wedding."

My eyebrows pull together. "How in the world do you know that?"

He's quiet for a long time. So long, I'm sure he's not going to answer. But he then turns to me, and it's all I can do not to swallow the lump in my throat because Maxim looks ... haunted. Which doesn't make sense, considering how he treated her, but he's clearly wrestling with something.

"She's my daughter, Kira. You don't think I keep tabs on her?"

I shake my head. "Tabs? What does that mean?"

"It means... Fuck." He grits his teeth and slams his fist down on the stone ledge. "It means I don't want anything to happen to her because of the life I lead. My enemies will go to any lengths to hurt me. That means she's a target. At least if she was by my side, I'd know she was safe."

My nails dig into my palms. "Seems like you should have thought about that before you abducted her and threw a ball in her honor, announcing to the world that she was yours."

"Word had already gotten out. The Black Company hacked into the DNA-test files that confirmed I was her father. It was only a matter of time before they used her against me." His smile is brittle, and his voice drops an octave when he says, "I believed she would accept me and this life in time, that she would see the opportunity to rule by my side as a gift."

"You could have told her all of this rather than taking her against her will and threatening everyone she loved! How did you think that was the better way?"

He sighs and crosses his arms over his chest. "I've grown used to getting my way with sheer force. It's been a long time since I had to negotiate." He's looking at me intensely, and I don't know why his words send chills up the back of my neck. "I ... regret the way I handled it."

My pulse whooshes in my ears. I'm used to the Maxim that is as cold as ice, untouched by human emotion unlike the rest of us mere mortals. I'm not used to the flesh-and-blood man who stands here, admitting his mistakes.

All at once, the pieces fall into place. "You married me to keep Alyona in your life?"

There's nothing vulnerable about Maxim, but right now, the tiniest flare of something tender crosses his expression. "I'm not completely dead inside, Kira. She's my daughter, my blood... I care for her, even if the feeling isn't reciprocated."

I think about what Liza told me, the rumors that Maxim may have had a kid with his first wife. The one he killed. With Maxim anything is possible, but I can't shake the sense that if there had been a child—a part of him—he would have fought with everything he had to keep them safe, to keep them close.

"And you didn't want Aly to spend her whole life hating you ... which she totally would have, by the way."

"That, and your brothers are very persuasive." His expression turns wistful. "Leo would burn down the world for her. He'll lay down his life to protect her. I knew she would be safe with him ... and happy."

Maxim is a force, all commanding masculine energy and dominance, so I'm momentarily stunned by this unexpected softness. I don't know how to feel about it. It doesn't mean he's not a monster. He is. But even monsters love their kids.

He clears his throat and looks at his watch. "We should go."

I shake my head. I had somehow forgotten all about the auction. "Right."

"Kira?"

"Yes." I look up at him.

"You look beautiful." His words are nearly a whisper as his

fingers brush through my hair, grazing my neck before he drops his hand to his side.

I take a step back and straighten. I refuse to be put under his spell by this new version of Maxim. He's still the enemy. I'm still dead-set on taking him down.

"Thank you," I reply without emotion. "Now, let's go so I can spend all your money at this auction."

Chapter Twenty-Two

MAXIM

"Mr. Belov!" Friedrich Müller, the auctioneer, lifts his hand to catch my attention and makes a beeline toward me across the room. The auction ended ten minutes ago, and now all the guests are gathered in the gallery, drinking champagne and lamenting about the money they lost in the way rich people do. Or, in my case, the money I made. Because three of my counterfeit bottles sold for a mint. Not that anyone knows they were my bottles. They were entered into the auction by an "anonymous collector".

"I thought I saw you in the crowd," Friedrich notes. "So nice of you to join us with your new bride. I noticed she was very active during the auction."

I swallow the smile that threatens to break out across my face. To say Kira was paddle-happy is an understatement. Right before the auction started, she told me she was going to spend my money like she earned it, and the little minx certainly did that. Not by purchasing my wines, of course, but there were plenty others up for offer. I am now the proud owner of a 1947 Château Cheval Blanc and a 1945 Château Mouton-Rothschild, spending over three hundred thousand a pop.

The press will eat it up. *Billionaire's new wife drops over half a mill on vintage wine.*

When I leaned over and asked Kira if she even liked to drink vintage wine, she flashed me a cheeky look and said, "I guess we'll see." I had no idea spending my money on her would turn me on so fucking much. But as I've learned, everything Kira does turns me on. From the way she laugh-snorts at her own jokes to how she tips her chin defiantly whenever I challenge her.

I sure as hell don't trust her, but I like her. And that was *not* in the plan.

"Yes, Kira got swept up in the spirit. It's because you did such a good job, Friedrich. Speaking of which, I can't believe you were able to authenticate the bottles of Romanée-Conti. They're very rare, I understand."

"Ah, they are. You have to be so careful with forgeries these days. That's why we put our best investigators on the case. The wine is authentic. As you can see, there is a huge demand for this kind of product."

"Very impressive," I agree.

As Friedrich drones on, I lock eyes with my lead guard, Konstantin, stationed near the entrance. He gives me a slight nod, confirming all is good. The rest of my men are fanned out around the room, trying to look like they belong with the wine-and-cheese crowd. Like wolves in sheep's clothing.

With my wines officially at auction, we're prepared for trouble with the Black Company. Auctioning it in New York helps—they'll be reluctant to attack on American soil—but I'm not taking any chances. To the Black Company, this is an official declaration of war.

My gaze snags on Kira politely talking with an older woman. Not the first time today, my heart skips a beat taking her in. She really is a sight to behold. I know she's too young, too stubborn, and too proud, but she's burrowed somewhere deep under my skin and I can't shake this need I have for her.

It's how she buries into my chest when I hold her during her nightmares, how she cares more about her family than herself, how solemn she looked when I admitted to her that I care for Alyona more than I've let on to anyone.

Now, Kira knows my one vulnerability in this life.

I've tried meeting with my usual hook-ups but as soon as I get to the door, I spin around and leave, knowing they'd leave me feeling empty and unsatisfied. Since I can't fuck her out of my system, I've resorted to fighting, attending underground fights most nights. My knuckles are raw and ugly—the only reason no one's commented on them is because people are too polite.

On autopilot, I smile and nod at something Friedrich says, but my eyes are still glued to Kira. She leans in and says something to the older woman. Then she pulls away.

Our eyes lock. She gives me the barest of smiles. Like maybe she doesn't hate me.

Kira tilts her head and starts walking towards me, and something prickles in my chest. Is it happiness?

No, it can't be that. I haven't felt that since Ilya's death. Since he was tucked into my side at bedtime and insisted I make up superhero stories for him and his stuffed bear. Since the nights when he would look up at me with those eyes full of wonder, seeing me not as the man the world feared but as his father.

Friedrich realizes my attention is elsewhere and follows my line of sight, a small smile tilting his lips when he understands what has captured my attention so thoroughly.

"Ah, that's the look of a happily married man."

Right, let him believe what he wants. I'll just enjoy the view.

When she's a few feet away from us, a waiter steps in front of her path, offering a glass of champagne. She shakes her head, preparing to pass him but he's much taller than her, built big and sturdy, and he won't let her move.

My gut clenches. There's something odd about their exchange.

Handing Friedrich my glass, I cut through the crowd, beelining towards Kira and the waiter still blocking her path. She looks at him, and something crosses over her face, something that tells me they're not having a friendly chat.

Motherfucker! I push people aside, desperate to get to her when she curses and raises her knee, slamming it into the waiter's gut. He stumbles back, clutching his abdomen in pain as a kitchen knife falls from his grip and clatters on the floor.

Before he can recover, I lunge forward, pinning him to the ground, my vision blurring in a red haze of fury. I land a series of punches to his face, his nose crunching under the force of my hits. As his blood pours from his nose, the room explodes into chaos. The auction's guests flee the place as if it's on fire while my men tighten rank around me.

Where is Kira?

Because this asshole isn't working alone, my guess is this is a coordinated attack. My head swivels, searching for her, and... Shit. I find her with her assailant's knife in hand, crouched low, engaging another so-called waiter.

"Get her out of here," I yell at one of my men. "If she's hurt in any way, there will be hell to pay."

He makes a move towards Kira, but she shoots my guard a fierce glare and he stands down. He's a head taller with at least a hundred pounds on her, and yet he cowers and backs up.

"I can handle myself!" she insists.

While that may be true, there's not a chance in hell I'll let her try. If she was hurt because of me... Shit.

"I'm serious, get her the fuck out of here," I growl, ignoring her.

Two of my men advance on her, and although she's fast and capable with a knife, they manage to usher her away.

Sensing my fractured focus, the man beneath me now gets the upper hand, flipping me over. I taste blood as his fist connects with my jaw. A sharp, searing pain shoots through my face, and that only pisses me off further.

We grapple, rolling around on the floor, when I spot a glint of broken glass nearby. With a rush of adrenaline, I twist my body and manage to knock him off me, landing a solid blow to his ribs. He gasps for air but is quick to retaliate with a knee to my gut. I clench and absorb the impact, then use my feet to knock out his legs from under him. He goes down hard, and I prepare to end this once and for all.

Around me, I'm aware of grunts and groans piercing the air as I pick up the shattered glass off the floor. Konstantin steps forward with a gun, but I raise my hand to stop him. This mudak is mine. I take the jagged edge of the glass in my hand and shove it into his neck, stopping short of severing his carotid artery. His face contorts, an agonized cry leaving his lips.

"You're a dead man and you know it," I spit. "Tell me who sent you, and we can end this quickly."

"Fuck you," he gurgles. Blood spills from his neck where I jam the jagged piece in deeper. He coughs, opening his eyes wide. "You know who sent me, and they won't stop until you're dead." He flashes his teeth, and dread washes over me. "Bonus points for killing your wife."

His threat ignites the beast inside of me. I twist the shard of glass deep into his artery.

He cries out as blood seeps from his neck like a faucet, coating my hand in sticky warm liquid as I continue to hold him down.

His death is slow and ugly, and I make him pay for daring to hurt Kira. For even accepting the job. When he's bled out, I drop his lifeless body to the floor, wiping my hands on my pants.

So the Black Company wants to play dirty, go after the woman wearing my wedding ring.

They better be prepared because I'm going to come at those fuckers with a wrath that even the deepest circles of hell haven't seen.

Chapter Twenty-Three

MAXIM

It takes me hours to sort out the mess the attack brought about. Both the press and police were all over the auction house by the time I sent Kira's attacker to his grave. With blood still coating my hands, I managed to spin a story that benefitted me: A group of thieves had infiltrated the auction house, posing as waiters, with the intention of stealing millions in valuable wine.

The press ate up the story, and the cops didn't dig too deep because, well, let's just say I have connections in high places. In the end, I came out looking like the hero. Most, including Friedrich himself, believed I had defended them from the intruders, leading to a flood of praise and favorable coverage.

It's midnight as I finally get back to the hotel, and I'm still vibrating with a mix of adrenaline and pure fucking anger at the Black Company. I don't even know who to direct my rage at since the Triad remains an anonymous force with a nameless, faceless leader.

Konstantin is waiting for me as I step out of my private elevator and into the suite. I thought about moving us to my private residence in New York, but a hotel is safer. Even the Black Company is not stupid enough to stir up shit in a public space after what they pulled earlier today.

"How is she?" Seeing Kira nearly get hurt, knowing she's a target because of me, has lodged a cold knot of terror in my gut. I hadn't felt that scared since I lost my son.

Ilya's memory is a wound that never closes, a sharp jab to the soul at the most unexpected moments. I can still hear his four-year-old laughter echoing through the halls of our home. His small hands, always reaching for mine, trusting and sure. The way his eyes lit up like the first star on a clear night whenever I returned from a trip, especially when I brought back gifts. His favorite was a miniature wooden ship an old artisan handcrafted in Turkey, claiming it held magic in its tiny sails—magic Ilya believed could sail him to any land he wished.

Konstantin cocks his head, and I realize he was talking while I was lost in my thoughts. "Excuse me?"

"Kira's angry."

I quirk an eyebrow at him. I was expecting him to say something along the lines of shaken, maybe upset. I wasn't expecting anger. But Kira manages to surprise me at every turn.

"Why is that?" I ask, stripping off my bloodied dress shirt while my guard passes me a fresh one.

He clears his throat. "She seems to be upset that we stopped her from fighting the assailants."

A full-blown smile lifts my lips because only Kira would be pissed off that my men removed her from a situation where my enemies were attempting to kill her. "Where is she now?"

He leads me to the open living area, where she's pacing the penthouse floor with the energy of a brewing storm. When I step into the room, she comes charging at me. Fury and frustration fill her gaze, and before I can brace myself, she raises her hand, about to slap me across the face.

My hand darts out and catches her wrist before her palm makes contact. "Go ahead and throw a hissy fit, but if you think I'm the kind of man who will ever put my woman in danger, you're wrong." I let the words hang between us.

She sniffs and tries to take a step back, but I'm still grasping her wrist.

In that auction house, I was more beast than man, protecting what belongs to me. What's mine. Business arrangement or not... She. Is. *Mine.*

This truth burrows into my veins and holds on tight.

She pulls her hands out of my grip and crosses her arms over her chest. "You seem to forget who I am. I've been playing this bullshit society-wife role, even excelled at it, but when shit hits the fan allow me to be Kira Kozlov. You wanted someone to rule by your side, so let me be that," she pleads.

"Tell me, what was your plan? We were surrounded by members of the Black Company—trained soldiers with knives. Did you really have a fighting chance?"

She tilts her chin up but remains silent.

Maybe she knows I'm right. Security was tight at the event, prompting the Black Company's men to disguise themselves as waiters. The only available weapons were kitchen tools and knives, but they were trained operatives and knew how to use them. Thank fuck my men, acting as guards, were permitted to carry arms.

"Let me make this clear," I continue, pushing Kira against the wall, my thumb drifting over her hammering pulse. "There's no fucking way I'll ever allow you to risk your life. Being my wife is dangerous enough on its own. I won't lose another person that—"

Means something to me. Fuck. What did I almost say?

Kira looks at me like she can see through to my soul. She can see the hurts and betrayals that I haven't released buried there.

Her voice is gentle when she speaks again. "What happened that you hold on so tightly to everyone in your life? You can't control everything in your perfect little world. Sometimes, bad shit happens."

Her words cut to the bone, and I don't like the feeling. I respond in the only way I know how—I rear back and sting. "Don't try to be more than what I need you for. It won't end well."

Her body braces like I slapped her, and she gazes at me, eyes brimming with pain.

I walk away because the heat in my blood is back. The restless energy that plagues me, day in and day out, and haunts my soul rises stronger than ever. Demanding an outlet.

Since it won't be between Kira's thighs—not after what I just said to her—I need to find a fight.

* * *

KIRA

Maxim storms out of the room and I watch his retreating form, shocked into silence. He's shown his true colors, and I shouldn't be surprised by his hurtful words. Except I am, and I don't know why.

He's a snake and has never claimed to be anything else, but something about the last few days made me lose focus. He kicked a flight attendant off the plane for me and admitted that he cared for his daughter. It's not like he's a good man, but at least I see his human side.

Did he save my life today? Maybe. As much as I hate to

admit it, I was outnumbered and the attack came out of nowhere. If Maxim didn't put his body between mine and the man brandishing a knife, ready to kill me, the outcome wouldn't have been good. I know that much.

But I also know he didn't even give me a chance to prove myself. He treated me like some damsel in distress, demanding his men drag me out of the auction house as if they didn't have more important things to do. The room was crawling with his enemies—men from the Black Company, I gathered based on the guards' conversation. I could have been useful.

I look out the floor-to-ceiling windows, staring at the starless night sky. New York is buzzing, and I'm feeling as restless as the city spread below.

Making my way through the hallways to our bedroom—the bedroom I will certainly not be sharing with him tonight—I hear low voices coming from behind the closed office door, and Maxim's is one of them. Checking to ensure the coast is clear, I press my ear against the door, barely breathing.

"I have a call with Viktor, Pavel and Roman now. After that, I'm going out for the night," my husband says. "But I need you to make sure..."

The rest of the conversation fades into the walls, and I can't make out what he's saying.

I don't need to. If Maxim is going out tonight, so am I. And if anyone thinks they can stop me, let them try.

Chapter Twenty-Four

KIRA

An hour later, I track down Konstantin, the head guard on duty, and tell him, "I'm locking myself in the bedroom for a movie marathon, and I'm not to be disturbed. Well, except when room service comes up with my food. Send the attendant straight in so they can lay out the meal for me." I tip my chin up. "I ordered everything on the menu."

"You got it, Mrs. Belov." He grins, relief evident in his expression.

He probably thought he'd have to deal with my monster mood all night. Welp, I'm making it easy for him. I won't even be here.

My eyes dart to the closed door of Maxim's office, where I can hear a tense meeting with Viktor, Roman, and Pavel taking place. Maxim is speaking quickly and sounds agitated. Good.

"Do you know if my husband will be joining me tonight?" I ask, blinking up at Konstantin.

"Ah, no." He pushes his hands through his hair like he's

worried about how I'll react. "He'll be leaving soon. He has business to take care of off-site."

"Good. More cake for me," I say, stomping off.

Soon, my hair is held back in braids and I'm dressed in a form-fitting, black ensemble, complete with a hooded jacket and sneakers.

Right on cue, a knock sounds at the bedroom door. "Room service."

"Come on in." I jump into bed and pull the covers up to my neck. "You can set up right there." I point to the little breakfast table situated by the wall.

"Not a problem," he responds, getting to work.

Looks like a nice enough kid. I'm almost sorry for what I have to do next. When he unloads the fourteen dishes I ordered with extra fries and a bottle of champagne on ice, he turns to me with a big smile on his face. Most likely expecting a bigass tip.

"What the—"

"Don't make a sound," I say to him, holding the pistol in my hand. "I don't want to use this, Russell," I add, with a glance at his name tag. "But I will if I have to. Nod if you understand." Eyes wide and horrified, he nods. "Here is what is going to happen. I am going to crawl into your cart over here, and you are going to cover me up with a tablecloth. Then you are going to roll me out of here, and on your way out, you're going to say to the guards outside of the door that I'm asleep but you left the food anyway. See how easy that is?" Again, he nods vigorously. "All you have to do after is drop me off at the loading dock and make sure no one sees. That's it. No one gets hurt, and you live a long life."

Poor Russell hasn't stopped nodding, but I'm convinced we've reached an understanding.

"Great," I say with a smile then quickly contort myself

under his cart, after which he drapes a white tablecloth over me.

His breathing is heavy, but a stern reminder to calm down does the trick. Impressively, he plays his part well. He informs the guards that I'm asleep, and I overhear what sounds like Konstantin tipping him. Before I know it, we're in the elevator, jostling through the hotel's back corridors. We pass the kitchens and then the garbage bins, their odor unmistakable.

Finally, he whispers, "Coast is clear."

I step out of the cart, offering the kid a smile while keeping my hood low over my face. "For your troubles, sir." I hand him a thousand dollars in cash. Maxim's fault for leaving so much money lying around.

Then I tell Russell to scram.

As arranged, a black town car is parked in the shadows across from where Maxim's chauffeur typically picks him up. The driver of the town car knows me well—he was my driver when I was with the Kozlov Bratva—so he knows better than to make conversation or ask any questions.

Tony nods at me as I enter the backseat, and I nod back at him. "When a handsome, dark-haired man gets into that vehicle," I instruct him, "follow it, but keep your distance. We can't afford to be spotted, and they'll be on the lookout."

"You got it," he promises.

True to his word, when Maxim slips into his car not long after, Tony discreetly follows at a safe distance.

Twenty minutes later, we pull up in front of a dilapidated building.

What in God's name is Maxim doing here?

From a distance, we watch him exit onto the street level. Unusually, his driver doesn't wait for him; instead, he peels off into the night. Maxim glances left and right before heading down the stairs to the basement of the building.

Weird. Really fucking weird. This is not the Maxim I know, the man who wouldn't be caught dead in anything but a bespoke suit and cufflinks that cost more than most people's rent. But tonight, he looks more like a member of a motorcycle club than a billionaire, dressed casually in worn jeans and a leather jacket, and damn if that's not a hell of a turn-on.

"Do you know what this place is?" I ask Tony, leaning forward between the front seats to get a better look. "A club of some sort?"

Maybe a sex club? The thought alone has my molars grinding together.

"I don't think so. Give me a minute," he says and types something into his phone.

"No one can know about this," I remind him.

"I got you." His eyes meet mine in the rearview mirror. "No one will know."

After we've watched a few other men surreptitiously enter into the building, Tony's phone chimes.

"Well, look at that." He fully turns in his seat to face me. "It's an underground fight club."

Oh.

"Totally anonymous, but no one steps into the ring here unless they're a top-tier fighter. Only big bets are on the table, cash only, no weapons allowed, and fights stop when one man can't stand or surrenders."

"I'm going in," I tell Tony.

"Want me to come with you?"

I shake my head. "I got this. Don't wait around. It might take a while."

I hand Tony my pistol, aware I won't be allowed in if I'm armed. Unlike Maxim, Tony knows what I'm capable of. He's seen me in action.

"By the way, maybe you can not mention this to my brothers."

He winks. "Call if you need me," he says as I open my door and step out of the car.

"Thanks again." I give him a final reassuring smile, but I sure as hell hope I don't need to take him up on that offer.

* * *

Following Maxim's lead, I head down the stairs to the lower-level entrance. A big burly guy that looks like he could be a fighter, broad and with a heavily scarred face, stands guard. A toothpick dangles from the corner of his lips as he gives me a thorough once-over.

I square my shoulders, refusing to be intimidated.

"No," is all he says to me.

"You can't turn me away," I argue. "I'm here to bet."

"Listen," he says, twisting the toothpick between his thin lips. "I don't know what a pretty thing like you is doing in a place like this, but it's better if you stay away." He dismisses me, going back to the phone in his hands.

Motherfucker, what's with all these men underestimating women? It really gets old after a while.

"You clearly don't know who I am," I drawl, crossing my arms over my chest.

"A princess?" He chuckles darkly, amused at his lame joke.

I smile widely. "You could say that. The Kozlov Bratva princess. I'm sure you're familiar with my brother, Andrei. Or maybe you know Daniil or Leonid?"

He freezes in place. His head slowly rises from his phone, his eyes widening in recognition. I don't give him time to get another word in. I swiftly pull out a thick wad of cash from my jacket, letting the green notes speak for themselves.

"Now, once again... Move over. I'm here to bet."

With a begrudging nod, he steps aside, granting me entry.

I push through the doors. Bloodlust, testosterone, and the heavy scent of sweat fill my nostrils. The vast, dimly lit area echoes with shouts and the thuds of fists striking flesh. The crowd is thick, lining the walls around the space, and at the heart of the commotion is the fighting ring. A makeshift square bordered by fraying ropes, with a ground stained by blood.

My eyes search the crowd for Maxim's tall lean frame, but it's too dark to make out any familiar features without getting in people's way, and I have no intention of doing that. It's hard to imagine a man as refined as Maxim choosing to hang out in a place like this, unless he has backroom business, but he didn't look like he was stepping into a meeting. He was dressed to fit in.

Without warning, a hush falls over the crowd. A massive bear of a man with a shaved head and bulging muscles steps into the ring.

"Tonight," a voice bellows, "a special match for our regulars and anyone who's got the balls to bet against our reigning champion. The Butcher is taking on ... The Russian."

My head snaps up, searching the ring as a chill seeps into my bones. There he is, standing at one corner of the ring. No fanfare, no pomp. Only raw power and a look that would make the bravest man cower.

My thighs clench at the sight of him because ... wow. It's the first time I've seen him shirtless, and he steals my breath away. Maxim's ripped muscles stand out against his golden skin. He turns around, and his back is a canvas of tattoos and scars—not what I imagined was hiding under his ten-thousand-dollar suits. He's not covered in tattoos, but the ink he does have on his back is simple and evocative—a broken chain and a chess knight, rendered in bold, black ink.

I push to the front of the crowd, desperate for a closer view. One thing is clear: Maxim is a born fighter. He appears completely at ease in the ring, every inch the predator on a hunt, unfazed by the beast of a man standing across from him.

A prickle of worry skitters across my skin. I mean, his opponent is named The Butcher! The bell clangs, and the fight begins.

I hold my breath as both men circle each other like gladiators in an ancient arena. The Butcher makes the first move, and it's on. They clash with the ferocity of a storm. The Butcher uses his sheer size, aiming heavy punches and trying to corner Maxim, but each time he lunges, Maxim dodges, countering with precise, calculated strikes to the giant's head and torso.

Like a bear that's been poked, The Butcher charges forward, delivering a swift and punishing blow to Maxim's exposed side. Maxim winces, a flash of pain crossing his expression. He recovers quickly, his focus lasered on his opponent.

Maxim moves like a panther, striking with a roundhouse kick to the gut that lands with surgical precision. He isn't a brawler; he's a tactician.

Watching him is doing funny things to my insides. The crowd is in a frenzy, matching the intensity inside the ring.

Maxim's eyes sweep over the crowd briefly, and then stop on me.

Shit! I try to pull up my hoodie, but it's too late. He saw me, and he looks *furious*.

On instinct, I turn around to run, but the mass of bodies makes it near impossible to get through. I'm trapped in place.

In a move that has the crowd gasping, Maxim ducks a wild punch from The Butcher, which throws the bigger man off balance. It's the only opening Maxim needs. He counters with a devastating uppercut, followed by a swift kick to the side of his knee, and The Butcher goes down hard, groaning in pain.

With a snarl, Maxim pounces, pressing an elbow into the other man's throat until he hits the mat three times, admitting defeat.

Maxim stands victorious, but there's no joy in his expression, no triumphant roar. Only a look of raw fury, directed straight at me.

Fuuuuck.

A chill sweeps through me, and now I run in earnest. Screw the crowd still buzzing from the adrenaline of the fight—I elbow people out of the way as I beeline for the door. I have enough sense not to look back, to keep moving towards the exit. When I'm out of here, I'll get in a cab and go straight to one of my brothers' homes.

Just as freedom is within reach, an unyielding arm snakes around my waist, yanking me back into a hot, muscled chest.

"Where do you think you're going, wife?"

Chapter Twenty-Five

MAXIM

My mind must be playing tricks on me. I blink hard, convinced my vision is blurred by The Butcher's punches. But no, there she is—Kira, standing amidst the chaos, looking so exposed, so vulnerable in this sea of unbridled male aggression. She thinks she can handle herself, but it's cold comfort when my enemies are actively pursuing her.

Rage replaces reason as my gaze fixes on The Butcher. Every ounce of me is driven by a single purpose to end this fight—now. That's exactly what I do seconds later with a swift roundhouse to his knee, bringing my towering opponent down like a sack of potatoes. I had hoped to toy with him a bit longer, but seeing her here changes everything.

I don't even stick around to bask in the roar of the crowd. As soon as my victory is declared, I vault over the ropes, my gaze locked onto the flash of Kira's blonde hair as she pushes through the frenzied crowd. My little lastochka thinks she can run from me. How wrong she is.

I let her get as far as the entrance. I let her taste freedom before I lunge for her, one arm wrapping around her middle like a seatbelt, lifting her right off the ground and bringing her flush with my body, adrenaline still pumping hard through my system.

"Where do you think you're going, wife?" I hiss into her ear.

Her breath catches, and she fights me. Of course she does. Wriggling and trying to break free of my grasp, but that's not going to happen. Ever again.

One nod at the bouncer, and he rushes to open a side door for me. It leads out to the alleyway between two looming brick buildings, dimly lit and echoing with the distant sounds of the city. The door slams shut behind us, the roar of the crowd cut off.

Before she can do anything else, I press her against the cold, rough wall. My hands shoot out, planting firmly on either side of her head, caging her in.

Her chest heaves with short, panicked breaths, her wide eyes locked onto mine. There's a wild defiance in them, but also fear.

My voice is a low growl, vibrating with anger. "Have you no fucking sense of self-preservation? Wasn't nearly being killed once today enough? You made it that much easier for my enemies to get to you."

She notches her chin and pushes against my chest with a dark glare, but I don't budge. I have a sudden pressing urge to turn her around, press her against the wall, and fuck her mercilessly until she chants my name like I'm her personal savior. Fuck that stubborn streak right out of her. But first, I'm going to make my wife spill all of her secrets—right here, right now.

"What about you?!" she explodes. Despite the tremor in her words, the fire in her eyes is unwavering. "You get to take off into the night, alone and with no word of explanation? You don't even have a weapon on you. Your double standards are bullshit." She punctuates her words with a furious stomp of her foot. "Fuck you, Maxim!"

I slam the underside of my balled fist into the brick above her head.

She flinches, swallowing hard, her delicate throat moving under the pale glow of a distant street light.

"Why did you follow me? What were you hoping to learn by trailing me?" Because that's the only way she could have known where I went. Other than my driver, who is a steel trap, no one else knew where I was headed.

"I ... I thought maybe you were going to see another woman." She takes a shaky breath, her resolve faltering for a moment. "I had to see for myself."

"Haven't we moved past this already?" I weigh her words, trying to gauge her honesty and finding it sorely lacking. "I'm not interested in any more lies."

Leaning in close, the heat of our bodies mingles in the cool air. I wrap my hand around her neck like a collar, feeling for the delicate pulse thumping under my fingers. "I'm going to give you one more chance to tell me the truth, and if you don't..." I squeeze the slightest bit, giving her a taste of what it feels like to have your air supply cut off. "I'm ending this right now."

Her eyes widen in horror and tears spring to the corners, glistening in the dim light.

"No, you wouldn't... How could you—"

"I would," I cut her off. "Start talking. Right. Fucking. Now." I lightly trace her pulse with my thumb, the tender touch contrasting with the veiled threat it carries. Not that I'd actually kill her, but I want her to believe I will. "Why do you think Roman's been your bodyguard all this time? I have eyes and ears on you, and you sure ask a lot of questions. You sneak into my office, and then you follow me here. Start talking while you still can. Because I'm out of patience."

She heaves a sob. "You are a fucking animal!" Her voice carries fierce, raw emotion.

"I am. No one would disagree." My fingers around her throat tighten again, only for a second. I want her to feel fear, to understand I have all the power here and we're not leaving this alley without a confession. But when she remains stubbornly silent, I've had enough. "Have it your way, lastochka."

I spin her around, still pushing her against the wall, ignoring her gasp of surprise. I was never going to choke her, but she sure as hell earned this punishment.

"Maxim." She tries to turn, but I don't let her. I grab the back of her neck and force her to face forward, away from me. With the other hand, I pull her leggings down right to her knee so her pristine pale skin is exposed to me.

"What are you—"

My hand connects with her ass cheek, delivering a hard smack that echoes in the quiet of the night. Lust shoots through me as I take in the pink imprint on her skin. I did that. I marked her, and it only makes me hungry for more.

Her breath stutters for a moment, before she regains control. "I swear to fucking God, if you—"

I don't wait for her opinion on the matter before delivering another slap. This one is hard enough that her flesh jiggles with the contact, leaving her skin the prettiest shade of crimson. She makes a noise that sounds like a whimper of need.

"I should have done this a long time ago," I growl. "And I'm not going to stop until you confess." I want the truth from her, but in this moment, I want her submission more.

The vixen doesn't argue with me. Instead, she subtly arches

her back, her body begging for my touch. I can hear it in her uneven breaths, and see it in the way she clenches her jaw and waits for my touch.

Shit, so much for spanking a confession out of her. She likes it too much. As do I. My cock is harder than it's ever been, but I won't let it distract me from what I need to do.

"Suit yourself," I say between clenched teeth.

This time, I brace one hand in the center of her back, and I let her have it. I'll extract a confession from her one way or another, whether through pain or pleasure. The sound of my hand slapping flesh reverberates in the small space between the buildings. She releases an audible gasp and turns her head, shooting me a look that suggests she's far from reaching her breaking point. So, I go harder. I spank both cheeks until her skin is bright red and adorned with my handprints.

Her chest rises and falls with heavy breaths as I lean in and whisper into her hair, "You brought this on yourself." How much more can she take until she breaks? I guess I'm about to find out.

A laugh spills from her throat, dark and bitter. "Spank me all you want. It doesn't change the fact that you are a monster. What kind of psychopath marries the person whose life you ripped apart?!"

Confusion churns in my gut. I spin her around so she's facing me and haul her leggings up over her ass. I don't know what she means, but there's an ominous undercurrent in her words.

"You want to know what this is all about? Fine!" Her lips tremble, her eyes brimming with tears. "You helped my father kill Masha! Led her to her horrible death like an animal brought to slaughter."

Her accusation lands like a punch to the stomach, disbelief coiling tightly within me.

She thinks I had something to do with killing Masha?

Before I have time to absorb the accusation, she strikes me, her small fists pounding against my chest. I can feel the weight of her anger and sorrow. It's a storm that needs unleashing, and even though I'm not the person she accuses me of being, I do the only thing I can to lessen the weight of her grief—I stand firm as she vents her fury. She wants to use me as a punching bag? I'll be that for her.

Kira keeps hitting me, her strikes fueled by tumultuous emotions. It's an ugly combination that I know all too well. That pain burrows under your skin and eats at your very soul unless you have an outlet.

Only when she's spent and exhausted, and her tears have slowed to a trickle, do I cage her against the wall and force her eyes to meet mine with a finger under her chin.

"I don't know where the fuck that accusation comes from, but let me be clear. If I have a reason to kill someone, I do it without a second thought. And trust me, I don't shy away from my sins." Kira's eyes narrow with suspicion. "I. Didn't. Kill. Masha."

"Of course you'd say that! Of course you'd deny it. But the night of Alyona's ball, Boris Ivanov told me everything. It's what people have been saying behind your back for years, and he was the only one who had the guts to say it to my face." She takes a deep, heaving breath. "It makes sense. You owed my father for bringing you into the bratva."

My eyebrows shoot up in surprise. "You're delusional if you think I owed your father anything. And Boris Ivanov is not a reliable source of information." I can't contain the laughter that spills from my lips until something even more absurd occurs to me. "Is this why you married me?"

"Yes," she hisses. "So I could kill you with my bare hands."

Amusement flickers to life. She's gutsy, even if she's off the mark. "Go ahead." I hold my arms open wide. "Get your revenge."

Fire courses through my veins. I've had enough of this bullshit, and we're ending it here and now.

Her lower lip trembles. "You're a snake," she shoots back but says nothing else.

"Do you believe I'm her killer?"

A flicker of doubt passes over her features. My shoulders lower a notch as she grapples with the truth. "You had a meeting scheduled with her days before someone convinced her to come out of hiding."

The memory slowly comes back to me. "I did have a meeting scheduled with Masha, about donating to one of her charities, but it never happened. I have documentation to prove it." Her red-rimmed eyes dart towards me, the fiery accusation replaced with a shadow of something else. Acceptance. "Look at me, lastochka. Look at me." Her gaze meets mine, and she nods slowly. "I'm sorry this is not what you want to hear, but it wasn't me. I had nothing to do with Masha's death."

She shakes her head and covers her hand with her mouth. A strangled sob escapes her. "She didn't deserve it ... didn't deserve what they did to her. It was all because of me."

Her knees buckle, but before she goes down, I swoop in and cradle her to my chest. She may still hate me, but I'm not letting her be swallowed by the abyss of guilt.

I want to tell her it's not her fault. Her aunt Masha was a big girl and made her own choices. But I know firsthand that hearing "there's nothing you could have done" only feels worse.

I study her face, tracing the soft curve of her jawline with my eyes. Every instinct in me screams to protect her, to shield her from this world, but it's too late for that. The scars are already etched deep into her soul, as they are in mine.

Anger bubbles up—not towards Kira, but at the sacrifices

she's made to get justice. Like marrying me. It's a painful echo of my own past. In Kira, I see a reflection of the grief I've carried within me since Ilya's death. She's felt loss and pain like I have, and her determination to get revenge strikes a chord.

I tighten my hand wrapped around her jaw. "I'm going to hunt down Masha's killer, and I'm going to do to them exactly what was done to her. You can even watch. Every ounce of pain they inflicted, I'll return tenfold. They'll know the true meaning of fear and despair, like Masha did." Slowly, I tip her chin up, but her eyes are still downcast, her brow pinched. "Look at me," I demand.

She drags her gaze up to mine. The anger she was hiding behind now gives way to something else.

Bloodthirst. Determination.

The same drive that consumed me when I sought vengeance for Ilya's death. I razed half of Moscow to get my revenge, and I succeeded. Annihilating the syndicate that dared to come after my family.

She meets my eyes without flinching, holding my stare. "Whatever they did to my aunt, I will do to them. I want to help."

"Whatever you want." I rub my thumb over her bottom lip and whisper, "Whatever you want, I will give you."

A mixture of vulnerability and hope dances in her gaze. "Why? After everything, why would you do that for me?" she asks, still in my arms.

"I don't fucking care if you married me for some twisted revenge plot—you wear my ring. You are my wife." Kira's eyes round in surprise, and truthfully, my words surprise me too. I don't want a wife and everything that comes with it, but the idea of leaving Kira alone to battle the world sets my skin ablaze. "You're a Belov now, and that makes you mine to protect. You'll never fight another battle alone."

Her teeth sink into her plush bottom lip, and my cock throbs in response. "I don't know what to say."

"Say nothing."

I cup her jaw and capture her mouth, teasing the seam of her lips with my tongue until they part, granting me entry. I delve inside, our tongues intertwining. Unlike the kiss after the mayor's house, driven by anger and possessiveness, this kiss is a wildfire, unchecked and brimming with lust.

She groans when I twist my hand in her hair and angle her head so I have better access to her lips.

Fuck, her lips. She tastes good. So good.

A rush of heat from my chest spirals downward, and I grind my rock-hard cock into her soft belly, reveling in her warmth.

A distant voice tells me this is a bad idea. Because I'm already addicted to how her lips taste. If I feast on her pussy and taste her cum, I'll be in too deep. Once my dick is buried in her tight, beautiful cunt, I'll be a goner.

Fuck, my wife is going to ruin me.

And I'm going to let her.

Chapter Twenty-Six

KIRA

The sensation of Maxim's tongue exploring my mouth and his hand grazing the naked skin of my stomach feels like bliss. My eyelids flutter closed, a whimper slipping out as I'm lost in the overwhelming taste and touch of him.

Fuck this man, and fuck what he does to me. How he makes me feel. How he destroyed my world only to build it back up. He let me cry and rage, and accuse him of murder, my body collapsing into his as years of grief poured out of me. And he didn't flinch, not once.

Maxim is many things, but he's not a liar nor a coward. Even through my haze of grief, I saw the truth shining in his eyes. He even offered up the proof, but somewhere deep inside, I know I don't need it.

I believe him.

Drained of emotion, the only thing I'm capable of right now is feeling. Feeling the hot slide of his tongue against mine, feeling his hand under my shirt and in my bra, pulling at my nipples. The way his cock pulsates against me. All I know for sure is I want more of this.

I pull back for a breath, trailing my hand down his hot bare chest. *This chest.* Despite the fall chill, it glistens with sweat. I was mesmerized by the sight of his physique during the fight. The body that this man hides underneath his tailored suits is fiiiine. He has the form of a fighter, lean and ripped. He rests his forehead against mine, our lips hovering inches apart as we pant against each other's mouth.

Is he going to push me away? Tell me this is a mistake? A physical relationship would complicate everything, except right now, I can't find it in me to care.

Something snaps inside of me, releasing a tidal wave of emotion. Instead of barricading it back, I crave to feel every bit of it, especially through his touch.

His fist tightens around my hair. "Fuck." His one word says it all. If only a kiss can feel this good, we're screwed. His eyes flutter closed for one long second, and I think he might end this. Instead, he says, "Turn around, baby. I'm going to show you how much I need you."

I can't turn around fast enough. My back is now to his front, facing the graffiti-covered brick wall of the building.

"Hands up," he demands.

My skin comes alive, and goosebumps break out at the feel of his hands pulling my hoodie off. I still have my T-shirt and bra on, but he doesn't take those off. Instead, he pulls both up so they're shoved above my breasts, giving him full access. He circles them with his hands, pinching and flicking a thumb over my nipples until my every nerve ending is singing with his touch.

I moan out, and he releases a satisfied chuckle. One of his large hands lands between my shoulder blades, pushing my front against the dingy brick. My puckered nipples brush against the cool, rough stone, and it feels ... so good.

"Stay like that," he bites out. "Now you're going to let your husband fuck you with his tongue until you come all over his face."

His thumbs hook into the waistband of my leggings and thong, and he sinks down. In one pull, he has them down around my ankles like a shackle.

I'm vulnerable and exposed to him—and anyone who dares wander into the alley for a breath of fresh air or a smoke. Fuck me, that only makes this hotter.

One of his calloused palms lands on my ass, a light caress over my heated skin. "Spread your legs as wide as you can," he commands.

I do my best, my leggings stretched to the max restricting my movement.

"So perfect, lastochka." One of his thick fingers slips inside of me.

I can't help but bite out a curse because, Lord help me, it fills me to perfection. But as quickly as it entered me, he pulls his finger out, leaving me wet and restless, and desperate for more of his touch.

"Do you know what I'm going to do to you?" His voice is a husky growl.

I huff out a laugh, my cheeks on fire. "I have an idea," I say, trying not to sound too hopeful. I arch my ass back flush with his hard cock.

He pulls back with a grunt. An unexpected, harsh slap to my pussy jolts my thoughts apart. The sensation sizzles in my bloodstream like a shot of adrenaline.

"What was that for?" I cry out.

"That was for disobeying me. Tricking my men, sneaking out, putting yourself in danger." He sucks my earlobe into his mouth and gives it a tug with his teeth. "Now, I'm going to give you pleasure. Be a good girl. Keep your hands glued to the wall" — he presses down again between my shoulder blades — "and your tits pressed against the rough brick. Keep your ass out, presented to me like this."

A low, needy groan slips between my lips in anticipation of his touch. I'm probably working through some messed-up trauma right now, with the man I thought was my aunt's killer. But messed up or not, it feels good. It feels cathartic.

Without hesitation, his powerful hand lands on my backside again, and this time I jerk forward, finding pleasure in my breasts grating against the brick. I'm desperate to feel the same type of friction between my legs.

"You're so much fucking trouble, and have been from the moment you stepped foot in my home," he hisses in my ear.

"You mean, from the moment you abducted me and held me prisoner?" I sass back.

It earns me another slap on my clit, and a sharp tug on one of my braids before he uses it to guide my head back and to the side, taking a deep inhale of my scent as he trails his nose down my neck.

"I need to taste you so fucking bad. I've wanted to suck your clit into my mouth for so long." He almost sounds pained, like I've hurt him in some way.

But I'm hurting too. My clit is hard and tense, desperate for release only he can provide. His mouth trails from my neck, down my back, and then... Whoa, I wasn't expecting him *there,* coasting over my most private hole. I clench on instinct, and he chuckles.

"It's okay, lastochka. Only a taste. I won't lick your ass properly until you're ready to take my cock here." A finger trails up and circles my puckered hole.

I stop him with a strangled sob. "Maxim," I plead, "I can't."

"You can, baby, when the time is right."

He doesn't give me any room to question what's coming next. Two hands grip both sides of my hips and I'm bent over further, my cheek against the wall while Maxim kneels behind me.

Holy shit, I'm spread as wide as I can go, so vulnerable right now. My feet are shackled by my leggings, my shirt and bra above my tits. If someone found us right now, we'd certainly make a lewd tableau—me bent over and exposed to him. Maxim looking like a Roman gladiator, half-dressed and glistening with a light sheen of sweat, his mouth inches from the apex of my thighs. So close, I can feel his hot breath coast over my delicate flesh.

Grabbing hold of each of my ass cheeks, he spreads me wide and swirls his tongue over my opening. I gasp at the foreign sensation. I'm no virgin—I've had plenty of one-night stands and hook-ups—but no one has gone down on me properly. There were some feeble drunken attempts that ended up feeling more awkward than satisfying, and I quickly put a stop to it, preferring penetration than having my labia licked because all of the men I've been with seemed confused as to the location of my clit.

Not Maxim. *Shit, not Maxim.*

He knows exactly what he's doing.

I bite down on my bottom lip as lust pumps through me. He dips his head and runs a gentle tongue over my clit, swirling over the bud and making me cry out, my fingers clawing at the brick wall in front of me.

"You taste perfect. Exactly like I imagined you would."

I'm too worked up to respond. Each pass of his tongue over my tight bundle of nerves is pure bliss. I close my eyes and tilt my head back in ecstasy. Shivers race through my body, and all I can do is surrender to the moment as he continues, his tongue expertly flicking and circling my clit, my dopamine levels off the charts.

Two of his thick fingers make their way inside of me. He scissors them, the feeling intense, like being stretched in the most delicious way. A low moan escapes me, and he chuckles.

"Mmm, I'm glad to discover what you like."

"Yesssss," I gasp. "More."

He gives me a third finger and captures my clit between his lips, deeply sucking the little bud. My nails scrape against the wall as I'm dragged close to the edge. One more hard suck, and I'll be crying out my release.

As if he knows exactly what I need, Maxim uses his two hands on either sides of my hips to pull my pussy back against his face, suckling my clit, savoring my pleasure while plunging three of his fingers into my channel.

If his tongue can make me feel this unhinged, I can't wait to find out what his cock can do. Picturing him rising from his position, notching the head of his hard length against me and surging forward, is all I need to unravel.

My pussy walls contract, and I clench down hard on his fingers, my legs shaky as I cry out. Intense pleasure blankets me, different from anything I've felt before. All the tension of the day, weeks, even months before this mounts and releases in one intense, limb-shaking, mind-numbing orgasm. I'm not even sure how I'm going to walk out of here on my own.

Behind me, he presses closer and gives my entrance a final lick. "Fuck, you did so good for me."

I can't move, my muscles lax, as he plants a kiss at my entrance and then rises, lifting up my pants and underwear.

Huh? Aren't we going to have sex? Because I'm only getting started.

With his chest pressed firmly against my back, his hands find their way to my breasts, cupping and gently weighing them. He finishes with a simultaneous pinch of both nipples, sending waves of pleasure coursing through me.

"Such pretty tits," he whispers in my ear. "I can't wait to suck on them. I can't wait to rub my cum into your beautiful pale skin."

"You can," I offer, "right now."

Every feeling is intensified, my body humming now that I came. I want him to fuck me right here, against this wall. But as he settles my shirt and bra back in place, it's clear nothing else will be happening.

"I'm going to, lastochka. Very soon, I'm going to slide my dick inside that tight little pussy of yours and savor how you feel from within. But not tonight."

I wheel around to find his commanding gaze fixated on me.

He's not acting on impulse. He's acting in my best interests right now, and that thought warms a previously untouched corner of my heart.

Chapter Twenty-Seven

KIRA

The first touches of dawn lighten the sky by the time we make it back to the hotel. Maxim is in the shower, and I'm curled up in an armchair, watching the sunrise and wondering if I am foolish to believe he didn't kill my aunt.

Maxim says he'll give me full access to his private correspondence, diaries—anything to prove he had nothing to do with her death. He's even promised to find her killer, and if anyone has the resources, he does.

At the end of the day, I have no reason not to believe him. Others might call me foolish, but I have to go with my gut and the lack of evidence that points to Maxim's involvement.

Personally, I'm not sure where we stand. I accused him of murder, broke down sobbing in his arms, and then let him eat me out against a brick wall, culminating in the most delicious orgasm of my life. It's not like we can go back to normal from here. There is no "normal" between us anyway.

The bathroom door opens and Maxim emerges wearing a towel, a puff of steam following him into the bedroom. I can't help but stare at his tight ab muscles as he reaches up to dry his hair with a small towel.

I thought I had this man all figured out. Turns out, I knew nothing.

"You keep on looking at me like that, lastochka, and we're going to end up right back where we started tonight."

A shiver coasts down my spine and settles between my legs.

He releases a slow, deep chuckle. "I see you wouldn't mind that. But first, you need some sleep." He disappears into the closet and comes out a moment later, wearing boxers and nothing else.

Pulse pounding in my ears, I stare up at the ceiling and grit my teeth, trying to loosen the lusty thoughts rattling around in my brain. He pushes a button on a remote control and the blinds lower, enveloping the room in darkness.

We've never gone to bed together like a normal married couple, which is probably why this all feels so damn awkward. To me. Not to Maxim, who is already in bed, lying on his back with his hands under his head, staring at the ceiling. And hot damn, the covers are bunched at his waist, showing off his fighter's physique.

Deep breaths, Kira.

What happened in the alley should have eased my hunger. But I swear, all it did was amp up my craving for him.

I lift the covers and settle into bed beside Maxim. It's not like we're touching or anything, but I don't know which way to look or turn, so I opt for curling up, facing away from him. I won't be able to fall asleep with the knowledge that if I open my eyes, Maxim is there beside me.

As my eyelids are getting heavy, he says, "You have nightmares. You cry out and thrash around. I thought it was about your father, but now I'm not so sure."

I'm quiet for a moment. "Masha's death is all my fault."

He makes a noise of acknowledgement in his throat but doesn't argue. He doesn't try to convince me that it's not on me or justify it six ways from Sunday. Instead of words, one of his strong arms wraps around my waist and hauls me into his body.

I stiffen, not used to being held like this, protected and cradled, but it feels good. Strangely, it feels familiar.

"They sent me pictures, you know, of her body, after ... after everything they did." I exhale sharply through my nose. Even though it twists me up to talk about it, somehow it feels like he has the right to know. "And a letter, describing everything they did to get her to talk. To put her in that state. When I close my eyes, that's what I see." He stills behind me, quiet. Listening. "The weird thing is, the nightmares have eased up recently. I have them, but I'm not waking up in a cold sweat." I chuckle silently. "Until the nightmare I had the other morning. I'll have you know, you were in it."

Maxim exhales, his breath fluttering across my neck. "Perhaps it's because her so-called murderer was comforting you every time you had a nightmare."

"What?" I turn in his arms so I'm facing him. What the hell is talking about?

His fingers gently brush over my face, the faint lines framing his eyes softening in amusement. "I couldn't stand to hear your cries," he says simply as if that explains it all.

"So you—"

"Held you. Like this." His strong arms tighten around me, and he turns me so I'm resting on his chest. The thud of his heartbeat reverberates in my ear, and the scent of *him* fills my nostrils.

Holy shit. Talk about unexpected. Being in his embrace is

comforting because it's familiar. My heart twists, a little twinge above my ribs.

Why does Maxim care enough to comfort me? I was sure he disliked me, or at the very least, that he was indifferent.

"I really thought it was you," I say. "When Anatoly told me your history with my father, coupled with the fact that you knew my aunt and she would have trusted you, all the pieces seemed to fit together."

Except, they don't fit together.

"Trusted me?" he asks.

"She kept a diary right at the end," I explain. "I found it at her cabin outside of the city, where she was hiding out. She talked about someone she knew and trusted reaching out to her in her final days, offering her protection from my father." I huff out a breath. "It made sense that it was you."

"I'm sorry to disappoint." His voice rumbles in his chest. "I'm also sorry I didn't give your aunt's murder enough thought before today. I didn't know the details, but I didn't take the time to find out." Even though his words hurt, he's not saying anything surprising. The world we live in has hardened us to death and violence, and Maxim sees it every day. "When we're back in Russia, I'm paying Boris Ivanov a visit."

My head whips up, and I meet Maxim's intense gaze. "Please don't hurt him," I plead. "He was drunk. When Liza asked him about it when he was sober, he denied the accusation."

"I'm no fan of Boris's, but even he's not stupid enough to make up something like this." His voice is lined with steel. "He's a gossipy piece of shit, but I want to know where he's getting his information from."

"Just don't kill him," I plead. "Even if he is a worm, he's Liza's father."

"If he talks, we won't have a problem." He pulls my mouth

close to his, and I want more than anything for him to fuse our lips together. "Lastochka, I meant what I said. I'll help you get your revenge. I won't let the crime go unanswered, but I still need you to play your part as my wife. Things are going to get even more dangerous, and I need to know that you're safe. No more sneaking around and no more lies between us."

A choked laugh spills from my lips. "You know I'm a trained fighter, right? I've been doing krav maga for years."

"I don't care." I can make out his smirk in the dark as his two hands travel down the length of my body, before landing on each ass cheek. The possessive squeeze he gives my flesh says it all. "Don't make me punish you again."

"Fine, I'll drop it for now." I pause to think. With everything out in the open, there's something I need to address. "You have to get Nadya to back off. She treats me as if I'm her lowly stepdaughter, not the lady of the house." I swallow, taking a moment to choose my next words carefully. "I think she's in love with you," I admit.

He laughs, like the idea is ludicrous. "She's not in love with me. She's just overly protective. I don't want you worrying about her," he reassures me, gently tucking a strand of my hair behind my ear. "I'll talk to her again. She needs time to come around. After Irina..."

I freeze. He's talking about his mysterious first wife. I hold my breath, waiting for him to say more, but he doesn't.

Roman and Nadya made it seem like Irina betrayed him. Even if she cheated on him, that's not a crime punishable by death in my books. But Maxim lives by a different moral code. I have so many questions I want to ask—starting with why he killed her—but he's staring at the ceiling, and I get the sense he doesn't want to talk about Nadya or Irina right now.

We're both quiet as I settle back on his chest, the only noise the rise and fall of our breaths.

Out of nowhere, Maxim's voice cuts through the dark. "Does Alyona know?"

"Huh?" His question startles me from my turbulent thoughts.

There's a moment of weighted silence. "Does she know you believed I killed your aunt and that's why you married me?"

"She knows I had ulterior motives for marrying you, but she doesn't know what they are." I snort. "If either she or my brothers knew the truth, they would absolutely lose their shit."

His voice is amused as his fingers slowly comb through my hair. I close my eyes—his touch is comforting. My body definitely doesn't think of him as the enemy.

"You're damn brazen, lastochka. I don't know many people who would have the balls to take me on like you did. Since you're far from stupid, you must be a little crazy." He gently pulls at a strand of my hair.

I smile into the dark. "That should be clear by now."

"Tell me something about Alyona. Something I don't already know."

I hold back expressing surprise at his question. "She has a real sweet tooth. Loves it all, especially sour candies and anything gummy. She loves dogs and hates cats. Well, 'hate' is too strong of a word, but you know what I mean. What else... She gets frightened during storms. Had a bad experience as a kid and doesn't like being alone when there's a thunderstorm."

Maxim is quiet for a while, staring straight ahead. "Thank you," he says.

"For what?"

"For sharing. These are things a father should know about his daughter."

As my hands dance over his chest, he releases a tight breath. And when I move my hand lower and lower, finally dropping beneath his boxer briefs, he hisses into my hair and bucks up into my hands.

"Are you tired?" I ask him. "I know at your advanced age getting hard is sometimes—"

He flips me on my back and settles between my spread thighs. "Shut up," he says, pushing his rock-hard cock against my panty-covered entrance. "Does it feel like I have issues getting hard?"

No. No, it definitely does not.

"Sometime soon, I'm going to show you how virile I am. Trust me, that demonstration will leave you sore for a week."

"Does this mean our one-month sex moratorium is off?" I taunt, and roll my hips up and into him.

"Fuck, yes." He lets out a satisfied groan. He kisses behind my ear, and the gesture is sweet and does funny things to my insides. "But now, you sleep."

"Sleep?" I pout. "Why waste time on sleep when we could be having fun?"

He makes an amused noise. "Because you've been through a shock. It may not feel like it, but your world has been turned upside down. Sleep now, so I can fuck you mercilessly tomorrow."

So I do.

Chapter Twenty-Eight

KIRA

I'm jolted awake far too early by raised voices outside the bedroom. Morning light filters through the curtains, and the distant hum of Manhattan traffic buzzes below. Considering I only slept a few hours, my body is heavy and tired.

I've barely propped myself up against the pillows when Maxim reenters the bedroom looking way too fresh despite the few hours of sleep he's had. Instead of his typical perfectly tailored suit, he's dressed in gray sweatpants and ... nothing else.

I find it hard to tear my eyes away from his chiseled torso. He's fine with a capital F. No, scratch that. I don't even try to look away as he grips the door frame overhead, causing his biceps to flex.

My breath catches seeing Maxim so unlike the uptight business oligarch who, up until last night, I would have happily killed in his sleep. It feels as if the world has shifted on its axis between yesterday and now. My chaffed breasts and sore thighs are proof of all that we shared.

He's looking at me with the same hungry expression I'm surely giving him. I crook my fingers, inviting him back into bed. If he's going to look that delicious, we need to finish what we started.

He stalks forward with a chuckle. "I wish we could, but we have guests."

Guests?

"So early?" I make a face.

"It's ten. Not too early. But I think you'll want to come out and greet them."

My eyebrows knit together as I tug the duvet up to my chin. "Why?" I'm not usually involved in Maxim's business.

"Because..." His thumb traces over the swell of my bottom lip. "It's your family."

"What?! My brothers? Why the hell are you being so casual about this?"

I fling the duvet off and stalk through the room, looking for something decent to wear. There's no one in the world I love more than my family and friends, but this seems like a very inopportune time to have a family reunion.

"And Alyona."

"Jesus Christ, you told me her and Leo are in Italy."

"They were, but now they're back. And they want to see you."

In the bureau mirror, I catch sight of myself—hair mussed, eyeliner smudged, lips swollen, my cheeks flushed with a satisfied glow. I consider taking a shower so I look less disheveled, but an insistent knock at the door relieves me of that idea.

"Kira? What's going on?" Alyona sounds worried.

"I'll be one second," I holler back, wrestling to get a T-shirt over my head while Maxim looks on with amusement.

I narrow my eyes. "What's so funny?" I whisper-yell.

"We're married. It's not a crime to have relations with your husband."

I hold up my hand so he stops talking. I can't even begin to go there. Maxim is Aly's father and the man my brothers hate. They'd probably declare war on him if they could. So yeah, them seeing proof that we've been intimate is beyond awkward.

I fling one of his dress shirts off a chair towards him. "Can you put on some clothes please? Your bare chest is distracting me."

He shrugs, leaning back against the wall. "I'm good."

"Ugh," I let out a thoroughly annoyed groan. He's doing this to torture me, I'm sure of it.

I dart into the bathroom, pee, brush my teeth, and run my fingers through my hair, but honestly, it's a lost cause. I can't put this off any longer, so I slip on last night's hoodie and head out of the en suite. Maxim isn't in the bedroom, so I assume he's already with our guests—or my guests.

I swallow down my pride and head to the main sitting area. Raised voices float to me as I round the corner into the open space.

"What the hell do you mean the Black Company was behind the attack?" Andrei, my eldest brother and the Kozlov Bratva pakhan, stands by the floor-to-ceiling window, his broad shoulders tense and his jaw held tight as he addresses Maxim.

Unfazed, Maxim doesn't respond when he sees me enter the room. Instead, he rises, pours a coffee, and brings it to me before I can say otherwise.

All eyes in the room shift towards us and his small act of thoughtfulness.

"Kira!" Aly is the first person out of her seat, her eyes filling with tears that she attempts to blink away. Her arms circle me tightly, her breath shaky against my neck.

The scent of her familiar perfume wraps around us, and emotions clog my throat because I've missed her so much. Trying to keep my best friend and brothers at bay this whole time has been exhausting.

"I was so worried when we heard..."

Heard about what? It takes me a minute for my brain to figure out she means yesterday's attack at the auction house. With everything that happened afterwards, the attack seems like a distant memory. Which is messed up.

"Sis!" Daniil's booming voice sounds beside me and as Aly releases me, my middle brother wraps me in his arms, kissing the side of my head.

Leo is the next to embrace me in his big, powerful arms, and finally Andrei steps in with a tense hug.

"You okay?" he whispers into my hair.

"I'm okay, I promise. Can we ... sit down and talk?"

In the space of a heartbeat, Maxim wraps a protective arm around my shoulder, lowering me beside him onto the couch. My brothers take a seat opposite us. It feels like a standoff, with tension lacing the air. Aly's eyes ping-pong between all of us before she lowers into the space beside Leo. Though it's probably a really bad time to squeal in delight at seeing my brother and Aly in love and finally together, I can't help but flash her a smile. She smiles warmly back at me.

My brothers don't. They're frowning, all three of them staring at Maxim's arm slung around my shoulder and how close we're sitting. I'm relieved to notice that Maxim threw on a T-shirt while I was in the shower. Still, we do look pretty damn cozy.

I clear my throat and try to put a few inches between us, but he straight-up stops me with a firm squeeze, his fingers lightly tracing circles on my knee. My brothers might look tense, but Maxim seems completely unbothered.

Talk about *awkward*. Last they saw us together, guns were pointed, Maxim was surrounded by legions of guards, and threats were being made. Now, well, the fact that Maxim practically pulled me down into his lap makes it pretty obvious where things stand.

Since no one speaks, I decide to break the ice. "I'm fine, really. I don't know what you heard, but Maxim was on my attacker so fast I didn't even register what happened."

Aly arches an eyebrow at Maxim. Her father. "You risked your life to save her?" she asks in a quiet voice.

Maxim makes a dismissive gesture as if to say, *Of course*. "She's my wife."

His words ignite a warmth in my chest.

Leo points accusingly. "It's your fault she was in danger in the first place. What the fuck were you thinking parading her out in New York if you're about to go to war with the Black Company?"

Beside me, I can feel Maxim bristle at Leo's aggression.

"You seem to forget," I say with a slight smirk, "I was born into this life. Danger is something I've always known."

Leo ignores my attempt at lightening the mood. He sees Maxim as a twisted opportunist who granted his daughter freedom only when a better opportunity was presented. From the outside, that's exactly what happened, but I know that in his own fucked-up way, he cares about Aly. He let her go because it was best for her.

Aly lays a hand on Leo's shoulder and whispers something in his ear, likely telling him to take it down a notch since he's still vibrating with anger.

"It's okay, Leo." I give my brother a weak smile. "We were well protected. Maxim's men surrounded the room. It was one of those things..."

Leo continues to shake his head in disgust and I hold my breath, not sure how this is going to play out.

Maxim speaks, his tone low and serious. "My head of security believed they wouldn't attack on American soil, and I agreed with him. We were wrong."

My head snaps towards him. Why is Maxim blaming himself? It was a private event and we were well guarded, but he seems to think everything that happens is his responsibility, which is messed up.

Andrei crosses his ankle over his knee, his expression intense. "So you're at war with the Black Company now?"

"Going to war," Maxim clarifies. "They don't appreciate competition in the wine fraud market."

Daniil cocks a brow, raking a hand through his hair. "You've got more money than you know what to do with. How can selling a few bottles of fancy wine possibly be worth going to war for?"

Maxim chuckles and runs a thumb along his bottom lip. "It's true, I'm not in it for the money." His warm hand lands on my thigh, causing a shiver to blast up my spine. "I'm in it to prove a point."

"And that is?" Aly asks, even though her eyes are glued to where Maxim rests his hand possessively on my body.

"There's nothing more pretentious than rich people with more money than sense. If these idiots think it's worth spending hundreds of thousands on a bottle of old wine, let them give their money to me and I'll make sure it goes to a better cause."

"What, like your palace on the sea?" Leo shoots back.

"Sure, something like that," Maxim says, but I know there's more to the story than meets the eye.

"Listen," I say to my brothers because I suspect they need to hear this. "I'm happy here. I'm fine, I'm well protected, and Maxim and I have a deal. I need to see it through."

"What kind of deal do you have?" Daniil asks, sitting forward.

I look towards Maxim, and he gives me a little nod of approval. "Our marriage serves as a distraction, something for the press to focus on while Maxim deals with the Black Company. And in the meantime..." I hesitate, feeling a little nervous sharing something I've kept locked away for so long. Aly and I have barely even spoken about it. "He's going to help me find the people that killed Aunt Masha."

Aly shakes her head, clearly confused. "Didn't your father kill your aunt?"

"Yes, he ordered the hit, but someone else carried it out. Whoever helped lure her out of hiding and killed her will pay." I laugh bitterly and stare down at my hands, not knowing how to tell my family this but knowing they need to hear it. "I thought Maxim was her killer. That's why I married him. To get revenge."

The whole room is quiet for half a second until everyone starts talking at once. I get it, my family has a lot of questions. My news is a shock.

Andrei's voice carries above the rest. "Jesus, Kira, talk about putting yourself at risk! Why is it that you're convinced he didn't murder her?"

"He can prove it."

Daniil scoffs. "Not if he needs you alive to keep up his important image."

Maxim rolls his eyes. "If I had killed Masha, I would have had a good reason and you'd know about it by now. Oleg and I had history, but it's not a good one. I disliked him as much as anyone."

"Maxim has no reason to lie," I speak up.

Defending him in front of my family feels strange, but I've spent a lot of time considering what motivation Maxim might have to lie, including not alienating Alyona. In my gut, I know deception isn't his style. He's always been brutally honest, even when it hurts.

Leo's face falls. "Why didn't you come to us? We would have looked into it for you. We would have helped you get your revenge so you didn't have to marry this ... this—"

"I didn't want to burden you with my past. I thought it was the best way."

"Well, that certainly explains a lot," Aly says, eyes wide. "I never understood your motivation for marrying him. My father."

When he glances my way, his eyes hold a trace of softness, a contrast to his usual guarded expression. "Kira is my wife, and I will find out who was behind Masha's death and help her get the revenge she deserves."

Andrei shakes his head. "You don't need to. She's our sister. We'll figure out—"

"Did you miss it when I said she's my wife and, therefore, my responsibility?"

I've never heard anyone interrupt Andrei like that and I tense, preparing for Andrei to lunge across the coffee table between us. But my brother doesn't move, just keeps glaring daggers.

Maxim lifts my hand and shows off the big, honking diamond ring that heralds to the world I'm a taken woman. "My. Wife."

My heart hammers in my chest—I'm not sure if it's anxiety or excitement at his possessiveness. Or both.

Aly rises from Leo's lap, cutting through the silence in the room. "Kira, can I talk to you alone?"

"Of course." I stand and follow her into a small room, closing the door behind me.

Nerves jump in my stomach because I don't know what to expect.

Before I say anything, she has me wrapped in her arms. "Fuck me. I'm so sorry." I pull away to find tears in her eyes and her face clouded with worry.

"You have nothing to be sorry for!" I insist. "How were you supposed to know?"

"That's the point." Her expression falls. "I knew you married Maxim for some other reason, and I didn't push the issue. I left you alone with him—a monster."

I pause, not sure how to explain that he's not entirely the big bad wolf we thought him to be. "He's not a monster." The words fall from my lips, revealing a truth I hadn't fully acknowledged until this moment. "He's complicated and dangerous, yes, but not quite the nightmare we thought he was."

He shields me from *my* nightmare. He made the mayor pay for his sins. He held me when I couldn't hold myself up. He's going to hunt down my aunt's killer. He gave me the best orgasm of my life.

Aly's brows pull together. "Huh?"

This is not easy to share, but Aly has a right to know that my feelings for Maxim are complicated. "Things ... have changed." A softness invades my tone. "I've seen a different side of him."

Her eyes take me in from head to toe. When she's done with her inspection, she frowns. "So you actually want to be married to him? Are you together now?"

"No. Definitely not," I'm quick to counter. We haven't talked about it, but it's clear Maxim has no desire for this to be real. "It's an arrangement until he deals with the Black Company and helps me get my revenge. And then..." I shrug because I don't really know what happens next. "We'll probably go our separate ways."

Her expression carries a hint of disappointment, as if I've let her down in some way. But I can't lie to her and continue to portray Maxim as all bad, because he's not. "Why would you trust him? After everything he did to you, to us?"

I shift from foot to foot, pulling at my hoodie like that's somehow going to distract her. "He's shown me a different side of himself. He's done some shitty things, I won't deny that, but he's not all bad. Give him a chance to explain to you why he did what he did. To show the other side of him. He's protected me, he's taken care of me during a terrible nightmare, he even kicked an attendant off our flight when... Whatever, that's a long story."

Her forehead creases. "Honestly, I'm not sure I can forgive him that easily. But if this is what you want, I'll support you."

Guilt washes over me, making me question if I'm siding with the enemy. But the truth is, the only thing I care about is Maxim helping me get my revenge. And I guess it remains to be seen if he'll actually deliver what he promised. "The only thing I want is to bring my aunt's killer to justice," I answer, truthfully. "After that, we'll go our separate ways."

It's impossible to imagine what happens after this. Would I like to go back to my old life working with my brothers and having my family and friends close by? Hell yes. But something inside me has shifted. I don't know what's next or what I want, but I do know that deep down, Maxim has left a mark on me that can't be easily erased.

"And in the meantime, you're gonna keep on sleeping with him?" She pulls a face, and I can't help but smile.

"I'm sorry, this is weird to talk about with you. Maxim is your father."

"That's not how I think of him."

My mouth tips up. "So you don't think of me as your stepmother?"

She snorts. "God, that's fucking weird. No." She heaves a sigh. "Okay, fine. Promise me you'll be careful. I still don't fully trust him, no matter what he claims about helping you find your aunt."

I lay a hand on her shoulder. "I'll be cautious," I promise. "But there is something you should know." Her eyes search mine, waiting. "Maxim didn't let you go because I offered him an alternative. He let you go because he didn't want you to be unhappy and he knew that Leo would keep you safe. In his weird way, he cares about you."

A long, slow breath leaves her lungs as she shakes her head. "I'll believe it when I see it. Right now, it sounds like a convenient story."

I understand Aly's wariness of Maxim, and honestly, I'm not sure if time alone will be enough to heal the wounds he inflicted. But I want her to understand that there's another side to Maxim. Not for my sake, but because it's tough to believe the worst about your own family. I should know—my father was genuinely evil. I don't know what Maxim is, but he's not that.

But now isn't the time to push the issue, so I take the opportunity to change the subject.

"How are things between you and Leo? I'm sorry I haven't been there for you, but I'm always a phone call away."

Her eyes go soft. "We're good. We're really, really good. I never imagined things would work out between us, but Leo makes me so fucking happy. We're planning the wedding, but I don't even care about that. All I care about is the life we're building together." She frowns. "To be honest, the only dark spot in my world has been worrying about you."

"I know, babe." I wrap my best friend, who is also a full head above me, in a tight hug. "But you don't have to worry anymore. I'm okay. I'm better than okay. I'm putting some old demons to rest." Knowing Maxim will use his money and power to find Masha's killer is a huge relief.

She keeps one arm around my shoulders. "Please don't get yourself hurt, crazy lady. You have no idea who or what you're dealing with."

"I won't," I promise, sincerely hoping I can keep my word. And then I take a chance. "Will you stay for tea? I think it would be good for us all to talk."

Aly twists her lips. "If it's important to you, I will, but I'm not ready to have a relationship with Maxim."

"I get it." I squeeze Aly's hand. "Just tea for now."

Chapter Twenty-Nine

KIRA

Rolling out the pelmeni dough is proving more challenging than I remember. Each push and pull seem to leave it lumpier than before. I glance around the unfamiliar kitchen, trying to find a better rolling pin or perhaps the bottom of a big jar to flatten the bunched-up edges. It's what I remember my aunt doing.

The penthouse kitchen has no amenities, other than the ones I asked Maxim's men to deliver to me when I got a hankering for pelmeni—small, meat-filled dumplings—earlier this evening. The truth is, they were my aunt's favorite dish—the only one she could make—and she taught me how to prepare them. I'm not a skilled cook, but making them always makes me feel closer to her.

I lift a small piece of dough and hold it up to the light. Not thin enough. A sigh escapes my lips as I brush a stray strand of hair from my face and attack the dough with a renewed vigor.

"What did that dough ever do to you?" That voice. Smooth with a rough edge. Deep. Commanding.

My nipples instantly stand at attention. I glance up to see him positioned against the breakfast bar opposite me. He's loosening his tie and shedding his cufflinks. His suit jacket is discarded carelessly onto a stool next to him. Leaning forward, his intense gaze captures mine, making my breath catch.

After Alyona and my brothers left, Maxim locked himself in his office with his men. He's been barking orders into the phone all day and I've mostly steered clear of him, spending the rest of the day in bed, reading. It was hard to say goodbye to my family, and emotion still roils around in my chest.

When will I see them next? Do they feel like I picked Maxim over them? I did what I had to do, what I felt was best, and I hope they can see it that way.

"It's not cooperating." I pout.

Maxim might have been caught up in meetings all day, but it doesn't diminish how delectable he looks. Rolling up his sleeves, he unveils strong, corded forearms. "Like what you see?" he asks, falling in line beside me.

"Would you believe me if I denied it?"

He chuckles, gently taking the roller from me. "Let me give it a shot," he murmurs.

"What do you know about making pelmeni?"

"A little bit," he admits, smoothing out the dough far more easily than I managed. "My grandmother raised me. I spent most of my boyhood in her kitchen."

I freeze, hand halfway to a dish towel. My thoughts drift to that photo I found of a young Maxim. Plump cheeks. Bright eyes. He looked happy. Innocent. Although, peeking at him right now, he's not the intimidating crime lord, just a man with soft eyes, kneading pelmeni dough.

"Tell me about your grandmother," I say, hopping on a stool beside him.

"She was actually quite stern." He chuckles. "You wouldn't call her a soft woman, but then again, few of her generation could afford to be. The only way they could get through life was by being hard. She was the only constant parental figure in my life. And she did teach me how to make a solid pelmeni." He pauses for a moment, reaching for the bowl of minced meat mixture that I prepared earlier.

I watch him take a small portion, placing it in the center of a dough circle and then folding it over before pressing the edges together to seal the filling inside.

"If the whole business-oligarch thing doesn't work out, maybe there's a career for you in the culinary arts."

His eyebrows raise, and he huffs out a laugh. "Something to consider."

Handing me some dough, we work side by side, stuffing each dumpling, making sure not to overfill them so they don't explode when they boil.

"Where was your father? You said he was sometimes around." It may not be my place to ask, but curiosity gets the best of me.

His face drops at the mention of him, his features settling back into their usual sternness. "My father was in and out of my life, but he lived hard and didn't take an interest in me until I was old enough to train as an underground fighter."

"Oh. Is that how you met Oleg?"

"It is. He noticed me in the underground circuit when I was fifteen. Saw an opportunity to make money. He'd bet on my fights and after a while, he decided to bring me on jobs as the muscle. I learned early on what kind of man Oleg was. The last job I went on with him was to collect payment on some guy in his debt. We went to his house that night, but he wasn't there. His family was." Maxim shakes his head and curls his lips in disgust. "Let's just say, Oleg took his pound of flesh from the man's wife and kids." My stomach turns at the mention of my sadistic father. "That was the last job I ever worked for your father. I cut ties with him as soon as I could."

I shrug sadly. "You won't hear any arguments from me. He literally ripped me from my mother's arms at birth and stole me away. Not because he wanted to raise me, but because he wanted to ruin the Kozlovs. And he nearly did. My mother killed herself not long after he took me away." Ragged emotion clogs my throat. It's a while before I can speak again. "I never got to meet her."

"I'm sorry, lastochka," Maxim murmurs, his fingers tenderly tracing the contours of my neck as he holds my gaze. "But you got your revenge. You should be proud of taking him down." His words are laced with unmistakable pride, and his eyes shine with genuine affection.

A wave of emotions floods my heart, leaving it pounding fiercely.

Plus, he's giving me a once-over. Probably has something to do with his dress shirt I have on, and the fact that I'm wearing nothing else.

He sucks air through his teeth, eyebrows pinching. "You look good in my clothes."

"Then why do you look so annoyed?" I tease.

"What are you wearing under there?"

I look down, catching my breasts moving freely under the fabric, and feeling the cool air flit between my legs and over my bare pussy. "Nothing."

His eyes darken. "Are you telling me you've been walking around the suite dressed in nothing but my shirt?"

I sense I'm in trouble, so I choose my words carefully. "I haven't been walking around. I've been cooking!"

He exhales sharply through his nose. "If any of my men saw a glimpse of bare legs, there would be hell to pay. Do you want to know what I'd do to you?"

I clear my throat under his intense gaze. "No."

"Maybe I'll show you."

"But we need to finish the pelmeni," I argue weakly.

"Do you remember how I spanked you last night? I would tip you over my knees and do the same thing with my belt." His voice slides over the words, thick with lust.

I blush, aware of my arousal coating my inner thighs. "Just for wearing your shirt?"

"For wearing *just* my shirt in front of my men. If they saw anything ..." He swears under his breath. "I'd have to kill them. Slowly. *Painfully*."

"I'm hardly naked!" I protest, but it falls on deaf ears. "I haven't seen another living soul since you wandered in here! Konstantin texted to let me know the items I asked for were waiting in the kitchen."

"Let this be a warning to you. Don't wander around naked again. Konstantin is one of my best—it would be a shame to lose him." He glances up at me, a hint of amusement playing on his lips.

"Jeez, caveman much?"

His gaze travels down my form, deepening in intensity with every inch it takes in. "Believe me, I meant every word. This" — he motions to my body — "belongs to me."

"Agree to disagree." I sidestep behind him, cranking up the stove's heat to bring the water to a boil while dodging his intense stare.

I hear him rinsing his hands under the tap, and then suddenly, his arms encircle me from behind, pulling me tight against the warmth and hardness of his body.

God, he feels incredible.

He wraps his arms around me, his hands gently cupping my breasts over the fabric of his dress shirt as he presses his hips upwards into mine. Looking down, I notice his defined muscles in his forearms. His chafed fighter's knuckles. He embodies raw, primal masculinity. I feel small and delicate beside him.

"Do I need to mark you? Tattoo you with my name so the world knows that this is my property?"

"Absolutely not," I bite back, preparing for a fight.

The power behind my words is lessened when one of his hands dives between my legs. He finds me wet for him, and he groans into my neck while stuffing me with his fingers. I look down to watch them move against me, so excited by the sight.

So much for playing coy.

When my head tips back and makes contact with his hard chest, it's like a switch flips inside him. His free hand winds around my neck as his lips graze my ear.

"Agree to disagree," he mocks me.

The warmth of his large palm ignites a fiery sensation between my legs. How could I deny how turned on I am now? There's no question he can feel my slickness, his hand coated in it.

How am I going to survive this man?

"The water is boiling," I choke out.

"So it is." His fingers move inside me with a newfound urgency, vigorous and demanding, each contact with my clit making me thrash against him. "Do you belong to me?" he demands.

The boldness of his question catches me off guard. My breaths are hard puffs of air, pleasure making me drunk.

"The pelmeni—"

"Will be fine." He pulls his fingers out of me for a moment and swirls them against my clit. His hard cock pulses against my back.

"Please," I beg, teetering on the edge of an intense climax, so close it's almost within my grasp.

"Answer me," he repeats, easing off a bit.

I shake my head. I want to hold back. I really do, but Maxim is like a freaking magician, those clever fingers of his delving inside of me, only to come back out, circling and rubbing my clit, and driving me half out of my mind before filling me up again. I'm writhing against his fingers, my head thrown back, chasing an orgasm I can no longer deny.

Then nothing. He pulls his fingers out, leaving me empty.

No, no, no. That will not do.

"Yes, Maxim. Yes, I'm yours. Now please, make me come!"

He grunts and brings his fingers back where I need them most. "Come on my fingers, lastochka." He sucks at my neck, the pain a counterbalance to the pleasure blooming between my legs. "Such a good girl. You're made for me."

As the orgasm hits, a loud cry bursts from me, the sheer intensity of it taking over. My hips jerk, riding the wave of pleasure, while his lips leave a path of searing kisses down my throat.

"And guess what?" he whispers. "I'm made for you too."

I nearly jump out of my skin when he slaps my ass with his open palm.

"Never deny me again." He turns around and drops the pelmeni in the boiling water like he didn't just break me into a million pieces.

Chapter Thirty

MAXIM

I'm so full." Kira moans as she drags the last dumpling on her plate through the remnants of sour cream and pops it between her luscious lips, her eyes fluttering shut in satisfaction.

"They are excellent," I say, unable to tear my eyes away when her tongue darts out the side of her mouth, chasing a dollop of sour cream.

Good God, that mouth. I haven't yet had the pleasure of seeing her lips wrapped around my cock, but damn, I'm ready.

Her eyes flutter open, shining with contentment, and something in me softens.

"I know it's good. It's my aunt's recipe. Literally the only thing that woman was able to cook."

At Kira's suggestion, we settled on the floor near the coffee table to eat. With the meal over, I shift back onto the couch, drawing her with me so she nestles against my front. She sighs happily against my body, and a slow realization hits—I like having her close.

"I can't imagine Masha cooking," I admit, testing the waters of discussing her aunt in life, not in death.

Kira is quiet for a while, drawing circles on my wrist, before she finally responds, "How well did you know her?

"Not all that well. She was an acquaintance." I shrug. "You know how it is in Moscow—we ran in some of the same circles. We'd bump into each other at parties and such. I remember her swanning around the room in bright dresses and cornering any minister whose policies she disagreed with. She was fearless. That's why when we first met, I said you remind me of her."

"I remember that," Kira says, her head nestling into my chest. "It was when we were walking in your vineyard a few days after you abducted Alyona and me."

"Are you still bitter about that?" I tease.

"Yes. No. I don't know. I still object to your methods, but if things hadn't played out like they did, I wouldn't be here. And you wouldn't be helping me track down my aunt's killer."

"True," I concede with a nod. "Now, tell me what you remember about your aunt."

"I don't know where to start. My father dumped me in her arms as a newborn, and instead of telling him to go to hell—as I'm sure she wanted to because Masha disliked my father as much as anyone else—she realized if she did, then I would have no fighting chance of a decent future. My father would have left me at the next orphanage without a second thought. He never really wanted me—he wanted to ruin the Kozlovs." She sighs deeply, and I feel it in my chest. "The funny thing is, I'm not sure Masha wanted children. She was made for glamorous parties, runway shows, weekends in Paris, and sailing through the Greek Isles." Her voice carries a hint of a smile. "Still, she raised me with all the love any mother would offer."

"Did your aunt ever reveal the truth about your lineage? About who your mother and brothers really were?" I ask, brushing her hair with my lips.

"No. She either didn't know it herself, or she chose not to tell me because she knew I would confront my father and he wouldn't take kindly to that." She shakes her head "I only discovered the Kozlovs were my brothers when I had a gun pointed at them, demanding they help me bring down my father. You should've seen the shock on their faces. They'd been looking for me all this time."

I kiss her on the head. "I'm glad you found them when you did. You deserve a family that loves you." Kira deserves more than a family that loves her—she deserves a man that worships her, that puts her above all else. If I still had a heart left in my chest, that could be me. Because I see how amazing she is—smart, capable, a fighter. But I'm too broken to give myself to any woman again.

She looks up at me as if she can hear my thoughts. "So do you."

Pain unfurls in my chest. My past is as tragic as hers. The only difference is that I've locked it away, never to be looked at again. "I have my family. They aren't blood relations, but Pavel and Roman are my brothers."

"And you have Alyona," Kira murmurs.

"Alyona is my blood, but I doubt she'll ever consider me her family." I say that with no bitterness. When I discovered I had a daughter, little else mattered. I wanted the best for her, to keep her safe, even if it meant she hated me for a time. I believed she would come around. But now, I'm not so sure.

"Give her time," Kira says gently and then with a sly grin, "Did you really think threatening her would work?"

I shrug. "My methods are persuasive, if not wise." Gathering Kira's hair in my hands, I tilt her head, exposing her neck to me. "Did you honestly believe you would be able to kill me?"

"Yes," she says with absolutely no hesitation.

I kiss up her neck, enjoying the little breathy moans she releases.

"I was going to stab you in your sleep."

I nip her earlobe. "It's like that, huh. What would you have done afterwards? How would you have hidden my body?"

"Uhh, hadn't thought that far," she admits.

Or maybe she has, but my prominent erection digging into her ass might be distracting her. I suck and bite on her neck, loving how she's losing control in my arms.

"That's not much of a plan, lastochka. You would have been killed by my men on the spot. Or worse." Unease presses down on my chest. The thought of Kira hurt or in danger twists my insides.

"I was prepared to die." She turns in my arms, straddles my lap, and starts kissing and licking her way up my neck.

The feel of her soft lips and warm tongue on my skin is a fierce turn-on, but I'm still stuck on what she just said.

I gently pull away from her. "No."

"No?"

"No. I don't care what your reason is, you're not allowed to risk your life again."

Kira looks at me like I've half-lost my mind.

Maybe I have. Because the thought of something bad happening to her feels like a vice tightening around my heart. Which is a problem. Because no matter how she makes me feel, a real marriage is not in the cards for me.

"You can't forbid me to get hurt or die." She reaches up and threads her fingers through my hair before trailing them down my neck, eliciting a groan from me. "These things happen," she adds quietly.

I hold her face so she can't look anywhere else except directly at me. "I can, and I will."

She snorts. "Do you have the grim reaper on your payroll or something?"

"I am the grim reaper," I tell her. Then I grab both of her ass cheeks and pull her flush against my aching length. "Now, get naked so I can make you feel alive."

Her fingers hover over the first button of my shirt when my phone starts to buzz. I manage to resist the urge to answer for a solid minute, but when the caller tries again immediately after hanging up, I know it's urgent.

"What is it?" I snap into the receiver, seeing Pavel's name on the screen.

"The Black Company hit one of our shipments in Vladivostok an hour ago. We're trying to make contact with our men on the scene. So far, no luck."

"*Gavno*," I curse.

This day is back to being a fucking nightmare, just when I thought it was about to get a lot better. I desperately need to taste Kira again, to have her sit on my face while choking on my dick. But that will have to wait.

"I'll call you back from the office," I say to Pavel, then hang up the phone.

"Is everything okay?" Kira raises an eyebrow.

"The usual. More shit I have to deal with." I roll down my sleeves and reach for my suit jacket. "This will take a while."

She nods and sits back on her haunches. "You know, I might be able to help. The Kozlov Bratva has come up against a triad before. I have knowledge about how they work."

I stand, shrugging my suit jacket onto my shoulders. Not much I can do about the raging hard-on. "I know you're smart and capable, but I don't want to get you caught up in my syndicate's drama. Sometimes the less you know, the better."

"Back to this 'delicate lady' act? As if I can't handle more," she scoffs.

I lean forward, brushing my lips softly against hers. "Please, let me protect you from all the bullshit."

She rolls her eyes. "Fine. Guess I'll go back to the room and get myself off tonight since you won't be around to do the job." The look she flashes me is pure evil.

I grip her wrists in one hand and lift her chin with my other. "What did we discuss earlier? Your pussy is mine, and you're not allowed to touch yourself without my permission."

She pouts. "I think that rule is bullshit."

"I'm serious—there will be hell to pay if you touch yourself below the belt tonight. Don't think I won't be watching. There are cameras everywhere," I warn her.

"Or you could let me be part of your meeting. My brothers always did. They valued my opinions. You might too."

I firm my voice. "I do value your opinion, but it's not happening." I know she's capable, but I can't bear the thought of her getting caught up in my tarnished world, even if it's the world she comes from. I want better for her. "I need to go now. Don't disobey me or I'll be forced to take action."

"Again with the spanking? I thought you'd be a little more creative."

Jesus, my wife is a brat.

"I'm plenty creative. Don't test me to see." Kissing her on the head, I leave the room with the distinct feeling that she has no plans to heed my warning.

* * *

"What do we know?" I bark as soon as I enter the office.

Konstantin has already set up a conference call with Roman, Pavel, and Viktor.

Pavel is the first one to speak. "They blew up our transport truck as it was coming out of the port. It only contained empty bottles and labels, but it will put our production behind by at least a week. All three of our men were killed on-site."

My fists clench on the desk in front of me. "How did they find out about our shipment?"

Viktor clears his throat. "One of our port guys was bought out. We found the digital trail showing he tipped off the Black Company about our shipment." There's a pause. "He was killed in a shootout with our soldiers, but we're hacking into his phone to see if we can ID his Black Company contact."

I slam my hand down onto the desk. "Fuck."

I'm already on a short fuse. I should be buried inside Kira's tight little cunt now, not managing this mess.

"I might have something to warm your cold heart," Roman offers.

"What is that?"

"We've captured Leung, the Black Company operative that turned Henri Blanchet. Caught him on the CCTV at Teatralnaya Station and figured out he has a flat nearby. He's being transported to the warehouse as I speak."

"That does warm my heart." I crack my knuckles, grateful that I don't surround myself with total idiots. "Start questioning him tonight. The sooner we know the Black Company's plans, the better. I'll fly back to Moscow tomorrow."

"We're on it," Pavel assures me.

The conversation moves on with Roman and Pavel talking about the measures they're enacting to contain the Black Company's damage, but my mind keeps wandering into the next room.

Is Kira behaving, or is she purposely disobeying me?

I pull out my phone and open the encrypted app that shows me all camera angles in the penthouse suite. It's the first thing we do whenever we're in a new location. At first, I can't locate Kira anywhere in our bedroom, and a small prick of panic builds. But soon enough, I find her luxuriating in the giant tub in the en suite.

I smile. She looks relaxed and comfortable, bubbles up to her neck. She's being a good girl.

As I'm about to put away my phone, something catches my attention. Something about her facial expression, the way her mouth hangs open. When she releases a little gasp, I zoom in closer, but I don't have a good enough angle to see what she's doing.

"Maxim, what's our timeline for that?" Roman's voice carries through the speakerphone.

My head snaps up. I have no idea what he asked me, but I don't bother making him clarify.

"Yesterday," I say.

There's a beat of hesitation, and Roman chuckles. "I see."

My gaze must be scorching the phone as I attempt to decipher Kira's body language. That's when she tosses her head back, a display of obvious pleasure. That isn't the expression of a woman luxuriating in a hot bath; it's the look of a woman touching what's mine.

There's shit to do. Serious matters to take care of. I shouldn't be pulled into Kira's little game, but I can't fucking help it.

Slipping the phone into my pocket, I stand and announce, "There's a situation that needs my immediate attention."

Stalking out of the room, I make a beeline for the bathroom. Throwing the door open without knocking, I find Kira looking straight at me, mischief in her gaze and no hands in sight.

"What are you doing?" I ask deceptively casually, leaning a shoulder against the doorframe.

"Taking a bath." Her eyes close, and she lets out a little moan. "What does it look like?"

"It looks like you're disobeying me, lastochka."

A slow grin builds on her face. "I'm not using my fingers. I'm using the water jets. I don't believe you specified that that wasn't allowed."

"All of your orgasms are mine to give or deny. Maybe I should have made myself clearer."

"Why would you deny me?" Her adorable eyebrows knit together. "Are you going to spank me again?"

"You're about to find out." I stalk over to her, stripping off my jacket, tie, and dress shirt, dropping them on the ground as I walk. I let her enjoy the view, drinking me in.

Bending so my lips are right by her ear, I say, "You're a greedy girl. You already came once tonight, but I see that wasn't enough."

Her eyes are wide, watching me as I slowly dip my hand under the water. Her rapt gaze gives me a little thrill.

"Have you been playing with my pussy?"

She nods, not looking the tiniest bit contrite.

"Spread your legs," I demand.

She does, but it's not enough.

"More," I say, slapping the inside of her thigh. My fingertips brush between her legs, my breath warming the skin of her neck. I sweep my thumb between her slick folds until I find her clit, circling it with an expert touch, allowing her a taste of pleasure.

"Is that nice?" I whisper.

"Yes," she breathes, her eyes closed.

My lips ghost over hers before I suck in her bottom lip. I give it a little tug with my teeth, and a copper taste fills my mouth. She cries out, digging her fingers into my shoulders, releasing a moan into my mouth as I lap up the blood from her lips.

She's close, I can tell. But I'm not going to make this easy for her. I keep stroking her clit under the water and plundering her mouth with my tongue.

"I need to taste you again. Don't you remember how good it feels with my tongue buried inside of you?"

She doesn't answer, just squirms, chasing her orgasm on my fingers. Her hips writhe under the water as her orgasm builds. It's going to happen soon.

I pull my hand out of the tub and sit back, watching her eyes shoot open, and she looks at me like I've stolen the last piece of her favorite candy.

"Noooo. I was so close," she breathes.

"I told you, baby, your orgasms are mine to bestow or deny. And I've decided to deny you."

"Why would you do that?"

"I think you know why. Now, out of the tub," I order.

She tips her chin up in defiance, and for a moment I think she's going to challenge me, but for once she doesn't push the issue. She stands up straight, water sluicing down her body, between her full breasts with perfectly pink nipples, continuing to her curved stomach and juicy thighs. I have to adjust my rapidly hardening cock.

The way she stands there with a self-satisfied smile, allowing me to drink in every inch of her, reminds me of the night I doused her in ice water and made her change in front of me. That clearly didn't teach her a lesson about disobeying me, but I hope this does.

"Dry yourself, and get on the bed," I rasp.

She grabs a towel, quickly passing it over every inch of pale, smooth skin. I'd love to see it covered in my bite marks, but that can wait. Tonight is about teaching her a lesson.

She lies down on the mattress, watching me with big, curious eyes as I reach for a few of my silk ties resting on the nightstand. First, I bind her wrists together above her head. Then I tie a quick, tight knot around one ankle and then stretch the tie to the corresponding bedpost, looping it multiple times before securing it with a tight knot. I repeat the same action with the other ankle.

I step back to check my handiwork, my breaths coming out in ragged pants as I take her in, spread-eagle, the view of her dripping cunt nearly making me come in my pants.

Does she know how every little thing about her turns me on? Kira is a fascinating mix of vulnerable and confident, seductive and innocent. Which makes me wonder something.

Positioning myself between her thighs, I ease down until my abdomen presses against the bed. "How many men have touched this?" I ask, trailing a finger over her slit.

She shivers. "What do you mean?"

"How many men have touched what's mine?"

Instead of responding, she makes a futile attempt to roll aside before realizing escape is not an option.

"Kira," I say in warning.

"I ... I don't know. I don't keep track of shit like that."

"Good. Forget anyone who came before me. Your body is Belov property now, and no one dares mess with what's mine."

I push my shoulders under her thighs, bringing her up to my mouth and plunging my tongue in her cunt, feasting like a starved man. I don't have it in me to go slow. In fact, if I was on death row, Kira's pussy would be my last meal request.

She closes her eyes and throws her head back with a sigh. The look of intense pleasure on her face is perfect.

"No one has ever done this to you before, have they?" I ask between swiping my tongue over her beautiful clit.

"You did, the other day." She can barely get the words out. They spill from her lips stilted and breathless.

"And I was your first," I clarify, flicking and circling her clit with my tongue.

"No. But the only one worth remembering." She cries out, clearly done with this conversation.

"Good," is that last thing I say before I go absolutely feral on her. Sucking her clit into my mouth with long, gentle pulls and plunging two fingers, palm up, into her sweet pussy, curling them in a come-hither motion, stimulating her G-spot so she loses complete control.

"Holy shit, Maxim." Kira shudders, and she thrashes at her restraints.

She's about to come. I can feel how ready she is, but I won't allow it.

I run my tongue between her folds a final time, savoring the taste of her pussy. Then, I pull away.

Chapter Thirty-One

KIRA

I'm so close, so very close. I'm not sure what kind of punishment this is—death by a thousand near-orgasms—but I'm not against it. Not when Maxim can make me feel so good. His tongue, his fingers, even watching him bob up and down between my legs, his mouth slick with my wetness... It's perfect. It's perfect, and I'm so close, and... Oh, shit, I'm going to—

Nothing. Because Maxim pulled away from me.

"No." I thrash about. "No, no, no! Maxim..." My hoarse voice betrays how desperate I am. "I need to come." I'm sure my eyes are blazing with fire as I look down at Maxim, still between my legs, his mouth glazed.

He's panting hard, and he looks as pained as I feel. "This is your punishment. Do you know what edging is?"

My lust-addled brain takes a moment to process his words. "Like ... orgasm denial?"

"Something like that." He blows on my overly sensitive clit, and I release a little whimper.

"That's cruel!" I argue.

He chuckles at that. "Consider it a lesson. I warned you, Kira. But you didn't listen. Next time, you will."

I stare down at him in horror.

With that, he goes back to laving me softly. A slow build-up. He doesn't use his fingers this time—he drags his hot tongue from my clit to my opening and back again. Usually, it wouldn't be enough to take me over the edge, but I'm so damn sensitive right now. It's like anything can set me off. But as soon as I come close to the edge, he pulls away and starts the process all over again.

My God, this man is going to be the death of me.

He does it again and again until I am a shaking, sobbing mess. Even when he's just fucking me with his tongue, no clit stimulation, I'm still seconds from coming. And it's so damn much. Too much. I can't hear, I can't think, can't feel anything beyond the blinding haze of lust.

As if Maxim knows exactly what he's done to me, he crawls over my body and kisses away the tears that pepper my face. "Shhh, my lastochka. You did so well. I'm going to reward you now."

His tongue finds its way into my mouth as he kisses away all my hurts. His mouth is covered in my juice, and I find the taste of us together intoxicating. The flavor of Maxim is deep, rich, and smoky with my own sweetness layered in.

I'm not even fully aware of what's happening when he undoes the belt that binds my wrist and then moves on to untie each of my legs. I'm still in a daze as he stands beside the bed and strips off his pants, followed by his boxer briefs.

My breath catches in my throat as I drink him in. Because damn, the view of Maxim naked is edging in its own right. His body is cut and powerful, like a work of art, honed in the boxing ring. My gaze travels down his form, from the solid muscles of his biceps, over the defined ridges of his abs, and finally rests on his impressive cock hanging heavily between his legs.

My mouth goes dry. His cock is glorious. Big and perfectly angled with an upward curve. And it's all for me.

Aware of my burning stare, he gives me a sly grin and lowers his hand to his cock, giving it a few lazy pumps, precum glistening on the head. It's so damn sexy I release a whimper.

"Is this what you need, wife?"

I nod furiously, fearful he's going to edge me some more. I couldn't take it if he did. I'd self-destruct.

Sensing my desperation, he joins me on the bed. He plants a single kiss on my lips, then positions himself sitting up against the headboard, lacing his fingers together, his head resting back in his hands.

"Use my cock, baby. It's yours. You've earned full control for being such a good girl."

I straddle his thighs, our mouths coming together. My nerve endings come alive as his hands drift over my skin, which seems to be everywhere all at once.

"No touching," I whisper. "I'm in control now."

The ghost of his earlier touch still pulses between my legs. I lift her hips so my pussy rubs against his length, from the base to the tip. He lets out a strangled groan.

I grin. "You're not the only one who knows how to tease, husband."

He wears a smug expression, his hands tucked behind his head. "Is that so?"

I circle my hips, suspended over him for a few interminable seconds. Even though I'm dying to lower myself onto his thick length, I want to torture him like he tortured me.

"Taste me," I breathe, presenting my breasts to his mouth.

His eyes flash with heat before he leans in and takes a nipple into his mouth, tugging on the tip and sucking it deeper. I whimper, unable to keep my eyes open as the sensation of his lips sends a fiery pulse low in my belly. Blood rushes to my head. I feel delirious with want. No, *need*.

I can feel how soaked I am as I continue to grind on him, rolling my ass over the ridge of his hard-as-steel cock, covering him in my juices. I'm panting, but I refuse to take him inside of me before giving him a taste of his own medicine.

"Kira," Maxim growls in warning. He's holding his jaw tight like it's costing him everything to hold back.

"It's only fair," I rasp.

I circle my hips once more and then freeze, realizing my pussy is hovering over his tip.

Our eyes lock, tension thick, as I lower an inch, his head pressing at my entrance. He snarls, his breathing ragged and deep, each inhale and exhale pronounced as he looks up at me with a fierce glare.

I can't take it anymore. I need Maxim inside of me like I need my next breath.

Lowering myself, the crown of his dick breaches my entrance. As I sink down further, I'm deliciously stretched, the feeling so intense that my nails dig into his shoulders once I'm fully seated. He brushes the hair out of my face as I slowly lift and descend on his shaft, getting used to the stretch. My mouth opens in a silent cry, and he uses the opportunity to slide his tongue between my lips.

Just like that, I'm lost in the fullness and intensity, the feverish sensation dancing and flaring within my veins. This feels like nothing in my past, nothing I could have ever imagined. I don't know if it's because of the weeks of simmering sexual tension or if his dick is really that good, but I'm lost to the feeling of him inside of me. Filling me to the brim while he kneads my tits and sucks at my neck.

I had no idea sex could feel like this. All-consuming, a combustive mix of explosives.

His mouth is my weakness. Warm and inviting, his tongue dances with mine, flicking and teasing in ways that leave me breathless. Rising onto my knees, I press my body tightly to his. I pant, winding my arms around his neck to pull him as close as possible. I like this position for that very reason. He groans and grabs a handful of my ass, squeezing my cheeks and forcing me down harder and faster on his cock.

So much for me being in control. He's possessive, using me like a fuck toy, and it's everything I never knew I wanted. But holy moly, it *is* what I want.

"God, Kira. Your pussy is as hot and perfect as I knew it would be. It was made for me." He slaps my ass with no mercy and pulls my hair.

The delicious bite of pain liquefies every nerve inside of me. I'm already teetering on the edge, my orgasm building so hot and fast after Maxim edged me to my breaking point. And now, as I writhe on his hard length, my control is a hairpin away from snapping.

"I am so close," I pant into his mouth.

His voice is a rough tumble as it vibrates against my skin. "Yes, lastochka, that's it. This cock is all yours."

His lips travel down to the base of my throat, and he nips the skin before sliding a rough hand between us, his fingers circling my clit with expert precision. Pleasure rushes to my core like a tidal wave, and I scream—yes, scream—against his neck as I let go entirely. It's the hardest orgasm of my life.

"Good girl. You gripped me so tight, and now I'm going to spray your pussy's walls with my cum."

His body tenses as he roars into my neck, and liquid heat fills my insides.

My eyes close as I will this moment to stretch. Both of us are still. Maxim's face is pressed into the crook of my neck, and my fingers rake through his thick hair. It feels right. Us together, how he's holding me so tight against his chest as we float down from the clouds.

When I finally lift myself off his lap, his seed spills down my legs. I shuffle over, needing to clean myself up in the bathroom, but Maxim stops me with a hand on my hip.

"Maxim," I plead. I gesture down to my body. Naked and dripping with his cum.

"Wait." He reaches out and swipes a finger along the inner seam of my thighs, coated with his release. "Open," he commands.

I do as he asks, our combined tastes mingling on my tongue. There's no denying we taste good together.

"I didn't have the pleasure yet of watching you choke on my cock and lap up my cum, but trust me, that will happen soon."

A frisson of excitement works through me. The idea of being on my knees for him makes the thought of giving a blowjob more erotic than I imagined. "I'll hold you to that," I promise.

Making my way to the bathroom, the pressing realization that I'm not on birth control hits me. He released a flood of cum inside of me. It's not like I was in my right mind. When he brought me to the edge continuously like that, all rational thought was swept away.

Wiping the dampness between my legs, I do the rough math in my head. I'm on day seventeen of my cycle. Not totally in the clear, but my periods are super regular, and it's far enough from ovulation that I think I'm alright. Since I won't be fertile for another month, maybe I can keep on enjoying Maxim bare, for as long as we're together.

Except ... Maxim doesn't want me to get on the pill. He wants me to bear his heirs. Or at least, that's what he wanted not too long ago. I have no idea where we stand now.

Maxim is sprawled on his back, head under his hands, as I come back to the bedroom. His eyes track me as I approach the edge of the bed, not sure what we're supposed to do now. Beyond the sex, I don't know what we are. The past few days have been chaotic. I haven't had a chance to overthink, but now... I bite my bottom lip.

Maxim grins at me. "What's on your mind? I can practically see the gears turning."

His large hand encircles my wrist, drawing me towards him until I collapse against his chest. His powerful arms wrap around me, holding me close. I tilt my head up to look at him, drinking in his distinct profile in the dim light. He might not have aristocratic blood, but his features are regal. Sharp nose, chiseled cheekbones, lips that curl just right.

"What am I to you?" I ask.

He shakes his head, locking eyes with me. "You're my wife."

"Yes, but we both know it's not real. Or forever."

His expression hardens. "While you wear my ring, we are as real as it gets."

"While I wear your ring?" I tuck a stand of hair behind my ears, not understanding why this conversation feels so fraught. "What exactly is the time frame we're looking at?"

The soft sound of Maxim's sigh travels through his chest. "You married me to avenge your aunt's death, and I married you to distract the press and keep Alyona in my world, however misguided that seems to me now. But after that..." He drifts off.

"But after that, we go our separate ways?"

He pauses, blows out a heavy breath. "I tried marriage

once. It's not an experience I'd like to repeat." He shifts to get a better look at me. "We still need to find your aunt's killer, and I'm at war with the Black Company—you're still needed by my side."

"Good. Great," I say with forced enthusiasm. I smile and soften against him, allowing my head to fall into the crook of his neck so I don't have to look him in the eyes as a weight settles over my heart.

I should be thrilled that he's helping me find Masha's killers and then allowing me to get on with my life, but for some reason, it feels like a lead ball in the pit of my stomach.

Chapter Thirty-Two

MAXIM

We've been back in Moscow for a few days. My return has been a whirlwind of meetings and strategy sessions, tackling the threat posed by the Black Company and overseeing my legitimate businesses.

Work consumes my days, but Kira owns my nights. The restless energy coursing through my veins finds release in her body. I've never experienced anything this intense and all-consuming, and that unnerves me. With each passing day, the fear creeps in—a fear rooted in a past where opening my heart led to a betrayal so profound, it cost me everything.

A knock on my office door pulls me out of my thoughts. "Come in," I say, adjusting my tie.

Viktor steps inside, tall and imposing, his military training evident in his posture. "You wanted to see me?"

"Did you get anything from Leung last night?"

We've been working over Leung, the Black Company operative in our dungeon. But even after a few days of brutal questioning, he isn't talking. *Yet.*

Viktor's frown deepens, displaying more emotion than he usually allows himself to show. "We've pushed him hard. He's been trained to resist—that much is clear."

I grunt, my frustration mounting. Viktor, Pavel, Roman, and I have taken turns torturing Leung, but the guy's a fortress. Somewhere in there, though, is a weak spot. We need to find it before the Black Company makes their next move.

"Try the electrodes on his feet again. He wasn't fond of that method."

"We will. We've been working around the clock—"

"Then make time stop," I cut him off, my words like cold steel. "I want the Black Company gone. Erased. When they targeted my wife, they signed their death warrant." I pause, letting the gravity of my words weigh heavily in the silence.

Viktor grunts in acknowledgement and takes his leave. He knows the stakes.

A familiar heaviness settles in my chest because no matter which way I look at it, violence is inevitable.

Things with the Black Company are reaching a boiling point, and the thought of Kira getting harmed because of me, like Ilya was, feels like an invisible band constricting around my lungs. Which is why she's not allowed to leave the estate for the time being. She gets it, but she's definitely not thrilled about having her movements restricted.

The only good thing to come out of the Black Company attack in New York was the opportunity to see Alyona. I don't know what Kira said to her when they were alone, but Alyona seemed to thaw a bit towards me afterwards. I can't say the same for the rest of the Kozlovs, but at least the lines of communication with them are open. They're aware of the need to increase security as the Black Company situation escalates, and knowing that the Kozlovs are vigilant in protecting Aly lifts a weight off my shoulders.

I rise from my desk, reaching for the vodka bottle I keep in the fridge in the corner of the room. The clear liquid flows smoothly into my glass. Taking a deep breath, I make my way to the window, a chill seeping through the panes. Below, the landscape is a mosaic of barren trees and fallen leaves. I take a sip, the vodka's bite mirroring the sting of the cold outside.

"Meditating on the meaning of life?"

My head whips around to find Pavel strolling into my office, an envelope in hand.

"Something like that," I say, lifting my glass of vodka.

Pavel holds up the manila envelope and places it onto my desk. "I've brought you something you'll want to see."

Abandoning my drink to the windowsill, I sink back behind my desk and snatch up the envelope. "Why don't you give me the Coles Notes version. I take it this is about Masha?"

When I was in New York, I asked Pavel to look into Kira's aunt's death because he's one of the few people in this world I trust implicitly. He hasn't bothered to hide the fact that he thinks I'm balls-on crazy for digging into something that is far in the past. Under normal circumstances, I would agree—we have enough important shit to focus on—except, when it comes to Kira, there's nothing I wouldn't do.

Maybe that makes me weak. I've spent most of my life keeping people at arm's length. Just this once, I'll bend my own rules. Knowing it's temporary. It can't be anything more.

Pavel fixes me with that intense dark stare of his, rolling his shoulders back. Dressed in a starched white shirt with the sleeves rolled up, he could pass for an accountant off to crunch numbers in a boardroom, especially wearing those glasses he reserves for office work. It's the snaking tattoos underneath his suit that reveal a different side of him. And the fact that he's unhinged. He's as straight as an arrow, deeply disciplined, until he's pushed too far like a taut string that has no more give. Then, he turns into a total psychopath.

"Very well." He sits down in the chair across from me. "The monogrammed Zippo Irina gifted to you on your second wedding anniversary was somehow at the scene where Masha was killed."

I furrow my brow. "How is this possible?" I eradicated every item tied to Irina's memory in the aftermath. That lighter should be lying at the bottom of some landfill, never to see the light of day again.

He leans forward, resting his elbows on his knees. "I'd like to know that too."

I tear the envelope open. Inside it, there are a series of glossy photos. The first few are of Masha, her lifeless eyes staring blankly, crimson staining the concrete beneath her mutilated body. Each subsequent image reveals more gruesome details of her torture and murder—the handiwork of a trained killer.

My stomach twists. Scenes like this don't sicken me—I've done much worse to people before—but to know that these are the same pictures sent to Kira after her aunt's murder is what burns. These are the images that haunt her nightmares.

There, amid the chaos of the scene but almost out of frame, lies my Zippo, or at least a damn good replica. I remember every intricate detail of its design—the way it felt heavy in my palm, the unique etchings of thorns and roses that Irina had custom-engraved with my initials.

I look up at Pavel, clenching the photographs so hard that the edges crumple in my grip. "Someone tried to frame me. There is no other reasonable explanation."

He shrugs. "If so, they didn't do a very good job of it. No one's come for you. You haven't been arrested, not that the police got wind of this murder. But we didn't even know about the rumors before Kira blabbed about her encounter with Boris. I'm just saying if someone tried to frame you, they pretty much failed."

I rub the back of my neck. "It doesn't mean we can ignore this. If anything, it could help us figure out who's really behind Masha's death."

"I agree." Pavel stands and collects the photos off my desk, organizes them into a neat pile, and places them back into the envelope. "But let this be my worry. I'll figure it out. You have bigger things to focus on."

I pinch the bridge of my nose. "You think I don't know that? It's been days, and we haven't gotten Leung to talk. I can fucking feel the Black Company breathing down my neck."

"This can wait." Pavel holds up the envelope to make his point. "Shit with the Black Company can't."

I shake my head. To Kira, Masha's death was far from insignificant. It's a wound that's never healed, a rawness she carries every day. I hate that, for the last four years, she's been tortured by the endless nights of grief and unanswered questions.

"I promised my wife," I say simply. "This is as much a priority as the Black Company."

Another thought occurs to me. Kira's hungry for something meaningful. She's a force in her own right, and it's time I acknowledged that.

"We haven't been able to break Leung yet. Our methods aren't working. I want to give Kira a chance to question him."

"Are you serious?" Pavel bangs his hand on the table. "You're going to trust a wild card like Kira? We barely know where her loyalties lie."

I shoot out of my seat. "*You are* confused about where her loyalties lie. I'm as clear as day." Pavel didn't trust Kira from the start, and in all fairness, his instincts were right. She did have an ulterior motive for our marriage. But things have changed. "When I first married her, you told me not to underestimate Kira. I'm asking the same of you now."

He scoffs. "I meant, don't underestimate her capability to murder you, not involve her in our syndicate's business. You're losing focus on what's important, and we can't afford any screw-ups right now." He shakes his head, not bothering to hide his frustration. "What's your endgame here? A real marriage? Kids? A life together? After Irina—after everything—you want to go down that same path?"

“I don’t know what I fucking want!” I growl and hurtle a lamp from my desk across the room. My chest heaves as the truth of my words settles in my veins.

All I know is that I can’t stay away from Kira. Not since she bared her soul and fell apart in my arms. If I’m truthful, the moment I laid eyes on her, my world spun on its axis and it hasn’t yet righted. But it doesn't mean we can make this real.

Emptiness gnaws at me at the thought of letting her go, but Pavel is right. Sometime soon, the terms of our arrangement will be satisfied, and then what? Walking away from her will damn well hurt, but how can I keep her? Because you can’t love someone when you no longer have a heart beating in your chest.

Pavel runs a thumb down the centerline of his lips. “Well, you better figure it out because we don’t have time to waste.”

“I don’t answer to you.”

“That’s fucking right—you don’t. But you know I have your best interests at heart.”

I busy myself by pouring another shot of vodka so I don’t have to make eye contact with my second-in-command. *My friend.*

He gives me one last hard stare before heading towards the door.

"Pavel," I call after him, my voice firm. "I'll end things when it's time." I'm not sure who I'm trying to convince—him or me.

His final look is one that says, *Keep telling yourself that, buddy*.

As the door closes behind him, the quiet click echoes like a period at the end of a damning sentence.

Chapter Thirty-Three

KIRA

Liza looks at me as if I've sprouted two heads, and from her viewpoint, it probably does seem that way. I've filled her in on the whirlwind of events that took place in New York. A week ago I was planning on killing Maxim, and now I can't keep my hands off him.

"It's a lot to digest," Liza says, sitting back and running a hand down her cheek.

"It is," I agree. I pick up a fiery-red nail polish from the table in front of us. "Do you think this color complements my skin tone?"

"Forget your skin tone," Liza snatches the bottle I'm examining and sets it down firmly between us. "I'm still wrapping my head around the fact that you followed Maxim to an underground fight in New York, accused him of murdering your aunt, and instead of killing you on the spot, he... well, you know what," she says, reddening slightly. "And then he promised to help you track down the real killer."

I let out a heavy sigh, leaning my elbows on the table cluttered with Liza's assortment of nail polishes and the latest issues of *Architectural Digest*. She's spending the day with me, catching up and helping me brainstorm interior design ideas. Much to Nadya's dismay, I've started to redecorate Irina's old sitting room to give myself purpose before I go out of my mind with boredom. With Maxim constantly working and at war with the Black Company, leaving the estate isn't really an option, so having a visitor is a welcome change.

"I know it sounds insane, but it's true. He's already begun the process of hunting down Masha's killer."

I've given Maxim all I could to help—my aunt's diary, a list of her contemporaries, and any other details and memories that might be relevant. The horrific images of her lifeless body and the menacing letter I received were burned long ago, but I described everything I could recall from them, the haunting visuals forever etched in my memory. It was hard to go there, but Maxim held my hand and talked me through it, not allowing me to slip down the dark rabbit hole of guilt and despair.

The fact that he's making finding Masha's killer a priority with everything else he has going on means something to me.

"And you're ... physical?"

I arch an eyebrow. No point in mincing words. "Very."

She smirks. "That certainly explains your glow."

"What are you talking about?" I bring my hand to my face. I'm not glowing.

"You seem, I dunno, happy. Relaxed."

I shrug, attempting to pull off a casual gesture. "The sex is good. It's been a while since I've been with a man who knows what he's doing."

"So what happens from here?" Her eyes widen to the size of saucers. "Does he still expect an heir?"

I pause in thought, examining an eggshell-blue nail polish. "I ... I don't think so. This is still an arrangement. It's not like we have feelings for each other." I bite my lip and avoid Liza's probing gaze because I don't want her to see the truth I can barely admit to myself. Maxim has burrowed under my skin. I've let myself get wrapped up in him.

It started in the mayor's basement when he broke the man's hand in my defense. He kicked a flight attendant off a plane mid-flight, and he didn't hesitate for a moment to try and save my life at the wine auction. But maybe I'm reading too much into his actions.

Maxim is still a mystery. He's opened up a little about his past, but there's something else he's guarding. A hurt he holds close to his heart. I assume it has to do with Irina. But with everything that's happening, he's been working so hard. When he does fall into bed beside me at night, I hardly want to bring up his past. It's none of my business, and I want him to take comfort in my arms, like I take comfort in his.

"Masha would love this blue color," I say, hoping to distract Liza from asking more questions I don't know how to answer.

"She definitely would," she agrees. "Edgy but still glamorous. It suits you." She takes the bottle of nail polish from me and gestures for me to lay my hand flat on the table, and I comply. "So, where's your shadow? I'm used to Roman always lurking around."

I have to hide my smile. For a girl who can't stand the man, she seems surprisingly curious about him.

"I don't need him by my side in the house. Only when I leave here, which won't be happening for a while." I stretch out my hand, watching as she applies the polish with smooth, careful strokes.

"By the way, I have those birth control pills you asked for. I'll drop them off tomorrow. Sorry it took so long to get them. I had to be careful so Anatoly didn't find out about it since me being a virgin is part of his deal with my parents." She sticks her finger down her throat, and I couldn't agree more.

"Thank you," I say with genuine gratitude. "You got it just in time. I'm expecting my period soon, but after that, I'll need to get on birth control."

"The doctor said to start the pill on the first day of your menstrual cycle." Liza's eyes narrow on me. "What have you been using for protection?"

I bite my lower lip. "Uh, nothing. I know, I know ... but before you say anything, let me point out that we only started having sex after ovulation."

She lets out a small whistle. "Girl, I might be a virgin, but even I know that's a terrible idea."

I sigh, my shoulders slumping. "It's a little late for regrets. Anyway ... I much rather we talk about a way for you to ditch Anatoly but keep all of his family's money."

She lets out a laugh, but it doesn't reach her eyes. I know this arranged marriage weighs heavily on her. How could it not? Being tied to someone horrible for the rest of your life sounds like hell.

"Yeah, maybe in a perfect world that would be possible." She pauses, her expression turning somber. "Someone came by the house yesterday to collect on Papa's gambling debt. The maid told him that Papa is still in Poland, but how long can we keep putting off these creditors? The next time they come by, who knows what they'll do."

Nails be damned, I reach out and firmly grasp her hand, offering a reassuring squeeze. "Let me tell Maxim. He can help."

"No. Please, I don't want to involve him. Or anyone, for that matter. As soon as I marry Anatoly, we'll have the money to settle all of my father's debts. I have to manage until then."

"If you're in danger in any way, you come to me."

"I will," she says, focusing on my nails again.

"Hey." I snatch my hand away so she has to meet my eyes. "Whatever you need, I'm here for you. Promise you won't shoulder this alone."

"I promise." She smiles wistfully. "It's so great to have you back here. Just having a friend to talk to ... it makes everything easier. I don't feel so alone."

My heart sinks thinking about the struggles she faced. "I'll always be here for you. No matter what. Even when I'm back in New York."

Her eyebrows knit together, a small crease forming on her forehead. "Are you planning on leaving soon?"

"Well, no, but at some point." I shrug. This isn't forever—how could it be?

Liza avoids my gaze, focusing on my hand, her movements slower as she resumes painting my nails. "Then, let's enjoy the time we have together now."

I smile sadly. "That's exactly what Masha would have said."

Because Masha didn't believe in wasted moments nor regret. She was a believer in living for the moment and letting the rest take its course. It would do me good to remember that.

Chapter Thirty-Four

MAXIM

"As you can see, the shipping routes are secure and operating at maximum efficiency now that we've doubled security," Viktor addresses me, pointing to a map spread across the table.

I listen intently, my gaze sweeping over my top lieutenants assembled here in the security of my home. It's a tactical decision—better to have them within these walls discussing the finer details of our operations than meeting off-site.

While we're reviewing financial projections, the door bursts open with a clamor.

"Maxim!" Kira's voice, sharp and irritated, slices through the room.

She stands in the doorway, clad in an oversized shirt splattered with streaks of paint, the hem barely grazing her thighs. Beneath it, barely-there short-shorts peek out, clinging to her curves. The shirt hangs off one shoulder, revealing a swath of creamy skin, and it's apparent from the way the fabric moves against her that she hasn't bothered with a bra.

The room, a moment ago filled with the hum of business, falls into abrupt silence, all attention snapping towards Kira.

Moments later, Nadya appears behind her, her face etched with fury.

"I was painting the new sitting room," Kira starts, "and Nadya barges in, saying it's 'shameful' for your wife to be doing such work!" She shoots Nadya a death glare, completely unaware of the captivated male audience around the table. Turning her fiery gaze towards me, she demands, "Can you please tell this witch to keep her opinions to herself and—"

"Eyes off my wife, now!" I cut her off, my blood boiling.

The men around the table instantly avert their gazes—some to the floor, others to the documents in front of them—a mix of embarrassment and fear etched on their faces.

In a swift motion, I grab my jacket from the back of my chair and drape it over Kira's shoulders. Her eyes narrow, but she doesn't fight me further.

"My office. Both of you," I say through gritted teeth.

Without another word, I grab Kira's arm and drag her down the hall and into my office, with Nadya following close behind. Once inside, I release Kira and turn to face her, my frustration barely contained.

"Don't you ever leave our bedroom looking like that again," I growl.

Her jaw drops. "I was painting. What do you want me to wear?" Kira shoots back. "If you don't want me to interrupt your meetings, do a better job of keeping your attack dog on a leash. I'm sick of her treating me like your whore!"

Outrage sharpens Nadya's features. "Well, if you stopped parading around like a whore, maybe I wouldn't need to treat you like one!" Her words are harsh and unapologetic. "Maxim needs a proper wife, not one who acts like a street artist, covered in paint and lacking any sense of decorum."

Something inside me snaps. "What did you say to my wife?"

A flicker of alarm crosses Nadya's features. "Forgive me. I spoke out of turn. I only want what's best for you."

I run my tongue over my upper teeth. "If that were true, you'd show my wife the respect she deserves, something I've already asked you to do," I point out firmly.

At our first meeting after returning from New York, I made it clear to Nadya that her behavior towards Kira needed to change.

What I didn't tell Nadya is Kira's real motivation for marrying me and how I'm going to help her avenge Masha's death. We're keeping that piece of information on a need-to-know-only basis, which means the only ones who know about it are Roman and Pavel.

"Of course, Maxim." Nadya bows her head slightly.

I'm not fooled by her act. There's no real remorse there, which pisses me off.

"I meant no disrespect to you or" — Nadya pauses, her voice straining as she forces out the next words — "your wife."

"We'll discuss this later," I say sharply, my firm gaze on Nadya, letting her know that this conversation is far from over. Even if this marriage is an arrangement, she *will* treat Kira with the respect due to the woman who wears my ring.

Nadya departs without another look, leaving us in uneasy silence.

"Nadya has a talent for drama. Don't let her get to you," I say to diffuse the situation. I know Kira thinks Nadya's in love with me, but that's crazy. Her affection is driven by an overprotective maternal instinct, nothing more.

"Drama? That's an understatement. She doesn't trust me because I tried to take down my father." Her shoulders slump on an exhale. "Does she think I'm going to betray you like ... like your first wife did?"

I close my eyes briefly, attempting to block out the rush of pain her words unleash. "Something like that," I admit, my voice hoarse.

Kira lifts her hand to my cheek. Her touch is gentle, almost tentative. "You can talk to me, you know. I'm here for you, and not just because of this arrangement," she says softly.

For a moment, I'm tempted to open up, to tell her everything. But the scars run deep, and the walls I've built around my past are thick and high. So, instead, I focus on the much more immediate issue—the one growing in my pants.

I reach out and gently grasp Kira's jaw, angling her face towards mine. My thumb lightly skims over her bottom lip as I meet her eyes. "I understand Nadya was out of line, and I will deal with her," I vow calmly. "But I already warned you to never let my men see you dressed like this." I grab her ass cheeks, my hands kneading the flesh I consider mine. "I'm going to have to kill everyone in that room now."

Kira's face drops. "No, Maxim, please don't."

"Maybe I'll only blind them." I release a heavy sigh. "Unless you can convince me otherwise."

Her eyes narrow on me. "And what could I do to convince you otherwise?" She languidly licks her lips, calling my attention to her plush mouth.

I sit down in my office chair and push out so she has plenty of room to kneel in front of me. "I'm sure you can think of something."

Heat blasts down my spine as she pulls her T-shirt off, flings it aside, and drops to her knees. She holds eye contact as she undoes my pants and pushes them down along with my boxer briefs, far enough down to free my cock. She runs her tongue over my length a few times, taunting me with her little licks.

"Put it in your mouth," I snap.

The moment her lips wrap around my stiff length, I release a guttural groan. *Jesus, this woman.* I reach down, grab her by the roots of her hair, and take control, thrusting into her warm, eager mouth. She hums her approval, and it sends arrows of pleasure straight to my balls.

As she takes me deep, I delight in the view of messy blonde hair bobbing up and down over my lap. It's like she's made for me, fashioned exactly how I like. Strong but soft. Demanding but submissive.

Kira pulls up, her mouth still coated with wetness from my arousal and her lazy, sloppy sucking. "Fuck my mouth. Use me how you need me."

"You want it rough?" I ask, pushing a strand of hair back from her face. "You want me to ruin your beautiful throat?"

She nods eagerly, stroking my cock with one hand.

I stand up, maintaining my grip on her hair to help me angle her mouth exactly where I need it. "Stay on your knees for me."

I take a moment to admire her body. Lush, curvy, and perfect. Thick thighs and a tapered waist. Could any man dream of more?

"Open," I demand, pulling out and rubbing the head of my cock along her lips, loving how ruined and depraved she looks with my tip trailing over her mouth. The moment she opens for me, I thrust between her lips, electric heat pumping through my veins as I feel her tongue slide across the underside of my dick. "Good girl. Keep your eyes on me."

I thrust deeper in her throat, the gagging sounds she makes as she struggles to take all of me music to my ears. She loves it too. Her little moans around my cock tell me everything I need to know.

"That's right, you're doing so good letting me fuck your throat."

Tears slip past her lashes and her eyes widen, but I don't let up. I smile down at her, admiring the view of her breasts bouncing and her mouth stretched. The whole time, she keeps her eyes glued to mine as if looking at me for approval.

"So good. Swallow around me. Let me feel your throat hug me tight." I use her hair like a leash, pulling her in so close that my pelvis brushes her nose, and saliva drips down her chin.

My God. This is perfection. She's so determined, my little hellcat.

I can tell that she's struggling. I'm a lot for her, especially in this position, but she doesn't give up. Watching her fight to breathe through her nose and swallow every inch of me is all that I need to send me toppling over the edge. My balls tighten, and my thrusts are uneven and desperate, pistoning in and out of her mouth.

"You're such a good girl, making me come so hard with that perfect mouth. Look at me, baby."

Even with the tears in her eyes, she holds eye contact.

"I am going to give you my cum now, and you're going to drink down every drop." My cock swells and I shout out my release, my grip on her hair unforgiving as my cum spills, coating the back of her throat.

She gags, and for a minute, I'm not sure she's going to be able to finish the job, but she steadies herself and does so fucking well. My lips curl as she smiles up at me, her pretty face looking wrecked and perfect.

"You couldn't look more beautiful right now." My thumb catches a dribble of cum that leaks from the side of her mouth, and I bring the bead of liquid up to my lips, savoring the taste. "Jesus, woman, you're going to be my downfall."

"I think the same thing could be said of you. I'm not sure my jaw will ever be the same."

I pull her onto her feet and bring her against my chest. "You'll tell me if I'm too rough with you."

"I think you know I like it rough."

I almost wish she didn't. Then, she wouldn't be so perfect for me and I wouldn't be so fucked. Because as it is, I'm addicted to her little moans, how her thick thighs wrap around my waist gripping me tight, the way her pussy spasms around my cock when I command her to come.

Shit. How did I get here?

Pavel's words from the other day are still front and center in my mind. She's a distraction, a liability. My head's not in the game. And he's right—my dominion is a solitary one. A realm for a king, not designed for a queen.

I don't know what our future holds, but I do know right now she's here in my arms and I'm not turning away from her. Not yet.

If Kira senses my spinning thoughts, she doesn't let on. Instead, she reaches for her T-shirt and pulls it over her head. Once she's dressed, I sit back down in my office chair and pull her into my lap.

"Don't you have to rejoin your meeting?" she asks.

"They'll wait. I have something to tell you," I say.

She lifts her head to look my way.

"Pavel's been looking into Masha's situation on my orders. There's something at the site of her murder that belonged to me."

"What does that mean?" Her eyebrows press together as she studies me closely.

"It was an engraved lighter, monogrammed with my initials

and a design. A gift from my first wife. I had thrown it out a long time ago. No idea how it ended up at the warehouse where Masha was taken. Unless someone wanted to connect me to her murder."

I debated telling Kira any of this because I don't actually have anything concrete. More than that, will she doubt my innocence in connection to her aunt's death? But I need to be honest with her, even if I have no real answers.

Kira's body tenses. "Who has access to your trash? Only people who live here," she points out.

I run a thumb over my lips. She's not wrong. The estate is not easy for outsiders to access. Then again, my enemies have been known to go to great lengths to hurt me. Paying off a sanitation worker to go through my trash wouldn't be unheard of. But Masha's murder was inconsequential in the lives of my associates. Why would someone go to any lengths to try and connect me with a death that, sadly, most people didn't give a shit about?

I brush a hand through her hair. "Until we fit all the pieces of the puzzle together, nothing will make sense. Give it time."

"I can help," she says. "Don't you think I have a right to be involved in this?"

"You do," I agree, kissing her neck. "But I need your big sexy brain for something else first."

She purses her lips. "What is that?"

"We've been questioning a high-ranking member of the Black Company for over a week, but the man is a steel trap. Refusing to talk, no matter what we do to him. And we've done a hell of a lot." With two fingers, I angle her chin towards me so she can't look away. "Think you could get him to spill his secrets?"

She sits up with sudden interest. "I can try. What information do you need?"

"We need to find out who leads the Black Company. They remain hidden, but it's widely believed that their leader is the brains of the operation. If we can capture them, we'll have a chance at bringing down the Triad."

She angles her head. "What makes you think I could break him if you haven't been able to?"

I trail my fingers down her cheek. "Something tells me you could do whatever you put your mind to."

She looks wary. "You think Roman and Pavel would appreciate me stepping in? I don't think so."

"It's not their decision to make, it's mine. I'm aware of your potential, and it's time they realized it as well."

Her fingertips dance over the lapel of my suit, avoiding my gaze like there's something she wants to say but can't get it out. "Why did you ask Pavel to look into my aunt? Why not ask Roman, or do it yourself?"

"Because he's the best," I admit simply. "He's damn good at what he does. If he weren't unhinged, he'd be a top-notch detective."

"Yeah, but he doesn't like me. I bet he thinks chasing down my aunt's killer is a waste of his time."

I swipe a piece of hair from her face. "Pavel doesn't like anyone. It's his way of keeping the world at arm's length. It happens when your childhood is painful. You learn to build walls around your heart, protecting it from the potential pain the world might inflict again."

"What does that mean?"

"It means some of us are broken, and it's impossible to put us back together." I don't know if I'm talking about Pavel or myself now. But she should know I'm just as damaged as my friend. Once you lose your reason for living, you walk around the world half a person.

Kira presses her forehead into mine. "I don't think you're broken," she whispers against my lips.

My heart squeezes. If that's the case, she sees a different man than the one I see reflected back at me in the mirror.

"We've all had our life bruises and scrapes, but you still get up and fight every day."

I run my hand through her hair, fingers weaving gently through the strands. I don't know what to make of this little hurricane that tore into my life and turned everything upside down. She makes me feel something—a spark, an energy. Something I haven't felt in a long time.

I bury my face in her neck. "You're the fighter," I insist. "You stood up to your father when no one else was willing to put him in his place. You fought like hell for a place alongside your brothers, and you never gave up trying to right your aunt's death. There's not many like you."

"Such high praise," she breathes out. "You should be careful, Maxim Belov, or I might mistake your intentions." As soon as the words slip out, she pauses, a hint of regret in her voice. "I didn't mean anything by that."

My arms tighten around her, and I choose my words carefully. "Are you ready to help me break this Black Company motherfucker?"

There's a pause, and I think maybe she can see through all the hardened layers that protect my heart. But she just rests her chin on my chest and looks at me with determination.

"Let's do it."

Chapter Thirty-Five

KIRA

Chun Leung's gaze is wild, flickering around the room as he sits bound to a chair in the dimly lit basement. His chest heaves with ragged breaths, eyes wide with terror. Strapped securely, he looks every bit the cornered animal he is, sweat matting his hair and darkening his shirt.

I step forward and tilt his head back gently, offering a stream of water from the bottle to moisten his parched lips.

Maxim's men ran him through the ringer—he looks like he's been dragged behind a train. I'm sure he expected the torture to ratchet up, which is why what I'm doing is so much more effective. I'm playing good cop. This isn't about force—it's about strategy.

His relief is evident as he gulps down the last of the water, the rise and fall of his chest slowly steadying. I've only been at this for two hours, but his will is slipping. I can feel it.

"Just give me a name, that's all," I coax gently. "Then this all ends."

The name of the Black Company's leader lurking somewhere in the shadows of Hong Kong is crucial for tearing down the syndicate that has become a relentless adversary for Maxim.

Leaning in, I make sure my eyes meet Leung's, offering a reassuring smile—one that I know is reflected in the two-way mirror for Maxim and his crew to see. Maxim is the boss so what he says goes, but I doubt his crew was very supportive of me taking the reins on this interrogation. Still, I know what I'm capable of, and soon his men will too.

With a steady, soothing voice, I press, "I understand your loyalty to the Triad. It's expected, honorable even. But let's face it—they've abandoned you. You've been trained to endure, to protect secrets at all costs. I admire that. But at what point does personal sacrifice become senseless?"

Leung's stoic expression doesn't waver, but I notice the slightest flicker in his eyes—a sign of doubt, maybe? This is when the good cop turns bad.

I press on, my voice soft but insistent. "It's your family I feel bad for."

Leung's eyes flash with a raw, untamed ferocity.

I continue to circle him. "Even if you stay silent ... we'll spread the word that you sang like a canary. That you caved and laid bare every secret of the Black Company." I lean in, my words laced with threat. "Consider what they will do to your family then. Their retribution will be ugly, won't it?"

Leung's anger ripples through the room, as tangible as the tremble of his hands straining against the cuffs. He pulls against the plastic ties, his breath coming out in ragged snarls. "You wouldn't dare," he spits, his voice rough. "The Triad knows loyalty."

"You think you're a hero? A martyr? Let me tell you what a hero is. A hero is willing to protect his family. The people who love him. Not some nameless, faceless organization like the Black Company. To them, you're nothing. A dime a dozen." I pause, letting my words sink in.

I don't actually know what family Leung has, but I'm taking a gamble that there is someone somewhere on this earth that loves him. Someone whose death he would do anything to prevent.

His face is stoic, but the slight twitch in his jaw tells me I've hit a nerve.

"They'll come after my family either way," Leung finally says, his voice less certain than before.

I tilt my head, crossing my arms in front of me. "If you give us what we want, we'll keep it under wraps that you talked. You'll go to your death honorably. Don't make the people you love suffer for your silence. Is the code of the Triad worth more than their lives?"

He looks away, a silent war raging behind his pained expression. I can see the walls he's built starting to crumble, brick by brick. It's a subtle shift, but it's there. The rise and fall of his chest becomes more pronounced, and he dips his head in surrender.

"He goes by the name Lai King," he confesses, the name emerging like a dark secret unfurling into the dim light of the room. "But he's not in Hong Kong right now."

"Where is he?"

"He has houses all over Europe, moves around all the time, so no one but the top Black Company officials know where he is. He does have a daughter in Paris. Kind of a bohemian type, refuses to take Dad's money or take part in the Triad, but he keeps a close watch on her."

Interesting. Very interesting.

My head snaps up to face the mirror. I'm aware of every inch of my posture, every breath I take as my eyes meet the reflective surface. Through it, I feel Maxim's intense gaze on me.

A small, triumphant smile forms on my lips.

I did it. I broke Leung.

* * *

MAXIM

Kira is on fucking fire. And she hasn't spilled one drop of his blood. She doesn't need to. She's wearing him down, slowly but surely, using nothing but pure psychological manipulation. It's a beautiful thing to witness.

Beside me, Roman is as fascinated as I am as we watch Kira through the one-way mirror. "Well, fuck." He whistles. "I think he's going to break."

I smile.

She moves with a dancer's grace, her figure outlined in a fitted charcoal-gray turtleneck and sleek black jeans. I was right —this is not her first interrogation. She walked into the room with her head high and a strategy firmly in place.

I glance at Roman. "What, you're not going to give me shit for involving her in syndicate business?"

He scoffs. "The moment you married Kira, she was involved in syndicate business. If you trust her, we might as well use her as an asset."

"Pavel doesn't share that sentiment. Neither does Nadya."

"Not a fucking surprise. Pavel doesn't trust anyone outside of this room, and Nadya, well... If we're speaking frankly, that woman needs a hobby. She's a little too focused on you."

"Isn't that her job?"

Romans snorts. "It's not her job to obsess over your marriage. Or be openly hostile to your wife."

"I put an end to that." My jaw ticks in annoyance. "How does Nadya treat Kira when I'm not around?"

He shrugs. "She's not a fan, that's clear as day. Nadya's old-school and conservative, and Kira is anything but that."

Action on the other side of the mirror catches our attention. Kira is leaning down, her face close to Leung's battered and bruised one.

"Don't make the people you love suffer for your silence," she gently coaxes him. "Is the code of the Triad worth more than their lives?"

Leung's expression morphs into a portrait of despair as he gives us a name. Lai King.

Holy shit. She did it. Kira fucking did it.

Roman pounds on my back in congratulations. I'm itching to burst through that door, grab Kira, and kiss her senseless. She pulled off what no one else could. Getting Leung to talk.

If he's holed up in Europe with a reckless daughter, that's an advantage. Family ties could be a weakness—I'm all too familiar with that fact. But it won't deter me from exploiting it to our benefit.

Kira looks up at me through the window, and I can feel her triumphant gaze settle on me. She's not only proven what she's capable of, she's also handed us the leverage we desperately need.

But all I can think about is tipping her over the table and fucking her senseless.

"Have Viktor gather up all the intel you can on Lai King and his associates. We're shutting down the Black Company once and for all."

"You got it," Roman says.

Kira bounds through the door, a wide smile playing on her gorgeous face. Roman applauds at her entrance, and she offers a shy smile in return. But when her eyes lock with mine, I see something totally different. *Heat.* I see exactly how my girl wants to celebrate.

"Get out of the fucking room," I bark. "We need some privacy."

Roman gives me a salute and heads out. Kira leaps into my arms, fitting perfectly against me.

"You did so good," I whisper, my lips near her ear. "Watching you... It was like a fucking masterclass in interrogation."

"Does that mean you'll give me some real responsibility now? No more bullshit society wife tasks."

"I'll meet you halfway. If you want a role in my organization, I'll make it happen." Maybe I'm still riding high from the Leung win, but the idea of her becoming part of my world feels right, like a piece falling into place.

Kira's lips curve into a teasing smile. "I'm intrigued," she murmurs. "What's the salary like? Benefits? Pension plan?"

"It's whatever you want," I say before my lips meet hers in a kiss that so easily turns into fire.

I'm not sure what I'm offering her, but I know I want her by my side, without an expiration date. Pavel would probably say I'm drunk on her pussy and making bad decisions, but I don't think that's it at all. For the first time in a long time, I am seeing the world clearly. I once thought love was a weakness, but now I see it's the bravest damn thing a man can do.

Fuck. Am I in love?

I don't have time to question that because Kira is on her feet and focused on undoing my belt. "I need you. Right here."

Her lips lower onto mine, hot and fierce, as I yank down her pants and underwear, rubbing my palm between her legs. She's already soaked for me, which is good because I can barely wait to get inside of her.

There's a table nearby with a computer and monitor on it.

With one swoop of my arm, everything falls to the ground in a loud crash, but I don't give a fuck. All I care about is pounding her into oblivion.

I wind my hand around her hair and push her down face-first, one hand on her back to press her into the table. "This is your prize, lastochka. You earned my dick for being such a good girl. Is this what you want?"

Her response is a husky groan.

I lower my pants and boxer briefs and push inside her, swelling with a need so fierce I feel like I might break her. But her body welcomes me like I've come home. I lean over her, covering her back with my front, resting my arms on either side of her.

I want to hear her moans as they spill from her sexy mouth. I want to hear her sobs as I ruin her so I can put her back together again.

"I need you, Maxim," she gasps.

"You have me," I kiss her neck. "You'll always have me."

With each thrust, she claws at the table and cries out my name—the sweetest sound I can imagine. I'm riding her hard, nipping and sucking at her neck, whispering words that tumble out in ragged breaths against her skin. Confessions that I hope she can't understand since I can barely understand them myself. I tell her how I love the way she smells. How goddamn beautiful she is. How she makes me feel whole again, even when I thought it impossible.

She lifts her head, arching her back, and straightens. With my two hands, I hold open her ass cheeks and spit on her puckered hole, lubing it up for what comes next.

Kira stills. With my thumb, I breach her entrance, feeling the ring of muscle give way as I push into her tight hole.

"It's too much," she says. "I'm so full."

"Give it a minute, baby. I'm going to make you feel so

good." I give her shallow hard thrusts as I twist my thumb in her asshole and pinch her clit, knowing she needs the edge of pain to bring on her release. "Come for me. I want to feel you pulse around my cock."

Her pussy is so damn hot and tight it's impossible to hold out any longer.

"Maxim!" Her body tenses in pleasure, and she cries out her orgasm as I come with a deep grunt, emptying myself fully inside of her. It's several long minutes before either of us can move, our breaths slowly returning to normal as the world comes into focus.

I drop a gentle kiss in the middle of her back, before pulling out of her and zipping myself up. Kira is still lying there, her chest pressed against the table, her ass cheeks parted, her pussy still on display for me.

"Stay like that," I order her. I hold her open to watch my seed drip out slowly. It's fucking filthy and the hottest thing I've ever had the pleasure of viewing. "God, Kira, I need to taste you like that."

"No, Maxim..." Her pleas fall on deaf ears because I'm already on my knees, licking out her dripping cunt like it's an ice cream formulated just for my pleasure. "Oh God," she gasps, "That's so good."

"Then come again for me, lastochka."

I keep on lapping at her beautiful pussy, fucking her with my tongue while my fingers circle her clit in slow, sure motions. It's not long before she arches into my mouth and cries as another orgasm washes over her, riding out the waves as her core clenches against my tongue.

When she's thoroughly spent, I gather her in my arms and capture her mouth, letting her taste our combined flavors. Her lips are warm and soft. There's a hint of vulnerability in the way she kisses me back that stirs something deep within me.

"That was the best reward ever," she breathes.

"It was well deserved." Although, giving her orgasms and filling her with my cum is as much of a reward for me as it is for her.

One of these days, I'm going to have to tell her I know she secretly put herself on birth control. Roman overheard Kira ask Liza to get her access to the pill. I assume she's been on it since then, considering she hasn't mentioned condoms.

"So, what happens now?" she asks, starting to put herself back together.

I prop on the edge of a desk and enjoy the view. "Now, we learn everything we can about Lai King and his inner circle. Once we figure out where he's hiding, we'll annihilate the Black Company from the face of this earth."

"Damn, Daddy. You're making me all hot. Do I get to come with you?" She looks at me with big hopeful eyes.

"Baby steps," I smile and kiss her forehead. "You don't want to give your husband a heart attack."

Her hand lands on her hip, and she gives me a saucy wink. "I'll have to try to keep your heart pumping in other ways."

And she does. I'm crazy for the way her laughter fills the room, her sassy mouth, the adorable way she blows her hair out of her face when she's deep in thought.

"You don't have to try, Kira," I say, my voice laced with emotion, because I know letting her go will be the death of me. Even if it's something that can't be avoided. "It comes naturally to you."

Chapter Thirty-Six

KIRA

"Aren't you a present I'd love to unwrap."

I jump a little at Maxim's voice as he enters into the walk-in closet behind me.

"Oh, this old thing?" I exclaim before giving myself a final once-over in the closet's full-length mirror. I've settled on a shimmering white evening gown with a split up the thigh. It's gorgeous, and even more so paired with the black stilettos I've chosen.

The best part is Nadya didn't interfere with my outfit choice this time. Whatever Maxim said to her must have sunk in. She's not exactly friendly, but at least she's keeping her distance, which suits me fine.

Maxim's arms slide around me from behind. I lean against him, feeling the solid strength of his body. In the mirror, he cuts a sharp figure, his tailored tuxedo perfectly accentuating his commanding frame. He reminds me of Bruce Wayne, Batman's alter ego. Ridiculously handsome and looking like all kinds of trouble, the kind of dangerous that makes butterflies take flight in my stomach.

This is our first time going out together since coming home from New York a couple of weeks ago. We're going to a big society fundraiser hosted by none other than Anatoly's family, but Maxim's head of security deemed it safe for us to go. Probably because everything's been quiet with the Black Company lately. Maxim's men are pursuing Lai King, and it's believed his top advisors have gone into hiding, huddling together to plan their next move.

"You can't unwrap me yet," I say teasingly.

The corners of Maxim's lips curl into a wolfish smile, a glint of heat in his eyes as he studies us both in the mirror. "If I start thinking about unwrapping you, we're never going to leave this closet."

As if to make his point, his hands inch up and cup my breasts—they feel heavy and swollen under his touch. It's almost too much. I close my eyes, marveling at how a brush of his hand over my skin can make me feel so many things.

I've never been in love before, so honestly, I don't know how to tell if what I feel for Maxim is that or intense lust. What I do know is that his smile can completely unravel me, and the thought of a future without him makes it feel like I can't breathe.

Maxim asking me to join his syndicate after I coaxed a confession from Leung felt significant. Like he was asking me for more than this marriage arrangement. Life has been hectic, so we haven't had a chance to discuss what his offer really means. And truthfully, I've been trying to sort out my own feelings. Do I want to be here, by Maxim's side, forever?

It's difficult to think about leaving my friends and family in New York behind, but living without the man who touches my soul feels impossible.

"God, your tits are so sensitive lately. I love it." He squeezes my nipples to make his point.

I smirk at him in the mirror. "For your advanced age, you sure have a healthy appetite," I tease, grinding my ass into his already hardening cock.

"Just for that, I'm going to tie you up tonight and smack this gorgeous ass of yours until you can't walk." His threats only serve to turn me on.

He rolls my nipples between fingers, and I release a throaty moan. It's true. My breasts have felt more sensitive than normal. In fact, my whole body's been more sensitive lately, and I've noticed my energy sapped even after a full night's sleep. I must be stressed with everything going on.

"What happened?" Maxim chuckles, releasing me. "One minute you're dying for my hand between your legs, and the next you're lost in your head. I'll try not to take it personally. We should probably get moving, anyhow." He swats me on the ass and then pulls away to start rummaging through his watch collection.

"It's nothing," I assure him. "Maybe I'm a little nervous about tonight. It's been a while since we attended such a public event, and I know there's going to be a lot of scrutiny on us."

"We wouldn't be going if I wasn't totally confident that it's safe." He kisses my forehead.

"I know that." I lean against the cabinet, watching Maxim move on to his tie drawer. It's still ridiculously organized by color shade and fabric texture. "Remember how I messed up all your drawers a few days after we got married?" I ask, smiling at the memory.

He turns to look at me over his shoulder, his eyebrows pressed together. "I didn't know that. The maid must have cleaned it up before I could take in the chaos you caused."

I snort. "Yeah, well, I was seriously concerned that I'd

married a psychopath. I was snooping and trying to piss you off. If I'm honest, I was looking to learn anything I could about you. You were such a mystery."

Maxim pulls a silver tie from the drawer and hands it to me. "Can you do the honors?"

I nod and step forward, taking the tie from his hands. The silk fabric slips through my fingers as I begin to loop it around his neck, standing on my tiptoes to get the length just right.

"What did you learn about me, lastochka?"

"Nothing, really. I did find that cute picture of you as a kid in your sock drawer."

He freezes, pulling back to look me in the eyes. "That picture... That's not me."

"Oh." I focus on finishing the knot, pulling the tie snug. "Well, whoever that kid is, he's adorable." I smooth down the front of the tie, stepping back to inspect my work.

Maxim's expression is unreadable for a moment, then he clears his throat. "That was my son, Ilya." His voice is soft, almost lost in the quiet of the room. "He was killed eleven years ago, when he was four years old."

My knees go weak, and I lean back against the dresser for support. There's a buzzing in my ears, like the distant sound of waves crashing, drowning out everything else.

"You had a son? I'm so sorry, I had no idea." I reach out, placing a hand on his chest, feeling the quickened beat of his heart under my palm. "How did he die?" My heart aches for him, for the loss he must have endured, a loss so profound that he kept it buried away, even from me. "You don't have to tell me if you don't want to," I add.

Maxim holds my gaze. "Not many people know, but it's time I told you the whole story," he says with a voice that carries the weight of unresolved pain.

He leads me into our bedroom, where he sits me on the bed

and pulls up a dressing stool so he can sit across from me. He leans forward, his elbows resting on his thighs.

Taking a full breath, he steadies himself. "Irina and I weren't exactly an arranged marriage, but it was close enough. She came from a family with influence, at a time when I had the money but needed the connections. It was never about love. I didn't think love matches existed. I thought it was a fairytale people told." He pauses, swallowing visibly, the muscles in his neck tightening. I wonder if his view on love matches has changed. A flicker of hope rises in me, but now isn't the time to delve deeper.

"A few years into our marriage, Irina and I weren't in a good place. I worked constantly, and when I was home, spending time with my son was my priority. She met a man at some point—he was a fling, or at least, that's what she told me—but she didn't know who he really was."

The look in his eyes is pure anguish, and I'd do anything to take away his pain.

"The guy was actually part of a rival syndicate. Through Irina, they were able to track my movements, anticipate where I would go. We were at a family Christmas party, one of the few nights we were all together." Maxim stops for a moment, closing his eyes as if to brace himself against an invisible blow. "It was getting late, but Irina and I wanted to stay longer. We sent Ilya home with the nanny." He bows his head. "The car exploded as soon as the engine started. A car bomb meant for me. I-I saw the flames from the window."

My heart pounds against my chest, the gravity of his revelation making it difficult to breathe. My words come out in a broken whisper. "Maxim, I'm so sorry."

He nods—a single, curt movement. "It was my life, my world that put him in danger."

"Is that why you killed Irina?" I ask, pieces of the picture falling into place.

He tilts his head. "Killed her?"

"I don't blame you at all."

He shakes his head, a bitter half-smile tracing his lips. "I didn't kill her," he says. "But after what happened, after Ilya ... I couldn't bear the sight of her." He pauses as if the next words cost him. "She's in exile, as far from me as possible."

"Where did she go?" Not that it matters. But curiosity gets the best of me.

After a heavy silence, he replies, "Argentina. I gave her no other choice." His hands clench and unclench, and I know it cost him something to share this with me. "She lives with the consequences of her actions, as do I."

I stand, carefully lowering in his lap, pulling him close with an arm around his shoulder. "Were you serious about wanting another child? Like we agreed to before getting married?"

He sighs and traces my jaw with a finger. "I said that to keep you in line. It was something I could hold over you. But the truth is, I lost more than a son that day. I lost a piece of my soul, and I don't have the heart to try again. My relationship with Alyona ... It's my second chance at being a father and the only one I'll take—if she can forgive me one day."

"I see." I pull away and give myself a moment to process. My voice is even, but inside there's a rising tide of uncertainty. "I suppose we should have been more careful."

"What do you mean?"

"I mean ... with birth control." For someone adamant about not wanting more children, he could have taken a few more precautions.

"But you're on the pill." He smirks. "Don't think Roman didn't run to tell me that tidbit of information."

I swallow. "I'm not on the pill. It took Liza a while to get it for me." When I see his stricken face, something inside me breaks. "It's fine," I reassure him. "I'm expecting my period any day."

Maxim stares at me intensely, and I have no idea what he's thinking—if it's good or bad, or somewhere in between. Finally, he stands and approaches me. "I really put the ass in assume. We should have talked about birth control earlier. I'm sorry."

I give him a reassuring smile that I hope appears genuine. "It's fine. I'm going to grab my clutch from the closet, and we can go."

I turn quickly, hoping to hide the sudden flush of anxiety that I feel painting my cheeks. I walk to the closet, my mind racing, and start counting the days in my head since my last period—a silent numbers game that adds up to a startling realization: my period is late.

How could I be so stupid? With everything happening, I lost track of time.

I reach for my clutch, my fingers trembling as they brush against the cool leather. There's no way I can tell Maxim what I suspect. Not now, not after what he told me.

I take a deep breath, willing my heart to slow, to silence the rapid drumming in my chest. I need to compose myself, to put on a mask of calm before I face Maxim again.

But as I glance at my reflection in the mirror, the woman staring back at me is holding onto a secret that could change everything.

Chapter Thirty-Seven

KIRA

As Maxim and I step into the grand foyer of the theater, a hush falls over the crowd. All heads snap towards us as we make our way through the mass of people, nods are exchanged, camera flashes flickering at the edge of my vision. I try to smile at those who approach us, but I can feel my hands shaking, betraying my nerves.

Maxim gives my hand a reassuring squeeze as we continue our path through the sea of faces.

"Are you alright?" he murmurs in my ear.

"I'm fine," I say because I don't want him to worry.

Maybe he thinks I'm still digesting what he shared about losing his son and exiling his ex-wife. That was a lot to take in. But there's more to my silence—the realization that I might be carrying his child. One that he doesn't want, and for good reason.

"Let me get you a drink," he offers with a frown. "You look a little pale."

"Seltzer water, please."

Before Maxim can turn away, he nods at someone behind me. Seconds later, Liza slides up next to me, wrapping me in a welcoming embrace, her jasmine scent floating between us. A scent I usually find lovely. But right now, it makes me feel like hurling.

"Keep an eye on Kira," Maxim instructs her. "I'm going to get her something to drink."

Liza turns to me, confused. "Water? We have something much stronger, you know." She lifts her drink to offer proof. "The bartenders are making this amazing espresso martini with vo—" Something about my expression stops her mid-sentence. "What's going on?" she asks, pulling me into a quiet corner of the cavernous room.

"I'm okay," I whisper, "but I need you to do something for me. Can you get me a pregnancy test and bring it over to the house tomorrow?"

Even though the war with the Black Company has gone quiet, I can't head out on my own to the pharmacy. There are guards with me at all times. I know it's asking Liza a lot, but until she's actually married to Anatoly, she has more freedom than I do.

"Oh my God, of course. Do you think you're..." She looks at me intently, her gaze searching mine.

"I think I might be."

Her eyes widen. "Does Maxim know?"

I shake my head, wringing my hands in front of me. "I want to be sure before I tell him. He may not be happy about it."

"I doubt that. You should see how he looks at you. Like the Earth orbits around you."

"He doesn't want another child." As soon as the words are out of my mouth, I bite my lip.

Shit. I don't think anyone knows about Ilya. Maxim must

have kept him a secret from the world to protect his son's life. In the end, his enemies got to him anyway.

"You mean other than Alyona?" Liza looks at me curiously.

"Exactly."

Liza's eyes soften. "Whatever you need, I'm here."

"You are the best," I say and mean it.

She gives me a quick hug. "I'm happy to help you. Now, plaster a smile on your face because Maxim is storming over here, and he looks like a charging bull."

I square my shoulders and pull myself together in time to offer Maxim a warm smile when he approaches me with a glass of seltzer and a worried expression.

"Thank you," I say and take a big gulp. "I was overwhelmed with all the attention on us, but I'm feeling much better."

"Are you sure? If you want to go home, we can leave."

"No, no," I insist. "You go work the room. I know you have associates here that you need to speak with. Go wheel and deal, and I'll make the social rounds later on with Liza."

He brushes a piece of hair from my forehead and drops a sweet kiss. "As long as you're sure. If things change, come and find me."

"I will," I promise him. "I'll find you."

* * *

MAXIM

I've spent the last ten minutes cornered by Mr. and Mrs. Petrovich while they drone on about my generous donation to their fundraising cause. Apparently, I donated a quarter-million dollars to help build a state-of-the-art luxury shelter for Moscow's stray dogs—something I will be having a word with Nadya about since she handles my philanthropic donations.

I'm all for animal shelters, but I doubt mutts need a sauna or a silver-plated water bowl.

"There you are." Roman mercifully appears beside me. "Mayor Rashnikov would like a word."

"If you'll excuse me," I say to the Petroviches, thrilled for any excuse not to hear about sheepskin-lined daybeds for dogs.

As soon as we're out of ear shot, I turn to Roman. "Are you serious about that mudak wanting a word?"

Roman chuckles and takes a sip of his drink. "Fuck no. As soon as he took one look at you, he high-tailed it the other way. He's probably hiding in the bathroom or something. I was liberating you from a conversation you clearly weren't enjoying."

"A state-of-the-art dog shelter," I grumble. "I worry about the future of humanity sometimes."

"Yeah, you and me both," Roman snickers, but his voice barely registers above the hum of the gala's chatter.

I scan the room for Kira for what feels like the hundredth time. Something is off with her tonight. I can feel it. Through a sea of glittering gowns and tailored suits, I spot her laughing with Liza.

A wave of relief washes over me. She looks more like herself—color has returned to her cheeks and her eyes are bright, but there is something about the way her expression falls when she thinks no one is looking. Something changed after I told her about Irina and Ilya. She was fine until that point, but in the car on the way over here she barely said two words to me.

Fuck, who could blame her? I'm a walking red flag. Burned and broken. Kira's got her entire life ahead of her. Even if I keep her, one day she'll wake up and want a man who's whole. Who doesn't bear the weight of past scars.

A cold pit grows in my gut at the thought of losing her, but I can't go there right now.

Beside me, Roman whistles through his teeth, pulling me

from my whirlwind thoughts. "Look what cockroach dared to show up."

My head snaps up, zeroing in on Boris Ivanov's stocky form as he edges through the crowd. We've been after Boris since Kira spilled that he's the source of the false rumors about my involvement in Masha's death. His associates have been covering for him, saying he's tied up in Poland with "critical" matters. More like drowning in vodka and bedding whores.

"He must be feeling pretty bold to show up here," I muse aloud.

Roman draws in a sharp breath, leaning in. "Any progress on tracking down Masha's killer?"

I shake my head, frustration evident. "It's a dead end. After discovering the photo with my Zippo, we've hit a wall." I turn to Roman with a sly grin. "Let's have a little chat with Ivanov."

"My fucking pleasure."

Roman and I split without a word. He veers left while I take the right. People try to catch my attention in the crowd, but I walk on by with no acknowledgement. Boris continues his path towards the bar, oblivious to the net closing in around him. It's too late for him to bolt without making a scene when he realizes Roman and I have him surrounded.

He clears his throat nervously. "Maxim, Roman ... nice to see you, as always."

"Is it, though? Is it really?" I throw an arm around him and lead him towards an isolated alcove near the back of the hall, away from prying eyes and eager ears.

When we turn the corner, Roman shoves him against the wall. I step in front of Ivanov's path, and his eyes go wide as the gravity of his predicament sinks in.

"We've been trying to get in touch with you." I make a *tsk*ing sound. "Apparently, you're a busy man. Unless you've been avoiding me."

"N-no ... absolutely not," he stammers. "Why would I do that?"

"Oh, I don't know. Because you're spreading rumors that I killed Masha Antonov." He opens his mouth to argue, but I don't even give him a chance. "Save your breath, Boris. Kira told me everything that happened the night of Alyona's ball."

"Please," he pleads, his hands splayed. "I don't remember anything from that night. I was drunk—"

"You're always drunk," I snarl. "But you seemed very sure of my involvement in Masha's death, so much so that Kira planned to kill me to get her revenge. Lucky for me" — I grin and hold up my finger to show off my wedding band — "she had to marry me first."

"I've never even heard those rumors. You know I don't follow gossip, Maxim."

The words are barely out of his mouth when Roman punches him in the stomach, and he flies back against the wall, coughing and sputtering like the pussy he is.

"Maybe that will help you remember," Roman suggests.

Boris wipes his mouth and stretches out his jaw. "What do you want me to say?"

I drag a hand down the side of my face. "The truth."

He swallows hard, and a thin sheen of sweat covers his brow. "It was talk at a poker game," he wheezes. "I was drinking with some wannabe gangster around the time Masha was killed. One of them—I don't remember who—had a picture from the scene where Masha was ..." He makes a slashing motion across his neck. "I was curious, that's all. We all were. I don't remember who pointed it out first, but your Zippo—the one that you would always use to light cigars at the gentlemen's club—was there at the scene."

I clench my teeth. "A lost lighter doesn't make me her killer."

"That's what I figured," he continues hastily. "When the whispers started, I ran into Nadya at the opera. Took her aside and told her what people were saying, about your so-called hand in it, especially considering your history with Oleg." Roman's eyes cut to me, and I shake my head. Nadya never mentioned anything. "She said it was all bullshit. That I should ignore what people were saying, to keep my nose out of it."

"You didn't do a very good job of that," Roman says dryly.

"It's the drinking." Boris hangs his head. "It makes me ... loose-lipped."

"You've already sold your daughter to the biggest mudak on the planet," Roman barks, referring to Anatoly. "Very soon, your drinking and gambling are going to get you killed."

"I'm trying to dry out. That's what I was doing in Poland." That's a lie if I've ever heard one—one of the many things that make it impossible to take him at his word.

Doesn't matter. We don't need Boris to figure out who killed Masha. We will get answers, eventually. I'll make sure of it.

Roman's phone buzzes with an incoming text. He glances at it, his expression turning grave. With a subtle tilt of his head, he signals to me that it's important. Time to wrap this up.

"So, what do you think?" I say to Roman. "Should we kill him?"

Boris pales, his face melting into pure terror. "Kill me? But I didn't do anything."

Roman shrugs. "You ran your mouth. That alone is a death sentence."

Boris squirms, spewing excuses and apologies. It's sad, really.

With one swift move, I grab his collar, yanking him close enough to share a breath. "The only reason you're still breathing is because Liza and my wife are friends. Mess up again, and you're done." My words are a knife, slicing the last of his defiance.

Boris scrambles away, stumbling over his own feet to escape.

"That was pathetic," Roman grumbles. "But I have good news. We've got a location on Lai King. He's holed up in a mountain safehouse in Switzerland."

A grin tugs at the edges of my mouth. "I hear Switzerland is lovely this time of year."

Roman rubs his hands together. "Jet's being prepped as we speak."

"I'll let Kira know what's happening and meet you out front," I say, already in motion.

I wish I didn't have to leave her tonight, especially after my intense revelation, but duty calls and I can't put this off any longer.

Chapter Thirty-Eight

KIRA

It's nearing the dinner hour by the time Liza arrives at our estate the day after the gala. I greet her at the front door—something I'm sure seems uncouth to our staff, but I don't care. I need to take the freaking tests and find out if I'm pregnant or not. Because if I am, it changes everything.

"Please tell me you brought them," I whisper when the door is closed behind her.

"Would I let you down?" Liza runs a hand through her dark hair as she gives me a kiss on the cheek. "It took me forever to get rid of Anatoly today, but I got three different brands to be sure. Had to convince my guard that I was getting tampons so he'd give me space."

"I owe you one," I say, dragging her upstairs towards the bedroom. "Actually, I owe you a lot more than one. I hope you're keeping count."

"Oh, sure, I have a spreadsheet and everything," Liza jokes. "Pregnancy test delivery counts as double, though."

"Yeah, well, let's hope this is a one-off thing."

Both of us freeze as we reach the top of the stairs to find Nadya watching us, her gaze sharp as knives. She doesn't say a word, but her eyes follow us with silent suspicion.

Shit! Did she hear what we were talking about?

But no. That's Nadya's usual stern expression, and truth be told, I have bigger issues to worry about right now. As it is, I barely slept last night, debating what I'd do if I was pregnant. On one hand, I feel a rush of excitement at the thought of a baby. Then there's Maxim, his stance on having children so clear and uncompromising. How could I possibly tell him when he's so set against it?

Even though I'm worried about Maxim leading an attack on Lai King, I'm grateful for this time alone because if I am pregnant, I'll need space to sort out my head.

My impatience reaches a new level once Liza and I enter my bedroom. She fishes in her purse for the three boxes, all of them various shades of pink and white, because apparently pregnancy tests have to look as cutesy as the potential results they're delivering.

"How do these things work?" I ask Liza as I head into the en-suite bathroom.

"How should I know? I've never used one. From what I've seen on TV, I think you pee on the stick."

"Right. I'll read the instructions."

In no time, I have all three tests out of the box and lined up on the counter. My hands are shaking, and there's a tightness in my chest that won't ease until I know for sure. It's awkward as hell trying to aim my pee accurately on the tiny test strip, but I manage to do it. Three times. Now, come the longest five minutes of my life. I set a timer on my phone and flop onto the bed.

Liza settles next to me, her expression soft yet serious.

"What will you do if it's positive?" Her question hangs in the air, heavy with implication.

I let out a shaky breath, my gaze drifting to the ceiling. "I don't know," I admit. "Part of me wants a child. I never had a mother, other than Masha, and the mother-child bond is something I really want to experience. But I'm also terrified that Maxim doesn't want this."

Liza turns on her side to face me and props her head on her hand. "Do you think Maxim would make a good father?"

I'd never really given it much thought up to this point because there was no reason to. The long-term future was never something we discussed. But after this, I realize we have to.

If there is a child, nothing would make me happier than seeing Maxim cradle a tiny version of us in his arms. Maxim is rough on the outside, but inside he's surprisingly sweet and caring. I can picture him melting into a smile as our child wraps a tiny hand around his finger. Imagining us as a family brings a lump to my throat.

"I think he would." A sober thought douses the warm flicker of my imagination. "But he's made it clear that he doesn't want a kid, so if I'm knocked up, I might be raising this child alone."

"Yeah, right." Liza's face falls with concern. "There's no way he's letting you walk away with his child."

"But where does that leave me? He'd force me to stay living here, under his roof, to raise a child he doesn't want and would resent me for having?"

Liza looks at me like I'm insane. "First of all, it takes two to tango, so this potential situation is as much on Maxim as it is on you. And second of all, you're missing the obvious—Maxim is head over heels for you, whether he's told you or not. He might surprise you."

"I hope so," I say.

Liza watches me, her brow creased with concern, but before she can say anything more, the alarm on my phone goes off.

"I can't do it. You look."

Liza disappears into the bathroom and comes back with the three sticks. Her expression is unreadable as she examines each test, a master poker player holding all the cards close to her chest.

The silence stretches until she finally turns to me, her eyes softening. "Three out of three pregnancy tests confirm you're pregnant."

My heart stalls, then races. It's joy, fear, a wild concoction of "what ifs" and "now whats". I take the tests from her, my hands trembling as I see the positive results for myself. Each little plus sign is a monumental shift in the life I've known.

I'm going to be a mother. And Maxim is going to be a father, whether he likes it or not.

Liza and I spend the next hour talking about what's next, but ultimately, I know there's only one thing to do. I need to call Maxim and tell him I'm carrying his baby, that I want to have it and raise it with him.

Because I fucking love him.

The timing sucks, but I honestly can't wait. I'll lose my shit if I can't speak to him tonight. I'm sure Maxim would want me to reach out to him, especially with all these crazy emotions banging around inside of me.

As soon as I say goodnight to Liza, I go back to my room and try to find the number to reach Maxim. He told me earlier that he won't have his regular cell on him, only a satellite phone, and he provided me with the number. I look in my clutch, but I can't find it there. I go to the closet and rifle through the pockets of my coat but come up empty.

Seriously?! I've somehow misplaced it in the craziness of tonight.

Nadya, of course, will have it. *Great.* Time to hunt down the witch.

I scour the mansion, my footsteps echoing in the empty corridors. Nadya's office is dark, the door slightly ajar—a sign she's not there. I try her room next, knocking softly at first then louder. No answer. Frustration mounts as I check the usual haunts: the kitchen, the back office, even the bloody laundry room. Nothing.

Frustrated, I trudge back to our bedroom. I'm halfway up the stairs when I hear a loud noise—is that an explosion?—coming from the east end of the property.

A chill runs down my spine, my heart pounding as my palms grow clammy, gripping the railing for support. Downstairs, the shouts of guards and hurried footsteps amplify my fear.

What's happening? Are we under attack?

Terrifying possibilities occur to me as I rush up the stairs, entering my bedroom and locking the door behind me. I lean against it as I try to catch my breath, but when I raise my eyes, an unexpected sight greets me.

Nadya stands there, a coldness in her eyes that chills me to the bone.

"What are you doing here?" I ask her.

She jabs a finger towards the pregnancy tests on the nightstand. "This was not part of the plan," she spits out. "You were supposed to be on your way out, not pregnant with Maxim's child. You stupid girl. You've gone and ruined everything ... again."

Confusion pins me to the spot, and for a moment, I'm speechless.

She's angry that I'm pregnant?

"Let's talk about this." I try to keep my voice calm to not provoke her since she's clearly not in her right mind. "I don't know what the issue is, but if you tell me, we can work through it."

It's too late for talk because when I look up, she has a gun pointed at my chest.

My heart thunders, my newfound maternal instinct roaring to life as my hands go to my still-flat stomach.

"I'm not discussing anything with you. Here is what's going to happen: you're not going to scream or cry; you're going to walk calmly through the house towards the west entrance and into the waiting car. I'll be right behind you. Make one wrong move, and I won't hesitate to use this." She waves the gun, her eyes drilling into mine.

"The property is under attack," I point out, a cold sweat coating my back.

Her smile is ugly. "That was my handiwork. Couldn't have the guards getting in my way, could I? They'll be occupied for the next little while, so don't try anything stupid."

My heart drops to my stomach. She's truly lost her mind, or maybe she was always unhinged. Either way, I underestimated what Nadya is capable of. She's not only protective of Maxim—she's obsessed with him. And soon, I'm going to learn how far she's willing to go.

I choose my next words carefully, hoping to appeal to her sense of devotion to Maxim. "I know we haven't always seen eye to eye, but I promise you that whatever happens, you won't lose your place by Maxim's side. He doesn't know about this baby, and I'm not sure how he'll react ... but I know he'd never want to lose you."

"Shut up. I'm not interested in your opinion." She stuffs the pregnancy tests into her pocket, but she only has two.

That's because I have the third one. I kept it on me to stare at it whenever disbelief set in.

"Walk." She waves the gun for me to move.

We slip through the shadows of the back hallway, the gun's cold metal against my back. As I fight against rising panic, I consider my options.

I could fight her. Distract her and try to take her down. I'm well trained and in better shape than Nadya, but she's crazy and has a weapon. That makes her a dangerous opponent.

It may be a long shot, but the only way I have to communicate with Maxim is leaving the test somewhere he will find it, hoping he'll recognize that something is wrong. As Nadya guides me towards the back door, I know this is my only chance.

With a sudden gasp, I cry, "Did you hear that?" I glance upwards as if listening for something far away.

She looks up too, and in that instant, I reach into my pocket and slip the test on the shelf next to me.

Nadya responds with a derisive laugh. "There's no one to hear your cries, little lastochka," she sneers, mocking Maxim's pet name for me.

We emerge into the chilly night, finding a plain dark sedan waiting. I recognize it as part of Maxim's fleet, but there's no driver behind the steering wheel. Is she working alone? She pops the trunk, her intention clear.

"Maxim will never forgive you for this," I threaten. "You know that as well as I do. If you let me go, we can forget th—"

"Save your breath."

There's a sharp pinch at the back of my neck, and then a flood of warmth hits my bloodstream. She drugged me! It shouldn't surprise me, but somehow it does.

She pushes me forwards into the trunk. I have no choice

but to curl up into a ball before she slams the top down with a final thud. The world fades to nothing.

My last thought is a whirlwind of desperation and fear. I don't know when Maxim's coming back. I don't know when someone will discover I'm gone. Hell, I don't know how deep Nadya's betrayal goes. The only thing I know for sure is that I need to keep myself and my baby alive any way I can.

Chapter Thirty-Nine

MAXIM

We wait until nightfall to make our move. My men and I have surrounded the Swiss villa where the Black Company's top lieutenants are hiding out. It's not often that I join on this kind of mission, my face too high-profile to be caught carpet-bombing the enemy, but I wouldn't miss taking down these mudaks for the world. These fuckers are the cause of my incessant nightmares. They came after Kira, and that alone sealed their fate.

But tonight, it ends.

I give the word and like a well-oiled machine, my team cuts the power. The villa plunges into darkness, a tangible silence spreading like a virus. Panicked shouts fill the night as Black Company guards wake up to the fact that something is happening.

On my mark, my men advance on the house. We're a small but well trained team. I took only my best men with me. Roman, to my left, signals two fingers—our entry point is clear.

We glide through the breached fence silently. Most of my team takes the left, towards the front of the villa, but Pavel, Roman, and I go right, around the back. Lai King is mine to kill.

A pair of guards emerge from the villa's rear, flashlights cutting through the blackness. They don't see us coming until it's far too late. Pavel and Roman take the guards out in unison, the silencers helping to mute the gunshots before the men crumple to the ground. Adrenaline surges as we step over the fallen and push forwards into the villa. We still have chaos on our side, but that won't last long, so we need to locate King before he figures out we're here and beelines to the safe room.

Through my ear-piece, Konstantin reports that Lai King is still above ground. "Second floor, office at the end of the hall," he says. "All guards on the ground floor were taken out."

"Copy that," Roman says, taking point, while Pavel covers the rear.

We take the stairs two at a time, turning the corner when we reach the second floor, pausing to make sure the area is clear and to orient ourselves. We studied the floor plan of the villa on the plane, but it's different when you're on the ground.

"Fuck!" Pavel's pained words ring out behind me.

I spin, gun at the ready, to find my friend staggering, holding his side where blood's coming out fast. What the fuck happened?

A shadow detaches from the wall, knife in hand. From a crouched position, Pavel raises his gun but doesn't shoot. Because it's not a guard who attacked him. It's a young woman, her face streaked with tears, the knife in her hand still bloody.

Woman or not, she has to go.

My finger tightens on the trigger, but Pavel's voice cuts through the tension. "Don't!"

My moment of pause buys her a precious second, and she's running before I can make a move, disappearing into the darkness. I curse under my breath. What the fuck was that? Does he know her?

There's no time for questions. Whoever she is, she's clearly not a soldier—she looked shaken and scared. While I won't count her out entirely, I'm also not going to change course to follow her.

Roman crouches down by Pavel's side, pressing down on his wound. "Go." He waves me off. "Get King. I'll get Pavel out of here and warn the others about her."

I hesitate, but I know Roman is right. I need to end this here and now before it spirals further.

With my weapon extended before me, I approach the office door, senses heightened. As I'm about to force entry into King's office, a single gunshot from inside the room stops me in my tracks. Fuck!

My stomach churns with the realization that I'm too late. But I have to see for myself.

Inside, I find Lai King's body slumped forwards over the desk, a pistol loose in his lifeless grip, blood painting the papers and wood beneath him. Fuck me.

He chose his own end over facing me. I almost can't blame him. I wouldn't want to face me either.

On the desk in front of him, the computer monitor flickers with the remnants of a data wipe, lines of code cascading down as the last of the files vanish into the digital void. A snarl rips from my throat. Lai King took the coward's way out, and he took the secrets I'd hoped to wrench from his lips with him. Not only did I not get the fight I came for, information that I want is all but disappearing before my eyes.

I grab the nearest thing—a crystal paperweight—and hurl it against the wall, where it shatters with satisfying violence. All this way, for a dead man and a wiped computer.

I scan the room, half-expecting some final trick, but there's nothing. Only the quiet hum of electronics and the faint scent of gunpowder.

I turn, about to leave when the satellite phone buzzes in my pocket. Pulling it out, the screen lights up with a message from Viktor that punches the air from my lungs.

Viktor: Kira is missing.

Chapter Forty

KIRA

Consciousness creeps back to me like a thief, slow and stealthy. My eyes flutter open, and it takes me a minute to realize I'm in a familiar room. The worn wallpaper, the sturdy oak dresser, a patchwork quilt on the wall. This is my aunt's cabin in the woods. What am I doing here?

Memories flood back in a torrent. Nadya, her gun, her cold voice as she ordered me into the car. The sharp sting of a needle. I have no idea how long I've been out or how the hell Nadya knows about this place, but my only priority is getting out of here.

As I try to roll over, I'm unable to move. My wrists and ankles are bound to the bedposts, the rope biting into my skin. Panic claws at my throat, my pulse racing. I thrash at my restraints and cry for help, even though I'm well aware of how isolated this cabin is. My voice comes out croaky and weak, but still, I have to do something.

"Don't bother. There's no one around to hear you."

That voice.

I scan the room, and there she is. Nadya, rocking methodically in the chair beside the bed, the clicking of her knitting needles filling the otherwise quiet space.

"Why are we here?" I rasp, swallowing the fear that's thick in my throat.

She doesn't bother to look up. "It's where your aunt was hiding before her death, and now it's where I'm keeping you until your final breath. Isn't that fitting?" A shadow of a smile crosses Nadya's face, and it's creepy as hell.

"Why ... why are you doing this?"

"You should have been put down a long time ago," she says simply as if that explains everything. "You were meant to die with Masha. I'm finishing the job since your father's not around to do it himself."

Dread pools deep in my belly. "*You* killed Masha?"

Nadya stops knitting, finally locking eyes with me. "No. I only lured her out of hiding. Your father did the actual torture and killing. Made a special trip from New York to ensure the job was done right. Of course, Masha wouldn't give up your location. It's why she died in such an ugly way—protecting you."

Bile rises in my throat. The ropes allow me enough leeway to turn and retch up my last meal over the side of the bed.

Nadya doesn't seem to notice or care—she's in her own world.

"How could you?" I gasp, tears of anger and heartbreak streaming down my face. "Masha was innocent. She did nothing to deserve such a brutal end!"

Nadya doesn't flinch. With an eerie calm, she sets her knitting aside, her hands resting in her lap. "Your aunt got exactly what she deserved, and so will you."

"No one deserves to die like that. What could you possibly have against us? All we did was rid the world of a madman."

With a sudden, violent motion, Nadya flings her knitting aside. "You killed the love of my life! Do you believe I should forgive that?"

My mind races, trying to process her words. "I don't know what you're talking about."

Nadya's eyes flash with fury. "Then let me enlighten you. I want you to go to your grave knowing exactly what you stole from me." A shudder races down my spine, the word "grave" echoing with a foreboding chill. "I was young once too, in love with a man named Arkady. He was a high-ranking member of the Antonov Bratva. A powerful man. And a married one—a typical bratva arranged marriage—but what we had was real. We were in love." She pauses, a haunted look in her eyes. "He moved to the US when your father expanded operations there, but whenever he visited Russia, it was our time to be together. We were discreet, of course—I'm not some common whore—but I was part of Arkady's world. It's how I met Masha, though we were acquaintances, nothing more. This was before she turned against your father and exposed herself as a deceitful backstabber."

"Masha was no traitor! She was loyal to the Antonov Bratva to the very end." Heat flares in my cheeks as a wave of anger courses through me.

Nadya doesn't stop there. "Arkady died during the bloody ambush that you and your aunt had planned at the Antonov's warehouse. He took the fatal bullet meant for your father."

"My father was the one who betrayed everyone's trust by manipulating the family's honor for his own ambitions."

My words fall on deaf ears. It's like Nadya is in her own bubble, completely oblivious to my protest.

"When I heard Arkady was gone, I couldn't leave my bed for a week," Nadya rasps, her eyes shadowed by the memory. "I hadn't seen him in years—life got in the way—but he was still mine. So when Oleg needed someone to draw Masha out, I was more than happy to help." She sneers at the mention of my aunt. "Masha saw me as a neutral third party. She had no idea of her role in Arkady's death. I used Maxim's power, promising Masha that my loyal employer would protect her ... and you. She gave up her hiding spot—this shitty cabin—like that." She snaps her fingers to make her point. "Masha trusted me and that led her straight to her grave, where she belonged for taking Arkady from me."

The air feels thick as her confession sinks in, suffocating, like a heavy stone in my chest. My heart aches—not for myself but for Masha, for the twisted path of loss and betrayal that's led us here.

But the past can't be undone. My only hope lies in convincing Nadya that killing me is pointless.

"Maxim loves me. He'll tear the world apart to find me." I can only pray my words are true. "You'll never get away with this. When he discovers what you've done, he'll kill you, and it will be ten times worse than what you've done to me."

"That's why Maxim will never know. In fact" — she looks at her wristwatch and gathers up her knitting — "his plane will be landing soon, and I need to go back to the estate to comfort him. His pregnant wife left him, escaped in the middle of the night. It's a terrible thing."

She's going to feed Maxim a story that I abandoned him after discovering my pregnancy. The worst part is, with no sign of abduction, he might believe her when he realizes I'm gone.

Dread washes over me. "You wouldn't!"

"I absolutely would." Nadya reaches down, grasping my

chin between her thumb and forefinger. I thrash my head to loosen her grip, but she's surprisingly strong. "You have no idea what I'm capable of. You think I'm a monster, but everything I've done has been in the name of avenging Arkady's death and shielding Maxim from more hurt and heartbreak."

"You're delusional. What you're doing to me will hurt him. This will break his heart."

She shakes her head vehemently, unwilling to listen to me. "You weren't there for the days after Ilya's death. I never want to see him like that again." Nadya's voice cracks, eyes clouded with grief. "Maxim is so much like my Arkady. I couldn't protect him, but I will protect Maxim."

My stomach twists. Nadya's judgment is so clouded by the past that she can't see the harm she's causing now.

She shrugs on her coat before turning to me and tilting her head. "Don't worry. I'll be back as soon as I can, to put you down once and for all."

Desperation grips my throat, panic lighting up every nerve. "No, Nadya. Please, don't do this. Listen," I beg, my voice cracking with urgency. "I'm carrying Maxim's child—think about what you're doing. You're not only killing his wife but also his unborn child. If you truly care for him, how can you do this?"

Her expression twists into one of pure rage, more horrifying than I've ever seen. "A child he never wanted! After one disastrous marriage, I'm saving him from another."

She hurls a glass vase against the wall and it shatters, pieces scattering across the floor. A single shard lands beside me on the bed.

"You stupid whore, you've done this to yourself."

With a swift motion, Nadya pulls out a needle and plunges it into my neck before I can react. The drug courses through my veins as she spins and leaves.

Hopelessness wraps around me, and my final thoughts before I'm dragged down into the darkness are of Maxim.

This can't be the end, not when I haven't told him how I really feel.

That I love him. That he's the only one for me.

That I'm willing to stand by his side—forever.

Chapter Forty-One

MAXIM

Right after takeoff, I'm pacing the aisles and calling Viktor for an update. I'm desperate to scream, rage, and drown my sorrows in vodka, but instead I force myself to push aside my emotions like I do before a fight, and focus on my next move. The decisions I make now are critical in the search for Kira.

"What the fuck is going on?" I growl the moment Viktor answers.

My head of security was monitoring the Black Company mission from a control center off-site. But since the early morning hours when it was discovered Kira was missing, he's been relentlessly trying to piece together what happened.

"It's not good," Viktor starts, his tone grim. "Just past midnight, an explosion was heard on the east side of the property. When the guards went to look into it, they discovered all the camera feeds were down. Believing it was a counter-attack by the Black Company, they secured the property and focused on eliminating the threat. Except ... there was no threat. We've scoured the property, and there's no sign of an outside breach. I was able to get the cameras back up and running this morning—that's when we discovered Kira missing. No sign of forced entry or struggle. It's like she vanished into thin air."

My grip on the phone tightens as panic sets in, a cold fear twisting my gut. "She didn't vanish. Get every available man searching. I want eyes on every inch of footage before the blackout. Someone saw something."

Viktor is quick to respond, military precision in his voice. "Already on it. I've put a team together, and we're doing everything we can."

"Update me as soon as you have something." I end the call, the silence left behind louder than a bomb.

How the fuck could this happen? Did someone take her? Did she leave on her own? I think back to every face, every ally and enemy. The staff, the guards—could I have missed a traitor among us? Was Kira's disappearance part of a larger scheme against me, the work of the Black Company or another enemy?

Questions gnaw at me, but the one that burns the hottest, the one that feels like acid in my veins, is simple.

Is she still alive?

I don't allow myself to consider the alternative, the grim possibilities that try to intrude. There's only one thing I'm sure of—I'll tear through heaven and hell, leaving only ashes behind if that's what it takes to find her.

* * *

Four hours later, I slam through the mansion's entrance, all raw energy and frantic urgency. My boots echo against the marble as I make a beeline for the security office, with Roman and Pavel flanking me.

As we turn the corner, Nadya steps in front of me, throwing herself into my arms. "I'm so sorry, Maxim. I can't believe it." Her eyes are swimming with tears, her usual composure shattered. "She must have planned this for days."

"Planned what?" I freeze in place as she shoves two plastic strips into my hands. "What's this?" I question, my tone rising with agitation.

"I found these in your bathroom. Two positive pregnancy tests."

The ground seems to shift beneath me. The word "pregnant" echoes in my head, a thunderclap that drowns out all else. My thoughts race, trying to grapple with the reality of what Nadya is saying.

I clench the tests in my fist, feeling the plastic crack under my palm. "Kira's pregnant?"

She nods. "It's why she ran away."

Panic takes hold. Kira is pregnant with my child and she's left me?

Beside me, Roman's voice is hard and unyielding. "Kira wouldn't run. It's not who she is."

"Do we really know who she is?" Nadya sighs, shaking her head. "There's no sign of forced entry or abduction. She probably cut the cameras and orchestrated the explosion." She grabs my hand, her sad eyes meeting mine. "She's so young. She probably doesn't want a child, but she knew an honorable man like you would never let her go if she carried his heir."

Dread floods through me, solidifying in my veins. The tests slip through my grip, onto the floor. Nadya has it wrong.

Kira didn't run because she doesn't want a child. She ran because *I* don't.

I grab the nearest thing I can find—a crystal decanter, its weight cold and solid in my grip—and launch it at the wall where it shatters, fragmenting like the fucking heart in my chest.

Hearing the commotion, Viktor bursts out of his office.

"Is this true?" I bark at him. "She wasn't abducted? She left me? Fucking escaped from her own husband?!"

"We can't rule out anything," he answers cautiously. "But I recently installed drone security, to keep an eye on—"

"That's ridiculous," Nadya snaps. "You don't need to confirm what's as clear as day. If we want to find her, we should be focusing on the train and bus station. Even the airport."

Viktor glowers at Nadya. "I won't rule out any possibilities. It's possible that this is Lai King's final 'fuck you' to us. He could have orchestrated everything before his death." He shakes his head. "But the evidence isn't adding up."

Nadya huffs and crosses her arms in front of her. "It's a waste of time to focus our energies in the wrong place."

"I'll decide what's a waste of energy and what's not," I snap.

"Maxim, I only wanted to help—"

"I understand," I say, forcing a softer tone. It's no secret that Nadya isn't a fan of Kira's, and right now, her help feels more like interference. "If you'd like to help, take Pavel to the medic. He needs to get stitched up."

Pavel steps forwards and nods at me, a conversation taking place in our silent exchange. Roman managed a decent field dressing, but Pavel does need stitches. More than that, I need him to keep Nadya busy while we sort out what the fuck actually happened.

Nadya gives me a final pleading look, but she doesn't push the issue.

Roman and I follow Viktor into his office. The click of the latch is a sharp note as he closes the door behind us.

"Tell me about the drones," I demand, pacing the small space.

"I launched them after New York. It's still in the final testing phase, but they cover every blind spot we have. If anyone approached the house or left unexpectedly, the drones would've caught it. The feed isn't live-streaming to our servers yet, only recording locally." Viktor's expression tightens with frustration. "Which means we'll need to manually retrieve the footage from each drone, which could take hours."

"Do it now," I instruct. "Roman will help. Until we know who to trust, this stays between us three and Pavel. Let me know when you have something."

As I turn to leave the room, Roman falls in step behind me, a silent shadow in the dimly lit hallway. I know better than to ignore him—he's a dog with a bone when he's got something to say.

I spin to face him. "Out with it." I cross my arms in front of my chest.

"Tell me you don't really believe Kira orchestrated all of this to escape you? Can't you fucking see how she feels? She *loves* you. She wouldn't—"

"What? Leave me?" I let out a bitter laugh. "That's where you're wrong."

"You know I'm not. Stop being a pussy, and admit that what you two have is as real as it gets."

Self-hate consumes me. Roman has no idea how I failed Kira, how I have no one but myself to blame for her running.

"Fuck you!" I explode, gathering the front of Roman's shirt in my hand and pushing him up against the wall. "You don't know what you're talking about." My breath comes out in a ragged huff. "I told her about Ilya. Told her I'd never have another kid, all while she's pregnant with my baby. And a day later ... fuck ... she goes missing. Nadya got it wrong. Kira didn't run because she doesn't want a baby but because she doesn't want one with a broken man like me."

"Says who?!" Roman yells.

We continue to grapple, crashing into a side table, sending it toppling over.

"You don't know if she ran—she could have been taken. Forced." Roman shakes his head and looks at me like I'm losing my grip. "Tell me what you know to be true, right here." He pounds on my chest, just above my heart.

I shake my head in disgust. "The only thing I know to be true is that if I were Kira, I would've run from me as well. Pregnant by a man too damaged to tell her how he really feels." She's probably on her way to New York right now, needing to put as much distance between us as possible.

Roman's grunt is laced with annoyance, his arms crossed tightly. "I don't know if you're buying your own bullshit, but let me lay it out for you. That woman is in love with you. I've seen how Kira lights up around you—she's genuinely happy. And so are you, whether you admit it or not. Wake the fuck up and face the truth already, so we can get serious about finding her."

His words sink deep into my soul. Does he see something I don't? I know I love her, but does Kira love me?

Memories flood my mind. The way she snuggles into my chest as if it's her safe haven. Her beaming face after she broke Leung. The way she held me when I told her about Ilya, her eyes full of tenderness and free of judgment.

Am I a fucking idiot for not seeing what's in front of me? Roman clearly thinks so. I'm no expert on the matter, but somewhere in the depths of my heart, I know it's true. She loves me as fiercely as I love her.

This revelation changes everything. Every instinct to protect Kira and our baby claws to the surface. Even though she deserves a better man than me, I won't let her go. Not now or ever. She bears my name and wears my ring, and she is *mine.* Body and soul.

"She wouldn't leave on her own," I say, my mind whirling with the stark clarity of the truth. "This was planned. Someone timed it perfectly and covered their tracks." But they underestimated one thing—my resolve to get Kira back, no matter what. I'll move heaven and earth to find her.

Roman pounds me on the back. "Thank fuck you came to your senses, or I would have had to punch you out."

"And then I'd have to shoot you." I smirk at Roman, my chest filled with appreciation for the stubborn bastard. "Now, go hunt down some drones. I have a wife to find."

Chapter Forty-Two

MAXIM

I have my most trusted men scouring the city, searching every street corner and alley. The tech team is hacking into city surveillance and tapping into traffic cameras. I've combed through the list of last night's duty personnel. Maybe I missed a sign, a shift in allegiance. Someone who had access and motive to take Kira. I'm doing all I can to find her, but it still feels like I'm missing an obvious piece of the puzzle.

My eyes drift towards the window, my heart heavy.

Is Kira scared right now? Harmed? Is the life growing inside of her safe? These thoughts hammer at my brain, but I shove them down and focus on what I need to do.

The sound of footsteps and my office door opening draws my attention.

Pavel stands in front of me, face set in stone. A wave of confusion hits me as he holds up a pregnancy test. "Discovered this near the back entrance of the west wing."

I shake my head, trying to make sense of what I'm seeing. "I don't understand."

"This is a third test that Nadya is not aware of. I confirmed it with her—she swears there are only two." He swallows hard.

I sit straight up in my chair, a sick feeling growing in my gut. "What are you saying?"

"After I got stitched up, Nadya said she was going to church to pray for Kira." His jaw hardens. "She left through the west-side back door. Unusual for her, wouldn't you say?"

He's right—Nadya doesn't like to drive. She prefers to take a chauffeured car that would pick her up from the main entrance in front of the home. It's a privilege afforded to her as my personal assistant.

A strange sensation knots my insides, suggesting a truth I don't want to face.

The disjointed pieces fall into place: Nadya's resentment towards Kira, her withholding of information from Boris, her claims that Kira had run away.

Damn. I've been blind to what's been right before me.

Rising, I'm driven by a fresh sense of urgency.

Pavel remains expressionless. "What can I do to help?"

"Tell Viktor and Roman," I respond. "There's something I need to do."

I make a beeline for Nadya's room, the cold feeling in my gut growing stronger with each step.

Finding the door locked, I growl. Too impatient to get a key, I draw the Glock from my waistband, take aim at the doorknob, and fire, blasting it apart. Metal and wood fragments scatter as the door bursts open, revealing Nadya's meticulously arranged room.

I start with her desk, flipping through papers, checking drawers. They're filled with neatly labeled files—nothing unusual for someone in her position. Moving to her closet, I push aside clothes, feeling along the back wall, searching for any hidden compartments. I don't know what I'm searching for, but I trust that I'll know when I find it. I check under her bed, behind paintings, even in the bathroom.

Nothing.

I sit on the corner of her bed and take a breath. Have I lost my mind tearing apart Nadya's room on a hunch? My eyes drift around the space, landing on a shelf above her dresser.

It's a ceramic teddy bear that catches my attention. A small memento gifted to Irina and me on Ilya's birth. What the hell is it doing here? Like many things from my past, this should have been destroyed after Ilya's death.

I stand to get a closer look. Beside the bear is a decorative box. I reach for it. Opening its lid, the air whooshes from my lungs. Inside are fragments of my past: silver cufflinks Irina bought me, a pair of leather gloves gifted to me on my birthday, and—the most shocking discovery—the miniature wooden ship that Ilya loved.

I'm knocked to my knees.

This is more than a morbid collection. It's an obsession, a twisted timeline of my life that she's been secretly hoarding.

The Zippo.

It could only have been her.

Before I fully register my actions, I'm storming into Viktor's office. Viktor, Pavel, and Roman all turn to face me, their expressions grave.

Roman gestures towards the monitors. "You won't fucking believe this."

I freeze, taking in the image on the screen. Even zoomed in and with shitty resolution, it's clear what I'm looking at—Nadya pushing Kira into the trunk of a car.

Horror ices my insides.

It's worse. Worse than I could have imagined. Nadya has

always been the loyal assistant, the ever-present right hand. Not *this*. Not a kidnapper. Not a traitor.

Viktor's hands fly over the keyboard, his eyes fixed on the monitors. "I've got something," he announces. He points to a map displayed on the screen, highlighting a blinking dot. "She's in one of our tracked vehicles. If it's the car Nadya used to abduct Kira yesterday..." Viktor hits a few keys, pulling up a log. "Yeah, here we go. The car's history shows it went north, to a wooded area outside of the city. Looks like she's heading in the same direction."

Without having to say a word, Pavel and Roman stand in unison, each swiftly checking the magazines of their guns for ammunition.

A silent agreement passes between us.

Adrenaline pulses through me. "Let's go."

* * *

Viktor stays behind to run point. It's Pavel, Roman, and me racing to catch up with Nadya. We're not involving anyone else. Partly because we don't yet know who can be trusted—Nadya may have had help—and partly because this is personal. She betrayed all of our trust, and that's not something we'll ever forgive.

I've filled my right hands in on the memorabilia of my life I found in her room—one part of this sickening picture.

Roman is driving, hard determination etched on his face as the cityscape gradually gives way to rural roads, the bustle of Moscow fading into the rearview mirror.

Pavel leans forward, squinting at the passing scenery. "Where the fuck is she going?"

"Masha's old cabin," I mutter. I know it in my bones, though I've never been there. Kira talked about it often.

Viktor's voice crackles through the comms, breaking the tense silence. "Her vehicle just stopped. You're about a mile away from her. I suggest you park and approach on foot so we don't spook her."

Roman pulls the car off the road, finding cover among the dense evergreens. We gear up and start moving through the thatch of trees. The sky is dark overhead, a reminder of how long I've been running on no sleep fuelled only by adrenaline and hope.

Hope that Kira is still alive. Unharmed. That our baby is too.

Nothing else matters.

Chapter Forty-Three

KIRA

I wake up groggy and disoriented, only to find myself still tied to the bed in the cabin, exactly where Nadya left me. I'm dehydrated and weak, fighting the effects of the drugs, but I won't give up. I have to try and free myself.

Time is lost on me. All I know is that dark turned into day and it's back to dark now.

For the last however many hours, I've been working to loosen the knots that hold me in place. Gritting my teeth, I contort my body, wriggling and twisting to loosen the twine's grip. I've already managed to gain a few inches of slack, and with each shift, the knots loosen, giving me enough room to maneuver.

I extend my arm, reaching for a glass shard that landed on the bed when Nadya broke the vase. The sharp edges glint in the dim light. It's still a stretch, but desperation fuels me. My fingers are numb, my muscles scream in protest, but every fiber of my being is focused on this single, vital task—to free myself from these bindings. To save myself and this child.

To see Maxim again and tell him straight up that he's the one for me. I've never felt this intensely before. Being his wife, building a real family together... It's not what I planned, but now it's all I want.

The rope bites into my skin, but I stretch my fingers, inching closer to the shard. My fingers brush against the cold, hard glass, and I nearly cry in relief. Carefully, I wedge the shard between my wrists, sawing at the twine with all the strength I can muster. Each movement is painstaking and exhausting, but I keep going.

The sound of a car door slamming freezes me in place.

Fuck. She's back, and I'm not free yet. Time is running out.

I can hear Nadya beyond the doorway. I stop all movement, hiding the shard in my palm, not wanting her to know what I possess. She strides into the room, her face expressionless, a gun held firmly in her grip.

"What? No knitting needles?" I say in a weak voice.

She gives a cold laugh. "No need. This won't take long."

My spine stiffens. "What won't?"

"You'll see. Let me remind you not to do anything foolish. Bleeding out from a gunshot wound would be a terrible way for Maxim to find you. He's already distraught, searching all over the city for his pregnant wife that ran away."

Anger simmers in my gut, hot and consuming. "You've completely lost it," I snap, my words as sharp as knives despite my precarious situation. "You think by getting rid of me, you're saving Maxim. Protecting him. From what? All you're doing is causing more hurt, unraveling his life thread by thread. You're not his savior—you're his downfall."

My words strike a nerve, and I see the flash of fury cross Nadya's face before she delivers a stinging slap across my cheek. "You weren't there in his darkest hours, after Irina had left him broken. It was *me* who helped him stand again. You see only the man he is now, not the one I saved. I refuse to let a harlot like you destroy him again. I couldn't protect Arkady, but I'll protect Maxim with everything I have."

"This isn't about you protecting him. It's about your sick obsession with him. You've lost your mind if you think Maxim won't discover the truth. He's already on the trail of my aunt's killer, and he'll soon discover what you've done."

Doubt flickers in Nadya's eyes, but she steels herself. "Finding Masha's killer won't be a priority once you're gone." Her voice hardens to ice. "Now, shut up and don't make any sudden moves."

With the pistol aimed at my chest, Nadya produces a pair of scissors and cuts the twine binding my ankles and wrists. With the gun still trained on me, she steps back, closely watching as I try to regain movement in my limbs. The shard digs into my palm, but I bite my lip and pray that it doesn't draw blood.

"Up," she commands.

I rise slowly, my legs unsteady beneath me. The room spins, a mix of fear and exhaustion clouding my senses.

Nadya gestures with the gun for me to move towards the front door, away from the familiarity of my aunt's cabin. The cold night air hits me as I step outside into the dark, silent woods. Shivering in a T-shirt and sleep shorts, the pine needles and fallen leaves jab at my bare feet.

"Where are you taking me?" I ask, desperate to understand her plan.

She doesn't bother to answer.

My mind races with every possible scenario playing out, and none of them seem good. I look back at her, but she's all hard lines and focus. I have no doubt she'll shoot if I dart into the woods.

At the back of the property, Nadya leads me down an embankment towards the river. It runs fast and deep, not to mention it's ice-cold this time of year.

Her plan is suddenly crystal clear—she's going to force me in the water. There's no better way to make my death look like a suicide.

A sob rips from my chest. Everything about this is twisted. Nadya has convinced Maxim that I've left him, and sent him on a wild chase across the city to find me. Meanwhile, in a day or two, they'll discover my lifeless body in the river.

She'll get away with murder. Not of me, but of this child.

I can't leave this earth with Maxim thinking I betrayed him. I won't let that happen.

I stop and turn towards her, desperation coloring my tone. "Don't do this. I beg of you, please, don't do this. There's another way."

"Go for a swim, Kira. It's so easy. Get in the water, and you'll float downstream." Her voice sounds like it's a million miles away.

I drop to my knees, tears pouring down my face. I bow my head as if in solemn prayer and bring my hands together, the shard hidden between my palms. "Fine. I will do as you say, but before I go, pray with me. Pray for my soul." I'm not a religious person, but she is. "Please, Nadya," I whisper, "join me."

She hesitates before slowly stepping closer, her voice a low murmur as she recites a prayer under her breath. Time slows to a crawl and my heart beats wildly, preparing for what's next.

Her eyes are closed, her expression one of reluctant devotion. I silently edge forward, bridging the gap between us. I tighten my grip on the glass.

It's now or never.

With a surge of adrenaline, I thrust my arm up, driving the shard deep into Nadya's neck. Her eyes fly open, one hand grabbing the wound while the other raises her gun. I dodge to the side, losing my balance on the uneven terrain. As a gunshot pierces the night, I fall backwards.

I plunge into the swift currents, landing with a splash. The cold is unlike anything I've felt before, a numbing shock to my system. Voices shout in the distance—male, urgent—but in my dazed state, nothing makes sense.

Struggling is no use. My limbs are heavy and uncooperative. Each breath is a battle, and the darkness at the edges of my vision threatens to consume me.

More shouting in the distance, but the world seems so far away.

My last thought is of Maxim and the baby we would have had together. I picture his brutally beautiful face as he holds a sleeping baby to his chest, tenderly singing her a lullaby.

It's a beautiful image to leave this earth with.

Chapter Forty-Four

MAXIM

As we come out of the thick forest, my heart races seeing the cabin with its lights on. There's someone in there, possibly Kira. Hope flares up, but I shove it aside. This isn't the time for emotion—I have to stay sharp. Think strategically.

I gesture for us to split, sending Pavel to cover the back as Roman and I advance on the front. We move swiftly, surrounding the cabin on all sides. Approaching the small structure, my instincts scream that something's not right because the front door hangs open.

Roman and I lock eyes. Is it a trap? There's no time to second-guess. We go in, guns at the ready, the cabin's soft lights still harsh against my heightened senses. After only one sweep of the main room, it's clear. Whoever was here is now gone. The hope that flickered moments ago now dies a cold death in my chest.

"Fuck!" I growl, my voice tight with frustration. I kick open every closet, pantry, and nook, but there's nothing. *Nothing.*

"In the back room," Pavel hollers.

Roman and I join him only to find an empty bed, with cut rope still attached to the headboard.

Pavel turns to us grim-faced, his hand on the mattress. "It's warm. We must have just missed them."

"Let's split up and search the perimeter," I instruct. "Pavel, search in an east-west grid. Roman, you go north and south. I'll head towards the water."

I'm reaching for my night-vision goggles when a gunshot shatters the silence. Adrenaline surges, drowning everything else. Instinct takes over, and we bolt towards the sound.

My feet pound the earth, cold sweat pouring down my back as I run towards the river.

"Kira!" My shouts are muted by the thick woods, but I can't help calling out her name, again and again, as hope battles with the unthinkable.

I won't let my mind go there. I can't.

The sound of rushing water mixes with the pounding of my heart, but nothing prepares me for what I find at its edge. Nadya, on her knees, clutching at her neck. And just beyond is Kira, barely keeping her head above water.

My whole world shrinks to Kira fighting against the river's force. A howl rips from my throat, sounding more animal than human.

In one motion, I strip off my tactical vest and discard my weapon before diving into the cold, unforgiving current.

"Kira!" My shout pierces the night, an urgent plea for her to hear me, to know I haven't given up on her. Despite my burning lungs and aching muscles, my sole focus is to get to her.

A light from the bank sweeps over the water, revealing Kira's arms battling the river's pull. Her energy is fading fast.

As I near her, she vanishes beneath the surface, out of reach. Time slows to a crawl, a nightmare unfolding before me.

Fueled by sheer desperation, I plunge beneath the surface, the murky darkness swallowing me whole. I descend deeper, my lungs aching for air, but the need to find her is more pressing.

Then my hand brushes against something soft, something like skin.

I grasp at her tightly, dragging her up with all my strength, bursting through the water's surface with her cradled in my arms. Biting back a wave of despair, I wrap one arm around her waist and swim frantically back to the shore, her lifeless body clutched tightly against me.

This isn't how it's supposed to end. She's supposed to be alive, breathing, full of energy. We were meant to watch her belly grow and raise our child together.

This is *not* how it's supposed to end. I won't let it.

As I reach the rocky edge, Roman tosses me a rope. I fasten it around my waist, and he helps with pulling us over the slick rocks, each second stretching like an eternity in hell. Reaching solid ground, I heave her out of the water, her form still motionless in my arms.

"Over here!" Pavel approaches with an armful of quilts from the cabin and gets to work wrapping her up.

The cold of her skin, the blue tinge to her lips... It's fucking terrifying.

"Lay her down. She's not breathing," I rasp, the words tasting like bile on my tongue.

We set her down, and I quickly scan her for injuries. To my relief, she shows no signs of bleeding or being hit by a bullet—a minor miracle.

But we're still not out of the woods.

I start CPR, my hands working mechanically, driven by the intense fear gripping my heart as she remains still.

I scream—a raw, primal sound that echoes into the night. "You're not leaving me. Not now, not ever." She's mine, and I will command her soul back into her body if it's the last thing I do.

Again, I try chest compressions, breathing my air into her lungs, refusing to give up. Because if I give up, she'll never again tease me for being old, or roll her eyes when I tell her what to do. I'll never hear her laugh again—a sound so pure it's burrowed deep in my soul.

So I keep going. For my wife, and our child. I once told Kira that I'm the grim reaper. But I won't be the one to claim her, not now, not when there's so much left for us.

Kira coughs, water spewing from her mouth. Relief floods through me. My hands tremble as I gently cradle her face, desperate to see life in her eyes. That she is in fact alive and breathing. I scramble to check her pulse—it's weak, but it's there. A low, guttural sound rips from my chest. Profound relief, mixed with an underlying current of anxiety, knowing she's not yet in the clear.

The distant roar of a helicopter grows louder, piercing through my haze.

"It's ours. We need to get her to a hospital!" Roman shouts over the din.

I rise, holding Kira close, her light body in my arms a reminder of her vulnerability.

The chopper descends into a clearing nearby, its rotors churning the night air into a frenzy, its bright lights out of place in the dark peace of the forest.

I glance back at Nadya, her form still and silent on the ground. "Make sure she lives," I growl at my men. "I'm not done with her yet."

Climbing into the helicopter, the noise and chaos fade into the background. All that matters is Kira, breathing in my arms.

She'll fight—I know she will. She'll fight for me. For our baby.

For our future hanging by a thread.

Chapter Forty-Five

KIRA

The world filters back to me in fragments: the low hum of medical equipment, the sterile scent of antiseptic, a stiff mattress beneath me. My eyelids open reluctantly, and an unfamiliar room swims into focus, bathed in the soft glow of fluorescent lights.

I'm in a hospital, that much is clear, but how I got here is a blur.

I turn my head slightly, wincing at the stiffness in my neck.

I find Maxim beside my bed. His head is bowed, elbows resting on his knees, hands clasped together. He looks like a man carrying the weight of the world.

"Maxim," I try to speak, but the word comes out as a barely audible rasp.

His head snaps up, his deep blue eyes meeting mine. There's a storm there—relief, pain, and love all swirling together. He looks like he's been through hell and back, his dark hair messy, his face tired and drawn, his usual polished exterior cracked and tarnished.

"Lastochka," he whispers, reaching for my hand. "You're awake. How do you feel?"

"Like shit," I croak, trying to sit up straighter.

He gently presses a hand against my shoulder, urging me to ease back onto the pillows. "Easy. You've been through a lot." Maxim stands and reaches for a glass of water on the bedside table. Carefully, he supports my head, lifting the glass to my lips.

I drink slowly, the cool liquid soothing my dry throat. "How long have I been out?"

"Thirty nine hours, four minutes, seven seconds."

Despite my throbbing head, a small smile grows on my lips. "Not that you've been counting."

He sets the glass down, his gaze never wavering from my face. "Do you remember anything?"

Disjointed images flash through my mind, but everything is a jumbled dark mess. "Nadya... The cabin," I say, my voice still weak. "I remember fighting ... and falling into the water." I shake my head, ignoring the throbbing in my temples. "You saved me, didn't you?"

Maxim reaches out to cup my cheek. The lingering terror in his expression tells me exactly how he felt about that moment. "When we got there, you were in the river. I thought I had lost you." His grip tightens on my hand. "But you fought, lastochka. You fought so hard."

There's something else dancing at the edges of my consciousness.

"The baby!" I shoot straight up but tubes restrain me, sending a jolt of pain through my body.

"It's okay," he says gently, his face softening. "Everything appears to be fine with the pregnancy. You're both safe now."

Relief floods through me, easing the tight knot of worry that had formed in my throat. I let out a shaky breath, tears welling in my eyes. "I want this baby, Maxim. I didn't plan for it, but I want to keep it. I'm sorry if this isn't what you want, but—"

"Stop," he interrupts, holding my face tenderly in his hands, his gaze intense. "You don't have to be sorry. This baby is a part of us. I thought I was too broken to do this again, but you've turned my world upside down, in the best possible way. I want this family with you." The words leave his lips with newfound softness, his thumb softly caressing my cheek. "I love you, Kira. More than I ever thought possible."

Tears blur my vision. I'm not sure if it's the pain medication or the ordeal I've been through, but I'm dumbfounded, never dreaming I'd hear those words from Maxim.

"I love you too," I whisper. "I was terrified you wouldn't want this ... or us."

Maxim gently wipes away my tears. "I'm fucking crazy about you. A life with you is more than I could dream of."

A flicker of happiness ignites in my heart, basking in the promise of our future together.

"I'd never run away from you." My hand glides down his face, coming to rest on his strong jawline. He briefly closes his eyes, savoring the contact, before opening them to meet my gaze. "I wasn't sure if this is what you'd want, but I was always going to be honest with you."

"I know. And I'm sorry I didn't realize it earlier." He pauses, his gaze tenderly sweeping over my face. "Nadya killed your aunt, didn't she?"

I nod, a pang of sorrow bubbling deep within. "My father did the torture and killing. But she was the one who lured her to the warehouse under the guise of helping her. She promised Masha your protection, but of course, it was all lies."

"I'm so sorry for not seeing what she was earlier." His voice is calm, but his shoulders are tight. "She will pay. I promise you that." A quiet fury radiates from him.

My stomach turns as reality sinks in. "Where is Nadya now?"

His jaw clenches, and when his eyes meet mine, the raw intensity in them makes my breath hitch. "Still alive. I will deal with her in time." Maxim changes the subject, his voice softer now. "Are you tired?"

"A little," I admit, feeling the weight of exhaustion tugging at my eyelids.

He smiles, a glimpse of tenderness. "Your whole family is here. They've taken over the waiting room. Luckily, we're in a hospital I built."

I tilt my head in question.

"You want to know what I do with the money I make from wine?" He gestures all around us.

A small, tired smile grows on my lips. "Of course. You steal from the rich and give to everyone else. A modern-day Robin Hood."

He shrugs, a sparkle in his eyes. "I call it 'wealth redistribution'."

I gesture towards the door with my head. "Tell them to come in. I'll kick them out when I need to sleep."

"I haven't told them about the pregnancy. It's still early, and I wanted it to be your choice when to share the news."

I nod gratefully. He plants a gentle kiss on my forehead before stepping out of the room.

Closing my eyes, I drop my hands into my lap, drinking in this perfect moment. So many emotions shift beneath the surface.

The reality of nearly losing everything hits hard. We've

been through hell and back, but somehow, it made everything clear. I need Maxim as much as I need my next breath. And I have him. For real this time. Nothing can change that.

Moments later, my husband returns with everyone. And I mean *everyone.*

Alyona is the first through the door. She rushes to my side, gently throwing her arms around me. "Oh my God, Kira, I've never been so afraid."

I doubt that's true, given the life we lead, but I can't deny this has been a terrible ordeal.

"I'm sorry you had to go through that."

She shakes her head. "All I care about is that you're okay."

I can't stop the tears—once they start, they flow like the river Nile. Alyona is quick to join in.

My sisters-in-law, Georgia and Bianca, are the next to embrace me. As if crying is contagious, they start tearing up too.

"How do you feel? Are you okay?" Georgia asks, her dark eyebrows drawn together.

"I am," I announce. "Although, I wouldn't be if it wasn't for Maxim."

Andrei approaches next, his embrace firm, but irritation flickers over his features when his eyes land on Maxim. "He might've saved you, but he's the reason you were in danger in the first place."

Daniil drops a kiss on my head while Leo grabs hold of my hand. I don't miss the way my brothers' glances flit towards Maxim, accusation hanging in the air. It's clear that despite everything, they blame him for not seeing what Nadya was earlier.

Maxim watches quietly as my family envelops me in their love and concern. It's subtle, but I see the shadow of self-reproach that darkens his gaze.

"Enough of the blame game," I blurt out. "Nadya was a master manipulator. She hid who she really was, but—"

Maxim shakes his head before I can finish. "You don't need to defend me. They're right. I should have seen through Nadya a long time ago. It was my responsibility to keep you safe, and I failed." His admission silences the room, and all eyes turn to him. "I've always prided myself on my judgment, on being able to read people. But with Nadya ... I was blind. That nearly cost me the most important thing in my life." His eyes fill with pain. "Kira, the thought of losing you is unbearable. I vow to you, now and always, I'll never make that same mistake again. I'll guard you with every breath in my body."

"I know," I rasp, reaching for his hand and intertwining our fingers.

He leans forward, gently pressing a kiss on my lips, igniting the spark of electricity that dances between us.

The room is still, the tension palpable.

Alyona speaks, breaking the quiet. "We all make mistakes. What matters is that Kira is still here."

Maxim acknowledges Aly with a slight nod, but I can see how much the words mean coming from his daughter. Taking a deep breath, his gaze sweeps the room. "Kira's not only my wife —she's my partner, my equal. In her, I've found my reason to be better, to do better, and I promise you that her safety and happiness will be my priority."

Andrei meets my husband's gaze, an inkling of acknowledgement passing between them. "We'll hold you to that, Maxim."

There might be a long road ahead to build trust between our families, but maybe they're starting to see the qualities in Maxim that I fell in love with. His strength, his loyalty, his fierce love and devotion.

My eyes begin to close. Exhausted but happy, I drift off, faintly aware of everyone filing out of the room.

Except for one person.

There's a gentle kiss on my forehead, a warm hand in mine. "Sleep well, lastochka."

Chapter Forty-Six

MAXIM

"Why?" The question rumbles from my throat, the sound echoing off the basement walls.

Nadya keeps her silence, a statue of defiance.

In a swift move, I grab the back of the chair she's tied to, jerking it closer. "Look at me and explain. Now." I lean forward, the intensity of my gaze drilling into her.

Despite her bandaged neck and the wound that we expertly patched up so she wouldn't bleed out, there's no chance of Nadya redeeming herself. But I need her to confess the sins she's committed before I send her to her death.

For a moment, Nadya looks as if she might maintain her steely resolve, but then her façade begins to crack. A single tear escapes, tracing a path down her cheek. "You're not the only one who's experienced heartache. I've loved and lost, and my loss is directly because of Masha and Kira. The man I loved died in the attack they launched on Oleg. They took everything from me," she spits. "Kira was going to take you too. I couldn't let that happen."

Her words send a jolt through me, upending everything I thought I knew about Nadya. "Kira didn't take me from you—I was never yours. You had no fucking right to play God with my life." I slam my palm against the stone wall behind her, a sharp crack echoing through the basement.

Kira was right. Nadya's loyalty was nothing but a twisted, unhealthy obsession with me.

I'm an idiot for not heeding Kira's warning, and it nearly cost me everything

Nadya's voice drips with venom, her gaze piercing me with a look of scorn. "You're too good for her, Maxim, like you were too good for Irina! With Irina, you didn't know, but with Kira ... it's obvious what she is. A traitor to her family."

In a swift motion, I grab the chair I was sitting on and hurl it against the wall. It crashes with a resounding thud, splintering into pieces.

"You're the traitor. You've been lying, manipulating everything around you—including me. You call that loyalty?"

Her lips thin into a hard line. "I did what I had to do."

I clench and unclench my fists, desperate for release. "I found your stash. Pieces of my life you insisted on keeping. It's fucking twisted. You're sick. And I am a fucking idiot for not seeing it sooner."

"You remind me of him ... Arkady." Nadya's voice breaks as she clings to her memories of the past. "The man I loved. Your sense of honor, your reverence for our heritage, and the way you uphold the bratva's loyalty oath. You brought back a part of him to me."

"Your lover? A man stupid enough to be loyal to scum like Oleg Antonov?"

"Stupid? No, he was wise in ways you can't comprehend.

His loyalty was to the code, to the bratva oath," she counters fiercely, her restrained position only intensifying the strength in her voice. "My devotion was always to you, wanting only the best for you. You're blinded by her... But you'd be better off without that whore."

"How very wrong you are," I say through clenched teeth. "She's the only thing in my life worth living for. The best thing that's happened to me since Ilya, and you nearly took her from me. You have no idea what it would have done for me if I lost her, and our child."

"Maxim, listen to me—"

"Shut up." There's nothing she has to say that I want to hear.

But there is one more thing I want to know.

I pull out the pictures of Masha's murder scene and show them to her, pointing to the corner of the frame where my Zippo lies. "What is this doing here? Were you trying to frame me for Masha's murder?"

She huffs out a heavy breath. "I ... I kept it as a memento. I know it was a gift from Irina, but it reminded me of you. It was carved with your initials. I couldn't throw it out. I had it on me that day in case we needed to destroy the evidence. I lost it in the chaos."

"You're pathetic," I growl. "Pathetic and deranged. I can't listen to another word."

The urge to get the fuck out of here overwhelms me as my worst instincts—the ones that lead to violence—rise within me. I yearn to see Nadya suffer as Kira did. I want her death to be slow and excruciating, a retribution for all she's done. But Kira pleaded with me to leave her execution to someone else. She doesn't want that stain on my soul.

"I did this for you. How can you not see that?" Nadya implores, her voice a haunted whisper.

I turn away, leaving her to the darkness of the basement. I nod at Konstantin on my way out the door—his cue to finish the job.

Nadya's fate is sealed. But it won't be me pulling the trigger.

* * *

Hours later, I'm sitting in my office, papers scattered across my desk, but my mind is elsewhere, with Kira. We've been home for a few days now, and she's doing remarkably well. Well enough that her doctors tell me as of tomorrow, there's no need for her to be on bedrest. I'm not sure if I agree, but Kira's practically climbing the walls with boredom. Moving around will be good for her.

There's a knock on the door, a brief interruption to my thoughts.

"Come in," I call out, expecting to see Kira's nurse with her hourly update.

But it's not the nurse who enters. When the door swings open, Alyona steps in.

My heart skips a beat at the sight of my estranged daughter. While the other Kozlovs went back to New York this morning, Alyona is staying for a while longer to be with Kira. To be honest, I'm looking forward to spending some time with my daughter as well. The last few days have been hectic with everyone around, but now it's just us.

"Hi," she says, her voice tentative. "Do you have a minute?" She stands inside the door, her posture rigid, unsure of how to proceed.

I clear my throat, pushing aside the papers to give her my full attention. "Always," I reply, standing to greet her. "Have a seat."

I gesture towards the couch on the far side of the room. She hesitates, her fingers nervously twisting around her engagement ring, before she lowers herself down. I sit in the armchair across from her.

A knot of emotion tightens my throat. I've made so many mistakes when it comes to her. But there's no going back in time to fix them. The only way now is to move forwards, for me to do better.

"I know things have been ... *complicated* between us," she starts, her hands clasped tightly in her lap.

"Yes, 'complicated' is one word for it," I say with a little smile. "And that's my fault."

"I won't argue that." Alyona swallows thickly. "But I want us to start over. Kira is my best friend and now, weirdly, my stepmother." She huffs a laugh and tucks a strand of dark hair—the exact color as my own—behind her ears. "If things are strange between us, it will affect my friendship with her."

"I owe you an apology." I swipe a hand over my face. "Fuck, I owe you more than an apology, and it should have come much sooner, but I didn't know what to say." My lips tip up at the corner. "Apologizing is new to me," I admit.

She crosses her arms and lets out a small, almost imperceptible sigh. "If you're going to stay a married man, it's a good thing to get used to."

I hunch forwards, resting my elbows on my knees. "Abducting you, threatening your loved ones... It was wrong. In my mind, it was to keep you safe, hoping you'd eventually be happy by my side. I see now how wrong I was."

Alyona smiles sadly. "I know you were doing what you thought was best, but it felt like being caged, not protected. You can't force happiness."

Alyona's words stir a part of me buried under layers of pain and regret. Ilya's death was a wound that never truly healed.

But now, sitting across from my daughter, knowing that I have forever with Kira and our child, I feel more whole than I've felt in a long time.

"I'm a slow learner," I admit. Nerves alight under my skin—Alyona deserves the full story. "There's something you should know. I had a son named Ilya. He was the light of my life, the best thing to ever happen to me." The next words emerge ragged and sharp, tearing at my insides. "When he was four years old, he was killed by my enemies in a car bomb meant for me."

Her hand rises to her mouth. "I'm so sorry," she whispers. After a moment, she adds, "I had a brother."

"It was why I couldn't bear for something to happen to you." I sigh. "When I learned I had a daughter, after that loss... It was *everything*. So I tried to protect you in my own backwards, fucked-up way."

Alyona reaches out, her hand tentatively finding mine. "I can't imagine the pain of losing a child."

"Hopefully, you'll never have to. I know Leo will protect you and any future children with his life." A small smile grows on my face. "I'll be the first to say the road here was bumpy as hell, but having you and Kira by my side is the best possible outcome."

"I've never seen Kira happier," Alyona admits, huffing out an amused breath. "But it'll always be a little weird that my best friend and father ... you know."

Oh, I know.

Speaking of the devil... My phone buzzes with an incoming text.

> Kira: I require a sponge bath. With your tongue.

Apparently, Kira is feeling a lot better than I realized. I'm more than happy to play nurse.

"It seems the patient requires my assistance," I say, standing.

Alyona rises as well, and to my surprise, she steps forwards and wraps her arms around me in a tentative hug. "Thank you for telling me about Ilya. I'd like to learn more about him when you're ready."

My eyes search hers for a sign of acceptance before I manage to ask, "How about a drink tonight? We have a lot to catch up on."

"I agree," she says, her voice soft. "I'd like that."

Epilogue

Two Months Later

KIRA

“Okay, so ... we have news,” I announce, glancing at Maxim and linking our fingers, aware of all eyes on us.

The room's full of expectant faces—our friends and family gathered in the Kozlovs' Long Island mansion. Everyone's on edge for our big announcement, the one I've been itching to share.

Andrei's got his arm around Georgia, looking every bit the protective husband, while Georgia's hand rests on her baby bump. Their toddler whirlwind, Anya, is doing laps around the room, her giggles bouncing off the walls. Daniil and Bianca are making themselves cozy by the fireplace, and over in the corner, Leo and Alyona are lost in their own little world.

“Don't tell me you're breaking up already?” Daniil frowns, causing his wife Bianca to hit him on the shoulder.

“Let the woman talk, will you?” she says with a smirk.

Maxim shoots Daniil a joking—I think—death glare. "We're not breaking up," he confirms. "In fact, it's the opposite."

Taking a deep breath, feeling the steadying presence of Maxim's hand on my back, I announce, "Maxim and I are expecting a baby."

Cheers sweep through the room. Georgia is the first to rush over, her eyes shining with happiness, pulling me into a tight hug. "Oh, Kira, that's wonderful! A cousin for Anya and the bun in the oven," she says, pointing to her round belly. Having just passed the twelve-week mark, it looks like our little ones will be close in age.

Before coming to New York, Maxim and I got a clean bill of health from the doctor—a huge relief after the harrowing ordeal I suffered at Nadya's hands.

Andrei claps Maxim on the shoulder, a broad grin on his face. "Congratulations are in order. Hard to believe I'm welcoming you into our family with open arms, but life is full of weird surprises."

"Don't I know it." Maxim's eyes glint with amusement, his lips curling into a knowing smirk that says more than words ever could.

My family is still adjusting to Maxim being a new, unexpected part of our inner circle. Not so long ago, he was at the top of their shitlist. Aly's cool with him now, but Leo and my brothers are still thawing out, considering their rocky history. Maxim gets it, though. He's patient, knowing time often fixes things. Plus, a new kid on the way doesn't hurt.

Bianca and Daniil are next to rally around us with warm smiles and jokes about lack of sleep and dirty diapers.

"Yeah, very funny," I toss back at Daniil. "Uncles change diapers too."

"Do they?" he scratches his chin. But when Anya runs by,

he scoops her up into his arms and twirls her around, eliciting giggles from the little girl.

My husband comes up behind me, his hands, large and reassuring, cradling my just-beginning-to-show belly. "Looks like he's already wrapped around his niece's tiny finger," he whispers.

His words draw a soft chuckle from me. "That's for sure."

In the midst of the laughter and teasing, my gaze drifts across the room, catching sight of Leo and Alyona. They seem a bit removed from the excitement, their expressions thoughtful. Maybe Aly is considering her own future as a mother, or maybe she's thinking about her new role as a big sister. I give her space, knowing it's a lot for anyone to take in.

As Daniil and Bianca head off after Anya, Maxim pulls me aside, away from the family buzz. With a feather-light touch, Maxim traces the outline of my jaw with his fingertips, his gaze holding mine with a hint of vulnerability in his eyes. "Kira, you've turned my life around in ways I never imagined. Having you and our baby ... it's more than I ever hoped for. And to think I came so close to losing it all ..."

"But you didn't," I say, both of my palms flat on his chest. "I'm still here, this baby is here, and I want nothing more than to stand by your side, every day."

"I was hoping you'd say that." He gives me the faintest of smiles before reaching into his pocket.

He gets down on one knee and presents me with a ring that's sheer elegance featuring a large, pear-shaped diamond cradled in a band of polished platinum.

I'm so overwhelmed that I'm speechless.

"This ring was your aunt's," he explains, his eyes never leaving mine.

"My aunt's?" Emotion builds in my chest and catches in my throat. "But how..."

"We found a stash of her jewelry in the cabin, hidden beneath the floorboards. The rest of her collection is at home. I had this one restyled and fitted for you. I think Masha would approve."

My hand comes up to rest over my mouth as all the emotions bubble to the surface. Joy, excitement, love.

"Will you marry me?" Maxim asks, on one knee before me.

"But we're already married," I argue as tears start rolling down my cheeks.

"We are, but this time you deserve a real wedding, not a bullshit society one. A day with your friends and family present. Only people that we love and care for."

I can't help but laugh through my tears, happiness beating a drum in my chest. "Jesus, yes! Of course I will marry you again." He slips the ring onto my finger, and it fits perfectly—like we do. "And again and again and again. The answer will always be 'yes'."

"You make me so damn happy," he says, leaning down and capturing my mouth with his. By capturing, I mean plundering. He's practically fucking my mouth in front of my family, and I have no intention of stopping him.

"Ahem." It takes someone clearing their throat for us to finally pull apart.

Aly and Leo stand before us, looking everywhere but at us.

"Don't let us interrupt you," Leo jokes. "We're not in any rush."

"Well, in that case..." Maxim makes a move to pull my face back to his, but I stop him with a hand on his chest.

"That was a joke, honey. He definitely wants us to stop."

Maxim growls his displeasure, but then his eyes land on Aly, who stands in front of her father with a hopeful expression. "A baby? I'm going to be a big sister? And you're going to be a father ... again."

His head dips briefly, then he fixes his eyes on his daughter. "Maybe this time, I won't fuck it up so badly," he says softly.

"You didn't totally fuck it up," she says with a small shrug. "We're here now, aren't we?"

Leo's eyes lock with Maxim. "Just don't go chasing this kid around the Mediterranean in a stolen yacht."

Aly frowns at Leo. "The yacht wasn't stolen, was it?"

Leo smirks. "I'll never tell." His eyes cut to me, and he kisses my head, wrapping me in his strong arms. "Big congrats, sis. I'm happy for you, even if you're with this mudak." He tempers his words with a small smile.

"Show some respect to your father-in-law," Maxim deadpans. With a little smile of his own, he adds, "And brother-in-law."

Men are weird, but I guess this is their way of making peace, slowly but surely.

Aly steps in front of me, her face lit up with excitement. "I can't believe this," she says, her voice trembling a bit. She wraps her arms around me in a tight embrace, a hug that speaks louder than words ever could. "You're going to be an amazing mom, Kira," she whispers, pulling back enough to look me in the eyes. "This baby is going to be so loved."

I smile, feeling a surge of affection for my best friend, my family, and for the man who showed me what it is to love and be loved.

"And to think you thought I was crazy for switching places with you in the wine cellar of Maxim's home," I point out.

"Oh, I still think you're crazy." Aly rests a hand on her hip, narrowing her eyes playfully. "But it's the good kind of crazy."

Second Epilogue

ROMAN

"Budem zdorovy," Maxim raises a toast to our health. Pavel and I clink our glasses with his, the sharp echo resonating in the quiet room. We knock back the shots in unison, the clear liquid burning a familiar trail down my throat. I don't know why Maxim called us to his office tonight, but in our world, both good and bad news is greeted with ice-cold vodka shots.

"I have an announcement to make." Maxim sits forward in his seat. He isn't one for fanfare or big speeches, but his tone is oddly formal, capturing both of our attention. "I'm stepping back from the day-to-day running of the business. I want to be there to raise this child with Kira. After everything..." he pauses, allowing the significance of his words to sink in, "there's not a moment of my life that I'm willing to let slip by. Time's too damn precious."

My eyebrows raise to my hairline. That's not a change, that's a quantum leap, but one in the right direction. "Damn, I'll toast to that."

Maxim's lips twitch with a flicker of amusement. We've come a long way, he and I. We met when I was working as a low-level drug runner for the Antonov Bratva, and he was Oleg's strong arm. To this day, I don't know what Maxim saw in me—I was drunk and wild, always chasing danger and the next hit of adrenaline. But nonetheless, when Maxim realized what a dirtbag Oleg Antonov was and struck out on his own, he took me with him, something I'll forever be grateful for.

Maxim not only got me out of a shitty situation, but he was also the role model I never had. He taught me discipline. He taught me how to temper my darker impulses and transform the pain and rage that lived inside me into fierce determination. It's what he does best, after all.

And up until the moment Kira entered his life, he lived with a single-minded focus to build his empire and little else. I never would have imagined that he'd loosen his iron grip. But since falling in love and learning his wife is pregnant, everything has changed, undoubtedly for the better.

Maxim steeples his fingers in front of him, his gaze shifting between Pavel and me. "You two, you're more than right hands, you're my brothers." Pavel and I exchange a look, unsure where this is headed. It's true that we've faced our fair share of pain and loss together, and maybe that's what has cemented our bond into a loyalty that can only be earned, not bought.

Maxim's dark blue eyes fix on Pavel. "Moving forward, you'll take over the counterfeit operations." Pavel nods. He's a man of few words, but a rare smile tugs at the corners of his mouth. Forgeries, whether wine, art, or currency, rake in millions for the syndicate, and with Pavel's sharp mind and unflinching resolve, he'll keep everything running smoothly.

"And Roman will oversee shipping."

With the Kozlov deal in place, it'll be the cornerstone of our business, but fuck me. I'd happily take anything but shipping.

Don't get me wrong, it's exactly the kind of logistical challenge I thrive on, especially now with Maxim's new partnership with his brothers-in-law, the Kozlovs. The plan is straightforward: we ship our product to the US for them to sell, and they send theirs back for us to distribute across Europe. It's a big operation, promising big returns, and I'd be all in if not for one ugly detail.

Anatoly fucking Petrovich. The biggest slimeball on the planet, whose family owns Russia's largest shipping fleet. The Petroviches made us an offer we couldn't turn down: unrestricted access to their ships, networks, and assets to distribute our products—whether it be drugs, fakes, or weapons—globally. The partnership will be invaluable for our syndicate, but it means I have to play nice with the mudak engaged to Elizaveta Ivanova. The one woman who makes my dick hard, my blood boil, and sets every nerve I have on edge.

So yeah, it's not ideal, but what in life is? And there's no way I'm going to disappoint Maxim. If he's trusting me with an essential part of his business, I'm going to step the fuck up and make it work. Honestly, after the shit he just went through with Nadya, I want to see my friend happy.

I'll just keep my distance from Liza, and everything will be fine.

After all, the Black Company has been brought to heel, and we rule the wine forgery business. Maxim is marrying the love of his life, and they have a baby on the way. He's slowly working to repair his relationship with his daughter, Alyona, and even more than that, he's ending the exile of his first wife, Irina. Forgiveness is not usually his strong point, but he's ready to move forward with his life. We all are.

After another round of celebratory shots, Maxim clears his throat, tapping his fingers on the desk in front of him. "There's one more thing I need from each of you." He lifts a folder from his desk and passes it to Pavel. "Does she look familiar?" he asks.

Pavel's eyebrows draw together as he pulls a picture from the folder and studies it closely. "Should I know her?"

Maxim leans back in his seat and lights a cigar, regarding Pavel through the swirl of smoke. "That's the woman who stabbed you in the back. Literally."

Holy shit. I stand and look over Pavel's shoulder. The picture is of a gorgeous young woman, thick dark hair pulled back in a ponytail; she's wearing some sort of flowy summer dress, and she's smiling bright as the sun in the picture. She doesn't look anything like the trembling young thing that stabbed Pavel during the Black Company raid, but it was dark and chaotic and I didn't get a good look at her.

"Who is she?" Pavel asks, voice rough.

"Her name is Hope, Lai King's daughter. And now that we let her escape, she's a woman on the run. Last seen in Madrid but I'm sure that'll change soon. She knows better than to stay in one place for long."

Maxim watches a smoke ring drift upwards, giving Pavel a moment to process. Like me, he's a fan of a quality cigar, but I'm guessing that'll change once his kid's born. His world's about to shift in a big way, a shift he's embracing with Kira at his side. Me? I don't do relationships. Ever.

I live for freedom. A smoke, a drink, a roll of the dice, a wild night out. The only commitment for me is my work. After the shit my father put my family through, I'm not about to walk the same path. If I learned one thing, it's the fewer entanglements in life, the better.

Pavel's still focused on the photo when he mutters her name, "Hope King," like he's etching it in his mind. Damn. His eyes haven't left that picture since Maxim handed it over. Lost in thought, he traces the photo's edge with his finger. "I couldn't kill her. Wasn't prepared for someone so..."

"Female," I suggest, easing back into my chair, crossing one leg over the other.

Pavel grinds his molars together, and lifts his eyes to mine. "I'm not against killing a woman if she deserves it, but she was doing what anyone would do. Protecting her family..." He swallows, a hint of vulnerability peeking through his hardened exterior. The death of his younger sister changed him forever, and he has a secret soft spot few will ever see. Still, I've never known him to avoid a job that had to be done, no matter how unsavory.

"She fucking stabbed you. I'd say she deserved it," I point out.

Maxim watches Pavel quietly. He knows the demons that haunt our friend. "We killed most of King's senior men, but I'm sure he has allies just waiting to rise up in Hong Kong. And she's his successor, the rightful heir to the Black Company throne." Maxim gives a small shrug. "It's up to you to find her before she decides to get revenge."

Pavel's lips curl in a sneer. "Revenge? She was terrified. What damage could she possibly do?"

"We're not going to wait around to find out."

Pavel's expression darkens. "And then what? Kill her?"

"That's our last resort. Find out what she's been doing, what her plans are, who she's spoken with. But if we deem her a threat..." Maxim's expression is stoic. "There's only one way."

Pavel huffs out a ragged breath. He's one of the most ruthless assholes I know, but there's something about the girl that left a mark on him. Still, when Maxim gives an order, we see it through. It's what's expected of us and what we agreed to. And Maxim's rarely wrong.

Maxim's intense gaze locks on me, and something tells me

I'm not going to like what he says next. "And I need you to accompany Kira and Liza on a girl's trip."

"Excuse me?" I sit up straighter in my seat. Did I hear him right? "I thought I was done playing babysitter."

"You're not a babysitter." A chuckle escapes him as he flicks ash into the tray. "You're the one person besides Pavel I'd trust with Kira's life..." he smirks. "Except she actually likes you."

"Yeah, yeah, very funny," Pavel grunts. He and Kira are slowly warming to each other. Pavel finally trusts her, and Kira takes great pleasure in needling him for being so damn serious at times.

But Maxim's request is still rattling around in my head. It's not like it's a tough gig. Kira's good company, and a few days away could do us all some good. Everyone except for my dick, which seems to really like the idea of spending time with the dark haired beauty I've vowed to steer clear of.

Fuck me.

Maxim snuffs out his cigar and leans his forearms on the desk. "Kira wants to go away with Liza while she still feels good in the pregnancy. I'm tied up with business for the next few months, so this falls onto your shoulders."

"It's fine," I busy my hands pouring another shot of vodka. I don't like how either of them is looking at me, like they can read my every thought and emotion. "Whatever you need," I say to Maxim, not meeting his eyes. "And I will guard Kira with my life. Do you have the details of the trip yet?"

Because I sure as hell need time to prepare myself to be in Liza's company around the clock.

The funny thing is, while I'm panting over her, it's pretty obvious she hates me. My whole casual, easy-going act gets under her skin, and for some reason, it makes me want to prove to her that I'm more than meets the eye. But damn, these are dangerous thoughts. The bottom line is there's no room in my life, or my heart, for feelings, for attachments, or love, whatever that bullshit is.

I've kept my life straightforward so far, and I'm not about to complicate it for a woman.

"Kira is planning it now. Coordinate with her," Maxim advises.

"I'll do that," I say, feeling a surge of irritation.

Maxim stands, brushes off his pants, buttons his suit jacket, and wishes us a good night. I'd wish him the same, but judging by the glint in his eyes, I'm sure he's going to have a great night with his wife.

I reach for the bottle of vodka because, fuck, I'm going to need a lot more alcohol if I'm going to calm the wildfire raging under my collar.

I'm pouring myself another shot as Pavel lays down the picture of Hope King on the desk in front of him. We're a real fucking pair, him and I. The future of any syndicate relies on its leaders making clear-headed, rational, often brutal decisions—but the look in Pavel's eyes is tinged with a storm I recognize too well, the kind that brews not from strategy, but from something far more volatile.

Before I can put the bottle back down, Pavel speaks up. "You better pour me one too."

I top off his glass and then mine, the vodka flowing freely. We exchange a look, a silent understanding.

I'm not sure what comes next, but I do know we're in for one hell of a ride.

Thank you so much for reading!

Want another spicy Maxim and Kira scene?
Download the bonus epilogue here:
https://monicakayne.com/bonuses

Also by Monica Kayne

KOZLOV EMPIRE SERIES

Merciless Heir

Cruel Deception

Fierce Vow

Shattered Crown

BRATVA KINGS SERIES

Ruthless Reign

Savage Reign

Brutal Reign

Acknowledgments

First and foremost, a world of gratitude to Nina. Editor, creative lifeline, therapist, and undoubtedly one of the most imaginative minds I've had the privilege to work with. I am forever in your debt for helping me shape this book that felt shapeless for so long.

To Chanel, my phenomenal alpha reader, author assistant, 'Daddy finder' - I couldn't have done any of this without you. Thanks for putting up with my neurotic ass!

Thanks to Sierra for the excellent manuscript critique.

A special thanks to Deb Peach, for her keen eye and invaluable feedback during the beta reading.

A huge thank you to my street team and the cheerleaders who are always in my corner, making edits on social media, posting TikToks, and supporting my books. I wouldn't want to do this without you.

And thanks to each and every one of you who picked up this book and took a chance on me. Your support has turned my author dream into a reality!

Love xo

Monica

About the Author

Monica Kayne is a former documentary TV producer turned proud romance writer. She writes dark and swoony romance novels with a liberal dose of sass and humor. Her favorite characters to write are sweetly possessive bad boys and the feisty, smart-mouthed heroines they can't resist. When she's not dreaming up sexy plots, she can be found searching for the perfect Negroni and her next K-drama fix. She lives with her family in Toronto, Canada.

Connect with me!

www.monicakayne.com

TikTok

@monicakayneauthor

Instagram

@monicakayneauthor

Facebook reader group

Monica's Mafia Queens

Printed in Dunstable, United Kingdom

64134168R00221